Dead End

By

Mauro Azzano

© 2021

For Alison. She has never failed to amaze and support me.

For Michael, Jennifer, Elisa, Aaron and little Archer. Live your lives with joy.

2

I am sitting in an armchair. In a field. In the middle of a wheat field, at that, on a hot prairie day. The sun beats down on my face, burning my skin, while I lean back in the chair and look casually off to one side.

A woman appears, gradually, eerily, from somewhere in the wheat and walks toward me. She is very pretty, wearing a navy skirt and jacket, with coiffed hair, deep red lips and slinky legs. Her black high-heeled shoes make no sound as she walks. She stops at my chair, puts her hands on her knees and bends down to talk to me.

"Excuse me, sir, can you fold up your table, please?" She askes.

I look stupidly up at her. I have no idea what she means. She points at me and repeats it.

"Can you fold up your table, please? We're about to land."

I sit up and rub my eyes, squinting to look at the horizon outside the airplane's window. Obediently, I fold up the plastic table covering my knees, latch it into place and slide my newspaper into the pouch below it. I breathe deeply, forcing myself awake, and brush cracker crumbs off my shirt. A minute later I again hear her voice, from a speaker in the ceiling.

"Ladies and gentlemen, welcome to Toronto." She says, cheerfully.

Chapter One

"First time flying?" Said a voice beside me.

I turned to look. Next to me was a middle-aged man in a polo shirt and double-knit slacks, slightly pudgy, balding. I hadn't paid much attention to him on the flight from Winnipeg.

"No, but then, I don't fly very often." I said.

The man touched my elbow. "It's very safe, you know. I know this for certain- I've read all the statistics. I'm in life insurance."

"Do tell?" I said.

"Yes. As a matter of fact, I'm sure I could get you more coverage than you have now, for far less cost." He was talking faster now, leaning toward me. " What do you do for a living?"

"I'm a police detective."

He nodded sagely. "I'm sure you realize that your job, wonderful though it is, can have some risk, right? You'd want your family protected if anything happened, wouldn't you?"

"They *were* taken care of- when I was shot." I said.

His mouth opened slightly, then snapped shut. "You're just pulling my leg, aren't you, fella?"

"Four bullets, collarbone, lung and shoulder, five years ago." I said.

He grunted and looked away, watching the ramp extend out from the terminal to the plane.

I waited patiently at the luggage carousel, picked up my suitcase and headed to the exit door.

The man from the plane appeared beside me, breaking into a light jog to keep up with me.

"So, listen, if you or any of your fellow officers needs insurance, have them call me, all right?"

"I'm sure we have it covered, thanks anyway."

"I understand." He held out a business card, a shiny green card with embossed silver printing. "But in case you need any estate planning, or supplemental coverage, or anything like that, you just call me, and I'll be happy to give you some free advice."

I sighed, trying to find a polite way of brushing him off. I stepped out into the blistering sunlight, squinted at the sudden brightness, and waited on the sidewalk. The man was still beside me, still talking, but I had stopped listening. He had a leatherette folio tucked under one arm, waving his finger at me as he lectured me about something I needed to buy.

Across the driveway, I noticed a man walking in my direction. He was tall, slim, wearing a pale grey suit. His eyes were hidden by sunglasses, the mirrored aviator type that were so popular, a slight sneer on his face.

I turned to the insurance guy. "Look, are you armed?"

He stopped. "What?"

"That man, coming this way. I think he's armed. Do you have a gun, or maybe a knife?"

He looked at the man with the aviator glasses and gasped, then he thrust his business card at me and shook his head. "I gotta go. Call me." He said, running back into the terminal building.

The man in the glasses walked up to me, slowly took his glasses off and stuck out his hand.

"Hey, boss, how was the flight?"

I shook his hand. "Patrick, good to see you. It was a good trip, thanks, a good flight."

He poked his chin toward the terminal building. "Who was the dick?"

"Some guy trying to sell me insurance. I told him you were armed."

Patrick laughed out loud, a deep belly laugh. "Priceless. Trust you to come up with that, boss."

We turned in unison toward the parking lot. "So, how's everything?" I asked.

"Well, we have an interesting one for you, once you're back." He said slowly.

"I'll be in the shop tomorrow." I said.

"I'm not sure you'd want to come back just yet, boss. We're having a mutiny."

"Come again?"

"I guess you haven't heard. Captain Hook quit last week. They're scrambling to find his replacement."

I stopped walking. "What? What happened?"

Patrick looked around to see we were not being overheard. "He was supposed to retire in August, but this guy from City Hall came in, one Ernest Pascoe, and he started throwing his weight around, making changes in the name of cost savings. Martin told him to leave running the detectives to him, and Pascoe pulled rank. Captain Van Hoeke told him to perform an impossible sexual act on himself and quit. He will be in later this week to clear his desk."

"Did Van Hoeke say anything before he left?" I asked.

Patrick shrugged. "He told us 'my job is to catch criminals and protect the public, not to save on paper clips. I quit.'"

"Holy crap." I muttered.

"Yeah, we were surprised too." Patrick said. "So, are you going to take his job now, boss?"

"Why does everyone still ask me that? I haven't decided. Besides, it was clear that the job was offered partly because I'm Metis. I don't want to be the token Indian on the force."

Patrick opened the passenger door of his car and I got in. He loaded my case in the back seat, started the engine and squealed the tires pulling out of the parking spot.

We were silent for a good five minutes as we drove south toward my house.

I turned to face him and sighed. "So, this case, what's so interesting about it?"

He glanced in the rear-view mirror and changed lanes. "Someone stole a body from the morgue."

"Really? Was it a student prank? Is it Engineering week at the University?" I asked.

He shook his head. "This was done by a pro- or a crew of pros. They jimmied the lock at the exit, got in through the back corridors and took just one body. They didn't take any cash, or rummage through desks, or anything, just straight in and out. Seems like pros to me."

"Huh. Well, let me get unpacked and do a load of laundry, and I'll stop by the morgue this evening. We can check it out then."

Patrick shook his head. "Sorry, boss, hot date. Can we wait till the morning? I'm pretty sure the body won't come back before then."

I smirked at that. "See you in the morning, then. Anything else new?"

"Nope. How was Saskatchewan, boss?"

"It was good to see my dad. My brother James has been offered a job teaching high school music in Esterhazy. He said he's considered leaving the band for a while, and this would give him the chance to work in one place, and not live out of a suitcase. Besides, he can always join them for summer gigs if he teaches, and he'd have the best of both worlds."

Patrick nodded. "Good for him. By the way, Frank has been checking your place every day or so, and he mowed the grass the other day."

"Frank did that? That's very good of him to do that." I said.

"Well, not him personally. He paid your neighbor's kid ten bucks to do it."

I laughed. "I only give him five. I guess I'm stuck paying more now. No harm done."

We turned in at my street, cruised down the gentle slope to my house, and Patrick stopped across my driveway. I got out and pulled my luggage from the back seat.

"Want to come in for a coffee or something?" I asked.

"Can't, boss. Hot date, remember?" He grinned.

Patrick waved goodbye, aimed his car up the road and raced off.

I fumbled for my keys, opened the front door and stepped in. After three weeks away, coming back here felt comfortable, familiar. Home.

This was our house, where my wife and children lived, where I'd found out that Karen was pregnant again. Where I knew with my eyes closed where every doorknob and light switch was.

Even though I'd grown up in Saskatchewan, in the house my grandfather had built, and I'd only been in this house a year or so, I immediately felt that *this* was my home. Our home.

I unpacked, threw the dirty clothes into the laundry hamper and changed to shorts. I put on the coffee and watched it slowly ooze out of the filter and into the pot, then poured myself a cup and wandered out to the back yard. I sank into a lawn chair and sipped the hot liquid, closed my eyes and fell asleep.

About twenty minutes later, the side gate opened, and I heard the squeal of small children. I opened one eye, tentatively, and looked up. A small boy was staring at me, nose to nose, his mouth open slightly. I paused for a second, then opened both eyes wide.

"Boo!" I said, not loudly.

He jumped back, startled, then laughed out loud.

"Hello, Theo, how are you?" I smiled.

"Fine, uncle Ian." He giggled. "You scared me."

"Yes, I did. Where's your sister?"

He pointed at the other end of the yard, to a three-year-old girl climbing the treehouse ladder.

"Hi, Melina. No hug for uncle Ian?"

She waved and went back to climbing. Other footsteps came closer- larger, slower paced.

I looked in that direction. "Hey, Helen, nice to see you." I said.

She sat beside me. Helen looked like she did the first day her husband had introduced us; he was my Sergeant, and I was only his Constable, and we formed an immediate friendship.

She patted my arm. "Hello, Ian. How was Saskatchewan?"

"Flat." I said.

"How's your family?"

"Everyone's fine. James was offered a position, teaching high school music, and my dad is talking about leaving the business to his wife's son and retiring to the west coast."

"Wow. Things change, huh? Karen and the kids OK out there? She hasn't called in a week or so."

I nodded. "Ethan is deliriously happy riding the horses, and Charlotte is riding a pony. They're having a great time. Karen's morning sickness seems better, too. Everything's good."

I pointed to the twins in the treehouse. "They seem to have grown in the last few weeks, or is that just me?"

Helen shook her head. "They grow in spurts. One will shoot up, then the other. I can't keep them in clothes, I tell you."

"Where's Frank?" I asked.

"Boston."

"Boston? Baked beans, Paul Revere, that Boston?"

"Yep. He's at a security conference there. He'll be back tonight, though. He sends his best."

"Good. Can I get you a coffee or something?"

"No, I'm fine, thanks. We're all just going for groceries. By the way, we loaded your fridge with some stuff to keep you going till you get settled back here."

"Marvelous. Thanks for everything, Helen."

She patted my shoulder. "You're welcome. Sorry, I have to go. Kids!"

She herded the twins out the side gate, waved goodbye and left. It was quiet again. I fell asleep.

The sun sank behind the trees in the back yard, and the house got very dark all of a sudden. I made a sandwich and poured myself a glass of milk. The Buffalo jazz station was running a series on Miles Davis, so the radio filled my kitchen with the sound of his muted trumpet, plaintive and haunting.

My watch said eight-thirty. I picked up the phone and dialed a number, waiting for a familiar voice.

The phone clicked, I heard a soft sigh, then a small girl's voice said "McBriar house."

"Hey, Charley, it's dad. How are you, sweetheart?"

She squealed. "Hi, dad. I roded the pony today. We went out in the field. Where are you?"

"I'm home, at our house. Where's your mom?"

The phone thumped as it was placed on a chair, then a thunder of small feet faded away, then I heard 'mom, dad wants you'.

A moment later, other footsteps, heavier, slower, came close, and the phone was picked up.

"Hey you, how was the flight?" Karen asked.

"Hello, sweetheart. It was fine. I miss you already."

"Miss you too." She sighed. "We're making cookies. I had a very long talk with Pam today.

She's lovely. I'm glad she and your dad got together, they're really good for each other."

"Yeah, I agree. Listen, I won't keep you. How are you feeling, though? Everything all right?"

"Yup. No morning sickness, no wooziness. I'm feeling good. Your dad treats me like I'm made of glass, but apart from that, nothing to report."

"Good to hear. Listen, I'll be at work tomorrow, but I'll call you Wednesday, about this time?"

"That's fine. How's things at work- is there anything new?"

"Interesting times. Patrick said Martin just quit, so it's going to be a circus when I get in there. Plus we have a quirky case I'll probably have dumped on my lap. I'll let you know once you're back."

"Be very careful, you know. You have three children to worry about now, after all."

"Yeah, I know. I'll talk to you Wednesday. Goodnight, sweetheart. Love you." I said.

"Love you too. Bye." She hung up.

Seven thirty in the morning, and the sky was a deep blue, dotted here and there with cotton balls of pure white cloud.

I put on my good blue suit, made sure my shoes gleamed a shiny black, and got into my Caprice. After a minute, as I got out of my roadway, I turned on the radio. The chatter was non-stop, a yammering of voices, barking out numbers, addresses, codes and names. I headed for Keele Street, then turned north toward the station house.

Finally, there was a brief lull in the conversation, so I picked up the microphone.

"Fifty-two zero six to dispatch." I said, mechanically.

"Dispatch. Go, zero six." Said an unfamiliar voice, gruffly.

"Hi, who's this?" I asked.

"Dispatch." Repeated the voice.

"Where's Nadine?" I asked.

There was a long silence. Nobody else cut in. "She left. Go, zero six." The voice reiterated.

"Zero six, any messages?" I asked.

"Negative. Dispatch out." The voice said, curtly.

There was another silence for a few seconds, then the chatter started again.

I parked in my spot, carefully locked the car door- for the first time I could recall- and went in.

Usually, on a Monday morning, there would be a cluster of men and women at a couple of desks, detailing who was going where, doing what, asking whom. Instead, today there was near silence, everyone at their desks, holding wads of stapled papers.

I sat at my desk and went through the stack of phone messages left for me. Most of the urgent memos had been passed to duty staff, and only personal messages were left. I thumbed through them, tossed out the ones that didn't matter, and put the few remaining ones to one side.

One of the secretaries walked up to me. Usually, she proffered a mug of coffee as she said 'good morning', but today she only held a bundle of paper, similar to the ones everyone else had.

"Hi, Ian. Welcome back." She frowned and dropped the bundle of paper in front of me.

"Something wrong?" I asked.

"It's the new directive from Mount Olympus." She said. "Mandatory reading, sign every page."

I fanned the stack. There were twenty or thirty sheets of paper, single-spaced, with a spot at the bottom of each page for a signature. "This is a joke, right?" I said.

She shook her head and shrugged. "You're about to meet the asshole behind this. He'll be in at eight thirty. He always is, and he leaves at exactly four-fifteen. Always."

I flipped through the first few pages. It listed codes of conduct, dress standards, telephone use and the like. On paper, this seemed reasonable. In practice, it was pure crap.

By the time I'd reached page twelve, I was fuming. It was a time sheet, to be filled in by detectives when they left the office in the morning, and detailing how they spent their day, in fifteen-minute increments.

I threw the papers down. It was eight fifteen. If she was right, the new guy, whoever he was, would be in within fifteen minutes, so I went to the lunchroom and poured myself a coffee.

A woman in a trim skirt and blouse came in and refilled her mug.

"Morning, boss." She said, softly.

"Hey, Alex. How are things with you?" I asked.

She slapped her mug down, hard, and leaned a hand on the tabletop. "Do I look like a ten-year-old to you, boss?" She asked.

I sensed where this was headed. "Go on."

She pointed at the doorway. "So, this dipshit tells us all to cut down on waste, to do less Xeroxing, to share a ride wherever possible, to save on gas. Does he have any idea what the hell he's doing?"

I shook my head and picked up my mug. "Keep your head down, Alex. Hold tight for now. I haven't met this guy yet, so give me the morning to get a sense for him."

"That won't take you all morning, boss. Five minutes, max." She said.

I went back to my desk and waited. At eight twenty-eight, the front door opened and a man walked in. He was slightly built, with a bald head crowned by a fringe of too-black hair, an aquiline nose and an expression that said he was smelling something foul. He wore a very good suit, a three-piece blue silk one with thin black pinstripes, and gleaming black oxford shoes that made mine look dull.

He carried a deep red leather attaché case, swinging it in front of him as if to clear the way, and walked past the detectives without acknowledging them.

He slowed as he came up to my desk; he nodded curtly and put the attaché case on the edge of my desk.

"Hello. You're Ian McBriar?" He asked genially.

"Yes. You are?" I answered.

"Ernest Pascoe. Pleased to meet you."

He held out his hand, and I took it.

"We'll talk shortly." He said, in a careful tone, and went into Captain Van Hoeke's office.

He flipped on the light, opened his case and took out a single sheet of paper. He placed the paper squarely on his desk, adjusted it slightly so it sat parallel to the edge, and closed up the attaché' case.

He took off his jacket, straightened his vest and looked right at me. He pointed to me and waved his hand in a sweeping motion, silently calling me over. That was his first mistake.

I stared at him, not moving. He scowled and pointed at me again, then pointed at the ground in front of him. Second mistake. I didn't move.

He stomped over to my desk and leaned forward, his knuckles on the papers I was supposed to sign. Everyone watched him, curious.

"Did you see me calling you?" He asked.

"Yes." I answered.

"Why didn't you come?" He growled.

"Do I *look* like a dog?"

The people around me snickered. The man glared at them. "Come into my office." He snapped.

"Please." I added, coldly.

He stared at me for a long ten seconds, then leaned back and smiled. "You're right. I apologize. Please come into my office, Detective."

"Detective *Inspector.*" I corrected.

He waved his hand toward his office door. "Detective *Inspector.* If you would, please?"

I stood slowly, resting my hands on the desk facing him as I pushed myself up. I stretched my spine as far as I could, lifting my head high. By the time I was upright, I could clearly see over the top of the man's head.

He craned his neck back to look at me, waited a moment, then stomped back into the office. I picked up a pen and the clump of papers on my desk and sauntered in after him.

He waved at a chair. "Please sit down."

I sat, and he ceremoniously closed the door. He went around the desk and sat at the other chair, Captain Van Hoeke's chair, and leaned forward, clasping his hands together on the desk. That told me, in body language, 'let's please work together'.

"How was your vacation in Alberta?" He asked.

"Saskatchewan." I corrected. "It was a memorial service for my mother. We lost her ten years ago."

"Was it an illness?" He asked.

"A drunk driver." I said.

"Oh, I'm sorry." He muttered.

He frowned, solemn. "I've been asked to help improve the function of operations in the division. That's why I asked you in here. I'm working with all the detectives, trying to find the best way to help them do it."

"Who exactly are you?" I asked.

"My title is Resource Manager, in the finance department of the police force." He said proudly.

"You're a bean counter." I said.

He smiled a grim smile. "That's one way of describing it. I'm also a Police Captain."

He opened his desk drawer and took out a manila folder, with 'McBriar' clearly written on the tab. He opened it up and read something.

"Now, Ian," He started.

"Inspector." I corrected.

He tossed the folder on the desk and threw up his hands. "Have it your way. I wanted this to be cordial, but I can see that's not going to happen. So here's the deal; I'm your new boss. Get used to it. You do what I tell you to do, or you are out of here."

"Fine. I formally request a transfer." I said.

He leaned back, surprised. "To where?"

"Twelve division, fifty-three division, anywhere you're not."

He looked to one side, thinking, then looked at me like a cobra ready to strike. "Can I ask why you would want that?"

"Because you're an asshole." I said.

"We've only just met. Why would you say that?" He sounded almost hurt.

I leaned forward. He inched back, instinctively.

"You know what I haven't seen so far this morning?" I asked.

He shook his head.

"Respect. That's what you *didn't* show me out there- respect. If you disrespect me, my men disrespect me, and I can't have that. Right now, every one of those guys is giving everything they have to this job. Your handout talks about 'maximizing time utilization' and 'minimizing waste', but what we do is go after bad guys. Until we can convince them to surrender voluntarily, we do *what* we do, *how* we do it. Period."

He sat silent for a good thirty seconds. Finally he nodded. "I see I misjudged you, Inspector. I took you to be someone I could work with, a man who understands the system, not a cowboy who goes off on his own. I suppose I was wrong."

He pulled a sheet of paper out of his desk and slid it my way. It had a letterhead I recognized, and the signatures of people way above both of us.

"This gives me the authority to run this department as I wish. In essence, it means I can fire you. What do you say to that?"

"Yes, you could. I could quit, too."

He glared at me. "It seems we're at a Mexican standoff."

"Except you don't have a weapon." I said. "You want to fire me? Do it. Maybe I'll quit first."

He pointed to the stack of papers in my hand. "I want those read and signed by noon. That's all. Good day."

I got up and walked out.

Alex Reynolds and Patrick Walsh were standing at my desk, across from my chair. They watched as I walked towards them, then I sat down and flipped pages on the stack of documents, signing as quickly as I could without reading anything. A minute later I was done, and I tossed the stack to one side.

"Now, where were we?" I asked.

Walsh poked his chin at my papers. "Should we do that too, boss?"

"I can't tell you to do that, but I'll back you up if you do decide to."

Reynolds chuckled. "Fine. One problem solved. Sergeant Walsh told you about the missing body?"

"Yes, last night as he dropped me home. What gives?"

Reynolds pulled out her Moleskine notebook and opened it to a paper-clipped page. "It looked like just another drunk, passed out in the street. A beat patrol found him lying in a gutter and tried to wake him up, then realized he was dead and called it in.

"It looked like a case of Sterno overdose or something, so nobody took much notice of the body. That night the security guard noticed a light on in the morgue- nothing odd there- but then he heard the back door open, and when the coroner's people came in the next morning, they were short one corpse." She said.

"I'm guessing we don't have an identity for the man?" I asked.

She flipped a page on her notebook. "No such luck. No ID, no wallet. We have his fingerprints, but there's no guarantee he's in the system anywhere."

"Good enough. Keep me posted." I said.

"Now, then. Time for the Monday morning roundup."

I grabbed the active cases clipboard. "Patrick, would you lead the group today? You were here last week- I wasn't. Go for it."

Walsh took the clipboard, stood at the end of the room and bellowed out "Listen up!"

The room went quiet. Walsh explained several outstanding investigations, asked each team where they were in their respective tasks, and assigned extra help to those who needed it. It took him less than twenty minutes to wrap it all up. The room emptied, and he handed me the clipboard; Reynolds waited for instructions from him.

"There you go, boss. All done." He smiled.

"Gosh. You should do this more often." I grinned.

"I done good?" He asked.

"You done good."

I checked my watch. "Nine thirty. Let's get this show on the road. Patrick, you follow up with the coroner on the missing body. Alex, talk to the uniforms that found him, and see if they remember anything interesting. I'll meet you both at the Bloor-Jane Diner, at twelve thirty."

She nodded. "Got it, boss."

Walsh went to his desk, quickly scribbled his signature on all the forms, and Reynolds did the same. They left the forms on their desks and walked out to their cars.

I got my coat and found my car keys. Ernest Pascoe was at his desk, writing, and glanced over quickly as he saw me head for the door. He said nothing.

I drove west along the 401 then north on Bayview, finally turning in at a small cul-de-sac called Feldbar Court.

It was a short street, with only about a dozen houses, all upscale, all older, all very well-kept.

One of the houses, rather modest here, but still somewhat larger than my house, and set back from the street a little more, had a burgundy MG TD parked in the driveway. I parked in front of this house and walked up to the front door.

I knocked, waited, and a few seconds later the light in the frosted glass inset of the front door changed. The door opened, and a woman smiled at me.

She was slim, older, with streaks of steel grey in her brown hair, a few strands hanging down over one eye. She wore a baggy white shirt loose over polyester slacks, and she had a pair of yellow rubber gloves on.

"Ian. What a wonderful surprise." She gushed. She went 'bfff' and blew hair away from her eye.

She wrapped one arm around me and gave me a kiss on the cheek. "You came to see Marty?"

"I guess." I shrugged. "Since, you know, you're not home alone…"

She laughed out loud. "You. He's in the back yard. Go on through."

I grinned and gave her a peck on the cheek. "Thanks, Becky. I'm guessing we'll be in for coffee shortly?"

"I would be insulted if you weren't." She said haughtily.

I walked through to the back door, stepped out and down three steps into the back yard.

Martin Van Hoeke had grown up in England, and this was the closest approximation of an English garden he could create. There was a long winding grassy path, a carpet of lawn that led to the back fence, and to either side raised beds of flowers.

At the very back of the yard were banks of rose bushes, one a fury of deep crimson, another a crisp white, a third bank of roses a delicate pink. The aroma was intoxicating.

Van Hoeke was in front of the roses, digging a trench for a new flower bed.

His back was still to me, and he didn't turn around as I approached him.

"So, how was Saskatchewan?" He asked, without looking at me. He kept digging.

"Pretty good, Captain." I said.

"Martin. It's not Captain anymore, it's just Martin, now." He corrected.

"What gives, boss?" I said, shaking my head. "Why throw in the towel over a pencil neck?"

He gently laid the shovel down and turned to face me. He wiped his hands on his shirt and reached out his right one.

"Welcome home, son. Glad to see you." He said.

I shook his hand. "Good to see you, too. I remembered to bring you back a Stetson, by the way."

He chuckled. "Thanks. Now I'll look like a Texan when I drive the MG."

"So, why did you quit?" I repeated.

He looked into my eyes. "Is Rebecca making coffee?"

"She said yes."

"Fine. Let's go in." He said.

I followed him in through the back door again, into the kitchen, and sat at their round table. Rebecca poured coffee into china cups, and I spooned sugar as she brought a cake out of the fridge and cut slices for us.

We made small talk- I filled them in on my trip, talked about how my family was doing, explained what was going on with my father's restaurant, lightweight topics, all of them.

A few minutes later, Van Hoeke raised his eyebrow slightly, an imperceptible signal, and Rebecca excused herself to 'go do something'. He watched her go then turned to face me.

"So, Ian, what did you want to know?" He said.

"Straight to the point, huh, boss?"

He smiled. "All right, then. I was planning to retire later this year, anyway. The city is trying to trim the fat, and I guess someone thought that we're a good place to start. That was a mistake, I think, but so be it. The decision was out of my hands."

He took a sip of coffee. "Did you get the stack of meaningless papers to sign?"

I nodded.

"Well, then, what they gave me was far worse. I was asked to do an evaluation on all my men - and women - and pinpoint areas where they could cut the fat. I told them to shove it. I don't need the grief, and I'm well past the point where my pension kicks in, anyway."

"So," I said, slowly, "You're going to spend your days puttering in the garden?"

He shook his head. "My brother lives near Falmouth, in Cornwall. I haven't seen him since our son's wedding, so I figure it's time to pay him a visit, drink his scotch and go fishing with him."

"Sounds like fun. Can I come along?" I grinned.

He pointed over my shoulder. "You have a position to fill, *Captain*."

I shrugged and swirled the coffee in my cup. "*Maybe* Captain. Frank has offered me a job with his outfit. It's very tempting. I'm not sure if I want to make the jump, but we'll see."

"Do you feel that the department wants you as a tick mark for the ethnic quota?" He asked.

"It had crossed my mind, yes."

"You're not very far wrong. Still, remember Hattie McDaniel? The black maid from 'Gone With the Wind?'"

I smiled. "I know what you mean. She said 'I'd rather earn seven hundred dollars a week playing a maid, than seven dollars a day being one.'"

He nodded. "There you are. The money's good, you get a nice office, and you get to boss around white guys. Life could be worse."

"Life could be worse." I agreed. "So, how do I handle Pascoe?"

He thought for a moment. "Whittle a forked stick."

Chapter Two

The Bloor-Jane Diner is a monument to Toronto hockey. From the crossed hockey sticks and the Maple Leafs logo on the front window sign, to the jerseys and memorabilia throughout the restaurant, it was almost a caricature of a sports fan's basement.

I parked on the street, in front of a familiar Ford LTD, and went in. Walsh was in a booth, smiling up at the waitress, who was also his current girlfriend. She leaned forward, her elbows on the table in front of him, and he spoke softly, glancing down into her smock as he did. She didn't seem to mind. I slid into the booth beside him, and she stood up, straightening the smock over her hips.

"Hi, Kelly, how are you?" I smiled.

"Hello, Ian. Nice to see you again." She said. "Do you need a menu?"

I shook my head. "Just a burger, no fries, thanks. And coffee."

Walsh nodded. "Same for me." He grinned a wolfish grin. "No onions."

She blushed slightly. "No onions. Right."

She walked away, and Walsh followed her swinging hips through to the kitchen.

"Onions make you less kissable?" I asked.

"They make me fart at…inconvenient times." He said.

I opened my mouth to comment, but at that moment Reynolds walked in, her Moleskine book under her arm. She sat opposite Walsh, placed her book on the table and unbuttoned her jacket.

She looked back and forth at us. "What are you guys eating?" She asked.

"Just a burger and coffee." I said.

The waitress came back out of the kitchen; Reynolds leaned back in her seat and pointed at me.

"Hi, Kelly. Same for me." She called.

The waitress waved and went back to the kitchen. Reynolds opened her Moleskine and leaned forward, reading her notes.

"So, this gets weirder." She said.

Walsh glanced over at me and I leaned back. Reynolds was *his* subordinate. I said nothing.

"Go on." He said.

"Well, Sergeant, we just found our dead guy, behind the wheel of a car in a parking lot up on Don Mills Road."

Walsh raised an eyebrow. "I'm guessing he didn't drive himself there?"

"Highly unlikely. The big question is, who put him there and why?" She asked.

"More than that, why take him from the morgue in the first place?" Walsh added.

I was paying less attention to the conversation; I was just watching the cook, through in the kitchen, as he flipped our burgers, flames rising around the patties.

"Alex," I asked. "Do we know anything about this guy, or whose car he was in?"

She bent forward, reading. "He was in a seventy-six Mercedes 450 SL, according to the uniform that found him. It's registered to a…Gail Fontaine. I called her home; her sister answered, and said that Gail is in Mexico on vacation, and she has been for a week. She didn't know the car was missing. Apparently, it's usually in a locked garage, and Gail's sister doesn't drive."

"So who was our mystery man- her boyfriend, her brother, a car thief? What?"

Reynolds shook her head. "I thought of that. I described our victim- she didn't think it sounded like anyone she knows."

The door opened, and a uniformed officer came in. He was young, slim, model handsome, with impeccably creased pants and a smooth tie. He nodded at me and tucked his cap under his arm, then sat beside Reynolds. She smiled broadly as she looked into his eyes.

He smiled back at her and turned to face me. "Inspector, good afternoon. Hope you don't mind me crashing your party?"

"Brian, good to see you. No, I don't mind at all. What would you like?"

He looked around at the empty plates. "Whatever you're having, I guess."

The waitress came out of the kitchen again. Reynolds pointed to the officer and said "Can you bring the same for Constable Webb?"

"Detective Constable." He corrected.

My eyes opened wide. "You put in for the transfer? I'm very pleased to hear it."

He looked at Walsh. "Sergeant Walsh put me up for it. He pulled some big strings, I guess."

"Bull." Walsh said. "I'd be damned if I let you waste your time in Traffic. We need you in Major Crimes."

Webb blushed slightly. I glanced over and saw Reynolds' expression. It was a mixture of surprise and delight.

"You never told me…" She said.

He shrugged. "I was going to tell you tonight. I guess the cat's out of the bag now, though."

She reached down and squeezed his thigh, then gave it a quick pat. He grinned and bumped her shoulder playfully.

"Jeez, you two. Get a room." I muttered.

The waitress brought out two plates of food, then went back for two more. Walsh started in on his burger, reading from a small notepad beside him. He stopped chewing, frowned, and looked at Reynolds.

"If you stole a body, what would you do with it, once you didn't need it anymore?" He asked.

"Pardon?" She asked.

"Whose body are we talking about?" Webb asked.

Reynolds brought him up to speed- the theft, where the car was found, what we knew- and asked for his opinions on the matter.

Walsh put his burger down. "I need a body for some reason or other. After I'm through with it, what do I do with it?"

Reynolds nodded. "Yeah, that's the direction we're thinking- you'd need a place to dump it."

"Now I'm done with it, I need to dispose of it. Where would I leave it?" Walsh reiterated.

Reynolds swallowed a mouthful of burger and gulped her coffee. "OK. So, they wouldn't want to sneak back into the morgue- too risky. We weren't watching the place too carefully before, but we'd certainly be aware of them breaking in a second time. So, they make it look like a traffic accident, or a heart attack, and leave the body somewhere obvious."

Webb frowned. "Why do that, though?"

Reynolds looked over at him and smiled the way Karen smiled at me. "Why do what?"

Webb leaned toward Walsh. "I steal a body. Why I do that in the first place, that's the big question, but anyway… Now, I'm done with it, and don't need it anymore. Why bother dressing it up and posing it in a car, why not just sink it in the Don River and let the carp deal with it?"

Walsh squinted, thinking. "What are you saying, Brian?"

Webb slid his index finger along the table. "They wanted the body found, and soon. They left it there on purpose, so it *would* be found."

Walsh looked at him for a long moment, wagged his finger and turned to me. "And *this* is why I want him in Major Crimes."

We finished lunch; I paid and left a good tip. It would have been unseemly for Walsh to tip his own girlfriend. Webb and Reynolds leaned against his cruiser and spoke in low voices, then she rubbed his arm and said something that made him blush. He patted her backside, got into his cruiser and drove off. I waited at a polite distance then went up to her.

"So, Alex, what do you have planned for today?" I asked.

She opened out her Moleskine and ran her finger down lines of text. "I'm going to talk to the car's owner- her sister, actually. I'm not sure about her story. Something about it smells off."

Walsh walked up beside me as she spoke. "Good. I'm going to talk to the coroner. He may have some more information for me about our stiff. Want to come along, boss?"

"Yeah." I said, thinking. "I'll follow you. I need to go somewhere later on, anyway."

"Tell Frank hello from me." Walsh said.

I smiled. "I will. That was a good guess, by the way."

Reynolds got into her car and drove off. Walsh went next, squealing the tires, and I followed.

The morgue had recently moved to a new building on College Street, nestled in amongst the high-rise buildings and the old Eaton's department store. I parked in an alleyway, put the 'police business' sign on my dash, and went in. The woman at the reception desk knew me, and she buzzed me in through the security door. Walsh was already there, waiting for the coroner. He was a very good Sergeant, and if I moved on up to Captain, bumping up to Inspector would be easy for him.

The coroner came out, a slightly pudgy man in a white lab coat, thick glasses and a halo of scraggly grey hair. He held out a manila folder and offered it to me, but I waved it away and he passed it to Walsh.

"You guys like to keep me on my toes, huh?" He asked.

Walsh opened the folder. "Well, we don't want you getting bored." He joked.

"No, I mean, you switched bodies." The coroner explained.

Walsh looked up. "S'cuse me?"

The coroner pointed to something on the page. "This is not the man that was taken from here the other day. It's a different person."

Walsh shook his head, puzzled. "How so?"

"This man has different fingerprints. He's not the same man who was here before. Same height, almost the same face, same build, but this is definitely not the same man. It could be his brother, but it's not the man who was here before."

Walsh looked down at the page. "You already took his prints? Right, Alex mentioned that."

The coroner nodded. "Normally, we'd take his prints at the time of the autopsy. It happened that we had a med student in the morgue, and I like to ease them into the job, so I asked her to take his prints before we opened him up. It was just luck, I guess. In any case, this is not the man who went missing two days ago."

Walsh put his hands on his hips and looked down the hall. "Why do I need a body? And why do I leave a different body in its place?"

The coroner shrugged. "That's where you guys get to have all the fun. I just work here."

Walsh made notes in his Moleskine and pointed his pen at the coroner. "Any identifying marks, warts, tattoos, anything like that on this body?"

The coroner flipped to the next page. "This man is missing part of his right pinkie. It's an old injury, probably a work accident, but it was severed above the distal interphalangeal joint."

"An old injury." Walsh repeated. "So this is definitely not the same body you had the first time?"

"Right. They pulled a switcheroo." The coroner joked.

"Gives us a hobby, anyway." I said. "No word on how long he was dead before we found him?"

The coroner shook his head. "At a rough guess, about twelve hours. I'll find out more later, but for now that's only a ballpark estimate."

"So he died after the first body went missing?" Walsh asked.

"Yes, I'd say so."

Walsh frowned. "Why would anyone do that?"

The coroner chuckled. "As I've said before, the *how* is my job, the *why* is yours. Good day, gentlemen." He walked away.

I watched him go. "All right, Patrick, let's figure out who the two dead guys were. Any thoughts on this?"

Walsh shook his head. "There's just not enough to go on yet. We should get a better grip on this if we get an answer from the prints back, though. I'm going to talk to the people in the buildings near where we found the car. Maybe someone saw who put him there."

"Fine." I said. "Be sure to log everything you do. Pascoe would want everything written down."

He stared at me. "You're kidding, right?"

I had been joking, of course, but I had an idea. "Actually, yeah, let's really give him what he asked for, and see what he does with it. I'm going to tell everyone else to do the same. Every time you make a pay phone call, or buy a coffee for a witness, or anything else, write it down. And write everything on a separate piece of paper, with your name, date and time on it. I want us to bury him in paperwork."

Walsh grinned. "You sneaky bastard, boss. Thank you, thank you very much. I love it."

Walsh headed out to his car, humming cheerily to himself. I followed him out, drove a short distance west on College then turned south on University Avenue, stopping at a large glass building, familiar to me now, and sprinted up the steps to the sprawling lobby.

Inside, three young women sat behind an immense desk, directing phone calls and visitors with military precision.

I walked up to the middle one, a petite brunette with a studious expression.

She looked up, recognized me and smiled. "Hello, Inspector. You're here to see Mister Burghezian?"

I smiled back. "Hi. Yes, is he free?"

She picked up a phone and pressed a button. "One sec, please. I'll check."

She looked off to the far wall, where a large clock was built into the marble, and waited.

"Hi, Frank? Inspector McBriar is here?" She listened for a moment then frowned. "Right away." She said.

She put the phone down gently. "Please go right up." She said.

"Don't I need an ID badge? I was always told to wear one before." I asked.

"That's quite alright. Go ahead." She said, almost apologetically.

I shrugged and headed for the elevator.

The elevator took me up, the door opened, and I turned right onto a long hall. My feet squirmed slightly, padding through the deep green carpet, and it took a moment to get used to the feeling. At the end of the hall was the door to what was Frank's office. Except it wasn't.

In place of the brass sign that said 'Burghezian' was a black plastic one which read 'Admin'.

Just before I got to that door, I noticed another door to the right, wider, in dark oak instead of the pine that had been his door. This one said 'F. BURGHEZIAN' in heavy brass letters on the oak.

Below that, in smaller brass letters, it said 'No Entry'.

I tried the handle. The door was locked, so I knocked and waited. There was the faintest sound, footsteps on thick carpet, then the door opened slowly. An unfamiliar face peered around the door and looked me in the eyes.

It was a middle-aged man, not lean, not heavy, but muscular, under a Brooks Brothers suit, with salt-and-pepper hair.

He smiled genially and opened the door wide. "Hi, you're Ian? Hello. I'm glad I had the chance to finally meet you." He said.

His voice was like a restrained growl, soothing yet menacing, all at once. He stepped back to let me in. I followed him into the office and looked around.

Frank Burghezian was standing behind a desk. Not like the standard one he had before, this one was very large, deep, red cherrywood with a leather inlay. There were exactly three pieces of paper on the desk, and a framed photograph of Helen holding their infant twins.

Frank waved a palm at me. "Hey, Ian. I was hoping you'd show up today. This is my boss, Barry." He nodded at the man.

Barry reached his hand out to me. "Hi, Ian, it's nice to meet you."

I shook the hand. It was firm, definite, and the brief handshake told me exactly who the top dog was.

He slouched back into an easy chair beside the desk. "Frank has spoken at length about you, Ian. He feels you'd be a valuable complement to our team."

"That's high praise, indeed, Mister…?"

I waited for him to reply with his last name. Barry smiled slightly, with the look of a chess master who's several moves ahead of his opponent. "No need to bother with that just yet. Barry will do just fine. Would you like a coffee, or a snack, or something?"

There was a tray on a table behind us, with a chrome coffee carafe, china cups, and a box of corn flakes, as well as some cinnamon buns and fruit.

I shook my head. "I'm fine, thanks."

As he waved his hand towards Frank, I noticed his watch. It did not look cheap, and it appeared to be made of a large block of solid gold. "So, Frank, what did you want to ask Ian?"

It appeared to be a prompt, more than a question he didn't know the answer to.

Frank looked at him for a long second then turned to me. "Yeah. So, listen, we were wondering how it's going, what with the changes and all?"

"Changes?" I asked.

He moved a piece of paper from one side of the desk to the other, absentmindedly. "Yeah, with the new guy, Pascoe, and all."

"And all." I repeated.

Frank's shoulders dropped slightly, and his face softened. "We hear he's a dick. You don't do well with dicks. What would it take for you to come over to our side of the fence?"

"What side would that be, Frank?" I asked.

Barry leaned forward, placed his hands on his knees, and rolled upright. "Look, Frank and I were talking over dinner today, and we figure you're absolutely the right man for the job.

You're smart, intuitive, and you don't take the short road to the answer. Your police department is going corporate; I suspect you don't do pointless corporate stuff real well, either."

I nodded slowly. "So, why would I jump over and work for a good ole boy like you?"

Frank glanced at Barry, smiled broadly, and looked back at me. Barry was still looking right at me, reading me. "What makes you say that I'm a 'good ole boy'?"

I shrugged. "You have a very faint accent. It's American, not Canadian, and it's from the south, but it's not deep south. It's not Alabama or Georgia.

I'd guess you're from southern Illinois, or possibly Missouri. Am I close?"

He grinned. "St. Joseph, Missouri. Want to guess what street I grew up on?"

I laughed. "No. I just got lucky with that first guess."

"What tipped you off?" He asked.

"What's your last name?" I countered.

"Kellogg."

"I don't think so." I said.

He tilted his head slightly. "Why would you say that?"

I pointed at the food on the table. "Corn flakes. That's why you said 'Kellogg'. But I bet your last name does start with 'K'. You said 'Kellogg' too quickly to think about it for long."

He reached into his jacket and pulled out a business card. "Barry Kirby, at your service, Ian."

He handed me the card, then shook his head. "I give up. What told you where I was from?"

"You referred to it as 'dinner'. In the southern US they call lunch 'dinner'. And they say it in the Prairies, as well, but you don't sound like a Winnipegger. That plus your accent gave you away."

He nodded, taking it in. "What else can you tell me?"

"Frank was an Army Sergeant. This whole time he has stood at attention, without looking like he was standing at attention. What were you- an Army Captain? A Major?"

He threw his hands in the air. "Jeez, Frank, if you don't hire him, I don't know what I'll do. Yes, Ian, I'm a Marine. I was a Captain in the Corps."

"So, now that we've played some party games, why do you really want me? There are lots of men who could do this job, aren't there?"

He nodded. "There are. But sometimes, what a man *isn't* is as important as what he *is*. You're not American, you're not from Toronto, and you're *not* part of our community- yet. You're an unknown quantity, and that makes you a very valuable commodity."

"Doing what, exactly?"

"Doing the same thing that Frank does. But he can only work within certain circles. He's an American, and while that does open some doors, it closes others."

"This has nothing to do with my ethnicity?" I asked.

"I was unaware of it until I was told- and not by Frank. It makes no difference to us."

That piece of information gave me a pleasant rush.

He pointed at Frank. "So; Frank says he would trust you with his life. I've heard the stories, where that proved to be the case. Would you trust him with your life?"

"Absolutely. Without reservation." I said.

He smiled. "That's good enough for me. Have a pleasant day, gentlemen."

He left the room. A tall young man appeared from nowhere and followed Barry at a respectful distance.

Frank picked up one sheet of paper, examined it briefly and dropped it back on the desk. "So, kid, do you want the job?" He asked.

"Can I think about it?" I said. "After all, I'd be giving up a great parking spot."

"You don't know what the offer is." He said.

He slid the sheet of paper my way. There was a number written on it, with a dollar sign in front of it. It was substantial.

I tried not to look too excited. "Is this the salary they're offering?" I asked.

"This is just the signing bonus. The salary is roughly twice what you're getting now." Frank said.

I winced. "Well, that's certainly tempting. Let me think about it."

"You sure you don't want any corn flakes?"

I shook my head. "Nah, in my house, cereal seems to lead to pregnancy."

He nodded sagely. "I'll bring some home tonight, then."

I walked out of the building, across the broad concrete apron, squinting in the dazzling sunlight, and got into my car. Automatically, I picked up the microphone and waited for a break in the conversation.

"Fifty-two zero six to dispatch."

The unfamiliar voice came back. "Go, zero six."

"Zero six, any messages?"

A slight pause, then "Roger, Inspector. Please contact coroner's office first possible."

'Inspector'? That was rather formal, I thought. "Roger, thanks. Zero six out."

The voice came back on. "Roger, Inspector is out."

That was truly curious. It felt like they were trying to say something without spelling it out.

I drove the few blocks back to the morgue and asked the frail woman at the front desk to call the coroner.

He came out a couple of minutes later, holding a clipboard and a plastic bag.

"Ian, good of you to come by on short notice." He said.

He gave me the plastic bag. "This was the cause of death, I believe."

There was a bullet inside the bag, slightly flattened, but clearly a bullet.

"Any clues about the gun that fired it?" I asked.

"I'm pretty certain it was a pistol, not a rifle. It's an uncommon calibre for a rifle bullet. I don't know guns all that well, but our people here should have an answer for you this afternoon, or tomorrow morning at the latest."

I gave it back to him. "Good, doc. Let me know when you get more news." I said.

I drove back to fifty-two division and pulled into my spot. As I walked through the door toward my desk, a half-dozen detectives looked up and grinned at me. That was odd. I sat down and looked around. They were busily writing, all of them filling in forms of some kind.

I sat down and read through the short stack of telephone message slips, then called back the people that needed to hear from me. I threw the rest into the trash.

The secretary came up to me, a very thick bundle of papers in her hand, grinning broadly.

"Here you go, Ian. Here's the first batch." She said.

"First batch of what?" I asked.

"First batch of activity reports, from the guys."

She dumped the papers on my desk. "This should keep the little weasel busy." She muttered.

I leafed through the papers. They were activity reports, from every single detective, detailing in exquisite detail what they did that morning. One man explained that he had spent an extra thirty seconds at the urinal because his zipper was stuck. Another pointed out that it took him four minutes to pour himself a coffee because he had to rinse out his cup. A third said that from nine forty-seven to nine fifty-eight he was signing a car out from the motor pool, but it had a flat tire, so it took him another seven minutes to sign out a different car.

The reports were massive, pointless, full of details that were inconsequential. Buried in each one, though, were real activities; interviews and phone calls to witnesses and agencies.

I picked up the papers, roughly squared them up into a neat stack, and walked into Ernest Pascoe's office.

"Here you go. This is for you." I said.

He looked up at me from something he was writing, stared at the papers and glared at me.

"And what exactly is this?" He asked, sharply.

"You asked for it. It's the documentation of today's activity from the detectives. This morning's, anyway." I said.

He pointed his pen at the stack, dismissively. "Very funny. Take it away and deal with it."

I shook my head. "No can do, boss. You're the leader of this squad now. It's your job to review their activity, not mine. Unless you want to give me the authority to administer the men as I see fit?"

He leaned back, studying me. "All right. You want to start a pissing contest, then. I'm going to go through every scrap of paper. If I find anything I don't like, I expect you to deal with it."

"Certainly." I said. "That is my job, after all. Work fast, though, because you're getting another pile later for this afternoon's activity."

I walked out of his office, smiling. Before I even got to my desk, my phone rang.

I expected it was Pascoe, dumping something on me. "Inspector McBriar." I said, automatically.

The coroner's voice came back. "Ian, we have some information for you about our bullet."

That caught me off guard. "Bullet? Oh, right, *that* bullet." I said.

He sighed. "Well, the weight of the slug and the rifling indicate a 7.65-millimeter round, and the most likely weapon it came from is a Walther or an Astra pistol."

"7.65?" I repeated. "I've never heard of that. Is that rare?"

"Also known as a thirty-two caliber. James Bond's favourite. Like in the movies?" He prodded.

"Right. He uses a Walther PPK in the movies, doesn't he?" I said.

The man chuckled. "Look at you- you're a firearms expert now."

"I just watch the films for the 'Bond girls.' Anything else on the dead guy?"

"He ate very well just before he died. He had lobster, arugula salad and chocolate cheesecake, roughly two hours before he was shot, based on the digested food in his stomach."

I wrote this all down. "Great. Anything else to add, Doc?"

"I'll let you know as I find out. Good day, Ian." He hung up.

I checked my watch. Three thirty. There wasn't much more I could do here, so I drove out and joined the highway eastbound. I picked up the microphone and waited for a break in the chatter.

"Fifty-two zero six to one five." I said.

Reynold's voice came right back. "Go, zero six."

"Hey, Alex, where are you?"

"Leith Hill and Don Mills, boss. I'm parked out front of an apartment building."

"OK. I'm on my way, be there in about six minutes." I said.

"Roger, one five out."

I made my way through the maze of exits and cloverleafs, turned right and left till I rolled to a stop behind Reynold's car. She was on the sidewalk, writing notes in her Moleskine, glanced up when she saw me, then finished writing her note. "Hey, boss." She said.

She pointed at a building beside her. It was a new apartment block, seven or eight storeys tall, with floor to ceiling windows and shiny aluminum balcony doors looking out on the street.

A few balconies had potted plants, placed beside easy chairs or patio sets. Others had gas barbecues, held tight with fabric covers. It was very classy, all in all.

"Here's where the car was from." She said. "We need the super to let us in, and we need a special key for the garage door. Very high security in this complex."

"So this wasn't a random steal. Whoever left our dead guy knew the building well." I said.

Reynolds nodded. "Makes me wonder about the sister's story. Why would anyone steal that car from her spot? Was it a message? A warning?"

"Let's ask her. Is she home now?" I asked.

Reynolds walked up to the intercom. She scanned the buttons, then pressed one beside a slip of paper that read 'Fontaine' and waited.

A woman's voice came through a tinny speaker. "Yes?" It snapped.

Reynolds smiled. It was an instinctive action to make her voice sound less formal. "Miss Fontaine? It's Detective Constable Reynolds. We spoke earlier. Do you have a few minutes?"

We heard a soft sigh, then "Yes, fine. I do have to leave shortly, but yes."

The door buzzed. Reynolds tugged it open and held it for me to follow her. The buzzing stopped and we went through a pale marble hall into an elevator lobby.

Three wide elevators, each with ornate bronze doors, sat side by side. Reynolds pushed the call button and waited. A second later, one of the elevator doors opened silently and we got in.

She pressed the button for the top floor; the door slid softly closed and we went up.

The door opened. I felt slightly disoriented, for just a moment. The upstairs area was bright, with windows along one wall, like on the ground floor, but with a pair of wide dark doors, one at either end of the area. One door had a steel plaque that read 'PH1' and the other, oddly, had a plaque that read 'PH3'. There was no 'PH2'.

Reynolds knocked on the door marked 'PH3.' Behind the door, I heard something clink, a soft sound, nothing dramatic. The door opened, and a face emerged.

Immediately, I thought it was someone I recognized. Audrey Hepburn, the actress. This woman looked exactly like her.

She wore a short black dress with large blue polka dots. Her hair, jet black, was tied in a deep red ribbon, exactly the same colour as her lips. She had the long slim legs of a ballet dancer, tapering down to her high heels, also a matching dark red. She took a quick puff from her cigarette and looked me up and down, disapprovingly.

Reynolds waved at me. "Miss Fontaine, Detective Inspector McBriar. Inspector, Miss Fontaine."

I stretched my hand out. "Hi, nice to meet you. Miss Fontaine?" I asked, probing.

The woman switched on a broad smile and took my hand. "Hello. It's wonderful to meet you."

Reynolds looked quickly over at me, said nothing, but took a tiny step back.

"This is a lovely place you have, Miss Fontaine." I said.

The woman waved over her shoulder. "Thank you. Abigail, please. Call me Abigail. Let's sit down, shall we?"

She sat on a snow-white sofa and waved at a pair of armchairs across a glass coffee table from it. Reynolds and I sat in the chairs.

I leaned forward. "Abigail, then. And your sister's name is Gail?"

She sucked on her cigarette some more. "Yes, that's right."

"Are you by any chance twins?" I said, cautiously. "Gail, Abigail, just asking."

She grinned, a genuine grin. "Very good. I can see why you're the boss. Yes, we're twins."

"So, where is Gail again?" I asked.

"Mexico. She's spending some time in Acapulco. I already told Alex."

"So you did. But it's summer; it's hot out. Mexico must be even hotter right now. Why would someone go there in the middle of summer? I would expect that you'd go to Mexico- I don't know- in January or something, when it's snowing here. Don't you think?

The grin faded. "We always tell people she's on vacation. We always say it's Mexico, because that way we can claim it's hard to contact her."

"So where is she really?" I asked.

She tapped the end of her cigarette against a faceted crystal ashtray on the coffee table. "She's in Ireland, on assignment."

Reynolds leaned forward. "Assignment?"

Abigail glanced at her then back at me. "We run a modeling agency. She's managing the girls."

Reynolds raised an eyebrow. "Modeling agency? Really?"

Abigail stared at her, open disdain on her face. "We get that a lot. No, it's a perfectly legitimate agency. Look, we have to keep the 'stage door Johnnies' away from the girls. It saves a lot of grief. The girls may be pretty, but not all of them are smart. Or savvy."

"When will she be back?" I asked.

Abigail looked up. "Five days from now. You have her car; will she have it back by then?"

"Probably. You don't drive, though, Alex said?"

She shook her head. "I'm blind in one eye- an old infection. It affects my depth perception."

I leaned forward, trying to see which eye looked different.

She laughed. "You can't tell that way. Nobody can."

I smiled at that. "The man who was found in Gail's car- any idea who he could have been?"

She shook her head slowly. "No. Alex gave me a description of him. He doesn't sound like anyone we know, or anyone I've met."

Reynolds was flipping through her Moleskine, reading and poking her head up occasionally.

"Abigail, do you happen to know a man who's missing part of a finger?" She asked.

The woman's expression didn't change, but I sensed something- it seemed she froze for a millisecond. "No, that doesn't sound familiar at all. We do hire some male models, but they have to look as perfect as possible."

She stubbed out her cigarette in the ashtray and reached into a small purse beside her. She pulled out a pack of cigarettes and tapped it against her left hand to coax one out. Gingerly, with the tips of two fingers, she extracted the new cigarette completely from the pack and placed it with precision between her lips.

She reached into the purse again, pulled out a matchbook, and peeled a paper match free before striking it to light the cigarettes. She tossed the matchbook onto the coffee table, took a deep drag from her cigarette and leaned back. She spread her arms out wide, resting them on the back cushions of the sofa. This gesture could mean 'I'm being honest' but in this case I was sure it meant 'you're in my territory'.

"Listen," She said. "I don't mind answering questions, but I have a car coming for me in a few minutes, and I really have to get to this important meeting. Alright?"

Reynolds closed her Moleskine firmly. "Certainly. Look, Abigail, we really appreciate your help with this. Is there anywhere we can contact you later if we need to?"

Abigail reached back into her purse and rummaged around, finding a flat silver box. She opened it and took out a business card. She presented it to Reynolds, who read it quickly and passed it to me. The card was glossy silver, with an image of a white flower.

In curly script it read "The Gardenia Agency" and gave a telephone number. I handed the card back to Reynolds.

"Gardenia." I said. "That's a neat name."

Abigail nodded. "My favourite flower. I love the smell, so that's the name I gave the agency."

"It's related to the coffee plant- that's one of *my* favourite smells." I joked.

Abigail tilted her head back and laughed out loud.

Reynolds stiffened slightly, a move I knew Abigail didn't see. She smiled softly. "Look, I'm sorry to ask you, but could I get a cigarette from you? I just ran out this morning."

Abigail nodded. "Certainly."

She tapped another cigarette out of its pack and proffered the extended tip to Reynolds. Reynolds smiled thanks, pulled the cigarette out with her fingertips and picked up the matchbook from the coffee table. She lit the cigarette and tossed the spent match into the ashtray. "Thanks, I was really feeling the urge there." Reynolds muttered.

At that moment, the intercom on the wall buzzed, and Abigail strode to the panel "Yes?" She said.

A muffled voice said something, and she pressed the button again. "Be right down, thank you."

She turned and picked up a black leather briefcase from a table. "I'm sorry, but my car's here. I really have to get going." She said.

Reynolds and I stood up. "No problem at all." Reynolds said. "We'll ride down with you."

Abigail shrugged. "Sure. Look, as I say, I don't know what else I can help you with, but you can call my service- the number's on the card. Let me know if you have any other questions."

We all piled into the elevator, went back downstairs, and watched her stride ahead of us onto the sidewalk. A huge black Lincoln was waiting, the engine running, and a small man in a grey suit stood by the back door. He opened the door as Abigail approached, waited patiently as she got settled, then gently closed the door, got into the driver's seat and drove off.

"What the hell was that all about?" I asked Reynolds.

She grinned and tossed the cigarette onto the sidewalk. She stood on the lit end with the tip of her shoe and crushed it flat. "You picked up on that, huh?" She chuckled.

"You don't smoke. What gives?" I asked.

She reached into her pocket and pulled out a matchbook. On the cover was a stylized star, with radiating lines and streaks in a starburst, with the words 'Starlite Motel. Lindsay Ontario'.

"And?" I prodded.

"I grabbed it when she wasn't looking. It's the same matchbook as one we found on the dead guy. Hell of a coincidence, huh, boss?"

"Nicely done. Good work, Alex."

Chapter Three

I went back to the morgue. The coroner was gone for the day, but his assistant was still there. He was a sad-faced young man, thin and pale, who always wore a white lab coat that seemed ready to slip off his narrow shoulders.

The assistant brightened up somewhat when I told him who I was, and eagerly rushed to the 'back room' where evidence was kept. He came back with a large manila envelope and handed it to me.

"It's ok, we've dusted everything for prints." He muttered.

That much I knew. The young man stood beside me, curious, like a buzzard on a telephone line.

I flipped open the flap on the envelope and slid the contents onto a table. They were few; there was a matchbook, like the one that Reynolds had shown me, from the Starlite Motel in the town of Lindsay. There was a Zippo lighter; I flipped open the cover and rolled the flint wheel with my thumb. A yellow-blue flame rose up, an inch high. The lighter worked. There was a business card for a scrap metal dealer outside Lindsay, and there was a small key. It looked like a key to a locker, or a bike lock, or something similar. It didn't look important. That made it interesting.

I held up the matches and the Zippo lighter. "Why would you have both of these?" I asked.

The young man looked up at me, puzzled. "What do you mean?"

"You don't wear a wristwatch *and* carry a pocket watch, do you? It's one or the other. Why would he carry matches with him when he has a perfectly functional lighter?"

I flipped open the cover on the matchbook. Several matches were missing, all from the left side of the book. I looked at the matches for a moment, then handed them to the young man.

"Here." I said. "Strike a match."

He took the matchbook, flipped the cover back, and peeled off a match, from the right side.

"See?" I said, smugly. "You're right-handed. You held the matchbook in your left hand so you could pull a match away with your right hand. He pulled his matches away from the other side. He was left-handed."

The young man grinned and handed the matches back. "That is so neat! You guys have such fun on the job." He chortled.

"Yeah, it's just one big carnival." I muttered.

The Zippo lighter was the kind that took lighter fluid, not the fancy new kind that used butane. I slid the lighter out of its outer case and looked in at where the cotton wadding was, the stuff that held lighter fluid. I just barely saw the edge of something- something metal.

I picked at it with my fingernails; it came out, grudgingly at first, then smoothly. It was another key, just like the first one.

I held the two keys side by side, comparing them. They were identical.

The young man peered down, his nose almost touching the keys. "Why would he have a second key hidden in there?" He mused.

"In case someone took the first one." I said. "It's the only thing that makes sense."

I turned the two keys over, looking for some clue as to what they might open. There were no numbers, no symbols, no brand names, nothing that would identify them.

I looked at the other items again. The matches- they tied this man to Abigail Fontaine. The business card- that made no sense. The keys- wait.

The business card. In faint ink, just below the phone number on the card, was the number 'seventeen'. It was so faint I almost missed it.

I signed out the keys and the business card and got into my car. I wondered how to muster the troops without giving anything away.

I got on the radio. "Fifty-two zero six to one five." I said, unemotionally.

Reynolds came on right away. "Go, boss."

"Hey, Alex, how about you and Brian join Patrick and me to celebrate his promotion. Just a quick bite at the Bloor-Jane."

There was a brief silence. She was digesting what I hadn't said. "Sounds great, boss. You're buying." She gushed.

Good. She understood. "See you in thirty." I said.

I waited a few seconds then picked up the microphone. "Fifty-two zero six to fifty-two ten."

Walsh's voice came back right away. "Go, zero six."

"Patrick, want to join us for a bite?" I asked, casually.

Another pause. He was thinking about what I'd said.

"Never say no to free food." Walsh answered. "Fifty-two ten, out."

Just before five, I parked out front of the diner, picked up my Moleskine and made some notes. A minute later, an LTD pulled up in front of me and backed in close. Walsh got out, took a long drag from his cigarette then tossed it into the gutter. The cigarette gave a last curl of blue smoke, then it sucked up water from a puddle and went out.

Walsh stepped onto the curb and waited patiently for me. I joined him and watched as Reynolds' car pulled up behind mine. She got out of the driver's seat and Brian Webb got out of the passenger seat. The four of us stood outside the diner, looking around furtively.

Webb looked directly at me, his eyes inquisitive. "I'm guessing this is not about food?" He said.

I shook my head. "I have a funny feeling. I don't why, and I don't know how to put my finger on it, but I want to keep this between just us four for now. That's why I didn't want it on the air."

"OK." Walsh said.

I waved at the diner and we all went in. As far as anyone was concerned, we were just having a meal together.

We shimmied into a booth, Walsh and me on one side, Reynolds and Webb close to each other on the other side. A waitress came, a shortish older woman with jet black curls held tight in a hairnet, and the expression of someone who would rather not be here.

We ordered coffee and pie and waited till she left. I pulled the two keys and the scrap metal dealer's business card from my pocket.

"The first key was on the dead guy." I started. "Along with a Zippo lighter. The second key was hidden inside the cotton wadding of the lighter. He also had a matchbook."

I looked at Reynolds. She reached into her pocket and took out the matchbook she'd taken from Abigail Fontaine.

"Like this." She said. "We interviewed her today. Her sister owns the car this guy was found in."

Webb stared at the key, then the business card, his expression intense, focused. He said nothing.

"Are you going EVA?" I asked.

He looked up. "Pardon?"

"Are you doing a space walk? You're not on earth anymore, are you?"

He shook his head. "Have you ever taken Karen out to a fancy restaurant?"

"Sure. On our anniversary, last year." I said.

"Whose car did you drive there?"

"We took a limo." I answered.

He leaned back. "Would you drive a Mercedes convertible to a scrap metal yard?"

We were all quiet for a moment. Webb grinned, satisfied. Reynolds looked over at him, waiting for his next idea. Walsh was scribbling something in his Moleskine, notes on who to call next.

My mind was racing. There was a common thread here- there had to be. I had no idea what, but I could sense that I was right.

"Ok, so I go to a scrapyard." I said.

"Why? Am I looking for work, or do I have something to sell? And why would I go to a motel in Lindsay? Am I meeting someone, or do I have a room there? Toronto's only an hour away. Why would I stay there instead of driving home?"

The waitress came back with a large tray, placed our pie and forks ceremonially in front of us, and went to the counter for our coffees. She came back a moment later, set down four steaming mugs of coffee, and left.

Walsh watched her go then turned toward me. "You're assuming he's *from* Toronto, though. What if he was just passing through? What if he went from somewhere else to Lindsay, if he had work there maybe, stayed at this motel while he was there, and *then* came down here for some reason?"

I nodded. "He was missing part of one finger, a work accident, possibly. That would make sense, then."

"I bet he was a welder." Webb said, slowly.

I shrugged. "Why?"

"It's sort of common with welders. They can burn a finger if they're lazy and let the hot electrode touch them, or some of them run hands over metal edges and get sliced badly. My dad worked in a metal shop; a fair number of the guys in the welding shed were missing digits."

I looked at the others. "Interesting. Any other ideas?"

Reynolds took a large mouthful of pie and shook her head. "He's got me on this one, boss."

"Fine." I said. "So I'll stop by the scrapyard and ask some questions, then. What do you say?"

Walsh shook his head. "Uh, boss, that's not our playground. The OPP handles that part of the province. Did you want me to give them a call? We can go in there with them."

I thought for a moment. "No. I have a funny feeling about this. I can't say why, I just have a funny feeling. I'm going to go out there on my own. And look, I may step over the foul line on this, so if any of you would rather not go there with me, I completely understand."

Webb glanced at the others and grinned. "Yeah, and let you have all the fun? No way, boss."

I sat back, collecting my thoughts. "All right. So let's make some really dumb-assed assumptions here. Let's say he was a welder, working at the scrapyard. Let's say he was living at the Starlite Motel, or at least he went there to meet someone. He had a key to something at the scrapyard. Maybe a car, or a truck, or a glove box, who knows. I want to connect the dots. I'm going there undercover, and I'll ask some questions."

"Maybe I should go instead." Webb offered.

"Or me." Walsh countered.

I shook my head. "Sorry, you both look like recruiters for the police academy. I'll go."

Reynolds snickered. "In your unmarked cruiser?"

I scratched my cheek. "Good point. Patrick, what beaters do we have in impound?"

He jotted a note in his Moleskine. "I can let you know first thing in the morning."

"Fine. Let's scatter. See you all back at the shop in the morning, and as far as anyone knows, this meeting was only to welcome Brian to the team."

Just before six, I warmed up a can of soup, buttered toast to go with it and sat down to eat and do the crossword puzzle. I was pleased with myself; the crossword clue was 'they hate foreigners using phone boxes', and the answer was 'xenophobes', an anagram of 'phone boxes', and that filled in a critical line. I was intent on the next clue when I heard the doorbell.

I put down my soup spoon and wandered to the front hall. The shadow in the frosted door was familiar; I opened up and let Walsh in. I almost didn't see Reynolds behind him.

"Hey, guys. Good to see you again." I said. "To what do I owe the honour?"

I knew perfectly well what they wanted to say. Walsh spoke first. "We'd like to know what you're doing, boss. You're still planning to go undercover, right?"

"Yeah, I thought it over, Patrick, I'm sure that's what I want to do."

"Why would you want to do that?" Reynolds asked.

I waved them both to sit. "You guys want coffee, or soup, or something?"

Reynolds shook her head. Walsh leaned forward. "OK, so if I was the Inspector in this case, what would be the reason for me to go under? Why do you think that's the right way to go?"

"Well put, Patrick. Look, we have nothing to go on here; no ID on the body, no ID from his prints yet. We could wait for six months till someone calls up and says that 'Bernie' has been missing all this time, or we can check out the scrapyard. If they don't know anything, then no harm done. If they are hiding something, though, then going in all official is like taking a marching band on a sneak attack. They'll clam up and hide stuff on us. Period."

Walsh sighed. "No way I can change your mind, huh? Let me go instead?"

"No. You look like a boy scout. These guys cut up cars and sheet metal. You don't look like them, but I do."

He shrugged and opened his Moleskine. "There's a sixty-four Valiant in impound. The owner died in March- natural causes- so we towed it two months ago. Nobody owns it. You want it?"

I grinned. "Yeah. Also, do you know any good forgers? I need some documents done."

"Really? You're kidding, right?" He said.

"Nope. And I'll need some out-of-province license plates, too. Saskatchewan would be best, if we can find them. It's easier to pretend that I'm from somewhere I know."

Reynolds stepped forward. "What forgeries do you need?"

"A driver's license from Saskatchewan, and a release certificate from the Regina Provincial Correctional Institution."

"You're posing as an ex-con, then?"

"Right. If they're on the level, they'll answer my questions to get me gone. If they're bent, they're more likely to confide in me."

Reynolds scribbled some quick notes in her Moleskine. "Great. So, will we see you at the shop tomorrow, or should we just put out an APB?" She joked.

"No, I'll be there first thing, checking on paperwork for Mr. Pascoe to review."

Walsh chuckled. "I've got so much CRAP, total crap, to give him, but I don't care." He said.

They left. Walsh squealed his tires making a sharp U-turn, headed downtown. Reynolds left a moment later.

It was almost seven. I picked up the phone and called a long-distance number, waiting the long few seconds until I heard a ring tone. Three rings later I heard a click, then a small familiar voice.

"McBriar house." It said.

"Hi, Charlotte, how are you, sweetheart?" I said, firmly.

She squealed. "Hi, da. We went fishing an' we got a big fish. It was real big, an' it flipped around." She gushed.

"Yeah? Did you eat the fish for lunch?" I asked.

She laughed. "No. Mom let it go. It went 'splash'."

"Good. Listen, sweetheart, is your mom there?"

I heard the phone clunk onto a table, then a patter of feet leaving, then 'mom, dad's calling'.

A moment later a rush of air as the phone was picked up, and Karen's voice. "Hey, you."

"Hi, hon. How are the kids doing?"

"Well, the big city will seem very boring after this trip. They're having a blast. I wish you could have stayed on longer, Ian. How are things there?"

"Oh, you know, the usual." I said, casually.

"What's wrong?" It was a sharp sentence.

"Look, I'm going to be gone for a few days, a week at most. I just wanted you to know in case you were concerned."

"What do you mean?" Now she sounded worried.

"I'm going out of town, checking out some leads, that's all. Nothing to worry about, just work."

She sighed. "Touch your nose." She said.

"Why?"

"Your nose grows when you tell a lie. You're lying now, aren't you?"

"Look, I'm just doing my job, hon. I'll be out of town for a few days, trying to get some information about a case we're working, that's all. I'll call you on Monday. I should be back in town by next Tuesday at the latest, a week from now."

"Be careful, all right? Be careful. I don't want to hear that you got hurt doing whatever you're doing, all right? Be careful."

"I will. Tuck the kids in, take care of yourself. How are you feeling, by the way?"

"I get a mad craving for Cheerio's. Your dad has bought a half-dozen boxes of them, just in case we run out. It's very sweet of him, actually."

"That sounds like him. Listen, say hi to everyone there. I'll call you on Thursday. Bye."

I hung up the phone and looked at the receiver for a long time.

What the hell was I doing? I had a pregnant wife and two children in Saskatchewan, and I was planning to go undercover at a junkyard. I would be out of my jurisdiction, away from my team, out on my own. I should forget about it, of course. Still, this is why I became a cop. I had to do it anyway.

Early the next morning, I woke up and made breakfast. Then I got my old gardening clothes out of the laundry, found the work boots I had put aside last year, and put these on.

I drove to the station, went around back and parked at the motor pool. I handed my keys to the mechanic and told him I wouldn't need my car for a few days.

Then I went into the detectives' room; on my desk were stacks of paper- notes, reports, meaningless details about everything the men and women had done since yesterday. I gleefully scoped them up into one tall pile and walked into Ernest Pascoe's office. He wasn't there yet- it was too early. I placed the paper on a bare spot and walked out.

Walsh came in a few minutes later, Reynolds right after him, and Webb with her.

The four of us sat together and went over what I had in mind. I would go to Lindsay, find out what I could about the Starlite Motel, and see if the keys from the dead man fit anything with a 'seventeen' at the scrapyard.

I would be there for a few days, but would check in regularly, I said, firmly. None of them seemed happy with the idea, but I pulled rank and insisted.

Reluctantly, Walsh took me to the impound yard beside the station. We walked through the yard, between rows of cars and trucks, then he stopped beside a mint green Valiant.

I looked it over, opened the doors and peered at the engine. "It's ugly as hell. It has torn seats, a cracked windshield, and it smells like the inside of a water buffalo." I said.

"Well, you asked." Walsh shrugged. "You wanted a beater, something invisible. You got it."

"Yeah, it's perfect." I agreed. "What about a Saskatchewan license plate?"

"We found you a rear plate. It's from a sixty-eight Malibu, though. That might be a problem, in case you're stopped."

"Actually, that's also perfect." I said.

The motor pool crew cut a key to fit the Valiant's ignition, then they checked over the car to be sure it wouldn't fall apart on me right away, and I drove it home. I wanted to look like someone who was not quite on the run, but who didn't really want to be found, either. I had a beaten-up suitcase that looked like something left behind at a bus terminal, and I stuffed it full of my roughest clothes. I made lunch, sipped coffee as I chewed my sandwich, and wrote a list of what to do next.

The phone rang. "Hello?" I asked.

Walsh's voice came back. "Hey, boss, you wanted a fake driver's license, you said?"

"And a release certificate from the Regina Pen." I added.

"OK. Under your name?" He asked.

I thought for a moment. "No. make the name 'Ian George Brewster'. Born November fifth of 'forty-six. That's great, thanks, Patrick."

I heard him writing. "OK, why that name?" He asked, curious.

"Long story, but I figure it's easier to remember if the first name is the same as my real one. If someone yelled out 'hey Norm' and I didn't turn around, then I might be in trouble."

"So much for the name. What about the home address on the license?"

I gave him an address I knew, for St. Gerard's Catholic Church in Yorkton.

"All right. I'll have all that for you later today- say five-thirty?"

"Boy, Patrick. I'm impressed. Who do you know that can do that so fast?" I said.

"Ask me no questions, I'll tell you no lies, boss. See you at the shop later?"

"No, can you meet me at home?" I asked.

"Sure thing. We'll see you then, boss." He said.

I finished my sandwich, ticking off boxes on a small slip of paper, things to arrange before I went, and circled the last two undone items.

I drove down the street to our family bank. The manager knew us well, of course, and knew what my job was. I asked to withdraw five thousand dollars in small used bills from my account. He asked, nervously, if there was a problem he could help with, and I assured him it wasn't anything personal, just something to do with work.

He went into the back room and collected stacks of withered bills, counting them meticulously until he was certain it was exactly five thousand dollars.

I put them into a paper lunch bag, went back to the Valiant, and drove off. The manager was staring through the glass as I left, no doubt wondering what I was up to.

It took me just ten minutes to get to my next destination; on Bathurst Street, around the corner from the fancy restaurants and clothing stores on Queen Street, was a series of run-down houses, Victorian relics that had somehow survived demolition. A couple of them were bookstores now, one was a sandwich shop, and one was a hairdressing salon. The one I was there to visit, though, was a storefront that had a grim black sign reading 'Tattoos'. I stuck the paper bag with the cash under the driver's seat and went in. The door opened with a ding-a-ling sound, a bell hanging inside the door, and I closed it gently behind me. The shop was not dark, gloomy, as I'd expected, but instead looked like a barber shop, or a dentist's office.

There were two chairs, with reclining backs and footrests, and on the walls were photographs of people with tattooed arms and faces. I waited patiently, then a beaded curtain in the back shook, and a small man came out. He looked like I imagined a tattoo artist would look; he wore a black shirt with the sleeves rolled up, a Cisco Kid moustache streaked with grey, and a head of dyed black hair slicked back onto his collar. He chewed some imaginary gum, looking me over.

"Yeah, help you?" He said.

"I'd like some ink done." I said, firmly.

His eyes scanned me up and down. "First time?" He said.

"Yes. Also, it has to be temporary. I want to wash it off in a couple of weeks. But I want it to look real-prison style, if you know what I mean."

He moved his lower jaw side to side. "Workin' undercover?"

That surprised me. "Why would you say that?"

"You're a cop. Seen your face on the TV. You stopped that bank heist around the corner."

I smiled. "I'm surprised you remember it. That was four years ago."

He shrugged. "I got friends in that bank. Nobody lost money, nobody got hurt. You did good."

"So, what can you do for me?" I asked.

He showed me books of standard tattoos, images of flaming skulls, rough crosses, buxom women, Celtic crosses, and dozens of others.

"I can put these on in black ink. Colour would fade sooner, maybe in three, four days, especially if you swim in a pool or something." He explained.

"No, black is fine. What can you do that would look like I had done time in juvie?" I asked.

"You mean 'HATE' on one set of knuckles, 'LOVE' on the other?"

I nodded. "Yeah, something like that would work."

"And a dotted cross on the hand between the thumb and first finger." He added.

I looked at my hand. I'd seen tattoos like that before, on criminals. "Perfect." I said.

"You realize, of course, I'd like this kept on the hush-hush."

"Won't hear it from me. Sit down." He said.

I emerged an hour later. I had 'STOP' painted on my right hand, one letter on each knuckle joint. There was an eagle on my upper arm, faint on the tanned skin, and a spiderweb on my neck, with a small spider dangling over my Adam's apple. The tattoos all looked very realistic. A cross, made up of dots, and about an inch long, was beside my thumb. It looked like it was done with a piece of wire and fountain pen ink. All told, it made me look like very much like an ex-con.

I'd been told to leave the designs overnight, then shower and see how much the ink faded. It should stay about the same after that for a week or two, the man had said.

I drove home and waited. I sat in a chair, dozing as I tried to read a book. Just after five, a loud knock startled me; I got up and opened the door.

Walsh stared at me, his eyes scanning the tattoos. "Really, boss? You got tats? Isn't that going a bit overboard?" He asked.

"They'll wash off. They're only temporary." I explained. "Come in."

He entered, furtively looking behind him, and pulled a large manila envelope from under his jacket, like a spy transferring state secrets.

"Here you go, 'Ian'." He said. "And if anyone asks, you don't know where they came from. I never gave them to you."

I opened the envelope. Inside was a paper rectangle- a Saskatchewan Driver's Licence, with the name 'Ian George Brewster', the address I'd asked Walsh to put on it, and details of my age and height. It looked very real.

Behind it was a larger piece of paper, very official looking, in heavy vellum paper with a legal seal on it. It stated that Ian George Brewster had served his full sentence and was hereby released from the Saskatchewan Regional Correctional Institution.

I placed the two pieces of paper on my dining table. "Thanks, Patrick. You'll never hear about these things again." I promised.

There was something else in the envelope, something heavy. I opened the flap wider, and recognized a license plate, a white Saskatchewan plate with green lettering, and a sticker that said it was valid until November.

Walsh shook his head. "I sure hope you know what you're doing, boss. Do you want us to stand by, to come out there with you, in case you're in trouble?"

"No, I think it's better if I go it alone. We need to keep a low profile on this case."

"What do I say to our fearless leader if he asks where you are?"

"Tell him the truth. Say that you have no idea where I am."

Walsh left, squealing the tires on his LTD as he turned toward downtown.

I made myself an omelet for dinner, watched something mindless on TV, then went to bed.

At seven the next morning, I was in the shower. I scrubbed my skin hard, weathering the ink on the tattoos to a dull grey, and toweled myself carefully off. I looked in the mirror; they looked as real as before, but now they had the patina of age, as though they'd been there for years.

I packed my suitcase, an old one I'd planned to donate to the Salvation Army. I had an assortment of rough clothes, torn sweaters and a threadbare sports coat, nothing that looked like I had money. I put it all into the Valiant, along with the five thousand dollars in the paper bag.

There was one more thing to do; I called Frank's house, and Helen answered. "Hey, Helen. Is your boyfriend still home?" I joked.

She paused. "What's wrong, Ian? Karen called me last night and asked me to check on you."

"I'll be out of town. I just wanted you to know."

"Is there anything we can do, Ian? Anything at all?"

"Would you mind checking my mail and stuff? I'd appreciate it."

"Certainly. Stay safe, all right?"

"Always." I reassured her.

Chapter Four

I left my police ID and gun at home, locked up the house and hid the key out back, under a large rock. I got into the Valiant, took a last look at my home, and drove north.

I took Yonge Street north and meandered east along Highway Seven till the road swerved south and east, just before the town of Lindsay. I followed the southern route for another five miles; Lindsay was behind me now, and I drove past the few houses, sitting forlorn in large fields, letting the road draw me further into clear farmland. According to my map, the scrapyard was only a half mile away, just up the road.

I turned off at an intersection with an abandoned gas station on one corner; to my left was more farmland, tall with corn, yellow and brittle in the summer sun. To my right was a bare dirt yard with a dozen or so semi-trailers scattered in a haphazard pattern. Just beyond the semi-trailers was a long, high chain link fence, and where the fence met the road was a four-by-eight sheet of plywood, painted to read 'Scugog Scrap and Metal'. Hanging under the sign was a piece of cardboard, about a foot square, a red and black sign that read 'Now Hiring'.

I drove past the scrapyard, went along for a good mile, and turned off on a farm access road.

I looked around to make sure nobody could see me, then I went to the back of the Valiant and took off the Ontario plate, replacing it with the Saskatchewan one. I looked around- nobody was watching. I took off the front plate, and threw both Ontario license plates into a ditch by the side of the road. They disappeared into the dark water.

I drove back to the scrapyard, pulled up to the front door of a building marked 'Office' and purposely parked in a spot labeled 'No Parking'.

I was wearing a khaki tee shirt, worn jeans and a plaid flannel shirt, trying to look as lowbrow as possible. I lumbered into the office, wavering gently side-to-side, and looked around meekly.

A woman behind a Formica counter glanced up at me and went back to sorting paperwork. She was somewhere over fifty, wiry, businesslike, wearing a cotton blouse that might have once been pretty. She slid a sheet of paper into a plastic desk tray and spoke without looking at me again.

"Yeah?" She said.

"Um, sign says you're hiring?" I said.

"Yeah. What can you do?"

She finished placing paper in the tray and looked right at me. She had a slightly aquiline face, grey hair pulled back in a tight bun, and eyes the same color that burned into me.

"I done a lot of manual work." I said. "What do you need?"

She scanned my clothes, looking me over more carefully, and her eyes slowed visibly when she saw the spiderweb on my neck.

"Where are you from?" She asked sharply.

"Saskatchewan. Yorkton, Saskatchewan." I said.

"You're a long way from home. Why did you come here to work?" She probed.

"I got family up in Muskoka, and in Peterborough. They said the jobs was better here." I said.

She paused for a moment then snorted. "You got a rap sheet?"

I pretended to be ashamed. "I done some time, yeah."

"You still on parole?"

I shook my head vigorously. "No, ma'am, I got my walking papers. I'm good."

She studied me for a moment, then held her hand out. "Show me."

I reached into the breast pocket of my flannel shirt and pulled out the Release Certificate.

I handed it gingerly to her, as though it was precious.

She unfolded the paper and read it over, carefully.

"What were you in for?" She asked.

"Bein' Indian." I answered.

"Since when is that a crime?"

I sighed. I had rehearsed this speech on the drive up, and I hoped it sounded genuine. "Me and some buddies went for a ride. I didn't know the car was stolen. Anyway, we all got sent up, and I just got out last month. So I figured I'd start fresh here, you know?"

She sniffed and folded the paper carefully, along the same crease lines.

"We pay eight bucks an hour, and a bonus if you work harder. You start at eight tomorrow. Does that work for you?"

I grinned. "Yes, ma'am. Thank you."

She nodded, and her shoulders softened. "All right. Tomorrow we'll get you a locker so you can change into coveralls for work. You'll have to pay for the coveralls yourself, but we'll take it out of your first paycheque. We pay every week, on Friday, in cash."

"That's fair. Sure." I said.

"You drink much?" She asked. The edge came back.

"Not on the job. Never when I'm workin'." I said.

She handed me the release document. "Fine. Come out and meet Mick. He's the foreman you'll be working with. I'm Sandra."

"You're the secretary?" I asked.

"No, I own this place."

I smiled sheepishly. "Pleased to meet you, Sandra."

She walked me through the office to the scrapyard. "When you come to work, you don't go in through this door. Go around the side, all right?"

"Yeah, sure."

I stepped down to ground level at the back door and looked around. There were the carcasses of abandoned forklift trucks, rusty engine blocks and rear axles, all tossed to one side like discarded toys. Beyond them was a rough-looking shed- a lunchroom for the men- with a long wooden table and benches. Along one wall was a series of lockers, in two rows high and low, numbered from one to twenty-four. My heart skipped a beat- I was sure the key in my pocket would fit the one marked 'seventeen'.

Sandra picked her way along the path, stepping carefully to avoid oil spills and sharp metal, then she stopped and looked at one man. She caught his eye and waved.

He pointed at a large piece of machinery, barked a command at someone, and strutted toward us.

He was not tall, barely coming up to my chin, but he looked like he was used to having people do what he told them to. He had a wide scar across his right cheek, a mop of curly hair that varied between silver and dark blond, and a set of tattoos that made mine look subtle.

"Yup?" He asked, not looking at me.

Sandra waved her hand my way. "This is Ian. He starts tomorrow. Show him around, all right?"

The man looked me over. "'Okay. Come with me."

He stomped along back the way he'd come, not waiting to see if I followed. He stopped right where I'd first seen him and waved at an immense pile of scrap metal.

"This's all going to a smelter. We separate the aluminum shit from the iron and send off the iron. You're working with Carl. He'll show you what to do. Be here for eight tomorrow. One minute late, you're fired. Got it?"

I nodded. "Do I get a locker, or bring my clothes from home, or what?"

He waved toward the office. "We'll get you a locker tomorrow. You get a key. We keep the other key. We do random checks, too. You bring booze or dope to work, you're fired. Got it?"

"Yeah, no sweat." I said.

"Where you living?" He asked.

"Nowhere, for now. There a motel or someplace I can stay at for a week or so? If this job works out, I'll get a room near here." I hoped it sounded sincere, plaintive.

He pointed north. "Just outside town, the Starlite Motel. Sandra's niece runs it. Tell 'em you work here and she'll give you a deal. It's not bad. It's clean, quiet. You don't party loud, right?"

I shook my head. "Nope, never."

"Good. The Starlite Motel."

He wrote the address on a scrap of paper and scribbled a map. It was about a five-minute drive away, further along the same road. I took the paper and nodded.

"Thanks. See you at eight." I held out my hand, but he just walked away, yelling at someone.

The Starlite Motel was like a mix of my father's hotel in Esterhazy and a hideout in a bad movie.

The main hotel was a long building, with a dozen doors facing the parking lot. The office was at one end of the main building. It had been one of the guest rooms, clearly; the wall facing the parking lot was now all windows and a high counter was stuck at one end of the room.

Beyond that was a handful of cottages, each one not much bigger than my living room, arranged in a U shape.

I pulled my suitcase out of the Valiant and swung it goofily as I went into the office.

There was a Coke machine, a pay phone, and a cigarette machine along the solid back wall, with a kidney-shaped coffee table in the middle of the floor, flanked by plastic stackable chairs.

A partition separated the main office from a back area, with paintings hung on its wall.

Nobody was behind the counter. I waited for a minute. From a back area I heard the tinkle of cutlery, of dishes being moved, two people talking softly.

Just down the counter, I saw a small metal bell, the dome kind you see in all the old movies.

I reached over and tapped it; it made a gentle 'ding' sound. The sound of dishes and cutlery stopped, and I heard the slap of leather on linoleum.

A woman came around the partition, wiping her mouth on a paper napkin. She looked like a younger version of the woman at the scrapyard, roughly my age, slight, quite pretty. She had auburn hair in a ponytail, tied with a plaid ribbon. Looking at her I could see how Sandra must have looked as a younger woman, before working with the men in her yard had made her tough.

The woman nodded. "Hi. Can I help you?" She said.

"Yeah. I just got a job at the scrapyard. Fellow called Mick said I should look for a room here?" I wanted to sound as harmless as possible. "You're Sandra's niece? Pleased to meet you."

She pulled a black binder out from under the counter and opened it up. "Yeah, hi. So, do you just need a room for yourself?"

"Yes, just for me."

She clicked a ballpoint pen and started writing, then looked sharply up. "You got ID?"

I pulled out the battered wallet I was using and showed her my fake ID. She copied down the address and license number. "Where did you work before this?" She asked.

I thought about how to answer. Surely she would talk to her aunt- there was no point in evading the question. "Nowhere. I was at the hill."

"The hill?" She repeated.

"I was in the Saskatchewan Correctional Facility in Regina. Everyone there calls it 'the hill'."

"When did you get out?"

"Three weeks ago."

She tilted her head slightly to one side. "What were you in for?"

"Hanging out with dumb friends."

She finished writing and slammed the binder closed. I felt worried that she might not give me a room. "Why did you choose to grace our community with your magnanimous presence?"

Too many big words- I couldn't let her know I understood them. "Sorry?" I said.

She spoke slowly. "Why are you here?"

I feigned sudden understanding. "Oh, yeah. I got family in Muskoka."

She held out a brass key on a plastic fob. "Room eight, at the end of the main building. We have maid service three times a week, Tuesday, Thursday and Sunday, so don't let the room get messy, or vomit on the sheets, or anything. Otherwise we charge extra. A lot extra."

She didn't wait for me to take the key. She put it on the counter and slid it my way. "No drugs, no dealing, no hookers, no campfires..."

"Campfires?" I interrupted.

She smiled slightly. "You'd be surprised. Anyway, it's a quiet motel; we like it that way."

She continued, reciting something she'd said thousands of times. "There's a bar fridge, toaster, hotplate, TV, and we check that they're all still there when you leave. Twenty dollars a day, a hundred a week. In cash, up front. Is that a problem?"

I shook my head and opened the suitcase. I pulled out the brown paper bag full of cash and counted out five crumpled twenties, then put the bag in my pocket.

The woman's eyes stayed on mine, but I was sure she was looking at the money in the bag.

I slid the hundred toward her, gingerly, as though I wasn't sure I could part with it, and waited patiently. She wrote me a receipt, placed it on the counter, and took the cash.

"There you go. Enjoy your stay." She said.

"Um, like, where can I buy some groceries an' stuff?" I asked.

She pointed her ballpoint pen toward the door. "Just before you hit Lindsay, there's a Valu-Mart on the left side of the road. And there's a laundromat in the same strip mall. Just up the road, as I say."

I nodded thanks, took the key, and stepped out into the hot sunlight. I walked to a painted wooden door with a peel-and-stick number eight above the peephole and unlocked it. The room was dark. Even after the blinding sunlight, the room was unusually dark. There was a double bed pressed to one wall, with a multicolored bedspread covering the sheets, and wildly patterned carpet on the floor. The drapes, thick and coarse, were in yet a different pattern, and they covered the single, undersized window. The walls were cheap wood panelling painted white, the grain of the wood still showing through the paint. At least the room didn't smell bad, just of Pine Sol and soap.

I pulled the drapes open; the sunlight streamed in, painting a rectangle of yellow on the walls, accentuating the wood grain. I dropped my suitcase on the bed, checked for a Gideon's Bible in the single nightstand, and casually opened it at random.

It fell open at First Corinthians, and a passage I knew well. Chapter thirteen, verse six: 'Love does not delight in evil but rejoices in the truth'. That would do. I was looking for the truth.

I unpacked my toiletries, placed them on the bathroom sink and turned on the hot tap, checking whether it worked. It howled like an injured goat, then as I opened it further it went quiet.

The shower curtain was not in bad shape, the rest of the bathroom acceptable. I went back into the bedroom and opened the small fridge. It was empty, clean, and it didn't smell. There was a set of dishes on a counter beside the fridge, some pots and a frypan, and cheap cutlery in a drawer. Good. There was time to set the stage for my next act.

I locked up, walked back to the car and looked off toward town. The woman behind the counter could still see me. I pulled the paper bag full of cash out of my pocket and dragged a few bills out, stuck these in my shirt pocket and put the bag away again. I wanted her to know I had all the money with me, so she wouldn't ransack the room.

Next, I drove to the grocery store she'd mentioned, grabbed a basket and wandered the few aisles. It was a small store, catering to those in the area, and I was hoping that the people here talked to her too. Most small towns were like that- a new stranger was the subject of fresh gossip, if nothing else. I wanted to be a subject of gossip.

After collecting a few days' worth of groceries I shuffled to the cashier's desk. I was the only person in the store, a lull between early morning and late shoppers, I guessed. The woman at the desk looked like the sister of the woman at the motel. Family businesses often overlapped in the country, so it was not unlikely.

"Hi, good afternoon." I said, softly.

She smiled mechanically. "Hey."

She started punching in prices from the stickers on the cans of soup and carton of milk. A couple of times, I was sure she had punched in a higher price. I said nothing.

She told me the total on the cash register, and I pulled out the bills from my shirt, counting out singles and fives. She took my cash and gave me some coins in return. I looked at them as though I was unfamiliar with money. She placed the groceries into a large paper bag, with the bread carefully on top, and slid it my way.

"Usually, don't you put the bread on the bottom and stack cans on top of it?" I joked.

"We only do that to people if we don't like them." She deadpanned.

I gave her a wide grin, and she smiled broadly. "You new in town?" She asked.

I sensed she was interested in me, and I wanted to act like I was interested back.

"Yeah, I just got hired- at Scugog Scrap Metal? Hope it works out for me." I said.

She rested both elbows on the counter and leaned forward. "You out here all by yourself?"

I smiled. "For now, yeah. It'd be nice to meet someone, though. Looks like a decent little city."

She blushed slightly. "Well, you know, it's a good place to meet someone who likes…"

The door opened, and a woman marched in, shepherding a pair of fast-moving children. "Stop! Stop running! No running! Darren! Darren!!" She howled.

I cringed at the sound, but it was a perfect time to get away. "I hope we meet again." I said.

The cashier looked disappointed by the woman's arrival. "Yeah, I hope so too."

I nodded goodbye and walked slowly out. The woman with the children glared at me, stared at my neck tattoo and shooed her children away from me. I ignored the look and wandered out to my car, put the groceries on the seat and looked around.

The strip mall had a few businesses; there was the grocery, then beside it a laundromat, further down the way was an auto parts store, and at the end of the mall, wrapping around to the back, was a bar.

The bar looked like a set for western movies- there was a hitching post, a water barrel for horses, a swinging door and a hanging wooden sign which read 'The Roundup'. I walked towards it, wondering if I could use it in some way.

I decided what to do and looked back toward the grocery store. There was probably a pay phone near there, and I didn't want to call from my room, because the staff might listen in. Sure enough, the pay phone was at the other end of the mall, beside a second-hand store.

I pulled out some coins and plugged them into the phone, then dialed a familiar number. It rang, and someone picked up almost immediately.

"Sergeant Walsh." The voice said.

"Patrick, it's me." I said.

He moved closer to the receiver. "Hey, what's going on, then?" He whispered.

"No time. Can you call me in fifteen minutes from somewhere else, not in the shop?"

"Sure. Boss." He was almost silent.

I gave him the number on the phone booth. "Can you get Alex to be there with you?"

He wrote quickly. "Done. Fifteen." He hung up.

I sat in the car, waited ten minutes, then went back to the pay phone. It rang a minute later.

"Hi?" I said.

"Hi, boss. We're at a hotel down the street. What gives?"

"OK, Patrick. I'm booked into room eight at the Starlite Motel. I got hired to work at Scugog Scrap and Metal, starting tomorrow. They have a series of lockers for the men- one of them is number seventeen. Incidentally, the driver's license passed muster with the hotel staff, and the Release Certificate passed muster with the scrapyard. The woman who owns the scrapyard is the aunt of the one who owns the motel. It all seems fishy, but more later. How are things there?"

Walsh let out a deep breath. "Captain Wonderful pissed off everybody today. One of the more.... vociferous guys offered to enlarge his digestive system, if you get my drift. He's hiding out in his office now. He asked where you were, and I told him I didn't know. In any case, he's a low priority for us right now. Good news is, we got a name for the dead guy in the Mercedes."

"Yeah?" I prodded.

"Robert Sankar. There's a problem with that, though. He was a cop- an OPP detective."

"Oh, shit. That really opens up a fresh can of worms, Patrick."

"Right. Was he working on a case, or was he just in the wrong place at the wrong time? We don't know yet. We'll find out more when Gail Fontaine comes back from Ireland. Anything else we can we do for you, boss?"

I thought for a moment. "Not yet. Tell you what, though, can you or Alex call me here on Friday night, around eight? I should have a better idea of where I'm at by then."

I heard him mutter something to Reynolds. He came back on. "Yeah. Alex asked if you would like one of us to show up to keep an eye on you?"

"Again, no, Patrick. The less attention, the better. I'll talk to you Friday night."

"Be careful, boss."

"Right." I hung up.

I brought the groceries back to the motel and filled the fridge. I might only be here a day or two, or a whole week, but either way I needed it to look like I was here to stay. I wanted to blend in.

I made myself a sandwich and warmed up a can of soup. The coffeemaker was adequate, and the can of coffee fit in the single shelf over the kitchenette's counter. I could drink coffee as I watched TV. There was an electric clock radio by the bed, and I set the alarm for six forty-five. I would probably be awake before then, but in case somebody went through my room while I was at work, I wanted to give the impression that I wanted to be up on time.

By ten thirty, I climbed into bed, tuned the clock radio to the country station, and endured some twangy music as I got drowsy. If the maid heard jazz on the radio when I was at work, it would have seemed incongruous. I reached over a few minutes later, clicked it off, and fell asleep.

The driveway of the motel was covered in pea gravel. Anytime someone walked past my door, the 'scritch-scritch-scritch' sound of gravel underfoot woke me up.

At three thirty, a long-distance trucker walked past my door, and his heavy footsteps woke me up. I fell back to sleep. At six fifteen, another sound woke me, more footsteps, hurried, then stopping just beyond my door. I heard the woman from the front desk, talking to a man's voice. The heavy outer drapes were open, but the inner ones, light and gauzy, were closed over, letting the morning sunlight in. I saw the outline of her body, a shadow on the drapes.

"Why is he here? Does he know?" She whispered.

I could barely hear her. She was standing to one side of my window, looking toward the road, then looking back to the man.

He spoke, soothingly. "He's just a drifter. Let it go. He'll quit soon and be gone. Forget it."

She hissed. "I don't like it. It's too soon after that cop. You should check him out."

The man again. "And draw even more heat? No, forget it. If he's fuzz, we'll know soon enough. If not, let it go. Forget it, Gillian. Let- it- go."

She grunted something and walked off, the sound of her shoes crunching briskly on the gravel.

I decided not to shower. Coming to work at a scrapyard clean-shaven and smelling good would make me a target. It also gave me another twenty minutes to finish breakfast and do the dishes. I wondered where I should leave the bag of money; if I was very sneaky about where it was, that would look suspicious, but if I left it our for anyone to find, that would be just as suspicious.

I decided to take it with me. I left the motel and drove off with the cash on the seat beside me. Half a mile later, I checked that nobody was around, opened the trunk and hid the cash under the Valiant's spare tire.

At a quarter to eight, I was outside the scrapyard, ready to start work. The yard was deserted, closed off, the chain link gate padlocked. Five minutes later, the foreman, Mick, pulled up, driving a rust-spotted Chrysler Imperial.

He walked past me, pulled a set of keys from his pocket and unlocked the gate. I waited patiently as he swung the heavy gate to one side, then drove his car inside and parked at a bare spot by the lunch shed.

I walked in behind him, stood a few feet away and let him come to me. He reached into the back seat of the Chrysler, came back with two pairs of heavy leather gloves, and approached me.

"Here. You can use these." He said.

"You'll get a new pair next week, but they'll come out of your pay. All right?"

I nodded. "Yeah, sure."

He watched as a half dozen men came through the gate; it was now five minutes to eight, and they clearly didn't want to give Mick any more of their time than they had to. Mick watched them wander to their spots, then turned to face me again.

"You'll be working with Jeff today. He's the one in the red tee shirt. He'll show you what to do."

"Jeff. Got it." I said.

Mick grumbled something unintelligible and walked away.

It was interesting to play at being stupid, to act dumb, but it was almost scary just how easy it would be to live like this, not pushing myself, not questioning.

I strolled up to the man in the red tee shirt. He was tall, wiry, with sinewy muscles and a grey stubble of beard. He worked with his head down, grabbing pieces of metal and tossing them into one of three bins, supposedly randomly. I waited till he'd stopped throwing one of the more jagged pieces and tapped his shoulder. He didn't turn around, didn't look up or even flinch.

"Yeah? You the new guy?" He asked, in a voice like a pained moan.

"Yeah. I'm Ian. You're Jeff?"

"Right. Sort the iron from aluminum and brass, then toss them in the right bin. That's it."

"OK." I said.

I spent the morning hunched over, scooping pieces of jagged iron and sections of cut-up girders into the bin marked 'iron', then tossing everything from gutters to flowerpots into the bin marked 'alum' and the rest, pots, lamp domes, water taps and the rest, into a bin marked 'brass'.

A car horn sounded at noon, and everyone stopped working. I turned to speak to Jeff. He had barely said a word all morning, and I wanted to sound like I was interested in the work.

"Do we have a lunch truck that comes by, or something?" I asked.

"Nope. Got to bring your own lunch."

"How long do I have?" I asked.

"Forty-five minutes." He answered.

I'd passed a burger place about five minutes away; I decided to treat myself for lunch.

"I'm going to go grab a bite. You want anything?" I asked.

He looked up at me, searching my face. "Why?"

I shrugged. "Hey, I'm just offering to buy you fries or something, is all. You want anything?"

He nodded slowly. "Yeah. A cheeseburger. With everything."

"Cheeseburger. Got it. I'll be right back." I said.

I drove quickly to the burger place; there was no lineup, and I ordered the food to go. I ate my hamburger on the way back to the scrapyard, slurping ginger ale, and scrunched to a stop back at the same parking spot. I handed the paper bag to Jeff. "Here you go, cheeseburger." I smiled.

He took it, incredulous, and looked inside. "Gee, thanks." He said.

He pulled the food out and started eating. He nodded approval. "Good. Thanks again."

I took a minute to look around. There were eight other men in the yard right now, plus Mick, the foreman, and me. The owner, Sandra, was in the office. I'd seen her poke her head out a couple of times and call something to Mick. Eleven people in total. That was a baseline, a place to start. I'd write notes later about anything I'd observed.

At a quarter to one, the car horn sounded again, and the men casually returned to work. Mick gave me another job to do; lining up metal conduit on racks at one side of the yard. These were sold in bulk to a construction company, he explained.

After I'd done that, he had me help him sort more metal. Finally, late in the day, he got into a forklift and scooped up the bin full of iron. He moved it further down the yard and tilted it on its side, spilling all the iron.

He dragged the bin away and used the forklift to flip it upright again, picked the bin up and brought it back. I watched this all, curious.

Then, another man climbed onto a large machine with an electromagnet hanging from a long metal arm and picked up the dumped iron. He swung the magnet around and stopped over a crushing machine. He turned off the magnet and the iron fell into the crusher.

The crusher ground the scrap metal down to soup-can sized chunks and fed them along a belt into another bin. I watched this for a good minute, fascinated, until Jeff tapped my shoulder and waved me to follow him. He led me to the back door of the office and yelled in.

"He's here!" He called.

I waited patiently, wondering what I had done. A minute later, Sandra came out with a thin clump of papers in her hand. She thrust them at me.

"Here, you'll need to fill these out by next Friday." She said.

I looked down at them; they were standard employment forms the government required for taxes, a letter of employment, and a waiver, in case I got hurt on the job.

"You want them by day after tomorrow, ma'am?"

"No, *next* Friday. If you don't work out, I don't want to do any more paperwork than I have to."

I took them and thanked her, then turned to leave.

"Wait a minute." She snapped.

I worried that I'd been discovered. She stepped into the office and came back holding something.

"This is a key to your locker. Try not to lose it. Number fourteen. Can you remember that?"

"Yeah, fourteen." I said. "Thank you, ma'am."

I took the forms and the key, opened locker number fourteen and placed the papers inside it. I now had a reason to be at this spot. Tomorrow, I would bring a lunch and keep it in the locker, and on Friday I would bring a nicer change of clothes, on the pretense that I was going to the bar after work. That would give me a chance to open locker seventeen, just three feet away from mine. So close, yet so out of reach. Still, I didn't want to rush and blow my cover. It might not be anything important in the locker, it might be nothing, or it might have already been taken away.

I went back to loading scrap iron into a bin and tried not to think about it.

At five minutes after five, the car horn sounded and everyone quickly finished what they were doing. We all filed out of the yard, Mick scanned the area to see nobody was left behind, and he padlocked the gate. The sound of engines, like a small Indy 500, filled the still air with a low rumble, and faded as everyone left.

I rolled down the window on the Valiant, fumbled for my keys, and almost missed the shadow coming up beside me. Mick poked his head into the window.

"Hey." He barked.

"Yeah?" I asked.

"Jeff says you do good work. Keep it up."

He patted the Valiant's roof and sauntered off. I smiled to myself, pleased. I started the engine, and looked around to see I wasn't going to hit anyone backing up.

Sandra came out of the office, scanned the yard and locked the door. I watched her step gingerly down to ground level, nod at me and get into a bright orange Monza. She drove off and I followed. She turned east, away from Lindsay, and I went north, back to the motel.

Dinner was just like last night's dinner. I warmed up a can of soup, made myself a sandwich from packaged ham and cheese slices, and watched some TV. What did they want to hide, I wondered? Why were they so afraid of who I might be, and why I was here?

The words of the woman from the office went through my mind. 'Does he know?' 'It's too soon after that cop.' Were they responsible for killing Sankar, or did they know who did it? How did they know he was a cop? It was frustrating- not enough puzzle pieces.

Maybe I was going about it the wrong way. Maybe instead of laying low, fitting in, I should stand out, make myself look vulnerable, a target.

That made sense. Do it that way. Tomorrow- I'd start on that tomorrow.

Chapter Five

At ten to eight I was pacing outside Scugog Scrap Metal, waiting for Mick to unlock the gate. Five minutes later, he screeched up, ran out of his car and fumbled with the padlock, mumbling an apology about some delay or other. He pushed the gate open, hard, jumped back into his car and raced in.

I walked in behind him, went straight to the lockers and opened locker fourteen with the key I'd been given. It was empty, slightly rusty, and smelled of shoe polish and stale leather. I placed the sandwich I'd made into it and locked up.

Mick yelled instructions to one of the men in the yard; I waited patiently till he noticed me.

"Yeah?" He asked.

"I had an idea." I said, slowly.

I pointed to the fresh pile of scrap metal I was supposed to go through. "Most of this pile is iron, right?"

He nodded, impatient.

"Well, instead of sorting it first, what about if you bring up the magnet first and pick up the iron? The magnet won't pick up aluminum or brass, just iron. Then we can sort what's left."

He looked at me, squinting in the morning sunlight, then his eyes widened as he understood.

"Shit, that's a really good idea." He muttered.

He glanced toward the office. I could tell that he didn't want me to get credit for the idea, or him to get blamed for not thinking of it sooner.

"Anyway, someone told me that once. I figured I'd just pass it on." I said. I walked away.

Mick grinned, stomped over to the crane with the magnet and drove it slowly down the path to the pile of metal.

He turned the switch, and the diesel motor groaned, generating power for the magnet. He lowered the boom until most of the metal stuck to the magnet, then he swung the boom and drove back, dropping the iron into the shredder,

The pile of metal, now just aluminum and brass, was a quarter of the size it had been.

Jeff had watched all this, intrigued. As Mick drove away, Jeff shook his head, curious, and slid his gloves on.

"C'mon, smart boy, let's go." He said.

We sorted the remaining pile into two bins, finishing by lunch time.

I opened locker fourteen, looked across at the tantalizing door to seventeen, and took out my lunch. I sat with the guys on a long picnic bench in the lunch shed. Some brought sandwiches, some had soup, some ate leftovers, from tin boxes or Tupperware containers.

One man, across from me, glared at me. I'd seen him in the yard, but never asked his name.

"So, where ya from?" He asked, loudly.

"Saskatchewan."

"Yeah?" He bit into some more of his lunch.

"Yeah."

"You got family?" He asked.

"Family. You know, a squaw, a papoose, family."

I could feel myself getting angry. "No."

He snickered. "So, are you in town all alone, or you looking to get lucky while you're here?"

"Always looking, you know."

He elbowed his neighbor, who was snickering along with him. "Got anyone in mind?"

"Yeah. Your sister."

He frowned. "I ain't got a sister."

"Is your wife cute?" I asked.

He roared like a bull and lunged over the table at me. Typical. I leaned back and let him flail at me.

The other men laughed, amused. I grabbed the man by the scruff of the neck and held him, face-down, against the table. I knew what would happen next.

A moment later, Sandra's shrill voice screamed across the room, at full volume. "What the bleeding hell is going on here? What are you doing, Dan?"

The men stopped laughing. I relaxed my grip and the man eased slowly away from me. I let go of his neck and he faded back to his side of the table.

Sandra glared at us, said nothing, and went back to the office. The man across from me, Dan, had his head low, but looked up at me, fuming.

"You think you're real smart, huh, Tonto?" He whispered.

"Hey, you started it, man." I said.

"I don't appreciate you slagging my family, Indian."

"No offense meant, man. I thought we was just playing around, is all."

He got up and went wordlessly back to work. I brushed breadcrumbs off my shirt and headed out to help Jeff with the afternoon's task.

From off to one side, I heard Sandra's voice, clear and sharp. "Ian, a moment please."

I sauntered over to her. "Yes, miss?"

She wagged a finger at me. "Dan is an idiot. He shoots his mouth off, and he's a bigot, but he's a decent man underneath, and one of my best workers. Let's let this go, all right?"

"I heard all kinds of names from everyone before, miss. He wasn't any bother, really."

"I'm happy to hear that, Ian. I understand you came up with a simple way to save us some time?"

Now she was smiling, speaking more genially.

"It were a trick I heard about a long time ago, I guess. Just glad it worked, is all."

"Is 'trick' just a euphemism?"

"A euphemism for what, ma'am?"

Right after that, I realized I had said the wrong thing. Why would I know what that word meant? It took me a few seconds to see how I could turn the gaffe to my advantage.

She smiled slowly. "Why are you acting so dumb, Ian?"

"Because, Sandra, people don't mind working with a dumb Indian. They get a little nervous around a smart one. Just like some people have trouble with a woman who owns a business in a man's industry. When did *you* stop telling people you were just the secretary?"

"How did you know I used to…"

She grinned broadly. "I'll let you get back to work, then. Have a good afternoon."

At the end of the day, I took off my flannel shirt, flapped it in the air to get the dust out of it, and opened locker number fourteen. I hung the shirt on a hook in there, ran my fingers through my hair and locked the door. There was nobody around; I had a few seconds to see what was inside the other locker. I took the key for seventeen out of my pocket, opened the door and quickly looked in. there was a small plastic box, smaller than a fishing tackle box, and a brown manila envelope.

I hurriedly closed the door, put the key away and wandered out to my car. As I opened the door, a large hand grabbed it, pulling me back. I turned around; it was Dan, the man I'd argued with.

"Hey, Ian. It's Ian, right? We're all going for beer. Wanna come?"

"Yeah, sure, man. Where?" I said.

He walked toward three other men in a rusty Pontiac. "Follow us." He called.

I followed the Pontiac past the motel, to the 'Roundup' bar at the strip mall. There were four other men from the scrapyard out front, waiting for us. We all filed in and found a large table at the far corner.

A waitress came by immediately. She was Native, or Eurasian- I couldn't tell- and she looked about fourteen. Some of the men ogled her as she walked past. One man said something and she came back with two large pitchers of beer and a stack of glasses.

He poured beer for each of us, expertly sliding the glasses along to the men down the table. I took my glass and waited for everyone else to get theirs. After the long, hot day at work, the beer felt good, cooling my throat and warming me up at the same time.

I nursed my beer, listening to the men talk about work, sports, women, anything they usually talked about. Most of them had poured their second or third drink and were feeling relaxed. The man who had egged me on earlier, Dan, leaned across the table and pointed at me.

"You move pretty fast, huh?" He slurred.

"I just got lucky. I'm sure you could have taken me." I smiled.

He wagged a finger at me. "No, like, you do that, like, kung-fu shit, or what?"

"Nope, nothing like that."

"Really? Where'd you learn them moves like that, man?"

"On the hill." I said.

I said what I wanted them to think was true. If any one of these men was involved in what happened to the dead cop, they might be more likely to talk to an ex-con.

Dan frowned. "The hill?"

"Yeah, that's what we call the Regional Jail, in Regina. I did a little time there."

He looked around. "What for?"

"Skipping out on a bar tab. Look, I gotta go, guys. This round's on me."

I stood up, pulled out a ten-dollar bill and placed it on the table.

"See you all tomorrow. Bye." I said.

They grinned at the money and said goodbye as they watched me leave. One man grabbed the bill and waved at the waitress for more beer.

I drove out of the parking lot and headed back toward the motel. Tonight, I'd lay low and just stay there. Tomorrow, I wanted to get at the contents of that locker. I had to get it without anyone knowing I had it, though. That was important. If I was still there for a few more days, I didn't want to raise any alarms in the meantime.

The trip back to the motel was only a couple of miles, and I drove cautiously, so as not to attract attention. Shortly after I left the bar, an OPP cruiser passed me, going the other way. In the rear-view mirror, I saw him pull over and come back towards me.

He raced up behind me, waited a few seconds, then turned on the lights and siren.

Dutifully, I put on the right turn signal, pulled over to the side of the road and turned off my engine. I put the key on the dashboard, a universal signal that I wasn't going to give him any trouble, and kept my hands on the wheel.

The OPP cop got out of his cruiser. He was alone, and he looked around to see if anyone was driving up on us, then he looked inside my car to see if I was alone. I sat still.

He squatted down beside me. "Evening." He said, simply.

"Good evening, officer."

"Mind if I look at your license and registration?"

"Not at all. I'm sitting on my wallet. OK if I get out and hand it to you?"

He stepped back slightly, his right hand above his revolver. He opened my door.

"Slowly, if you please." He said.

I turned, slid both knees out, placed my hands on the door frame and roof, and eased myself up.

I pulled my wallet from my back pocket and fished out the fake Saskatchewan driver's license.

"Here you go, officer."

I folded my arms and leaned against my car. The cop glanced at me, looked at the license, and tapped it against his other hand.

"Can I see your ownership as well, please?"

"You bet."

I tried not to look worried. I slid along the bench seat and opened the glove box. I reached in, pulled out a slip of paper, and glanced at it. It said that I was the owner of this Valiant, and it was also from Saskatchewan. Thank you for that detail, Patrick. I handed the registration to the cop.

He read it over.

"Do you still live in Saskatchewan?" He asked.

"No. I just moved out here for work."

"Where do you work?"

"Scugog Scrap Metal."

"And where do you live now?" It sounded like more than a casual question.

"I just got a room at the Starlite Motel, till I find an apartment or something."

He studied my face.

"Please wait right here." He said, firmly.

He strutted back to his car and picked up the microphone. He spoke, reading my registration, and waited a few seconds. Then he frowned, looked up at me, and spoke some more. He hung up the microphone and came back towards me, his hand now gripping his revolver.

I had my arms folded in front of me, not moving, not presenting a threat. He walked past me and leaned his left hand against the Valiant's roof, his right hand still gripping his revolver.

"So, your name is Ian Brewster, huh?" He said. There was a hint of a smile.

"Yes. Can I ask why you stopped me, officer?" I said, casually.

"Because you don't have a front license plate."

"No. In Saskatchewan, we don't."

"And why exactly are you in Lindsay, mister 'Brewster'?"

"Like I said, I moved here for work."

He nodded slowly. "I see, I see."

We waited for about ten minutes. He said little, and when I asked him any questions, he was evasive. I wasn't too worried; a call to the division would get me out of any trouble, and anyway, at the worst all they could get me for was a fake ID.

I heard an engine, and the sound of crunching gravel behind me. Another car, an unmarked car, pulled up behind the first cop. The door opened, and a familiar-looking man stepped out.

He was older than me, solidly built, with short red hair and a bushy moustache. He wore a suit, with a small pin on the lapel that indicated he was someone of importance.

The first cop stiffened noticeably when he saw the man. The man placed a hand on the cop's shoulder. "Good work, Zach. I'll take it from here. You can go."

The cop looked back and forth between us. "Don't you want me to stay here, sir, just in case?"

I grinned. "I don't believe that will be necessary. The inspector and I are well acquainted."

The cop shrugged, handed my documents to the man, and drove away. We both watched him go, then the man turned to face me and held out his hand.

"Ian, how the hell are you, and what the hell are you doing in our patch?" He said.

I shook his hand. "Hey, Josh. I'm just doing a little work under the radar."

He tilted his head. "Anything you can talk about?"

"Jeez, I'd rather not, you know."

He studied my expression. "Fair enough. It wouldn't have anything to do with a dead detective your lot asked us about? Rob Sankar?"

"Possibly. What can you tell me, Josh?"

He looked around. "Rob was a good guy, one of our best. Straight shooter, clean liver, a lot like you. We don't know what he turned up, but he sent us a message that it was a big deal. You wouldn't know anything about that, would you?"

"I haven't gotten that far. How did he lose a fingertip?"

"Accident- he was in the Caribbean, and he got a metal fishing line looped around his finger. A big marlin took the line and yanked it tight, cutting the pinkie off. He was always pleased to talk about it- said that despite that he landed the marlin."

"Sounds like something I might do."

He laughed. "Yeah, me too. Gotten far with your investigation?"

"Not yet, no. Do you want me to keep you posted, though?"

"Please. Rob went missing three weeks ago. All we can figure from his messages, he stirred up a real hornet's nest. Don't get yourself killed, Ian. Karen would never forgive me."

"Yeah, you don't want her pissed at you."

"How's she doing, by the way? And the kids?"

"She's in Esterhazy, visiting my old homestead. She's pregnant again, by the way. This will be number three for us."

"That's terrific. Meg and I will stop down and say hi before the end of the summer."

"I look forward to it. By the way, why did the Starlite Motel hit a nerve for your man?"

He shook his head. "We've been watching it for a while now. Everything looks right, everything seems legit, but there's something odd about the place, and we just can't figure out what."

I decided to not mention the conversation I'd overheard. I liked Josh, and I trusted him, but I wasn't sure about who he might talk to. The less he knew, the better I felt.

A rusty Pontiac rolled past us, with the four men from the bar in it. They slowed and stared at us as they went by, then picked up speed and drove off. They clearly recognized the ghost car. Good- that made my story about being an ex-con more believable. Josh hadn't seen them, and I kept that to myself, too.

He handed me the license and registration. "Keep me in the loop, Ian?"

"Shall do, Josh."

He frowned. "By the way, where did you get the name 'George Brewster'?"

"Do you really want to know?"

"Sure do."

I rubbed my nose, sheepishly. "When my brother and I were growing up, we sent away to one of those 'Columbia Record Club' things, you know, ten records for a cent, then you buy ten more at a ridiculous price."

He laughed. "I remember them, yeah."

"Well, we figured we'd get the freebies, but never buy any others. So we sent in the card with the made-up name 'George Brewster'. After the free records came, our dad was furious that we were cheating someone to get something, even from a big company, so he made us buy all the records we'd agreed to buy. It took all our allowance and paper route money. But it taught us a lesson."

"So that's why you used that name?"

"That's why." I confessed.

He looked up the road, thinking. "Rob Sankar was a good guy. I want to find the people who did this as much as you do, but I'd rather not add you to the list of casualties. Stay safe."

"Shall do, Josh."

I got to the motel, opened the door to my room and immediately panicked. Someone had been through the room. Wait- Thursday. Today was Thursday. The woman at the motel office had said the maid came on Tuesday, Thursday and Sunday. That's why things were moved around.

That gave me another idea. I drove out to the grocery store; like most general stores in small towns, they sold lots of odd things; tennis racquets, swim masks, car wax, things like that. There was an area at the back of the store that sold jeans, jackets and gloves. There were also a few tote bags, the kind one would take to the gym. I bought a rough-looking one, made of grey nylon.

Once I'd left the store, I drove partway back to the motel and pulled over. I looked around- nobody nearby. I threw the tote bag in the dirt, kicked it around, and stomped it, hard. Within a few seconds it looked beaten-up, old, and filthy. I shook off the loose dirt and tossed the tote into the back seat. It would come in handy later.

I parked in front of my room, brought the tote in with me, and made myself dinner. In the long evening of this summer day, I was too restless to sleep, too tired to do much, too worried about Karen and the kids to think clearly. What was in locker seventeen? Why was it so important that the dead cop had kept both keys? Was I on a wild goose chase? I'd find out tomorrow.

At seven in the morning, I was wide awake and eating my third slice of toast. I watched some mindless television, a gleeful woman describing how baking soda could remove stains from bathtubs, or something equally banal.

The sun beat in through the window and promised that this would be another scorcher of a day. That was what I'd hoped for. I threw a clean tee shirt into the tote bag, wore a scruffy one with my flannel shirt over it, and drove to the scrapyard.

Promptly at ten minutes to eight, Mick unlocked the gate and drove in. five minutes later, like clockwork, the other men walked in, ready to work.

I came in with them, swinging my dusty tote bag. I opened my locker, took off the flannel shirt and threw it into the locker, then placed the tote on top of it.

Jeff met me in the yard, eyeing a brand-new pile of scrap metal. Like the day before, we got the crane to lift out the iron, then sorted the remaining metal into bins.

At lunchtime, I opened my locker and fished a sandwich out of the tote. I felt in my pocket for the other locker key; the sound of voices made me reconsider- two of the men grabbed their own lunches from their lockers, standing by them and arguing sports as they did.

One of the men invited me to join him at the lunch table, and I followed him. Locker number seventeen would have to wait.

We went back to work. At four fifty-five exactly, Sandra came out of the back door to the office and handed out paycheques. I looked at my pay envelope; written on it, neatly in rows, was;

Three days, 24 hours. Gross pay: $192   Taxes: $29.67.   Deductions: $11.32 Net pay: $151.01.

I opened the envelope and counted the money. There were seven crisp twenty-dollar bills, a new ten, a single, and sliding along at the bottom of the envelope was a lone penny.

I folded the envelope up and stuck in into my pocket. Ten minutes later, we all wrapped up for the week, Mick shooed everyone out of the yard and closed the gate. Everyone drove off, giddy at their fresh cash. I waited till they'd gone and ran up to Mick.

"Hey, I forgot- my tote bag, it's in my locker still. Can you open up for me, man?"

He sighed and looked at his watch. "Gee, I gotta go. It's my weekend with my kids, you know?"

"Please, Mick, it'll just take a moment." I begged. "I forgot my license and shit in there."

He shook his head. "Ask Sandra if you can go through the office. Ask Sandra."

He got into his car and drove off. Sandra was at the front door, turning to close it behind her. I raced up to meet her.

"Sandra, Mick said I should ask you. I forgot my tote in my locker. Can I just run through and get it?"

She rolled her eyes. "Thirty seconds, then you're locked in the yard for the weekend." She said.

I grinned. "Great, thanks."

I ran through the office, opened my locker, took out my tote, and quickly opened number seventeen. I scooped everything from it into my tote, then closed both lockers, checked they were really closed, and raced back to the front door. It had taken about twenty-five seconds.

I reached into my tote and held up my wallet. "Can't go out without this. Thanks again."

We drove away together, then she turned south, away from Lindsay, toward Lake Scugog, and I drove north, toward the motel.

Halfway to the motel, I looked around. There was a short farm road between two corn fields, and I backed into the road, stopping just short of a wooden fence. The corn was tall; anyone passing by would never notice me unless they slowed to a crawl. Through my windshield I could see the road ahead and keep an eye on the few cars speeding by.

I opened the tote and pulled out my shirt, resting it on the seat. Onto that I carefully placed the manila envelope and plastic case I'd found in locker seventeen. I examined the case carefully; I wanted to be sure it wasn't booby-trapped or that opening it would spill anything. Carefully, slowly, I flipped open the plastic latch on the front of the case and lifted the lid.

Inside was a passport, in the name of Victor French. The picture looked like the morgue photo of the dead cop, sort of. It could have been his brother. This was the other body from the morgue, obviously. Still, if he was a drunk who died on the street, why did he have a passport?

I put the passport down. Below the passport was an airline ticket, first class, to Dublin, Ireland. That sent chills up my spine. Now we had some meat to bite into. Gail Fontaine was in Ireland, her car had a dead cop in it, and here was an airline ticket to Ireland for the guy who had gone missing from the morgue.

Lastly, I opened the manila envelope. Inside was a stack of travelers' cheques, twenty of them, a hundred dollars each. Two grand, right there, in travelers' cheques.

I looked at my watch; five-thirty. I'd told Walsh that he should call me at eight. I wanted to have a plan for how to pass this evidence on to him, without giving myself away.

Maybe I could do a dead drop- leave the stuff somewhere out of the way and let him pick it up when nobody was around. Or maybe I could have him drop by the motel and just give it to him.

The word 'euphemism' went through my mind. I had almost gotten myself into trouble by letting Sandra know I was smarter than I pretended to be. That was not a mistake I would repeat.

I drove to the motel, took the paper bag of money out of the trunk and stuffed it into my pocket. The woman from the front desk had spoken to someone outside my room, a conversation that told me she was involved somehow. I wanted to push her into making a mistake.

I went into the motel office, looked around sheepishly and waited for her to come out front.

She rested her elbows on the counter and smiled. Of course she smiled- she had seen my cash.

"Hi, anything I can do for you?" She purred.

I pulled the paper bag out of my pocket and clumsily peeled a twenty out of the stack.

"Um, could I get some change, for the Coke machine?" I asked.

"Certainly."

She opened a cash drawer, counted out a number of bills and change, counted them in front of me again to assure me it was all there, then took my twenty-dollar bill.

I grunted thanks, fed quarters into the vending machine, and bought two cans of Sprite.

I put the bills into the paper bag; she was watching, closely, without being too obvious. She wrote something in the daily ledger as she kept one eye on my money.

I took the Sprite and sauntered back to my room. Six o'clock. I had time to think up a plan, wait for Walsh to call me and tell him what I wanted to do. I made myself a sandwich and soup. This was food I was not used to eating, it gave me a bellyache and I didn't enjoy it. Once again since I'd come here, I really missed my home.

At seven fifty, I was sitting outside the pay phone, waiting for it to ring. In the pause between lunch and drinking time, nobody was around. A few people wandered into 'The Roundup' and the noise level had gone up slightly, yelling across the room, but nobody was out front.

The phone rang, softly at first, but only because I was expecting it to be louder. I jumped out of the car and picked up the receiver.

"Hello?" I said, tentatively.

"Boss?" Walsh's voice said.

"Hey, Patrick, yeah, it's me."

He sighed, relieved. "Good, so, when are you coming back?"

"Not for a bit. But I did get some information I want to share."

"Go for it, boss."

"I found a passport, belonging to our missing body, I think."

"I can be there in an hour." He said.

"No, I need you to hold the fort in town. Listen, is Alex there with you?"

I heard him say 'here' and the phone went quiet.

Reynolds' voice came on. "Yes, sir?"

"Alex, how would you like to spend a night with me?"

"*Excuse* me?"

"Can you meet me at The Roundup- it's a bar just south of Lindsay, tomorrow night?"

"Feeling lonely, are we?" She joked.

I laughed at that. "I need to set a scene for something. Can Brian drop you off at the bar? And I'd like you to wear something kind of slutty, if you would."

There was a long silence. "You know that I wouldn't do this for anyone else, right?"

"I appreciate that, Alex. And tell Brian that this is completely on the level. He'll understand on Sunday morning."

"What time do you want me there?"

"Around nine. If you show up too early, it won't look right. So, listen, you come in, I'll pick you up and take you back to the motel where I'm staying. I'll explain later."

"All right. Nine o'clock it is. See you tomorrow, boss."

"Thanks. Can I talk to Patrick again for a moment?"

Walsh came back on. "Yeah, boss?"

"Patrick, I've been identified by the OPP. A DI called Josh Klassen, good guy, knows that I'm here on a case. If I go missing, or if you think I could be in danger, contact him. He'll help you."

"Josh Klassen. Got it."

"Anything else going on I should know about?"

"No. We're managing the regular stuff just fine. Pascoe is feeling overwhelmed, I think. He's backed off a lot, lately. Still, it'll be good to have you back, boss."

"Good. Thanks for this, guys. I'll give Alex more details tomorrow."

I drove back to the motel. I pored over the passport, the airline ticket, the travelers' cheques. The passport was real; it didn't look like a fake, it didn't have a glossy coating over the photo, or a blurry stamp, or any of the other hallmarks of a fake.

The ticket was a return flight, Toronto to Dublin. It was for a week from now, in the name of Victor French. So; with money, a passport, and a ticket to Ireland, why did he die in the street?

I decided to stop thinking about it for now. Tomorrow, I'd call Karen and reassure her that I was alright. Then I'd do the charade with Reynolds. Hopefully it would convince the locals, and if I was lucky, word of what happened would get back to someone who was involved.

Too much to worry about all at once. Too many variables, too many ways for it to go wrong. At the worst, I could call in the OPP and have them bail me out. I decided to stop thinking for the night. I took a shower, watched some more mindless TV and went to bed.

Chapter Six

At eight the next morning, I decided to treat myself. After all, I had over a hundred and fifty dollars that I'd earned working in the scrapyard. I put the passport, cash and other things into my tote bag, stuffed it under the seat of the Valiant, and drove along the highway back toward Toronto.

I'd seen a nice diner on the road to the scrapyard, and I missed eating real food. I parked by the entrance, walked in and waited by the front cash desk. A waitress in a pale blue smock and shorty apron came up to me, slowing as she saw the tattoos.

"Can I help you?" She asked, carefully.

"Hi, just a table for one, please."

She tilted her head. "Um, I don't know if we have a table available..."

"You have a number of empty tables, miss. Just a table for one, please."

She looked up at me for a long while. "Let me get the manager."

She disappeared into the kitchen, came back a minute later, and waited till a man came out too.

He was older, wearing a rumpled white shirt over a white undershirt, and a baggy pair of checked pants, like many cooks wore. He glanced at the waitress and came up to me.

"I'm sorry, but we don't have a table for just one." He said, firmly.

"Fine, then give me a table for two. I'll buy two meals." I countered.

He waved his finger back and forth. "No, no, no. Look, we want no trouble. You just go now, OK?"

I sighed. "I don't want any trouble either. I just want scrambled eggs and pancakes. Period."

He flapped his arms, frustrated. "Listen, this is a nice place, a Christian place. The bible says 'My people will live in peaceful dwelling places.' That's what we give our customers, all right? A peaceful place to eat."

"I agree. You also know that Hebrews, chapter thirteen, tells us to 'show hospitality to strangers, for thereby some have entertained angels unaware'."

He studied me for a moment. "Fair enough. Please come with me." He said.

I followed him to a table in the corner, against a window and away from most patrons, but not completely out of sight. He motioned for me to sit down and waved for the waitress to bring me a menu.

She placed a folded, laminated menu in front of me and gave me a plastic smile.

"Yes, what can I get you?"

I looked the page over, quickly.

"Two scrambled eggs, coffee, buckwheat pancakes, and a side order of bacon, please."

I handed her the menu. A number of people in the diner- farmers, middle-aged women and families with children, glanced at me without wanting me to see they were looking. A few others, notably a table with four farm boys, were looking at me as though watching a zoo exhibit.

The waitress brought my coffee, and a few minutes later my food. I thanked her and ate, enjoying the first real meal I'd had in a couple of days. I ate slowly, savouring the taste and texture of the food. As I finished the last wedge of pancake, I looked out the window, thinking about Victor French. Why was he dead, and why was he found lying on the street? How was he tied to Robert Sankar, and had they both gone to the Starlite Motel?

I hadn't thought of that. If I could get a chance to see the guest book for the Motel, would I find both names in it? And where would that lead me? What was the next pebble in the stream, the next bread crumb?

"More coffee?"

The voice surprised me. I looked up and nodded.

"Yes, thank you. By the way, could you compliment the cook? He makes very good pancakes."

She actually grinned, pleased at the comment. She poured coffee carefully into my empty cup. "You know, you don't talk like you'd expect, to look at you, do you?"

"I've been told that before, yes."

She leaned back, resting the coffee carafe on her hip. "So, hon, what do you do for a living?"

"I work at Scugog Scrap Metal."

"Yeah? Been there long?"

"No, I just started there."

"But you're not from here, right?"

"No. I'm from Saskatchewan."

She grinned again. "Really? Me too. Where are you from?"

"Yorkton."

"I grew up in Melville. We're practically neighbours."

"Yes, I suppose we are."

She leaned forward slightly. "So, where did you go to school?"

As I tried to think of a way out of the conversation, a patron across the diner called the waitress by name, and she excused herself. I breathed a sigh of relief.

I paid the bill and left a tip. I found my keys and walked out to the Valiant. The four farm boys were outside, talking and laughing. I ignored them and unlocked the driver door. A hand tapped my shoulder, and I looked at the reflection in the car's side window before turning around. It was the biggest of the four boys.

Slowly, I turned around. "Yes?"

"Hey, where ya from?" He asked.

"Saskatchewan."

"For real?"

"Actually, I'm from Mars, but the license plate says Saskatchewan. What do you think?"

The other three snickered. He turned bright red. This might not go well.

"You're a real asshole, huh? What are you doing out here?"

I waved at the diner. "I was having a nice meal, and now I'm going home. Why do you ask?"

He waved his hand in a circle around his face. "How come you got the... spiderweb stuff?"

"My tattoos? You get kinda bored in prison, you know?"

He took a half step back. "You was in jail? What was you in for?"

"Beating the shit out of five guys. Why?"

He looked at his buddies. It was clear to me now; they had egged him on, wanting to see if he could 'take me' or at least scare me. Then he'd be respected in his peer group, I supposed.

I was in no mood to stroke his ego. "Tell you what. If you boys want to go a couple of rounds, I've got some friends coming. They should be right here. You want to hang around?"

One of the boys tugged on the big one's arm. "C'mon, let's go, man."

He shook the boy loose. "No. He's shittin' us. He ain't got no friends comin'."

A four-on-one fight usually doesn't go the way most people assume it will. For one thing, the movie thing of two guys holding the solo man's arms while a third punches him out never works.

All it does is to take two guys out of the equation. The third guy is the only threat, and the fourth guy sits back and watches. Kick guy number three in the balls or the head, and you have two guys at arm's length waiting to get pummeled. Guy number four then usually runs in panic. Besides, most guys don't have the coordination to fight side-by-side. They wait till their buddy is out of the way, which slows them way down, and makes them far more vulnerable.

In any case, I didn't want to explain this to these kids, verbally or physically.

Over the rise of land behind us, a familiar car cruised up- the OPP officer who'd stopped me, in his cruiser. He parked beside my car and got out. The farm boys looked distinctly nervous.

He nodded at me. "Afternoon, mister Brewster."

"Hello, Zach." I said.

"These fellows bothering you?"

"Nah, we were just discussing the weather." I said.

The four piled into a pair of pickup trucks and drove off.

The cop smiled and turned to face me. "The weather, Inspector McBriar?"

I grinned at the recognition. Clearly, Josh Klassen trusted him enough to tell him about me.

"I was deciding 'whether' I would beat them up or just scare them. The 'whether'."

He looked around. "Want to buy me lunch?"

"Yeah. Let's go in."

We sat in a corner booth, at my request, with my back to the window. The officer put his hat on the seat beside him and leaned forward, speaking barely above a whisper.

"So, the Starlite has some funny goings on." He said.

"Such as?"

"Last month, this big black limo pulls up to the motel, and this woman gets out. She looks like a model. Tall slinky brunette. Body by Fisher, legs up to her armpits, face that would stop traffic. Why would a woman like that go to a fleabag motel?"

"I've met her. Her name is Abigail Fontaine. She runs a modelling agency." I said.

His eyes widened. "She look that good up close?"

"Oh yeah."

He looked off into space. "Wow."

"It gets better. She has a twin sister."

He shook his head and rubbed his eyes. "I won't get *that* image out of my head for a while."

"Have you ever heard of a man called Victor French?" I asked.

"There was a guy with that name went missing last year. We found his boat on Sturgeon Lake, half full of water. We found an empty case of beer and a tackle box in the boat, but no rod or reel. We just figured he got drunk and fell overboard."

"Except we found his body in Toronto last week, on the sidewalk." I said. "No fishing rod."

The cop leaned back, thinking. "So, what the hell is going on here?"

I decided to confirm something. "Robert Sankar; was he a friend of yours?"

"Yeah. A real good guy. Crazy about fishing, Bob was. Good cop, too."

"Fishing?" I prompted.

"He used to take all his vacations in Florida. In his basement there was this big stuffed fish, and he told us about how he lost a finger but got the fish."

"Crazy."

The cop sawed his bacon in half, the plate jiggling on the table as he did. He stuffed it into his mouth and chewed, staring out into the road.

"So, what do you think happened there? We tried to get a line on the goings-on at the motel, but we're not getting any nibbles." He said.

"No clue. I think they're involved. I don't want to say any more than that, but as soon as I get something definite, I'll let you know."

"Want me to keep an eye on the place for you?"

I shook my head. "Absolutely not. If we let them think we're watching them, whatever they're doing will stop. Let me run with this, and as I say, I'll keep Josh posted."

He patted his mouth dry and leaned back. He took a bug swig of coffee and looked around to be sure nobody was near us. "So, what should I call you, then, if anyone asks?"

"For now, just tell them my name is Ian Brewster. The less you have to worry about, the better."

He nodded and looked at his watch. "Fair enough, Inspector. Thanks for lunch."

I waved the waitress over, paid the tab and let the cop leave first.

I started the Valiant and noticed it was low on gas. A gas station on my way back to the motel would be open, and it had a convenience store and pay phone. I wanted to call Karen and the kids, let them know I was alright.

I pumped in a half tank of gas, bought some sandwich bread and ginger ale, and got change for the pay phone.

The phone was just outside the station's little store, on the sidewalk.

I called Saskatchewan, spoke with Karen, and let her know that I'd be back in town in a day or two. I'd call her on Wednesday night from our home, I assured her.

I spoke with both children, gave them my love, warned them to behave, then I hung up and turned to step out of the phone booth.

The four farm boys from the restaurant were outside the booth, a few feet from me.

First mistake; they'd given me enough room to step out of the booth. The big kid was five feet in front of his buddies, his knuckles on his hips. He sneered, trying to look intimidating.

I stepped forward, nose to nose with him. He was almost my height, burly, with the fatty muscles of someone who does a lot of manual labour but eats too much.

He poked my shirt with his finger. "You trying to make me look stupid, huh?"

"I don't think you need my help for that, kid."

He turned beet red. "You think you can take us all on?"

I grew impatient at this game. "Should we see, then?"

His knuckles were still on hips. I could have done the next part blindfolded. He turned to look at his friends, laughed slightly, and his right knuckle tensed as he turned back to swing a punch.

Second mistake. I hooked his elbow with mine then swung down in a wide curve. His body followed, a clumsy dancer doing a flip as he flew over my hip and landed on the gravel.

"Would you stop now, and just go away?" I asked.

Third mistake. He growled and got up, swinging at me with both fists. This probably worked in the local bar. I waited till he got close and planted my foot into his gut. He bent in half, moaning.

"School's in session, kid. Here you go, first lesson free." I said.

I went behind him, got his neck and right arm locked in a choke hold, and tightened my grip.

"See, when you do this, your opponent can't swing at you. If I keep this up for thirty seconds, you'll sleep. If I do it for two minutes, you're dead. So how about I give you a wake-up call."

I let him go and he fell to his knees, unable to stay upright. His friends did not move.

"Here's where I have some interesting options." I said.

I rested my foot against his ankle. "If I step on your calf, you'll limp for the next week."

He yelped in pain, panting to stay conscious but clearly very aware of my foot.

I pressed down harder, against his calf. The kid groaned in agony. "Now, if I stomp your leg, it breaks the bone. If this was a real fight, you couldn't run, and you'd be dead meat. If I was only trying to disable you, however, you'd still be in a cast for the next three months."

I stood back. "So, what will it be? Did you learn the lesson?"

He brushed himself off and nodded.

"You won't try anything that stupid again, will you?" I asked.

He shook his head.

I shooed them away. "Class dismissed."

They drove off.

It was not noon yet; I had several hours before I met Reynolds in the 'Roundup' bar. I decided that I'd take some time and get away from people. Anyone I spoke to, anyone I met, especially the four rubes, could blow my cover. I pulled a map out of the glove box and looked it over. To the northeast, about thirty minutes away, was Bobcaygeon. It was on Sturgeon Lake. I could look around, see if anyone had any information about Victor French, and at the very least I would stay out of sight while I waited for Reynolds to show up.

I stopped at a low building on the east end of Sturgeon Lake, basically a prefab garage with a sign that read 'Sturgeon Lake Boat Rentals- fishing boats and live bait here'.

I went in and waited at the rough plywood counter. A man came out from a back workshop, slowing as he saw my tattoos.

"Afternoon. Help you?" He asked.

"Hi. I wonder if you have a boat available for rent?" I asked.

He rubbed his chin. Obviously, he was looking for an excuse to not let me have a boat.

"Well, I dunno. We ain't got a lot of choice right now, you know?"

"That's quite alright. Any small boat will do. I just wanted to go out for a couple of hours and see what I can find out."

He looked me over, suspicious. "You're just sightseein', then?"

"Sort of. Actually, I'm writing a book about local mysteries. I understand there was a boating accident here, a year or so ago? About some man who disappeared after he left the dock."

He leaned against the counter. I had intrigued him. "Yeah. That were that French guy. French was his name, not saying that he was French, you understand."

"Right, I think that was the name I heard. Now, I don't suppose you rented the boat he took?"

The man shook his head emphatically. "Nope. That were the Kenstone Marina. They rented the boat, I heard. Found the boat, but never found the guy. He's fish food now, I guess."

"Ah. Where did they find the boat?"

"Birch Point. Walking distance to the marina. Funny- if he'd run out of gas, he coulda rowed to shore and walked back to Kenstone. Instead he gets drunk and drowns."

I nodded. "Great. So, if I visit Kenstone Marina, who should I talk to?"

"Yeah, talk to old Bill. He's run the place since the war."

"Bill?"

He nodded. "Bill Fontaine. Like I say, he's had the place since forty-six."

That last name was not uncommon, but it still gave me chills to hear it. Was it a coincidence? I couldn't let that go without checking further.

"Great. I still wanted to rent a little runabout, what do you have available?"

"You got ID?"

I nodded. "I've just recently moved here from Saskatchewan, so I still have my old ID."

He wrote down the details off the driver's license, accepted that I'd leave the Valiant as security, and walked me to a pier. At the end of the pier there was a fourteen-foot aluminum boat with an anemic outboard motor. Both had seen better days. He shook the gas container, assured me there was enough fuel for a short ride, and pushed me away toward the open lake.

I waved thanks, cranked the throttle and chugged slowly toward Kenstone Marina.

Sturgeon Lake looks like a long, sideways letter Y. At its east end is the town of Bobcaygeon, and just beyond that is Pigeon Lake, attached to Sturgeon Lake through waterways and channels. Pigeon Lake, a thin, twenty-mile-long strip of water, is connected through waterways to a series of other lakes further east. According to the map I'd been given with the boat, it was possible to go another forty miles beyond that, zigzagging between islands.

I motored toward the bridges that crossed Bobcaygeon, waited as the double lock connecting the lakes filled up to let me through, and sailed out into Pigeon Lake.

Pigeon Lake was deeper, bigger, and probably had more fish. If Victor French was really out here to catch fish, why hadn't he gone to Pigeon Lake instead? More to the point, if his boat was found waterlogged and with empty beer bottles, why was his body found on a Toronto street?

I puttered around for a while, dodging faster speedboats and small cruisers. I was convinced by now that Victor French had stayed on Sturgeon Lake for a reason, and it wasn't to fish.

Kenstone Marina was classier than the place that had rented me the boat. The pier's walkway was clean scrubbed, the sides of the pier freshly painted, and a crisp sign over the walkway read 'Welcome Boaters'.

I tied up, left the gas container beside a fuel pump at the back of the main building, and wandered into the office.

A man behind the counter looked up at me. He was somewhere in his late fifties, I guessed, with a pale green polo shirt and black hair combed back over a bald spot. He had a Clark Gable moustache and a pipe on the counter, all of which made him look something like a park ranger.

"Hello. Can I help you?" He growled.

He looked at the tattoos, but then he locked eyes with me, intense.

"Hello. Are you Bill?"

"Who wants to know?"

He bent down, hunting for something under the counter. It could have been paperwork, but I had the strong feeling it was a weapon. I didn't want to spook him.

"Hi, I'm Ian Brewster. Did you get my letter?"

His hands came out from under the counter, and he folded his arms in front of him, relaxing.

"What letter?"

"Ah. I figured it might have gone missing when I didn't get any reply. I'm writing a book about local mysteries. Five years ago, there was a farmer who lost a cow, but the next day it turned up three hundred miles away. Do you remember seeing that story in the papers?"

He shook his head. Of course he hadn't seen it- I'd just made it up.

"Anyway, the next chapter is about some guy who disappeared after he rented a boat here last year. They found the boat, I hear, but there was no sign of him. Do you remember that?"

He stiffened at that. "Yeah, look, we talked to the cops and the insurance people, and I got nothing more to say. He got drunk and drowned, we figure. He shouldn't have been drinking."

"Fair enough. There was no next of kin, I suppose? Someone else I could talk to?"

"No idea. We gave his wallet to the cops, after we found it in the boat. Beyond that, got no idea."

I nodded. "Well, that gives me something to work with, anyway. Do you run this marina all by yourself, or do you have an employee that might be able to give me more details?"

"No, it's just me."

"It's just that you said 'we' found his wallet. I figured there were others working here."

"My daughter was here for the summer, but she's gone now."

I wanted to ask about her, without asking directly. "Oh, I'm sorry for your loss."

"No, no, she's just gone back to the city. She has an apartment there."

"Oshawa." I prompted.

"Toronto. Like I say, she's gone. She wasn't the one who found the boat, anyway, I did."

"I'll have to write about something else, then. Anyway, can I buy a couple bucks worth of gas?"

He walked out with me to the gas pump, took my two dollars and stuck the pump nozzle into the container. He pulled the trigger and watched the wheel slowly roll around to two dollars, then snapped his fingers away from the trigger and hung up the nozzle.

I thanked him and turned to leave.

"So, what's it called?" He asked.

"Excuse me?"

"This book you're writing, what's the name of your book?"

"Tales of the Bobcaygeon Triangle." I said.

He snorted. "Catchy. I'll look for it in bookstores."

I took the gas container back to the boat and pulled away. The man watched me go, paying far too much attention, I thought, and didn't move till I'd headed out of sight, around the point.

According to the map, I'd just passed Birch Point, the spot where the dead man's boat had been found. The first man was right; if the boat had run out of gas, French could have rowed or even paddled the fifty yards to shore.

Even if the boat was taking on water, he could have swum to shore. A quick prod with my oar confirmed that the water here was barely waist deep. He could have walked ashore.

So, why had he gone missing? Had he fallen overboard and walked away, drunk? Had someone mugged him and left him in Toronto, on the streets? His wallet was found in the boat, though, the man had said. If he had been mugged, they'd have taken his wallet. Nothing made sense.

Thirty minutes of aimless boating later, I was no closer to an answer. I returned the boat.

Maybe I was looking in the wrong place. If I'd gone to Bobcaygeon, I would have stayed in a hotel. If this was a vacation, I'd stay somewhere nice. If it was just a fishing trip, I'd stay somewhere cheap.

My map of Bobcaygeon showed a number of tourist spots on Canal Street, and I'd seen them from the boat earlier, so I drove up to a spot marked on the map as a hotel and parked.

A brass sign out front said 'Lockview Inn'. The building looked like an old woolen mill or brewery, with red brick on all sides and small leaded windows. A dark green awning over the raised entry, with 'Welcome' in scrolled white letters, didn't make it look much more inviting. Still, it was the nicest hotel on the street. The only other two I could see looked like prefab vinyl motels.

I went up the four steps to the front door and opened it. The entry was completely different from what it looked like outside.

There was a wide lobby, with thick patterned carpet, sumptuous wing chairs with elegant side tables to rest teacups, and a long mahogany counter which served as the front desk.

Behind the desk, a small, middle-aged man in a pale grey blazer regarded me with suspicion.

He straightened up as I approached him, clasping his fingers together on the counter in front of him. This gesture meant 'no further' and 'my space'. I stuck one hand in my pocket and placed the other on the edge of the counter. It communicated 'I'm not a threat, but I'm not backing off'.

"Good afternoon." I said.

"I wonder if you could help me. I'm writing a book about mysterious events in this part of Ontario, specifically around town here."

His nose wrinkled. "Yes?"

"So, do you know any stories about odd happenings, ghost stories, things like that?"

His hands came down and he shuffled side to side, thinking. "Well, we got that old story that's ben told every Halloween since I was young." He started.

"Yes. Go on, please."

"About the spirit that wanders up and down Canal Street. The story goes that back in the eighteen eighties this young woman's husband drowned one year, trying to save a horse in the river. She threw herself into the water at the spot where he died, and every year on that date, people swear they saw this ghost walking up and down the riverbank, looking for her lost love."

I nodded enthusiastically. "That's wonderful. It's certainly the type of story that's going into the book. You of course have heard the story of the local farmer, the one whose cow ended up three hundred miles away overnight."

He waved his arm dismissively. "Oh, yeah, you hear lots of those stories. I never believe them all, though."

He was smiling now, joking and chatting with me, his guard down.

"OK, how about this?" I asked. "The guy that drowned or something? He went fishing last year and disappeared. His boat was found near shore, but his body was never found."

"You're talking about Victor French?" He asked casually.

I tried not to seem too excited. "Yeah, was that his name? I don't know the whole story. Would it sound interesting in my book?"

"Oh, yeah. That one's a real mystery. Did you know- he stayed here before he went missing?"

"Really? Well, that's something I could write about." I said.

"Yessirree. Had a room up on the second floor. You want a real spooky twist? He booked for four nights, only stayed two before he disappeared, but he paid for all four nights on the night before he went missing. Wild, huh?"

"Did he leave many belongings behind? A note, or photos or something?"

He shook his head vigorously. "Clean as a whistle. Didn't even leave a toothbrush. Go figure."

"Well, that's curious, for sure. Did he talk to anyone here, get friendly with the staff or anyone while he stayed here?"

"Nope. Barely spoke to anyone. He was polite, but he didn't say much."

"Someone said he had beer in the boat when they found it. Had he been drinking much while he was here?"

"The cops asked me the same thing. The only thing he drank was coffee. Maybe he was a reformed drunk and just fell off the wagon, you know? Why else would he bring a bunch of beer on the boat? Like I say, though, all he drank here was coffee."

"Well, that certainly gives me a lot to work with. If I come back next week, could we chat some more?"

"Yeah, sure. Any time." He smiled.

Two in the afternoon, according to my watch. It was the end of July, and it was stifling hot. I was hungry, thirsty, and I still had some things to do before I met with Reynolds. There was a beer store on the main street; I'd seen it as I drove in.

I bought a case of beer, making sure to call it a 'two-four' when I paid for it. Then I stopped at a roadside burger place, bought a remarkably acceptable burger and fries, and drove back to the motel.

The young woman was behind the counter at the motel office; I loped in, asked her for change, and bought a couple of cans of Coke. She watched me, curious, out of the corner of her eye, pretending to not notice me as she filled out some forms.

I took the cans in one hand and opened the door with my other.

"Um, before I forget, I got a question." I said.

She looked up and plastered on a smile. "Yes?"

"Like, when does the maid come on Sundays? I was kinda hoping to sleep in, you know?"

She tapped her pen against the form she had been writing. "Let's see. Normally, she gets here around eight, but on Sundays she gets here around nine, nine thirty. Would that be all right?"

"Sure. That's fine. Thanks."

I'd been watching the other rooms. As of last night, there were only three other rooms occupied. That meant the maid would show up right around ten in the morning on Sunday.

Perfect. I drank a Coke, put the other cans in the fridge, and took a nap.

My eyes opened slightly, and I woke with a start. What time was it? Check my watch. It was still light, so it wasn't that late. I had to squint to see the watch face clearly; seven fifteen. Good.

Dinner, again, consisted of a can of soup and a sandwich of lunch meat. God, how I missed having real food.

Chapter Seven

At eight fifteen, I drove to the Roundup bar, parked very visibly out front, and went in. I ordered a beer, found a spot in the corner to watch a wrestling match on TV, and waited.

At ten to nine, Brian Webb came in. He was dressed in a rough shirt, with a John Deere cap and torn jeans. He saw me, blinked slowly to indicate recognition, and I sipped my beer, winking at him. Nobody else saw it. He glanced toward the door and back at me. I had no idea what he was trying to say. He looked around to be sure he wasn't seen and banged together the knuckles of his two forefingers. 'Staging an argument'. I understood.

Five minutes later, Reynolds came in. I almost didn't recognize her. She was in a black leather mini skirt, patterned black panty hose, and a tight red tee shirt. When she came in, half the men in the bar turned to follow her.

She sat by herself, and Webb wandered over to her table, hovering over it.

"So you came here anyway, bitch?" He growled, not very loudly.

She swatted her hand toward him. "Piss off, Gary. Forget it- I told you, we're done."

He grabbed her forearm and shook it. It looked quite convincing. "You don't walk out on me, Irma. You do not walk out on me, you hear?"

I tried to keep from laughing- the performance was quite good. I got up and stood nose to nose with Webb. I was a couple of inches taller than him, but I was sure he was squatting down slightly, to enhance the height difference for anyone watching. By now a good number of the people in the bar were paying some attention to us.

I stared at Webb. "This guy bothering you, lady?" I said.

She looked up at Webb then smiled at me. "Yeah, he is."

"Piss off." I said.

He put his hand on my chest and pushed. I swung it away and pushed his chest, not very hard. He tumbled backwards, as though I'd used full force. He was a very good actor.

He stumbled to the floor, knocking his hat off his head, and lay there for a moment. He got back up, put the hat on, and sneered at me.

"You want her? You keep her. Bitch is too much trouble, anyway." He stormed out. A number of the men laughed, then everyone ignored us.

I invited Reynolds to my corner table, and she grinned, following me to the spot. A waitress asked what she wanted, and she simply said 'vodka'.

I waited until she'd been served her drink then leaned in close to her and whispered. "Thanks for coming, Alex. And thank Brian for the floor show, that really helps the scenario here."

She tilted her head back, laughed as though I'd told her a funny joke, then leaned close to me too and whispered. "Sure thing, boss. What are we doing, then?"

"We're going back to my motel room in a minute. I need to give you something."

She laughed, less loudly this time, and caressed my face with her hand. She stood up and whispered in my ear. "Time to leave."

Reynolds put her arm around my waist and led me out of the bar. Again, half the men in the bar watched us go.

I unlocked the doors on the Valiant, fought the urge to hold the door open for her, and she let herself in. We drove away, with a couple of hangers-on watching her from the bar's entrance.

Once we had driven a half-mile, her shoulders relaxed. "How did I do back there, boss?"

"I'm going to have to think about you two in a different light, after that episode."

She chuckled. "Well, Brian has said I should dress like this more often, at home."

"Any other news from the shop?" I asked.

"Nothing important. Captain Fantastic has been notably low-key. Sergeant Walsh is doing your job, in your place. Everyone respects him. I could see him being an Inspector soon, boss."

"I agree. Anything more on our missing body?"

"No. have you got anything, boss?"

"Yeah, lots."

We pulled up to the motel, and I waited until couple of the guests were around before we got out of the car. I wanted people to see me with Reynolds. I wanted them to think I'd picked up some easy woman.

The motel room was dark, and even with the blinds open there was not much light from the parking lot lamps. I turned on the lights and pulled the drapes closed.

Reynolds looked around at the room and sniffed. "Not exactly the Ritz, is it?"

"It's dingy and sombre, but it's home." I joked. "Be right back."

The beer was still in the trunk of the car. I went to the Valiant, pulled the two-four out and tucked it under my arm. Again, the same people were around, and they saw me take the beer into my room.

Reynolds sat on the single chair, pulled it up beside the bed, and waited for me.

I placed the beer on the counter by the small sink and sat on the edge of the bed.

"So, Alex, first off, thanks for going out on a limb and doing this."

"Again, no problem, boss."

I reached under the bed and pulled out the tackle box and the manila envelope. Reynolds opened the box, gingerly. She opened the passport, read the name and looked carefully at the photo.

"So, this is the guy we found on the street?"

"Yep. Victor French- don't know much about him, but there's too many things about him that set off bells for me."

She opened the flap on the airline ticket. "Ireland? Where have we heard that before?"

Reynolds opened the manila envelope next. "And money. A guy could have a good time with this much spending money, I would think."

"OK, get out your book." I said.

Reynolds dug her Moleskine out of the brown denim purse she'd brought and opened it at today's date.

"First, Victor French went missing last year, presumed drowned. He rented a fishing boat on Sturgeon Lake, and it was found half full of water, lots of empty beers, no fishing rod."

"Got drunk, fell over, drowned. Supposedly." Reynolds said.

"Right. But we found him on the streets of Toronto a year later. Now, a man called Bill Fontaine rented him the boat."

Her eyes widened. "Any relation to…"

"No idea. He did mention that he has a daughter in Toronto. It could be a coincidence, but then again, too many common threads for my liking. The name, the boat rental, Ireland."

She shook her head. "How does that tie him to our other dead guy?"

"Robert Sankar left this stuff in the locker we found the key for. That means he either knew Victor French, or he was investigating his disappearance."

She looked at everything spread out on the bed, thinking.

"OK, so, Robert Sankar." She said. "He must have been working at the same place you are, because he was looking for information on Victor French. It's the only possible reason he'd be there. You found the key and the business card from the scrapyard. What sent Sankar there?"

"Right. Something else; I heard a conversation between the woman who runs this motel- she's the niece of the woman who runs the scrapyard- and she was telling some guy 'not so soon after the cop'."

"So, you think they're all in this somehow, boss?"

"Yeah, Alex. I have a plan."

I sighed. It sounded stupid, as stupid as it had when I'd thought of it earlier. But it felt right.

"I'll pretend you robbed me and stole my car. One of two things will happen; they will kick me out, or they will see me as a possible stooge and offer me some dirty work. Either way, I should be done here by Tuesday, Wednesday at the latest."

She nodded. "So, how do we convince them?"

I turned up the radio, almost drowning out any conversation we had. Any time I heard people walking past my door, Reynolds would laugh out loud. We opened all the bottles of beer, poured most down the drain, and left a couple of half-full ones by the bed.

I waited till after midnight and peeked out to be sure nobody was outside. I leaned in close to her and whispered.

"Here; take my car. There's a bag under the seat with five thousand dollars in it. It's my money, and I'd really appreciate it if I got it back. Take the passport and stuff with you, too, and tell Patrick what we said. I'll call him on Monday night, at his home, around seven. If he doesn't hear from me, send the cavalry, OK?"

She noted all this down, nodded agreement, and closed up her Moleskine.

Reynolds took the key to the Valiant, checked again that nobody was around and crept out. She drove down the road, then turned on the headlights. Good thinking, Alex. That made it look even more clandestine if anyone did see her.

I closed the drapes. The maid would be here around nine thirty or so. I wanted to set the stage.

The beer made the room smell like the Roundup bar, but even more so. I put on a pair of boxers and a tank top and spread out on top of the bed. I tried to sleep, but I wasn't very tired, mostly anxious, and the smell of beer made me nauseous.

I woke up around eight, surprised that I'd dozed off. Had I missed anything? I took my wallet, pulled out the hundred or so dollars I had in it, and hid the money in an envelope wedged under the kitchen sink. I left the wallet wide open, my ID scattered on the bed.

The waiting was interminable. Finally, just after nine thirty, the maid arrived. She was short, waddled as she walked, and her violet track suit was rumpled. She hummed a tune as she opened the door.

I was sprawled on the bed face-down, seemingly asleep. The maid yelped as she saw me. Clearly, she thought I was dead. She came close, heard me snoring, and shook my shoulder gently. She muttered something in Spanish, which I knew to mean 'dead fish'.

"Mister? You OK?" She whispered.

I rolled over. "Huh?"

I sat up, rubbed my eyes and looked around. "Where is the girl?"

The maid looked around, too, puzzled. "No girl, mister. No girl."

I grabbed my wallet, flipped through it, looking for cash, and tossed it down, dejected.

"Oh shit. She robbed me." I said.

I ran to the window. "My Car! Oh god, no, my car."

The maid said something else in Spanish, quickly, and ran out. I sat on the edge of the bed, trying to look bleary-eyed and hung over.

A few minutes later, the woman from the office came in. she was in sweatpants and a baggy tee shirt, her hair disheveled. Clearly she had just been woken up by the maid.

"What happened?" She snapped.

I rubbed my eyes. "I dunno. She came over, we had some beers, and then…"

The woman threw her arms up. "You got robbed! Great! That's all we need- the police coming around, asking questions!"

I had to bite my tongue to keep from smiling. I shook my head. "No, no police. Please don't. No police. No."

She pulled over a chair, sat and looked into my eyes. "Why no police?" She said.

"Why don't you want me to call them?"

I rubbed my eyes again. "He gave me ten grand. Ten grand. And he said to give him the package, but now she has it, and I don't have the ten grand to give back to him. Man, I'm screwed."

The man from the office came in next. He was in jeans and a tee shirt that matched the woman's.

She glanced up at him then leaned forward. "Ten grand? Ten grand for what?"

I reached over to my crumpled jeans, beside me on the bed, and pulled out the locker key. "He said to open this locker and give him what was in there, and he'd give me another fifteen grand. That was going to be my new life. That's what I needed to start fresh. I left it in my car. Now I got shit, and he'll want the ten grand back."

I tossed the key across the room. The woman didn't even look at it.

"What locker? What did you find in the locker?" She asked, quietly.

"Locker seventeen at the scrap yard. It was a tackle box and a paper envelope." I said.

"And what was inside them?"

I shook my head. "No idea. I never looked. No idea. If I don't know, I won't get tempted, you know? I never even looked."

She stood up and walked to the phone on the wall. She dialed a number and waited.

"Hey, it's Gillian." She said. "We have a problem."

She waited, listening. "No, Ian Brewster found the package. The cop left it in a locker."

She listened again. "He says he doesn't know. I don't think he does, no. But someone does. They gave him cash to dig it up."

Another pause. "He picked up one of those truck tramps and she rolled him. Took his car, his cash, and the package."

She listened for a minute, then nodded. "We'll wait for you." She said. She hung up.

I sat on the edge of the bed, shaking. It was only partly an act. This could go one of a couple of ways. I hoped it wouldn't go badly for me. Looking around the room, I felt sure I could handle both Gillian and her boyfriend. I only hoped that whoever came wouldn't bring much muscle with them.

Gillian went to the small kitchen and set up the coffeemaker. She waited, her back to me, until it had filled the small carafe with coffee, then poured me a cup and brought it over.

"Here. You must be pretty hung over." She said, gently.

I took the coffee and nodded thanks. "Yeah. I shouldn't drink that much. And I wouldn't, usually, but she was really cute, and she came on to me. I don't get that a lot."

Gillian nodded. "Did you think maybe she set you up? That she came to do just what she did?"

I looked up at her, wide-eyed. "You mean… oh, shit. I've been had, haven't I?"

Gillian shook her head and patted my knee, consolingly. "Listen, we may still be able to help you. If you work with us, we'll get you out from under, plus we'll give you…"

She looked up at the man. "Five thousand?"

He nodded. "Yeah, five grand. Maybe more. Maybe ten thousand."

The casual way they said that told me that I would probably never see any money, if they had their way.

"Gosh, that's great." I said.

"At least I'll be able to move up to Muskoka and start over, with that much cash."

The other man, behind Gillian rolled his eyes, ridiculing my naivete, I sensed.

I sipped coffee, waiting. After about twenty minutes, a car pulled up outside the window, its shadow blocking some of the morning sunlight. I saw another shadow as a person got out.

The door to my room opened, and Mick walked in. He glanced at Gillian, then walked straight over to me. He sat on the bed beside me and put an arm around my shoulder.

"You got yourself into some bad trouble, huh, Chief?" He said.

The words were warm and syrupy, but I sensed anger behind them.

"You came to work with us. We gave you a job, we took you in, we paid you, and all the time you were spying on us. Is that how you treat your friends, huh?"

His arm had slipped up and around my neck as he spoke. His grip tightened, pinching me in a head lock.

He leaned close to my ear. "I do not want to ever see you again, do you hear? I want to know who paid you to spy on us, then I want you to get as far from here as you can get. Got it?"

I leaned back, a hurt expression on my face. "But she said she'd give me five thousand dollars."

He shook his head, slowly. "Screw that. Tell us who paid you and get lost. I don't care if you *walk* back to Shit-skatchewan. I want you gone."

I sighed. "I get it. I'm sorry, you're right. He was using me after all."

Mick let go of my neck and stood up. "Get him here. Get him here now. Or else."

I walked slowly to the phone and dialed a number. All the while, as it rang through, I was hoping that Walsh would not pick up.

Three rings later, I heard his voice. "Hello?"

"Mister Walsh? It's Ian Brewster, sir." I said.

There was a long pause. He was thinking. "Yes, Ian?" He said.

Mick was standing beside me, close enough to hear Walsh's half of the conversation.

"Mister Walsh, you wanted me to find those things for you?"

Mick tapped my arm and whispered. 'You have them with you. Bring him here.'

Walsh spoke slowly. "Yes. What did you find, Ian?"

"I never looked at them, Mister Walsh. I never looked. But if you want them, they're here."

"And where is that, Ian?" He asked. "Are you in the same place as before?"

Clearly, he was asking if I was in trouble.

"No, I'm in room eight of the Starlite Motel, in Lindsay. When we spoke before I was in number one twenty-nine in the old place, but now I'm at the Starlite Motel, in Lindsay."

"All right, Ian. I can be there in two hours. Stay there and I'll come and get you." He said.

"I'll be here. Goodbye, Mister Walsh." I said. I hung up the phone.

Mick stepped back, reading me. "So, he doesn't have it, then?" He said.

"I guess not, no."

"Any idea who this girl was, the one that took your car?"

"She said her name was Irma, I think. I don't know any more than that."

"Irma what?"

I shook my head. "I don't remember."

Mick turned to look at Gillian. "We could be in luck. Maybe she doesn't know what she took."

She shrugged. "We can only hope. Let's find out what this 'Mister Walsh' has to say."

I rubbed my face and scratched my neck. "Look, I appreciate you all trying to help me. Do you mind if I take a shower and get dressed before he shows up?"

Mick poked his chin at the door. "Yeah. We'll give you some time to get cleaned up. Just don't run out on us, all right?"

"No, no way. I just want to get out from under this, and I need your help to do it."

Mick grunted agreement and everyone left. I quickly washed and dressed. I bundled my few clothes into my tote bag and cleared up anything I'd left out. I remembered the cash under the sink and stuck it in the tote, under my clothes.

I just hoped that Walsh picked up on the hidden message; 'number one-twenty-nine'. 129 was police code for 'hostages held'.

An hour later, I was sitting on the edge of the bed, sipping the now-cold coffee.

Gillian walked in, along with the man from the office, and Mick came in right behind her.

Gillian turned to Mick. "Does she know about this?"

"No. she'd crucify us both if she found out. Look- if this blows over, we go back to business as usual. Wait till the fall, go back to the way it was."

That told me a few things. Sandra, the woman from the scrapyard, was not involved. Mick and Gillian were. But involved in what?

It was noweleven-fifteen. The sound of gravel crunching came through the partly open door, and a shadow filled the doorway. Everybody looked at the door.

An immense man, taller than me, stepped in, turning slightly to fit his shoulders through the doorway. Mick and the other man took an involuntary step back.

The man was Sam, the Walsh family chauffeur and bodyguard. He scanned the room, satisfied, then turned toward the driveway and nodded.

Walsh came in, wearing a midnight blue silk suit. He stepped into the room and looked around. He smiled at Gillian, walked straight over to her and held out his hand.

"Hi." He purred. "You are?"

The other man stepped forward. "Gillian is my wife."

Walsh glared at him, a look that froze the man. "I'm sorry, I believe I was asking the young lady."

"Gillian." She said. "My name is Gillian."

"Where is the package, Gillian?" Walsh asked.

Gillian shook her head. "He was lying. He doesn't have it. Some woman stole it from him."

Walsh slid out a chair, ceremoniously dusted it off with a scarlet handkerchief, and sat down.

"Now, then, Gillian, in that case, what should we do about Mister Brewster here?"

The others in the room looked around, nervously. Walsh looked at each of them in turn.

"You people have cost me a substantial amount of money. Not to mention the inconvenience of having to come all the way out here. So, what are we going to do about him?"

The man with Gillian took a step toward Walsh, wagging his finger.

Sam moved about two inches forward, and the man stopped. "Listen, you." The man said. "This guy has cost us a lot, too. He's meddled in our business, and he's taken something of value."

Walsh slowly took out a gold cigarette case and chose a cigarette. He lit it with a slim gold lighter and drew in the smoke as the man spoke.

"That may well be." Walsh said. "But a passport and some travelers' cheques don't really matter much to me. I'm far more interested in the diamonds."

The man's eyes opened wide. "Diamonds?"

Walsh sneered. "You didn't know? Well, that *is* interesting."

I was trying very hard to look worried, to not laugh. Walsh had them in the palm of his hand.

"You see, Victor French had a shipment of diamonds with him when he died. They were mine. I want them back. Now, how do I get them?"

Gillian shook her head. "Look, mister, we don't kill people here, and we don't steal from them. All we do is give them an escape route. That's all."

Walsh's eyes sparkled, for just a moment. I knew that nobody else in the room saw it. She had blundered, and both he and I knew it. "I see. So, French never told you. You never searched his room after he left?"

Gillian made another blunder. "We always do, yes, but just to look for anything they left behind- that's all. Nothing else. And we never found any diamonds, that's for damn sure."

He sighed, stubbed out his cigarette on the kitchen sink, and stood up. Everyone else took a step back. He looked at Sam and waved my way.

"Bring him." He said, simply.

Sam grabbed my tote bag and my arm and lifted me right off the bed, pulling me outside. Walsh glared at the people in the room, stomped out and got into the back seat of a massive Mercedes. Sam sat me beside Walsh and got in the front. We drove away.

We were almost a mile away from the motel when Walsh laughed out loud.

Sam, at the wheel, grinned broadly and glanced at me in the rear-view mirror. "Sorry if I hurt you, Mister Ian." He rumbled.

"Not at all, Sam." I said. "Thanks for sending in the cavalry. Thanks to both of you."

We drove on for another minute, silent. Walsh turned to face me. "So, what do you think is going on there, boss?"

"I have no idea, Patrick. That was really good improvisation on your part, by the way."

"Thanks. I was making it up as I went along. I'm just glad I clued in on the 'one twenty-nine.'"

"Yeah, me too. Diamonds? What made you think of saying 'diamonds'?" I asked.

"I wanted them to think there was more at stake than what they're doing. Maybe it'll shake the tree. Maybe."

I grunted. "Gives us a lot to chew on, doesn't it, though?"

Sam drove on for another few miles then pulled over at a spot by the side of the road. A familiar car had stopped in front of us; Reynolds got out, wearing sensible clothes, and Webb got out the passenger side.

Reynolds waited for me to step out of the Mercedes. "You OK, boss?"

"Yeah, Alex. And thanks to you and Brian for that scene last night, by the way. Nicely done."

Webb looked around at us. "So, what do we do now, boss?"

"Well, first off, I have to get rid of these ugly tattoos."

Reynolds reached into her car and handed me the manila envelope and tackle box I'd given her.

"We dusted everything for prints, and we took photos. Check out the passport."

I opened the passport; the photo was of the man who'd gone missing from the morgue, Victor French. It listed his home address as a trendy apartment downtown, and his date of birth indicated he was in his thirties. Walsh looked as I turned pages, reading with me.

I flipped pages, looking for stamps. Reynolds crooked her head to look too, curious.

"When we went on our honeymoon," I explained. "Karen said she wanted stamps in her passport from the Italian customs, to keep as a memento."

I stopped at the first page. "Miami, Florida. Nassau, Bahamas."

I flipped to the next page. "Dublin, Ireland. Where have we heard that place mentioned before?"

Walsh chuckled. "Well, now we can tie this man to the Fontaine girls, I guess."

"You think they took him to Ireland with them last year?" I asked.

"Sure, but where did he go when he came back? And why hide the passport in a crappy locker?"

I handed the passport to Walsh. "Here, Patrick. This is your project. Find out where our man went, and when he came back. Let's work from there."

I looked at the manila envelope. "Alex, the traveler's cheques- they have serial numbers. Find out which bank issued them and see if anyone at that bank remembers who picked them up. A couple thousand dollars isn't a lot, but it might be a large enough sum that somebody remembers handing it out."

She took the envelope and nodded. "Same with the airline ticket, boss?"

"Yeah, and if you do get any information, let me know right away."

Reynolds and Webb drove off, and I got into the Mercedes with Walsh. Sam eased onto the road and we headed south, back toward Toronto.

Sam looked at me through the rear-view mirror. "Would you like to go home, Mister Ian?"

"I would really appreciate that, Sam."

They let me off at my house; I went around back, found my door key, let myself in and threw the tote full of clothes on the floor. It occurred to me that I'd left my old suitcase in the trunk of the Valiant. No matter, it was empty.

I put on the kettle, grateful for the small luxury of a good cup of coffee. A knock at the door surprised me, and I cautiously investigated. The shadow in the frosted glass was familiar.

I opened the door. "Hey, Alex, forgot to tell me something?" I asked.

Reynolds stepped in. "I just wanted to see how you were doing, boss."

She thrust a fat envelope at me. "Your five thousand dollars, before I forget."

I put it on the front hallstand. "Thanks, Alex. What's really on your mind?"

"How are you doing, that's all."

I wasn't convinced. "Same as I was thirty minutes ago. Now, what's on your mind?"

She shook her head. "I don't know, Ian. How do I explain it?"

She rubbed her nose and put her hands on her hips, the gesture for trying to simplify something complicated.

"Did you ever see that optical illusion? Look at it one way, it looks like a duck, the other way it looks like a rabbit? Or the one of the young woman and the old woman, in the same drawing?"

"You have very good instincts, Alex. What are you getting at?"

"Abigail Fontaine. OK, so she's a fashion model, or she runs a modeling agency, whatever. We were in her apartment, and I didn't see any copies of Vogue or Glamour on the coffee table. That's like a trade magazine for someone like her, right?"

"Go on."

"She was wearing nice clothes. It figures she would. But you'd think that either she has an office where she works, or she works from home. If she worked at an office, why was she home when we called on her? And if she works from home, then why doesn't she have racks of clothes, or fabric swatches, or copies of recent photo shoots, you know, things like that lying around?"

"One of those saddle burrs that gets in your head, huh?"

"Yeah. It doesn't make sense, somehow. And another thing that just occurred to me."

She reached into her jacket pocket and pulled out a matchbook.

"This is the one I got from Abigail, when we were in her apartment." She said.

She lifted up the flap and showed me the matches. "She smokes left-handed. When she gave me this matchbook, I hadn't noticed that the one we found on Robert Sankar, in the car, was torn the same way- all the matches were taken from the left side."

I looked at the matchbook. She was right.

"You figure Sankar's matchbook came from Abigail? That's kind of a stretch, I suppose. Then again, did he know her? And did she or her sister kill him, or do they know who did?"

Reynolds gave an exaggerated shrug. "It's just one of those niggling things, boss."

According to the man at the tattoo parlor, either alcohol, cold cream or scrubbing with soapy water would remove the tattoos.

I slathered on some of Karen's cold cream, let it sit for a while, then wiped it off. After a couple of applications, and a long soapy shower, the ink was almost completely gone. I felt like myself again, except with very smooth skin.

Later, I called Saskatchewan, told Karen I was back home, and spoke with the kids. My father and brother came on the phone, talked with me for a while, then hung up.

For a few minutes, I sat on a chair in the kitchen, listening to the clock in the hall. Somehow, the tick-tock-tick-tock seemed to be emphasizing in its own way that time was passing.

Charlotte was growing up. In two years she would be in school. A couple of years after that, Ethan would be in high school. Our new baby, when he or she came, would be walking and talking before I knew it. Would I still be chasing bad guys? Maybe.

I spent the afternoon puttering around the back yard, then I called Frank to let him know I was back. I washed my laundry, made dinner as the clothes went through the dryer, and spent the evening listening to the Buffalo jazz station. I went to bed early, tired, and missing my family.

Chapter Eight

Monday morning was blistering hot. The sun beat against the wall behind my pillow, waking me up before five. After a long shower and a leiaurely breakfast, I looked at my watch. Six forty-five; it was still really early. What the heck- I got dressed and ready for work anyway. It was the first time in days I'd had my holster strapped to my shoulder, and the police revolver seemed heavier than I remembered. That much, I knew, would pass quickly. A 'thwap' sound against the front door signalled the morning paper, so I thought I'd skim the comics and the crossword puzzle before heading in to the office. I stooped down to pick up the paper, vaguely aware of a car stopping in the driveway.

It was unfamiliar, a big burgundy Chrysler, driven by someone who looked about twelve. Its front door opened, and the driver got out. He was the young man I'd seen in Frank's office, the tall kid who shadowed Frank's boss. He looked around quickly then opened the back door.

Barry Kirby got out, brushed the dust off his navy wool suit, and said something to the driver. The young man gave a short nod and sat back in the car. I stood in the doorway, waiting to see why he was here. Kirby turned back to the open back door, reached in and retrieved a package. It was a cardboard box, about the size of a large flat shoebox, about three inches deep. He stuck it under his left arm and marched up to me, his right hand out.

"Good morning, Ian. I hope I'm not getting you too early?" He asked.

I shook his hand. "Not at all. Would you and your driver care to come in? I can make you some coffee or breakfast?"

He studied me for a moment. "That's very gracious of you. Certainly, if it's no bother."

"No bother at all, Mister Kirby."

"Barry, please."

"Barry, then."

The man turned to his driver and made a motion like spooning food into his mouth. The young man sprang out of the car and both men followed me into the kitchen.

"Eggs, toast, coffee?" I asked.

"Yes, please." The driver said, then looked at Kirby to see if he'd overstepped himself.

Kirby grinned at him and faced me. "Whatever isn't too much trouble, thank you."

He placed his package on the far side of the kitchen table and slid onto a seat. "So, Ian, what is it you're working on right now?"

"You must know that I can't discuss an open case with you, Barry."

He nodded. "True. I respect that. Now, what if I were to tell you that we have information about an old case, one that involves you?"

I slid a large plate of scrambled eggs and toast in front of the driver and set his coffee beside it. He began to devour his food.

I put Kirby's food in front of him, and he ignored it. This was his way of telling me he was in control of his emotions.

"What case would you be referring to?" I asked.

He leaned down and took a scoop of his food. "Mm. Good. Very good. How do you get these eggs so fluffy?" He asked.

"Start with a hot pan and don't over-flip them. It keeps the air in."

"Very, very good." He patted his mouth dry.

"In any case, when we spoke earlier, that was the first round of tests. You passed, by the way, with flying colours."

"And the next round?" I asked.

He swallowed some coffee and slowly patted his mouth again. This delay was a clear way of saying 'I'm in control of the conversation'. I waited patiently.

"We always investigate everyone that we consider for membership in our rather selective club. Frank has a military background, and his record indicates that he's willing to go right to the edge if required. Your record is somewhat more… diffuse. Your background is also more interesting. You were in the seminary, training to become a Catholic priest?"

"That's not exactly a secret, though, is it?"

He nodded. "Agreed. However, your transition from a seminary student to a police detective is a little out of left field, don't you think?"

"It was either that or become a Mafia hit man." I joked.

He laughed out loud. The young man snickered behind his fist and went back to devouring his eggs.

"And you have a sense of humour, Ian. I like that. Now, there are two more parts to the test. And I'm only going to tell you about part two."

"When do I learn about part three?" I asked.

"Never."

"No?"

"If you pass, you'll know it. If not, it will be irrelevant. That's all I'm going to say about it."

"So, what's part two?" I asked.

He tapped the cardboard box with his fork. "Don't look at this until you've finished with the case you're currently working. Once you resolve your case, please feel free to look this over."

I picked up the box, carefully. It was held shut with wide paper tape along the sides.

"What's in here?" I asked.

"Can't tell you. That's part of the test." He shrugged. "In any case, I don't know what it means."

I considered this for a few moments, then I picked up the box and put it up on a high shelf, above the good china. "There's nothing there that will leak or ooze, or anything?" I asked.

"No, nothing like that."

For the next five minutes, nobody spoke. The only sound was a soft clatter as forks scooped eggs onto toast, and a slurp as Kirby and his driver drank coffee. I watched them, resisting the urge to speak. It occurred to me this might be another test- would I feel compelled to open my mouth?

The young man finished his food, leaving the plate almost spotless, and sat still, his hands down in his lap. Kirby finally finished too, patted his mouth dry one more time, and gave a tiny nod.

The young man stood up straight, almost at attention. Kirby slid his chair back and reached his hand out to me.

"Ian, thank you for showing us the hospitality of your kitchen. We both appreciated it."

I shook his hand. "Any time. I'm sure we'll meet again?"

He smiled softly. "Well, that rather depends on you, sir. Good day."

The young man turned to follow Kirby. I had an idea.

"Sergeant! Ten-HUT!" I barked.

The young man snapped to attention, bolt upright. A second later, he relaxed and looked over at me, sheepish.

I grinned. "Thought so. You go, gunny."

The young man glanced at Kirby, embarrassed. Kirby glared at me, annoyed.

"Y'all enjoyed that, huh?" He grumbled.

"I was pretty sure that I was right. He was a Sergeant in the Marines, wasn't he?"

Kirby waved at the young man. "Speak up, son."

He glanced at Kirby then looked at me. "Yes, sir. I served in the Corps."

His voice was low, soft, but he had a determined tone about him when he spoke.

"Glad to meet you, Sergeant." I said.

He nodded quickly. "Thanks for the chow, sir. Good food."

He opened my front door, let Kirby out ahead of him, then softly closed it behind them. I was alone in the house. Again.

At eight in the morning, I pulled into the lot of fifty-two division, parked at my spot and went in. The chatter of men and women, a low rumble occasionally punctuated by clear words, filled the air. As I placed the small stack of paperwork I had on my desk, one voice came through, clear.

"Here he is. Let's ask him." I heard.

One of the detectives walked up to me, a sheet of paper in his hand. "Hey, boss." He said.

He thrust the paper at me. "We're trying to decide whether to list a pack of gum as an expense."

I read the paper over. "Really? It's gone that far, has it?"

He shrugged. "I spend fifteen minutes a week filling in bullshit, just so that waste of space in the office leaves me alone. Works for me."

I cringed slightly at the blunt insult. "If I was Captain, would you talk about me that way?"

"Would you make us do that too?"

"No, I wouldn't."

"Well, then, there's your answer, boss."

He walked away.

From another room, a secretary came up to me and placed a mug of coffee on my desk. I nodded thanks and took a sip. She didn't move; she just stood there, looking at me.

"Something on my nose?" I asked.

"We're glad to see you back, Ian. The jungle drums say you were working undercover?"

"They don't lie. It was interesting, to say the least."

She nodded approval and walked away. I flipped through telephone message slips, threw out the old and pointless ones and stacked three or four important ones for later in the morning.

Out of the corner of my eye, I saw Walsh, Webb and Reynolds walking towards me. They were smiling, laughing, and they looked about ready to break into a musical number.

Walsh moved closer, the other two deferring to him. "Hey, boss. Good to see you without the decorations."

I scratched my neck. "Yeah, thanks, Patrick. It's still a bit itchy, but they should be all gone soon. Where are we?"

He turned to Reynolds, and she slid up a chair beside me. She opened her purse and pulled out an envelope, then she dumped its contents onto my desk.

Victor French's passport dropped out, along with the travelers' checks and airline ticket.

"I did some checking on the airline ticket." She started. "The ticket was bought in cash, at a travel agency a couple of blocks away from Abigail Fontaine's apartment. That's according to the code on the ticket, so the person at the airport said. I'm going to visit the agency this morning, as soon as they open, find out who sold it, and see if they remember who bought it."

"Good work, Alex. Did you want to take Brian with you?"

She grinned. "Sure, it'll give him a taste of plain clothes."

She pointed to the travelers' checks. "Same with these. I'm going to ask the folks at my local bank if we can track down where these were purchased, and by whom."

"Whom? I'm impressed." I joked.

"OK, you guys run with that. Patrick, can you find out more about Victor's movements? Why the passport, why the Ireland stamp? And how on earth did he end up as a body on the street?"

"You want that done by lunch time, boss?" He asked. The others laughed.

"Yeah, it's a lot to digest, I know. I'm going to ask my friend at the OPP if he has any leads for us."

I looked at my watch. Eighty thirty-five. The front door opened, and Ernest Pascoe strutted in, nodded quickly at me and went into his office.

I waited for five minutes, then went into his office. "Mister Pascoe? How are we doing?" I asked.

He seemed surprised at the pleasantry. "Fine. Why do you ask?"

"Everything seem OK from your end?" I asked.

He leaned back. "All right. What are you setting me up for?"

"You came in, and you never asked me where I was all week. Why is that?"

"I assumed you were working on the current case."

"Which case is that?"

He looked around furtively. "Ah, the current one you mentioned, of course."

"Can you name our victim? Can you give me any details on the case?" I pressed.

He waved the back of his hands at the papers on his desk. "My focus here is on improving the work process. I'm doing my best to improve workflow. Catching bad guys is your job, not mine."

"Right. So, does this mean you're giving me control of the department, as far as the detectives are concerned?"

He leaned back and scrutinized me. "Why are you doing this to me right now, Ian?"

"I'm dealing with a very complex case. I can't have my people spending their time filling out meaningless paperwork."

He picked up a stack of papers. "So, was this your idea, to swamp me with confetti?"

"That was my first volley. I could make it much worse for you, believe me."

"How, exactly?"

I waved at the room outside his office. "These guys are detectives. They detect. Is your life squeaky clean, or do you want some things kept out of the light?"

He glanced out and leaned forward. "Why? What have you heard?"

"So, I hit a nerve. Good. Now, let us do our jobs. You can file reports, and say you've made changes, and whatever else you need to do, but I need you to just stay out of our way. Period."

He sat back. "Agreed. In exchange, no more stacks of paper."

"Agreed. Good day, Captain."

I picked up a clipboard and waited till all the detectives were looking at me.

"Good morning all. Regular Monday meeting." I barked.

"First off, Captain Pascoe thanks you for the input to help him write a report to city hall."

There was a confused muttering.

"Second, now that he has your data, he will no longer require those reports. Thanks to all, again."

The muttering changed to a soft chuckle.

"Next, we have a name for the first body, missing from the morgue. Victor French. Detective Reynolds has the details. The body in the Mercedes, Robert Sankar, was a cop, OPP."

There was total silence now. Of course, they had heard this before, but they were waiting for more information.

"We're working on the supposition that there was some reason Sankar was killed, a reason that ties him to French. We don't know what the common thread is yet, but we'll keep you posted. Meanwhile, what other cases do we have on the go?"

A number of the men spoke up, gave progress reports on the cases they were working, and what their next moves were going to be.

One man talked about a robbery at a sporting goods store; expensive equipment had been taken.

Another mentioned that there had been a series of assaults on panhandlers and bums who were hanging around the area where Victor French had been found. A uniform suspected that it was the work of a disgruntled landlord, he said, but we had no firm leads.

That got me thinking. "Do you think that French came back to see someone?" I asked.

"If he'd been in Ireland, maybe he came back for a reason, and that's why he was in that area."

The detective nodded. "I'll ask around- maybe he has family or a girlfriend or something in the area. I'll get back to you later today, boss."

"Good, let me know. Meanwhile, I think I should head back to the morgue, see if I can get any more information from a dead man."

It took me almost half an hour to drive to the morgue. Traffic was unusually heavy for a Monday morning, and the sun, heading south on Yonge, was directly in my eyes. To make matters worse, the car was stifling hot. I was tempted to stop home and borrow Karen's Pontiac. It had air conditioning, and I could wear a fur coat if I wanted to, sitting in her car. I fought the urge; her car was her car, and I didn't want to just take it- that was a slippery slope.

Mercifully, I found a parking spot in the shade on the street outside the morgue. I placed my 'police business' sign on the dashboard and went in.

The receptionist smiled recognition and let me into the back. I zigzagged through the office, between partitions and toward the small office the coroner had. It was a glass box, ten feet by six feet, with stacks of paper on one desk, and a backless swivel stool opposite the only chair in the room. The coroner was in shirtsleeves, his tie loose, writing something in a folder, and he only glanced up briefly as I sat across from him.

"Miss me already?" He asked.

"Haven't you noticed that I wasn't here for a week?" I answered.

He tossed down the folder. "Hell, Ian, I figured you'd wrapped this case up already."

I shook my head. "No such luck. What else can you tell me about our Mercedes victim?"

He pulled a manila folder out of the stack on his desk, checked the name on the tag, and opened it up. "Robert Sankar; well, he's still dead. What else can I tell you?"

"You said he was shot- a Walther or Astra pistol."

He flipped over the first page of the report. "Right. What else did you want to know?"

"It was just one bullet that shot him?"

"Yes, and I'm sure it was quite painful." He added.

"Painful? Didn't the bullet kill him?"

"It did, just not right away. The bullet nicked his pulmonary artery. He could have lived for a half hour or so before he died."

"So, he might have gotten into a car and driven away before he died?"

"Easily. One lung was full of blood, but he could have walked for a few minutes before he lost too much blood. I'm sure he could have driven for quite a while before he died."

I nodded. "Do you know what this means? We thought he was dumped there. I bet he wasn't- he was trying to get away. That changes everything."

I found an empty desk and picked up the phone. I dialed the station and asked for Patrick.

"Detective Sergeant Walsh." The voice said, firmly.

"Patrick- got news." I said. "Our dead cop- Sankar- he didn't die immediately after he was shot. He may have driven for a while- he might have been trying to get away and collapsed."

There was a long silence. "Really? Wow, that changes things, boss."

"Yes, it does. Now, he'd eaten a very fancy meal just before he died. Lobster, salad, cheesecake. That's not something served before lunch, usually. What if he ate it at a restaurant, somewhere near where he was found?"

I heard him writing this down.

"Let me work on that. I'll get Alex and Brian to canvas the area. I've got a photo of Sankar, so they can pass it around and see if he was remembered at any of the eateries."

"Good. Let me know." I hung up.

I called the station again and asked for Reynolds. She picked up after two rings.

"Detective Constable Reynolds." She said, firmly.

"Hey, Alex, got a question for you."

"Yeah, boss?"

"Patrick is going to fill you in, but it turns out that Robert Sankar was probably not killed in his car. The coroner says he was mortally wounded by the bullet, but he could have lived for a while before it killed him."

"Really? That's interesting."

"Yeah. He had a fancy meal before he died. Patrick will have you check out any local restaurants where he might have been seen, but I'm curious about the spot where he was found. What can you tell me?"

"It's a commercial building, just north of Fairview Mall. Don Mills and the 401 Highway."

"OK."

"It's a surface parking lot facing Don Mills, and he was found outside the offices of... hold on."

She paused as she opened her Moleskine to a page.

"Yeah, boss. He was found outside a customs brokerage, a company called Paramount Shippers. Also, his car was in parking space number seventeen."

"Seventeen." I repeated.

"Right. You think he was trying to make sure we got his message?"

"In case we didn't pick up on the number written on the business card? I suppose so." I said.

I looked at my watch. "Listen; I'm going to check out Paramount Shippers. You do your thing. How about we meet up at the Bloor-Jane for lunch, say one, one-thirty?"

"Fine, I'll pass the word. See you then, boss."

I thanked the receptionist for the use of her phone. She seemed fascinated by my conversation; she asked me if it was always this exciting being a police officer. I politely told her that this was the fun part of the job, but it also involved being away from home for long hours, in the cold and rain. That seemed less appealing.

Yonge Street was busy this morning. I decided to risk the Don Valley 'Parking Lot' as the Don Valley Parkway was affectionately known, so I headed east on Bloor Street to loop onto the Don and join the traffic headed north.

Luck was with me. I made it past the major exits without any bottlenecks, took the exit for Sheppard Avenue and made three right turns, ending up at the office building where Robert Sankar had been found.

It was a standard, two storey concrete slab, a long yawn on the landscape, with strategically placed shrub beds and breaks in the long apron around the building, designed to give it a more human feel. It wasn't working all that well. In the summer sun, the asphalt baked the air over the asphalt. I parked in spot number seventeen, got out and looked around.

There were other cars in the lot, not many for a Monday, but several of the windows facing Don Mills Road had large 'For Lease' signs on them. This wasn't a very busy complex, then.

I stood beside my car, trying to figure out if there was some reason that Robert Sankar had parked here. Was it just convenient, or did he meet someone in the lot before he died?

Had he stopped because he was weak and tired? Or did he feel himself slipping away, and he wanted to park before he collapsed? Which one of these was the truth? Was it something else?

A man in a black shirt and slacks came out of one of the offices, smiling as he approached me.

I stiffened slightly. He was probably going to ask me to move my car, or maybe he wanted to sell me something, I couldn't tell. He had a small stack of folded brochures in his left hand, and he patted his right hand with them as he walked.

"Hello." He said, his voice both soothing and welcoming.

He waved at the building. "Are you here for the meeting?"

I shook my head. "What meeting?"

He shrugged. "Ah. I thought you were part of our group. I'm sorry." He turned to leave.

"What group?" I asked.

He turned back, slid a brochure out of the stack, and handed it to me. "Here you go. Everyone is welcome, of course. We don't judge here. It's a safe place to be."

I glanced at the brochure. "Alcoholics Anonymous?"

"We think of it as a way to come together with others in the same situation. We work to help each other."

He paused. "Are you a friend of Bill W's?"

I shook my head. "We lost my mother to a drunk driver ten years ago. I don't drink, no."

He waved the handful of pamphlets in the direction of my car. "It's just that, you know, we don't get many people here on a Monday morning, mostly those who come to the meetings."

"I'm Detective Inspector Ian McBriar, Toronto Police. And you are?"

He stuck his hand out. "Reverend Elijah Turner. Everyone just calls me 'Rev'."

"You're a vicar?" I asked.

"I'm a pastor at the Calvary Evangelical Church, on Finch Avenue. Are you here about one of our congregation?"

"Actually, I'm here because of a body that was found here. You wouldn't know anything about that, would you?"

"You're talking about Robert?" He asked.

"We heard he was found here last week. Terrible thing, that. Do you know what happened?"

"I'm afraid I can't say much about it. Did you know him well?"

The man waved at the building. "He first came to meetings over a month ago, and we saw him about twice a week. He was dedicated to the program, very devoted. A nice person."

I scratched my head. "Do you know if anyone in the group remembers him? Was there anyone he was friendly with? Someone I could talk to?"

The man rubbed his nose and looked down, a gesture which meant he was thinking, or remembering. "Well, there was one fellow in particular. Victor, yes, that was his name, Victor. He'd been gone for a long time, but he came back a month or so ago."

It suddenly felt like a number of things fell into place. "Victor is in his mid-thirties, average height?" I said.

He seemed surprised. "Why, yes, that's right. Do you know him?"

"I've never actually met him." I said, cautiously.

I pointed at the building. "Any idea what they talked about in the meetings?"

"Fishing. Robert loved fishing. He showed everyone a picture of some massive fish he caught, one time. Apparently it lost him the end of his finger, but he still landed this fish."

"What about Victor?" I asked.

"He's in finance of some sort. A real high-roller, from what I gather. The last time he was here, he drove a foreign something-or-other. He had a number of cars, it seemed. Always something fancy, always something expensive. As I say, he hadn't been around for a year or so, then he showed up last month."

I pulled out my Moleskine and made notes. "Thanks, Reverend. Could I give you my card? If you remember anything, or if anyone says anything, can you let me know?"

He took my card and read it. "You were shot about five years ago, right?"

I was surprised by that. "Yes. I'm astonished that you'd remember that from the news."

He shook his head. "I was the hospital chaplain when you were wheeled in. A number of us prayed for you."

"Well, I owe you. It worked."

"Do you have time to come to the meeting? I'd like you to be here." He said.

I grinned. "How could I say no? lead the way."

It was now ten fifteen in the morning, and the room was set up like a small auditorium. Three rows of stacking chairs, plastic and chrome, were set facing a desk and a lone chair at the front of the room.

One by one, people wandered in. they nodded at others they recognized, or sat with them and spoke in low voices.

By ten thirty, there were twenty-odd men and four women in the room, and the mood seemed to lighten as they all got comfortable around each other.

The pastor set up a coffee maker and placed Styrofoam cups beside it, then he walked to the front of the room. He looked around like a conductor surveying his orchestra.

He sat in a solitary chair, facing us. "Good morning. Welcome one and all." He started.

He bowed his head and said what I later learned was called 'The Serenity Prayer'. Most of the people in the room said it along with him. He looked up, smiled and put his hands on his knees.

"For those of you who don't know me, and I see a few new faces here today, my name is Elijah. The rules, as you know, are simple. No smoking and no drinking, of course. First names only, don't interrupt, and you only need to speak if you feel like it. Who wants to go first?"

A woman, small, rather pretty, in a print dress that was now a size too tight, coughed and leaned forward.

"Hi." She started, speaking softly. "My name is Greta."

Everyone answered in unison. "Hello, Greta."

She swirled the coffee in her Styrofoam cup, looking into it for inspiration. "As some of you know, I have been coming here for quite a while now. Things have been better at work, lately, so that helps. I'm still being blamed for what happened, even though it wasn't my fault, but then, that's life, isn't it?"

Elijah leaned forward and waved his upturned palm at the woman. "Greta, you said last time that you were struggling, that you had broken up with someone close to you?"

She shrugged and studied her coffee. "Well, yeah, I thought I'd found someone that was right for me. He had everything going for him, you know? And I couldn't believe that he'd betray… Anyway, he ended up being a frog, not a prince."

Elijah nodded, agreeing with her. "Sometimes, we have to experience pain before we know joy, isn't that the case, Greta?"

She looked quickly up at him, anger in her eyes. "That's bullshit, Elijah. That's fortune cookie bullshit. I'm not talking about losing some guy to another woman, or losing him to war. That bastard screwed me out of my life savings, and he used me to steal from the bank. You want pain, Elijah? Spend three weeks in front of a criminal review board, having them pick your life apart. There's pain for you."

She looked down again, suddenly quiet. Elijah kept his eyes on her.

"Greta, I'm so sorry for what happened to you. Do you want to say anything else to the group?"

She stared at her coffee and shook her head.

One man raised his hand. Elijah pointed at him. "Yes, Travis?"

The man spoke for a while, describing how he had lost his job, his home, and his family over his drinking. He sounded angry, but he also said that he understood how it was his fault, and that the solution was in his hands, too. A number of others mumbled agreement. The man leaned back and rubbed his face.

After that, a few others spoke, giving stories about their lives, some revealing, some dismissive, others stating that they were there because a judge had told them to come.

Finally, Elijah faced me. "Hello. You're new here. Would you like to say something?"

I told myself to keep quiet, to just shake my head. I took a deep breath. "Hello, I'm Ian."

As one voice, everyone intoned "Hello, Ian."

I nodded. "I don't drink. Let me be clear; I may have a glass of wine with dinner, once or twice a month. Other than that, I don't drink. But ten years ago, my mother was run down and killed by a drunk driver."

A few people in the room winced, or sucked air. Others said nothing.

"Anyway, I was studying to become a priest. When they told me what had happened, I realized I didn't have the strength or the faith within me to forgive the guilty. I knew that I could let anger destroy me, or I could do something good with it."

Elijah waved his hand at me. "That's when you decided to become a policeman?"

"If I can't forgive the guilty, I can at least lock their asses up." I said.

A few people chuckled. The woman who'd spoken, Greta, stared at me. Another man spoke, then one of the women, then Elijah had us all recite the Lord's Prayer, and everyone got up.

A few people poured themselves a second coffee, some said goodbye and left. The woman who had spoken first, Greta, stood to one side and watched me. As soon as the few people who introduced themselves to me left, she came over.

"You're a cop?" She said, simply.

"Yes. I am."

"Why are you here, if you don't drink?"

"I came because I'm working on a case. As well, because Elijah invited me in."

She tucked her hands behind her back, a gesture that meant she was making herself vulnerable but also that she wanted to hide something.

"I thought maybe you were here because the bank sent you."

"No, I'm not. However, can I ask you- who was the person you were talking about?"

"Victor. I met him here, and he seemed wonderful. We went out for months, then he just vanished. He left without saying he was going. He left me a note. All it said was 'sorry- Victor.'"

"Was his name Victor French?" I asked.

She glared at me. "Was? What do you mean, 'was'?"

"I'm sorry. We think Victor may have passed away."

She stared down at the now-empty coffee cup. Her eyes filled with tears. "Bastard." She said.

I looked around. "Listen, Greta, is there somewhere we could talk? Somewhere private, away from everybody?"

The looking around was mostly to give her the feeling that I was keeping her story a secret.

She pursed her lips and nodded. "There's a coffee shop at the corner of Don Mills and Sheppard. I'll meet you there in five minutes." She said.

She got into a pale green Vega and drove away.

I thanked Elijah for letting me stay and walked out.

Five minutes later I was in the coffee shop, looking around. Greta was in a booth at the back, fiddling with a folded napkin.

I slid in across from her and picked up a menu from behind the ketchup bottle. "So, what's good here?" I asked.

"Nothing much, but it's quiet." She said.

A waitress came by offering coffee, and we both nodded. She filled our mugs; I ordered a bowl of ice cream, and Greta shook her head, sticking with just coffee.

"Gotta watch my weight." She sighed.

"I was really hot stuff, two years ago. Then I got involved with Vic, and it was great for a while, but after he left, I let myself go. I gotta get back in shape if I want to start dating again."

"Nonsense. You're a very pretty woman." I said.

She looked me up and down. "Yeah? You're married, right?"

"Yes. Two and a half kids." I smiled.

She smirked. "Congratulations."

She poured a large amount of sugar from the dispenser into her coffee and stirred it up. "Yeah, so, about Vic." She started.

"How did you meet him?" I asked.

"At the AA meeting, over a year ago. He took a shine to me right away. He just liked the way I looked, I guess. Anyway, I had just gone through a divorce, I was drinking a lot, and I felt really shitty about myself. Still, he started talking to me. Within a couple of weeks, I got to feeling pretty good about myself. I mean, he was in high finance, and he had this fancy car and everything. He had this gorgeous apartment, and from his balcony you could see all the way to Buffalo on a clear day. I mean, it had a pool and a sauna and… well, anyway, that was then."

I grimaced. "What happened?"

She shuffled her coffee mug back and forth. "He asked where I worked. I told him that I was the assistant manager of my bank branch. He didn't seem surprised by that. It's almost like he already knew that. In any case, we started dating. Soon I was staying over at his place. We talked about moving in together, about getting married. Then one night, I'd brought home some paperwork, and I caught him going through it. He said he was just curious, but now I realize it was more than that."

She looked over her shoulder for the waitress. Greta pointed at my ice cream. "Can I get one of those, hon?"

The waitress nodded and went back to the kitchen. Great took a long sip of coffee and continued.

"So, next thing, he asks if I can open a bank account for him at the branch where I work. I mean, shit, a monkey with one bad eye can open an account. Why did he need my help?"

The waitress brought over a bowl of ice cream and Greta picked at it, carefully, slowly. She swallowed and nodded.

"Anyway, he opens an account and puts a hundred thousand dollars into it. Everyone in the branch was gaga over him, and all the girls hated me for having him. It was great.

"Then, he moves the money around. Takes it out, puts it back, takes it out, puts it back. He explained that he buys and sells securities, and that's why he does what he does."

"Then he asked for a line of credit." I prompted.

I continued. "He got your bank to OK it, based on your say-so, then he took the money out and disappeared. Am I right?"

She snickered and wiped her nose. "You've seen this act before, apparently."

"It's an old scam, Greta. I'm surprised your manager didn't catch it."

"Our bank examiner was furious. My old manager is now an assistant manager in Markham. Five employees. They couldn't get rid of him directly, so they put him out there hoping he'd quit. And the worst part is, it wasn't even his fault. He let it go through as a favour to me. The review board later found out that he had done this to three other women, all bank employees, all single. They figure he took as much money from each of them as from us."

"A hundred thousand dollars?" I asked.

She shook her head. "We gave him a line of credit of a quarter million. If the review board is right, he took off with over a million dollars."

"What about his apartment, his cars?" I asked.

"None of it was his. The cars belonged to some rich guy who was out of the country. The apartment as well. Turns out that Victor had been in the bank before, asking about a loan, and he heard me talking to one of the other girls about my drinking. One of the things we're supposed to do in the program is apologize to people we've hurt. Victor found out where I went to meetings, and he pretended to be an alcoholic. That's how he got the apartment. The real owner of the place asked him to house-sit while he was doing some big real estate deal in Colorado. Victor just moved in. He had the apartment, he knew where the car keys were, so he had everything. He got me, and he took the money, and then he simply screwed off."

I winced. "If it's any consolation, it didn't do him any good. It didn't save his life."

She looked up. "Really? What happened to him?"

"If the person we found is Victor French, he did not end well."

The waitress brought her a bowl of ice cream, ceremoniously set a spoon beside it, and topped up my coffee.

"Listen, Greta, you know that nothing I heard in that meeting goes beyond here, right?"

She nodded. "Thanks. I really appreciate that."

"That said, can I contact you if I need to- if I think of anything you could help me with?"

She shrugged. "Yeah, sure. Absolutely."

"Listen, I understand that you're still bitter. Anything I can help you with?"

"It's just life, that's all. Shit happens." She said.

She scooped some ice cream out of the bowl and wrapped her lips around the spoon, sucking the ice cream into her mouth.

"It's been a long time since I had dessert like this. This is good." She mumbled.

She took a larger spoonful of ice cream, savouring the cold. "Mmm."

We finished our coffee. I gave her my business card, took hers, and promised I would be as low-key as possible if I spoke to her again.

She thanked me and we walked out into the blinding sunlight. I stood between our two cars, trying to think of what I should say to her.

"Look, Greta, you really are a lovely woman. Victor was a predator. He preyed on you, and I'm sure he preyed on other women, too. Not because they were dumb, but because they were nice. That's what men like him do. It's not your fault. Remember that. You're better than that."

"Thank you. I needed that." She grinned.

She threw her arms around me, hugging me tight. Instinctively, I hugged her back. I rubbed her shoulder, trying to convey empathy.

She looked up at me, serious, and pulled my face down to hers. She gave me a long, warm kiss that sent a rush through me, from my ears to my knees.

I stepped back. "Like I said, you're a lovely woman. Remember that."

She covered her mouth, suddenly embarrassed. "I don't know what came over me. Sorry about that. I'm not usually so… forward."

"I'm just glad I still have that effect on women." I joked. "Take care, Greta."

I got into my car, watched her smooth her dress flat and wiggle the hemline down, then she got into her Vega and drove away.

It was twelve thirty, and I could be at the Bloor-Jane Diner in forty minutes, if traffic wasn't atrocious.

On the cruise downtown I tried to think of what the connection might be between Victor French and

Robert Sankar. Something had brought them together, I was sure of it now.

I got to the Bloor-Jane about ten minutes after one. Walsh's car, Reynolds' car and my car lined up outside like boxcars. I went in, temporarily blinded by the relative darkness of the diner, and looked around. Walsh, Reynolds and Webb were in the same booth they always sat in, all talking over one another.

Walsh saw me first, slid over and let me in. he flipped open his notebook. "Hey, boss, I found some interesting stuff."

"French was a con man? He took off with over a million dollars a year ago?" I said, smugly.

Walsh closed his book and rolled his eyes. "All right, what number am I thinking of?"

I laughed. "No, I'm not psychic."

I explained the AA meeting, parking in spot number seventeen, Greta's story, and French's scam. I left out the parts about the hug and kiss.

Walsh made notes as I spoke. Reynolds leaned forward. "So, did French's death have anything to do with him coming back here, if he really was in Ireland?"

I shook my head. "How do you mean?"

"Maybe he pissed off the wrong people. Maybe someone wanted their cash back. Maybe a scorned woman went after him. Or maybe he just tried the same scam again and got caught."

"Yeah, all possibilities. How does it link up with Robert Sankar's death, though? And do we know how Victor French died?"

Reynolds pulled out her Moleskine and flipped to a page with a torn corner. "He was stabbed."

"Stabbed?" I asked.

"Yeah. The coroner didn't get much time to do anything with him. He disappeared right after they wheeled him in, after all. But one of the med students there says he noted a what appeared to be a stab wound in his back, upper right side."

"So he was stabbed from behind, by someone right-handed." Webb asked.

Reynolds thought for a moment. "Lets out Abigail Fontaine, doesn't it? She's a lefty."

Webb smiled. "Or, how about this? Stand up, Alex."

He and Reynolds got out of the booth and stood, facing each other. He picked up a drinking straw from the dispenser and put it in her left hand. "Now, hug me." He said.

She grinned and wrapped her arms around him. He nodded. "Stab me."

She poked the straw harmlessly into his back.

"See? A lefty, from in front, stabs the guy in the back, and it looks like a right-handed person from behind."

Walsh watched, curious. "Could a woman to get close enough to do that?"

I snickered. "You tell me, Patrick."

Walsh shook his head. "Erase, erase, erase. Forget everything. Let's concentrate on the why, and then the who should be easier to figure out."

I was pleased to hear him say that. He was clearly ready for promotion. "What are you thinking, *Inspector*?" I asked.

Walsh looked down at the table, thoughtful. "OK. So, we know he has stolen a bunch of money. The passport indicates he went to Florida, then the Bahamas, a year ago, right?"

Reynolds flipped the page on her notebook. "July of last year, he went through customs in Florida. The next day, he cleared customs in Nassau."

I pointed to her. "Remember what I asked Abigail Fontaine? Why would anyone go to Mexico in summer- it's too hot. Same here. Why would he go to the Bahamas in summer?"

Walsh smiled. "To open a bank account."

Reynolds wagged her finger at him. "Bank account- of course. He takes his loot from Canada, in a cashier's cheque or something, and deposits it in the Bahamas. Nice."

"Then what's the deal with Ireland?" I asked.

"Maybe he was doing the three-country monte." Walsh said.

"Enlighten me."

"It's what my father calls it. Some people we know have done it, especially after a divorce."

He took a paper napkin and laid it on the table. He pulled a thin gold pen from his jacket and started drawing boxes on the napkin.

"You leave Canada with a suitcase full of cash. Now, you like Canada and you want to live here, but you don't want the government or your ex to take your cash away."

He drew a line from one box to another. "So you set up a bank account in the Bahamas. They charge a small handling fee, but it's nothing compared to paying alimony or taxes."

He wrote 'Ireland' in another box. "You set up a business in Ireland. It's an investment company, and it takes money from the Bahamian account, and 'lends' it to you in Canada.

"Canada doesn't care whether the Irish company makes money or not, neither do the Bahamas. But you get to spend the cash you 'borrowed' in Canada, tax free, and nobody's the wiser."

I looked over the diagram. "So he came back, and either someone wanted their share, or they wanted revenge for what he did to them?"

Walsh shrugged. "Yeah. But how does the Starlite Motel enter into it?"

I'd almost forgotten about them. "Right, them. What do you think, Patrick?"

"Maybe they provide the escape route?"

"How would we find out?" I asked.

"You and I can go back there and ask."

We agreed that we'd go back to the Starlite Motel. Walsh would wear a radio microphone and Webb and Reynolds would wait nearby. Walsh would get the motel people to talk, and I'd return as his dumb lackey.

We had a couple of code words for various situations, signals to let Webb and Reynolds know we needed help. It was all settled.

I went back to the station house to do some paperwork. By five thirty I was tired, my eyes hurt, and I just needed to rest. I drove home, made myself dinner, and listened to jazz on the radio for an hour or so.

I went to bed early, trying to decide what I'd do in the morning. Everything went through my mind at once, all the parts of the puzzle. I fell asleep.

Chapter Nine

Tuesday morning, the coroner confirmed that Victor French had indeed been stabbed. His assistant hadn't done an autopsy, but it appeared that he had been killed by a thin blade, possibly a fish filleting knife. That much was written down. Beyond that, everything he had was from memory.

From the position of the wound, his assistant said, Victor French would have died right away. That left an interesting question; was he killed on the street, or was he killed somewhere else, and left on the street where the uniforms found him?

The clock on the wall chimed eight thirty. I drove to the station and sat at my desk, flipped though a short stack of memos, called back a couple of people who needed to hear from me, and waited.

Just after nine thirty, Walsh came in. he sat across from me, reached into his jacket and pulled out a folded sheet of paper.

"So, boss, found out some stuff." He said.

He unfolded the paper and placed it in front of me. "Victor French. Talk about a natural-born con man. He got into university with forged credentials and spent a year there before he got caught."

"What was he taking?" I asked.

"No, he got hired as a prof. He taught English Lit for two semesters without anyone clueing in that he was a high school dropout."

I read over the sheet of paper and chuckled. "Well, I guess we should count ourselves lucky he wasn't teaching medicine. Where did he go after that?"

"He went into securities sales and did pretty well, by all accounts, but he wanted to do better. Anyway, he got fired for drinking on the job. Takes quite a bit for a salesman to get fired for drinking. After that, he fell off the map."

"When was this, exactly?" I asked.

"A year and a half ago."

I scratched my head. "All right. So that jives with Greta's story. He used her, and other women too, presumably, then he took the money and disappeared. But where did he go, and why did he come back?"

"Maybe he blew it all? He came back to the well for more?" Walsh said.

"That would make sense. If it worked once, it'll work again? How would we find out?"

Walsh looked off, thinking, I had an idea.

"Patrick, if he was a drunk, then was he at the AA meetings for real? Not just as a cover?"

"Could be, boss. How does he tie in with Robert Sankar, then? Was he a drinker too?"

"According to Reverend Elijah, he was. Then again, maybe he'd been dry for a while, and he only went to the meetings to stay dry."

I leaned back, thinking. Walsh fiddled with his Moleskine, reading his notes.

He furrowed his brow. "Why take the body?"

"Sorry?"

"Throughout all this, boss, we never asked, why did they take the body? French was already dead, and he couldn't tell us anything, so why take his body?"
"Hmm. Good point. Maybe that *is* the point. Maybe if we'd had the chance to autopsy him, we would have found something out?"

Walsh read his notes again. "He had a ticket to Ireland in the envelope."

"Right." I said.

"But he hadn't used it. Maybe he was supposed to go to Ireland, and he never went. Maybe that's the point? He was supposed to use the ticket, to fly to Ireland, and he never did."

"So," I repeated, "Why take the body?"

Walsh leaned back and closed his eyes. He sat perfectly still for a few moments, then he opened his eyes and sat up.

"There's an old comic book I read once." He said.

"All right, I'll bite."

"I was at a friend's house, some time back. He had teenaged kids, and one of the boys was really a fan of comic books. Anyway, the kid read those 'Inner Sanctum' and 'Creepy Stories' comics.

"I was waiting for my friend to get ready- we were going to a movie, I think- and I flipped through one of the comics as I waited. The story was about this rich guy who paid a gang to help him disappear. He thought the sexy woman heading this group was going to sneak him across the border, or something, but it turns out she was a cannibal. She ate him."

"Charming." I said. "Your point?"

He shook his head. "The point is, boss, what if French paid someone to make him disappear, and instead they offed him? If he was a bunko artist, and trying to get away with the loot?"

"So, they promised him a new life, and they took his money instead, then killed him?"

He nodded. "Yeah."

He wrinkled his nose. "But why wait a year? No, that doesn't make any sense. Sorry."

"Still, you might be right, Patrick. We'll go back to the Starlite tomorrow; see if we can find out what they were doing with French. Maybe they did the same thing with others, too. After all, they were talking about going back to 'business as usual' after this."

"Fair enough. Let's get out there bright and early, boss. You dress the part, and I will too."

I got home around six, made myself dinner and watched the sparrows in the back yard, taking turns drinking and bathing in the shallow fountain along the back stand of trees.

After dinner, I called Karen.

"Hey, you." She said.

"I'm so relieved that you're back in town. How is everything?"

"Pretty good, hon, we're just wrapping up some details. Patrick is doing more of the heavy lifting, letting me manage the team. He'll make an excellent Inspector soon."

"That's good. Listen, someone here wants desperately to talk to you."

I heard the phone clunk as it was handed off. Charlie's voice came on. "Hey, dad, guess what?"

"Hi, sweetheart. You bought a giraffe?"

She laughed loudly. "No, silly. Grampa showed us where the horses live. It was fun. We got on the ponies an' we went around the fields."

"Wow, that sounds like so much fun, pumpkin. I miss you, you know?"

She sighed. "Miss you too, dad. Got to go. Bye."

There was a pause for a second, then Karen came back on. "Hi. Um, there was something else I meant to mention."

That sounded ominous. "Yes?"

"Lizzie Walsh called me. She said they were landing in Regina a week from now, when they head back to Toronto. She asked if I wanted to ride back on their plane. Would you mind if we took her up on it?"

I rubbed my forehead. Walsh's family had a private jet. I had declined their offer to fly Karen and the kids to Saskatchewan, because it felt like a bribe. Now, Karen was asking me to let them fly her back to Toronto, for the comfort and convenience it offered. I couldn't say no.

"Sure. I'm certain it will be more comfortable." I said.

She almost squealed with delight. "Great. I'll let you know when we're coming back, and you can meet us at the airport, all right?"

"All right. Talk to you soon, hon. Bye."

I hung up. One week. I had one week to wrap this up. Tomorrow would be very interesting.

At eight in the morning, Walsh was in my kitchen, wolfing down a three-egg omelette and toast.

I topped up his coffee, and he muttered thanks in between mouthfuls.

"Jeez, Patrick, don't you eat at home? I mean, your girlfriend works in a restaurant, after all."

"Kelly's leaving the diner. She got a microbiology fellowship at McGill." He said.

"Really? Congratulations from me, then. I hope she does well."

"Yeah, but it kind of sucks that she'll be out in Montreal while I'm here."

"That's life, Patrick. Crap happens while we're making other plans."

He snickered. "To scramble quotes, yeah."

I had purposely not showered or shaved, and I was in my worst work pants and plaid shirt, with a thin turtleneck hiding the fact that I no longer had tattoos.

Walsh was impeccably dressed, in a pale grey suit, navy tie and shoes that looked like black mirrors. He slid the empty plate away, thanked me for the meal and took a deep breath.

"Shall we go, boss?" He asked.

I followed him out of the house and turned, expecting to see his car. It wasn't there.

"Where's your car?" I asked.

He pointed down the way at a deep red Jaguar E type. It looked like a cigar, the sleek, fluid look of liquid mercury on four wheels.

"I figured I'd look the part of a crooked businessman today." He said.

He got in and I shoehorned myself into the passenger seat. Walsh placed his hand on one of the switches and buttons on a bewildering row of controls, and the engine roared to life. Walsh glanced left and the car pounced out onto the street, collecting admiring glances from about half the people we passed.

I settled back, relaxing.

Walsh glanced over. "You OK, boss?"

"Yeah. I'm just thinking how glad I am that you didn't meet Karen before I did. If she'd been in this car, I might still be single."

He laughed out loud. "I think the term is 'crumpet magnet'. I've heard that before about this car, yeah."

"So, where are we meeting the others?"

He got serious. "Alex and Brian are going to be a couple of miles from the motel. I'm wired for sound, and they'll follow us to the motel. The transmitter has a range of a couple hundred yards, so as long as we stay close, they'll hear everything we say."

"Do we have any code words set up?"

"Yes. If I say 'Africa' it means I'm in trouble. 'Bolivia' means come in, tell me that there's an urgent problem, and that we have to leave right away. Lastly, if I say 'China' it means 'stay outside but follow me when I leave'."

"Got it. Let's hope we don't need to use any of them." I said.

Walsh drove quickly, easing the long nose of the Jag through turns, accelerating on the straight roads, as he raced along the highway towards Lindsay. Again, we got more double-takes and waves from approving motorists.

This morning, the typical puffy clouds of an Ontario summer were back. Crisp white cotton balls floated by, the deep blue of the sky behind them making them seem like they were just above us.

Walsh roared up Route 35, then slowed and stopped behind a plain grey Monaco. Reynolds and Webb got out of that car and walked over to us. I rolled down my window and stuck my arm out.

Reynolds nodded and pulled out her Moleskine. "Morning, boss. Ready to do this?"

"Yeah, Alex. Do we have the radio working?"

Walsh got out and spoke to his jacket. "Testing, testing." He said.

Reynolds held a hand to her head, covering the earphone in her ear, and gave him a thumbs up. Webb walked straight over to the Jaguar, and stared at it, mesmerized.

"Is this the new one? The seventy-three?"

Walsh shook his head. "Seventy-five."

"It's got the four speed, right? With overdrive?" He said, softly.

Walsh nodded.

"And the straight six motor?"

"Vee twelve." Walsh corrected.

"Oh, man." Webb muttered.

"Brian, do you and the car need a moment alone?" I asked.

Reynolds snickered. Webb blushed slightly and backed away, still ogling the car.

We went over the code words, then our two-car convoy drove north towards the Starlite Motel.

Walsh and I were in front; Walsh pulled into the lot of the motel, the gravel crunching loudly under the fat tires.

Reynolds and Webb drove past, as though they weren't with us. They parked down the road, around a slight bend, out of view. Walsh fumbled with the microphone hidden in his lapel.

"Honk if you can hear me." He said.

In the distance I heard a horn beep. He seemed unconvinced.

"Two beeps, please." He said.

From the same faraway place, I heard two toots of the horn. Good; the radio was working.

"OK, here goes nothing."

He sprang out of the car and straightened his jacket. I tumbled out of my side, pulled my shirt smooth over my shoulders and slumped slightly, trying to look submissive.

Walsh glanced my way, his face pointed forward, and strutted toward the motel office. "Listen, boss, just follow my lead, OK?" he said softly.

I mumbled "Uh huh."

Walsh pulled open the door to the motel office and stepped in. The woman behind the counter was the same one as before, Gillian. She looked up sharply and jumped back a half step when she saw us. I was sure it was a reaction to seeing Walsh, not me. She looked around furtively, as though looking for a place to run.

Walsh casually placed a hand on the counter.

"I want to see your boss." He said, firmly.

"Well, I own the hotel, me and my husband." She said.

"No, that's not what I mean, and you know it." Walsh said, with an edge to his voice.

The woman shook her head. "I'm not quite sure I under.."

"Yes, you do. I know what you do, and I want to talk to your boss."

I stood quietly, trying to look bewildered. Walsh simply glared at her.

She leaned forward, feeling more confident now. "What exactly do you think we do here?"

"I know exactly what you do here. I need an exit, and you provide exits."

She stood straight, pursed her lips and picked up a pencil. "Just what exactly do you mean, Mister Walsh?"

"You remember me. Good. For the last time, I want to talk to your boss."

She tilted her head to one side slightly. "Why?"

Walsh reached into his jacket pocket and brought out a small velvet pouch, smaller than a fist. He undid a thick gold cord holding it shut and shook out its contents into his hand.

"Do you know what uncut diamonds look like? Have you ever seen them before?" He asked.

In his hand was a half dozen rough, cloudy stones, the size of the end of my finger. I tried not to gasp. Gillian was not so subtle. She cooed and reached out to touch the gems.

Walsh closed his hand around them and carefully dropped them back into the pouch.

"Now, it's Gillian, right? Gillian, I need an escape route. As well, there are several others, friends of mine in similar circumstances, who also need escape routes. I want to talk to the top man. Only him."

The woman kept her eyes on the pouch and licked her lips involuntarily. That could either mean she was worried, or she was relishing the possibility of a big payday.

"Well?" Walsh snapped.

She looked up at him. "Let me make a phone call."

She disappeared into the back area. I heard her speak but couldn't make out the words.

A minute later, she came back out. "He'll be here in about ten minutes." She smiled.

She waved at a pair of chrome stacking chairs against the wall. "Would you care to sit while you wait? And would you like a coffee, or tea?"

She looked only at Walsh. I was invisible. That suited me fine. Walsh glanced at the chairs and sneered. "No. I'll stand."

The woman shrugged and stood behind the counter, not knowing what to do. Eight minutes later, a rusty Chrysler pulled up. Mick, the foreman from the scrapyard, got out.

He strutted into the office, ignored me and walked up to Walsh. "You don't have your bodyguard with you, I see." He sneered.

"I don't need him." Walsh growled. "And I wanted to see the captain, not the cabin boy."

Mick frowned and got nose to nose with Walsh, looking up at him. "I'm the boss here."

Walsh slowly shook his head. "No, you're not, and we both know it."

Mick took a short step back, surprised. Walsh stepped forward and poked a finger into Mick's chest. "You get me the top dog right now, or I take our business somewhere else."

Mick sneered again. "Why should I believe you? Maybe you're just trying to muscle in on a good thing. I'm the head of this organization- you don't know who you're dealing with."

Walsh sighed, irritated. "Look, don't insult my intelligence. Either I talk to your boss, or I leave now. Your choice."

Mick glanced at the woman and back at Walsh. They all ignored me completely. "You call it, Gillian. What do you think?"

She took a deep breath. "Get him in here."

Mick walked to the door then waved at his car. He came back and leaned against the counter, eyeing Walsh.

Walsh put his hand into his jacket. Mick and Gillian both seemed very nervous at that. He pulled out a gold cigarette case, and they both relaxed. He opened the case, extracted a slim cigarette with a thin gold band around the filter, and snapped the case shut.

He put it away, reached into his outside pocket and came up with a gold lighter, with an ornate design that matched the case. He pressed a square button on the lighter, and a flame popped up. He lit his cigarette and put the lighter away.

The door opened, and we all looked. In came Jeff, the man I had been working with in the scrapyard. He glanced my way then walked straight over to Walsh.

"You wanted to meet me?" He said.

Walsh stubbed out the cigarette. "You're the one in charge of this enterprise?"

Jeff's voice was now much more precise, far more measured. "You have me at a disadvantage, sir. Who are you and how do you think we can help you?"

Walsh smiled. "You can call me Mister Walsh. I'm a businessman, and in my business, I hear things. I heard a rumor that you can help me disappear. Am I right?"

Jeff rubbed his nose. "Now, why would you want to disappear?"

Walsh pulled the pouch out of his pocket and picked out a stone, holding it near Jeff's nose. Jeff's eyes widened. Walsh had it between two fingers and let the light catch it.

"As I explained to your associates here, some of my friends are in the same position as me. We would all like to disappear, quietly. Now, how can you help me?"

Jeff licked his lips. He was hooked. "We can get you a fresh passport, a drivers' license, and a new SIN number. If you want to stay in Canada, we can relocate you, with a background deep enough that it would take years to crack it. If you want to leave the country, we can arrange that as well. That would be more expensive, of course."

Walsh put the stone back in the pouch. "How expensive?"

Jeff thought for a moment. "Fifty thousand dollars up front, another fifty thousand once we deliver. Bank transfer to our Bahamian account, and we do the rest."

"Where do you recommend that I go? I only speak English." Walsh said.

Jeff shrugged. "Anywhere. The States, New Zealand, Australia, the UK, you pick. We find you a place to live, and you just blend in."

Walsh smiled. "And if I were to arrange for some friends to do this, would I get a discount?"

"You get six people through the pipeline, and I'll let you go for free."

"How do I know you'll keep your word? How do I know you won't just take the cash and leave me stranded?"

Jeff shook his head. "We never do that. We operate on a basis of trust, period. If it makes you feel better, though, you can create an insurance policy, something that will ensure we deliver."

"Like an 'open if I don't contact you by next month' letter at my lawyer's?"

"Whatever you like. As I say, we operate on a trust basis."

Walsh pointed at me. "What about him? He has lost me a good deal of money."

"That's between you two. It's not our doing, and none of our concern."

Walsh glared at me. "He owes me, and he won't bother you again. How do I contact you?"

Jeff poked his chin at Gillian. "Call the motel, talk to her. She will make all the arrangements."

"Will I see you again?"

"Nope. Never."

Jeff turned and left. Mick followed him, and they drove away.

Walsh crooked a finger at me, calling me over. I walked meekly up beside him.

"I'll be in touch. You, come with me." He said.

He turned and left, and I followed. Gillian watched us get into the Jaguar and drive away. Walsh leaned forward slightly and spoke into his lapel. "We're out. Follow me at a distance, and we'll meet up where we stopped earlier."

We were almost a mile away from the hotel, headed back to Toronto, before I saw Reynolds' car slide in behind us. We drove until we got to the spot where we'd pulled over before. Walsh stopped by the side of the road and shut off the engine. The quiet, after the low rumble of the Jaguar's engine, was almost surreal. I heard the tic-tic-tic of the engine cooling off, then the crunching of gravel as Reynolds and Webb pulled in behind us.

Reynolds got out first. "What was that all about diamonds, Sergeant?" She asked.

Walsh smiled. "I said I needed to smuggle some diamonds out of the country. They took the bait. Now, we'll contact them later and set up a sting. "

I shook my head. "Diamonds, Patrick? Where did you get them?"

He pulled the pouch out of his pocket. "Funny, isn't it, how much they look like rock salt?"

He handed me one of the crystals. "And vice-versa."

I touched my tongue to it. "It's salt." I said.

"It's salt." He repeated. "From my garage."

"Nice. Let's get back to town and we'll figure out our next move." I said.

Webb pointed at the Jaguar's hood. "Mind if I ride with Sergeant Walsh?"

I chuckled. "Fine by me. Just don't ask to drive it."

I got into Reynolds' car and sat, waiting. She spoke with Webb for a moment, stroked his arm then came back and got in the driver's seat.

Walsh and Webb roared off, the Jaguar kicking up a small cloud of dust as it raced away.

Reynolds watched it go then started the engine and pulled out onto the road.

"So, Alex, how's it going?" I asked.

"Good, boss. I hope we get a break soon, though. It feels like we're getting somewhere now."

"I meant about you and Brian, actually."

She blushed. "Ah. Yeah, it's getting serious. I don't suppose that's much of a secret, though."

"No, not really. Look, as long as you two can work together, and your personal life doesn't rock the boat, it's none of my business."

She nodded. "Good to know. Thanks, boss."

"Then again, what if you become a Sergeant, and he's still a Constable?"

She laughed. "Hey, I already wear the pants. No change there."

We drove on for a while, neither of us talking. Something was bothering her, I could tell. She pursed her lips and shook her head, as though talking to herself, then shrugged, almost imperceptibly.

"What is it?" I asked.

"Why kill French? It just makes no sense." She said simply.

I smiled. "All right, I'll bite. What do you mean?"

She tapped three fingers on the top of the steering wheel, thinking. "OK. So, you have this guy who stole a bunch of cash. He disappears, but his last sighting was right up the road from your motel there. Got to be a connection, right?"

"Yes."

She continued. "So the options are; one, he came back to scam some more people, or two, he came back for a different reason."

"Go on."

"But, if he saw someone he'd cheated, would they kill him, no matter how much they'd lost?"

I could see where she was going. "Keep talking."

"He scammed banks. He didn't take individual people's savings. At most, as you said, someone might be pissed at being demoted. So, if I bumped into him on the street, I might say 'you asshole, I'm calling the police'. I wouldn't kill him."

It made sense. "So, Alex, then there are two other possibilities. Either he was killed by someone who knew him, or by a total stranger."

"A stranger might stab him for his wallet, or in a fight, but not from behind. That spells hatred."

What she said was reasonable, but it led to a brick wall. "So he was stabbed by someone who knew him, and not someone he cheated. Could it have been the motel people?"

She shook her head. "No."

She pulled over, put the car in park and turned to look at me. "I've paid you a bunch of cash to disappear, and I show up again. No skin off their nose. What's he going to say- 'hi, I was in Costa Rica, thanks to you folks at the Starlite Motel?' even if he had come back for some reason, the next logical thing for him to do would be to contact them again."

I shook my head. "Explain."

"He goes back to the motel and says 'hey, I'm back because my grandmother died, or I left the stove on, or there was more cash in the mattress, whatever. Can I get another escape route?' Then they just charge him for another trip."

She was right. It was pure, clean logic. And it left me with no answers. "You're right, Alex. Nobody had a reason to kill him, and nobody had any inkling he was back in town, if he came back with the same ID he used to leave."

"So, again, boss, the questions are, who killed him, and why did he come back?"

"Beyond that, why did someone take his body, and who did it?"

She nodded, agreeing. "And did the same people kill Robert Sankar?"

Chapter Ten

Reynolds dropped me home, waited till I opened my front door and drove off.

I changed into a suit and drove to the station. From his office, Ernest Pascoe glanced up at me, then ignored me and went back to writing something. I went through phone messages, made a couple of calls, and leaned back, thinking. Reynolds was right. There was no reason to kill French. But someone had. Had the same person taken him out of the morgue? Too many questions, too many puzzle pieces, not enough information.

The phone rang. I picked it up automatically. "Inspector McBriar."

"Boss, come for lunch." Walsh's voice said.

"Patrick? What's up?"

"Bloor-Jane. Twenty minutes." He said. He hung up.

Pascoe was still in his office. He had his back to me and didn't see me leave. I headed south on Keele, driving as quickly as I could without the gumball on the roof. Radio chatter was light; a hot Wednesday afternoon, with no reason for most people to be out of their offices, so I got down to Bloor Street in under fifteen minutes.

Just three minutes later I crossed Jane Street and parked behind Walsh's cruiser. I jogged up the short steps and went into the Bloor-Jane Diner; Walsh was in a booth, Webb and Reynolds were sitting with him. I slid in beside Webb and leaned forward.

"What's up, Patrick?"

He looked around, cautious. "I think I found out why French's body was taken." He said.

Webb and Reynolds watched him.

"Why?" I asked.

Walsh pulled out his notebook and flipped to a marked page. "The woman at the motel- Gillian."

He turned the page. "I did some checking. Your buddy, Josh Klassen, was very helpful. Her full name is Gillian Westlock. Not a very common name. Her husband, the guy we met at the motel, is Adam Westlock. Adam has a brother, Terry Westlock. And Terry Westlock, until last week, worked for our coroner in the morgue."

My mind quickly put it all together. "So, a body comes in, they take the name and ID, and create a new person with that name."

"Right. You have the ID of someone who will not show up to spoil your party. You had a case a few years ago, right, where the same thing happened? Canada doesn't cross-reference birth and death certificates. I could take the ID from someone on the slab pretend to be him for years, with nobody the wiser. It's perfect."

"So, where is Terry Westlock?" I asked.

"He quit. Normally, the coroner wouldn't have paid much attention to him, but Terry had worked there for a couple of years, so he mentioned it."

"And in that couple of years, how many names did he steal for our friends in Lindsay?"

"Right. One question answered. More questions crop up. Why kill French, and why kill Sankar?"

"Why indeed." I agreed.

Webb leaned forward. "Inspector, who was the second guy that showed up? The older voice?"

"That was Jeff, one of the workers at the scrapyard. I suppose it's a perfect cover; he works in a place where nobody would suspect him of being a criminal mastermind."

Webb shook his head. "I don't believe he is, not alone, anyway. I think he's just the frontman."

I frowned. "Explain."

"Um, I didn't mean to be disrespectful, sir, it's just..."

"No, it's quite all right, Brian. What makes you think he's not the boss?"

He looked down, collecting his thoughts.

"He works in the yard forty hours a week. He can't just come and go as he pleases, because people would notice. There must be someone else who does the work- creating passports, identity documents, Social Insurance cards, and so on. That's more like what a forger would do, or a notary or someone like that. I bet he just delivers the orders to that guy."

Walsh nodded agreement. "And that's why I wanted you in Major Crimes."

I sat back and thought. "OK, Patrick, if you were to go give them cash to change your identity, what are the steps they would take?"

"Well, they'd take photos of me, figure out what documents I need, and so on. Basically what we did for you with bogus papers, boss. Only more so."

"Then, how do we get these people?"

Webb coughed. "We say that that I'm one of the people Sergeant Walsh is trying to sneak out. That would give him credibility- they'll think there's more to come. I show up and they find me an escape route. We nab them and everyone lives happily ever after. Sound good?"

"Yeah, that would be a no, Brian. Too dangerous."

"Come on, boss. Think about it. They've met you, and if the Fontaine sisters are involved, one of them has met Alex, too. The only two of us who can show up are Sergeant Walsh and me. It makes sense, admit it."

I rubbed my face. Unfortunately, he was right. Reynolds glared at him, angry.

"You're an idiot, you know that? How stupid do you have to be to stick your neck out like that?"

He smiled at her. "Yeah, I know, hon, but what do you want me to do- give out parking tickets for the next thirty years?"

She shook her head. "Don't 'hon' me, lambchop, this is serious. This could get you killed."

"Lambchop?" I asked, curious.

Webb shrugged. "Don't ask. Anyway, what do you say, boss- it's your call?"

Walsh looked off, thinking. "I say we go for it. Either we nab them now, or we spend the next six months chasing them. I say we go for it."

Webb grinned. "Good. Do we get to go in your Jag?"

"Yeah, I wish there was another way to do this." I said.

"Still, let's do it right and make it work."

Walsh went to a pay phone down the street. We all stood around him, listening as he spoke. He asked for Gillian, and when he heard her voice he said 'do you remember me?' then he said 'I have a very important package for you to deliver, and it has to leave this week'.

He paused as she spoke, then 'the shipping for that is a hundred and fifty dollars? We agreed on a hundred.' Another pause, then 'ah, for the rush job, fine. How soon can we get all the shipping documents arranged?'

He pulled out his Moleskine and started writing.

"An item description, preferably two graphic ones?... oh, I understand. Of course. In colour? Right. Plus item weight, size, and so on." He said.

He listened some more. It seemed none of us breathed as we watched him.

"Where and when? Fine. You want the number?"

He said the phone number of the booth we were at and hung up. "So, they want me to get them a photo or two of Brian, for a passport and driver's license, and to be here tomorrow at this time. They will call me. Then they'll set up a meet and arrange the payment."

"Well, they didn't get this far by being stupid." I said.

Walsh patted Webb's shoulder with his Moleskine. "C'mon, Brian, we have to get you a couple of passport photos. Pronto."

They drove off, and I was left on the sidewalk with Reynolds. She seemed worried. She had her hands on her hips, shaking her head, watching them leave.

"Penny for your thoughts, Alex?" I quipped.

"You know damn well what I'm thinking, boss. A month ago he was ticketing jaywalkers, and now he's play-acting with killers."

She looked down and sighed. "How does Karen handle it, Ian? How does she cope with you heading out every morning? How does she feel when she sees you strap on the holster?"

I leaned against her car. "Five years ago, she watched me bleed into the sewer when I was shot. For two days, she didn't know whether I'd survive or not. In some ways, it was easier to be me. I was just unconscious, but she had to lie awake and worry.

What if it was the other way around? What if you were the cop, and Brian was a mailman, or a teacher? What would you want him to tell you as you left for work every day?"

She looked down the road, to where Walsh's car had gone. "Take care." She said softly.

"That says it all, Alex."

She drove off, and I was left on the sidewalk, all by myself. I didn't want to go back to the station- I had nothing to do there, anyway. I was restless, worried about what we were going to do, what would happen when we met with the people from the motel. I needed some perspective. That was it, I needed some perspective.

Captain Van Hoeke's MG was still parked in front of the house on Feldbar Court. Rebecca Van Hoeke was in the front yard, attacking a clump of dandelions with a long-handled shovel, expertly hacking them out with a quick sweeping motion.

I stopped out front and she put down the shovel even before I'd gotten out of the car. She stood there, hands on her hips, then she casually looked down and swept dried mud from the knees of her polyester slacks.

"You're back. Good." She grinned. "Martin was wondering when you'd show back up."

I gave her a quick hug. "Hello, Becky. You're looking as lovely as ever, I see."

She grabbed my jaw and pulled my face down, then gave me a quick kiss on the cheek.

"Nice to see you too, Ian. You know, you're the only person from the old place who has ever visited more than once. I'm sure Martin appreciates you coming over."

She waved at the front door. "Go on in. He's in the den, doing something or other."

I opened the front door and stepped in. From the back of the house, the sound of something clattering on wood echoed through. I followed the sound.

Martin Van Hoeke was sitting at a desk in a small room, carefully examining what looked like a bumblebee in a vise. He glanced up as he saw me and looked back down.

"Hello, Ian. Good to see you." He said it casually, as though passing a near stranger on the street.

"Hi, Captain. I just wanted to stop by and say hello." I said.

He picked up a fine pair of pliers and did something to the item in the vise. It was now obviously a fishing lure, a fly he was tying. He dropped the pliers on the table.

He leaned back, took off his thick reading glasses, pinched his nose with one hand, then he opened his eyes wide.

"Nonsense. You're here because you want to ask me something."

"Yes, I do, Captain."

"Martin."

"Maybe, but you'll always be 'captain' to me, boss."

He leaned back in his chair and smiled a fatherly smile. "Go on, Ian."

"We're doing something rather dangerous right now. It might break up a criminal ring, but it may also place my people in danger. How far do I let them go?"

From the other end of the house, I heard Rebecca's voice yell 'coffee-five minutes.'

Martin looked at the door. "We'll be there, love." He called.

He looked back at me. "Remember when you and Frank went to meet the man who had shot you? Was that a very smart thing to do?"

I rolled my eyes. "Well, if you're going to be logical, I'm not going to talk to you."

He chuckled. "It's different when it's not you, isn't it? When it's us, we believe we can do it, survive, prevail, accomplish the task. But when those who work for us do the same thing, then we worry about whether they're in peril."

"Yeah, but, I have a keener of a Sergeant and a brand new DC who are trying to out-macho each other. They're good, but they're young, brash, and they don't see the pitfalls."

"Like you did?" He asked.

"Right."

"So, if one of them went off to interview a wanted killer, one who'd already shot and wounded them, it would be a bad idea, but when you did it, it was right?"

"It was necessary."

"Is there any other way to do what they're doing? Don't give me any of the details, Ian, it's no longer my job. Just answer the question."

"No, there is no other way." I conceded.

Rebecca called from the kitchen, and I followed Van Hoeke through, sat at the end of the round table, and watched her slice a wedge of cake for me, then place it beside my coffee.

I thanked her and took a large forkful. "Mm, Becky, what flavor is this?"

"It's a lemon custard cake. Quite simple, really."

I took another bite. "I need the recipe, please. The kids will love this."

She shaved a small wedge off her own piece of cake and pulled it off the fork with her lips, then pointed the fork at me. "Trade you for the salmon orange glaze recipe."

"You drive a hard bargain. Deal."

She swallowed the cake and took a sip of coffee. "How's Karen doing?"

"She's well, thanks. I call her a couple of times a week. No more morning sickness, no aches or pains. The kids are well, having a blast out there."

"Do you miss them?"

It was a simple question. Still, it made me think for a long time. "Very much, yes. I try not to think about them when I'm working, though. It throws me off."

She nodded and took another sliver of cake onto her fork. "How about that offer at Frank's outfit? Have you given that any more thought?"

I looked at Van Hoeke. "Gee, Martin, I never realized before that I was working for your wife."

He shrugged. "Get used to it, Ian. That's the way it works."

Rebecca shook her head. "You're a very good investigator, Ian. Whether you work for the department, or for Frank, you'd be doing the same job. It just means that you'd have different perks in one than the other, but both have advantages and disadvantages."

That intrigued me. "How do you mean, Becky?"

She stirred her coffee and tapped the spoon inside the cup before placing it on the saucer. "If you stay in this job, you'd have more security- not a lot more, but more. You could retire comfortably at sixty and spend your days tying fish lures."

"Flies." Martin corrected.

"Lures, flies, zippers. On the other hand, you could go to a nice shiny office every day, be home at five for dinner, and not worry about getting shot. Again. Plus, you could retire at fifty with a very healthy bank account and spend your days watching your grandchildren grow."

Grandchildren. I hadn't thought that far ahead. That part was certainly appealing.

She shrugged. "Look, Ian, you have to do what you think is right. You're the only one who can decide which path to take."

Van Hoeke leaned forward. "Does the idea of doing what you do scare you?"

"No, it doesn't. I can live with the risk."

"Then don't you owe your people the same choice? If they want to do something, and it's something you've done already, why hold them back?"

We finished coffee, Van Hoeke thanked me again for the cowboy hat, and Rebecca gave me a kiss on the cheek and asked me to pass it on to Karen and the kids.

I got into my car, drove around the corner, and pulled into a parking lot as soon as I could. I wanted to think. There was something that Martin said, something that just didn't make sense.

I would think about that later. For now, I realized that Rebecca and Martin were right.

There was a break in radio chatter. "Fifty-two zero six to fifty-two ten." I barked.

Walsh's voice came back right away. "Go, zero six."

"Hi, Patrick. Can you and the others meet at my house, eight tomorrow morning?"

"Shall do, fifty-two ten out."

Reynolds' voice came through right after that. "Roger. Tomorrow at eight."

Four in the afternoon, and I was already home. I didn't feel guilty- I'd put in more than enough hours, day in and day out, and I cleared my cases in good time. I deserved to take it easy once in a while. I made myself a snack, turned on the jazz station, and sat back in my easy chair.

Sunlight poked in through the back window, a trapezoid of bright yellow on the floor, reflecting the shiny linoleum onto the ceiling. Karen had insisted we buy air conditioning when we moved in, and today I was grateful that we had. It was cool and pleasant inside, even though the glaring sunlight told me how hot it was outside. I leaned back and fell asleep.

Chapter Eleven

My grandfather is beside me; we crouch behind a bush, waiting for the deer he has seen darting through the trees. He knows it will come out, and he says it will come this way, past us, on its way to the only water hole in the area.

He knows this land well. He bought the two sections of dense brush, over twelve hundred acres, with money he earned serving in the First World War. Back then, the land north of Prince Albert was worth far less, and he bought as much as he could afford.

The land is close to his reservation, the place where he was born, and he tells me that he will leave it to me and James, as long as we show the same reverence for the land that he has shown all his life.

I open my mouth to speak; he places a hand on my arm and slowly pulls me down lower. The deer, sniffing the air, looks around then bounds quickly toward the water.

My grandfather brings his rifle up in one smooth motion. He presses the butt of the stock against his shoulder, takes aim and squeezes the trigger. Just ten seconds ago we were talking, waiting. Now we have venison for the winter.

The old clock in the living room clacked loudly, then chimed eight times, waking me. Why had I dreamed of my grandfather, there? Were we the hunters? Webb and Walsh were going to meet the people who were creating false passports, false identities, spiriting people out of the country.

Could they be the same people who had killed Victor French and Robert Sankar? It had to be related, somehow, but why kill someone after they'd paid you? It made no sense.

I went through the evening on autopilot. I laid out my suit for the morning, then decided it would be better to go in casual clothes and put it away. A little after ten, I climbed into bed and tried to figure out what to do next.

This was the part of the job that I enjoyed, but which also bothered me. The people who worked under me expected me to be firm, decisive, certain. I didn't always feel that way. Sometimes I had no idea which way to go, but it was crucial that they didn't see that.

Should I ask Van Hoeke about that the next time I saw him? Was he ever lost, did he ever feel he had no idea what to do next? It certainly never seemed that way, but now I wasn't so sure.

Maybe the difference between a great leader and a poor one was to not let people see when you were out of your depth. Maybe the most important thing for them is to believe that you know where you're going, even if you don't. Maybe I was just tired, and spouting crap. I fell asleep.

At seven forty-five, as I expected, the first knock at the door was Walsh.

I yelled 'come!' from the kitchen and he walked in. He was wearing a charcoal grey suit, with a navy-blue lining that flashed in the light when he unbuttoned his jacket. He slid onto the stool across from me and smiled, expectantly.

"Morning, boss. What's on the menu?" He said, cheerily.

"Sausages, eggs, pancakes, bacon. Take your pick, Patrick."

"All of the above?" He asked.

"Yeah, I kind of thought so."

I filled a large plate with food and placed it in front of him.

He took a bite of everything and grunted approval. "You know, if you ever get tired of the department, you could always open a restaurant, boss."

"Yeah, been there, done that." I joked.

I poured a coffee and he nodded thanks as he pulled the mug close. He took a slurp and scooped another forkful of eggs into his mouth.

"Hell, Patrick, don't they feed you at home?"

He shook his head. "Not like this. Is this real maple syrup, by the way?"

"Of course. We were up in the Caledon hills last year with the kids. We picked up a big jug of it from a maple sugar shack."

He grunted something unintelligible and sawed a piece of pancake free. Someone knocked at the door, and again I yelled 'come!'.

Reynolds and Webb came in, separately. Reynolds walked ahead first, an expression on her face that said they had been arguing on the drive over. Webb's expression said that he would rather walk through fire than say anything to upset her.

Reynolds sat firmly on an end stool beside Walsh, away from where Webb could sit. "Just coffee, please, boss."

"You sure, Alex? You don't want eggs or something?"

She shook her head. "No. Just coffee."

Webb sat on a stool with Walsh, away from Reynolds and placed his elbows on the table. "I'll take whatever you made, Inspector. Thanks very much, sir."

I filled his plate with food. He watched, fascinated, as I slid his plate in front of him, then carefully sliced a piece of bacon off the rasher and used it to scoop up eggs.

He munched happily, then glanced over at Reynolds. She was frowning, glaring at him.

Time to step in, I thought. "Look, Alex, what's going on? Why the dark cloud?"

She sneered and looked up at me. "Oh, I don't know. Maybe because a dumbass I know is putting his ass on the line for NO GOOD REASON!"

Webb put down his fork and looked over at her, irritated. "It's not a gunfight, hon. It's a meeting. A *meeting*, that's all. It comes with the territory. Don't you want me to be a real detective?"

Walsh stood up and wandered to my side of the counter. He put a couple of pancakes on his plate and went back. He stood beside Webb, pointed to the stool beside Reynolds, and said 'move'.

Webb meekly shifted over and pulled his plate along with him.

Reynolds swiveled in her seat and leaned forward to talk to him.

"I don't like the idea of you doing something stupid, lambchop. I don't want you to get hurt, that's all. You do understand that, right?"

He grinned and touched the end of her nose. "I'd be an idiot to risk hurting myself. You know that. Besides, Sergeant Walsh will be with me. You know he'll keep me safe, no matter what."

Reynolds frowned, picked bacon off his plate and nibbled it. "Just watch it, buster." She said.

She pulled his plate in front of her and took his cutlery. She started eating his food, silently.

Webb smiled at me. "Could I get some more food, please, boss?" He asked.

I smirked and filled another plate. Reynolds glanced up quickly. "And more bacon."

Webb grinned. "With extra bacon, please."

The rest of breakfast went smoothly. By nine o'clock, Reynolds was smiling, and when nobody saw, she playfully scratched Webb's knee. He responded by rubbing her thigh.

I brewed another pot of coffee and we retired to the living room.

"So, Patrick, what's the plan for today?" I asked.

"You're leaving this up to me, boss?"

"Sure. If you're going to bump up to Inspector, you'll need to manage the troops. This is a good time to learn."

He thought for a moment. "Fine. So, we're going back to the diner at lunch. They'll call us to set up a meet, and we'll wing it from there."

"'Wing it?' Any idea what you'll do if they want to meet right away?" I asked.

"Do you think they might want to?"

I shrugged. "Look, we should wire Brian up, like we did you. You two will meet them, and Alex and I will hang back somewhere. Use the same code words- say Africa for 'get here now', Bolivia for 'get ready to come', and China for 'back away'. How's that?"

Walsh nodded. "Africa, Bolivia, China. Got it. By the way, Brian, have you decided where you're planning to go, in case they ask?"

Webb grinned. "Mobile, Alabama. It's a big enough town, and it's remote enough that if I had problems back here I could hide there from people looking for me. Besides, warmer weather- that makes it sound more plausible, I think."

"Nice. I like that train of thought." Walsh said.

He pulled an envelope out of his pocket. "We got a couple of photos done, for passports and a driver's license and so on. We're still trying to decide what name to give him."

"How about 'Brian Reynolds'?" Webb offered.

He glanced at Reynolds. She smirked and playfully elbowed him in the stomach. "Now you're just trying to suck up, aren't you?" She asked.

"Is it working?" He joked.

"Yeah, you're out of the doghouse."

We went through some scenarios that might come up, then Walsh went out to his car and came back with the transmitter for Webb to wear. Webb took off his shirt and we taped the wire to his back, led it under one arm and up to near his neck.

Reynolds peeled strips of adhesive bandage and taped the wire down. Webb flexed his arms, waved them in a circle and shook his wrists. He could move without feeling the wire tug, he said.

He put his shirt on again. I noticed a wide scar on his side, the length of a pencil, as broad as a thumb. I pointed to it.

"What's that from, Brian?"

He glanced at the scar and back up at me. "Why do you ask?"

"Just curious, that's all. It looks like a knife wound."

He shrugged casually, but his face said 'don't ask'. I let it go.

The three of them sat as I loaded the dishwasher, then we all headed out to our cars. I decided I would ride with Reynolds, and of course Webb and Walsh would go together. This was in case anyone knew the location of the phone booth and was watching it.

Walsh walked down the road a few houses and tossed Webb a set of keys. He pointed to a shiny black Porsche. "Here, you drive."

Webb stopped and stared at it. "Really?" He almost squealed the word.

"Yeah, really, Brian. Once we close this case I'll lend it to you, alright?" He joked.

Webb opened the driver's door and peered in. "You're a lot of fun to work with, Sergeant. I'm going to enjoy this job."

Walsh shook his head. "It's not all fast cars and slinky women, Brian. Let's go."

Webb slid into the driver's seat and fired up the Porsche. He revved the engine slightly, then gently eased out onto the road, before stepping on the gas and roaring off.

Reynolds shook her head. "What do you think, boss? Is he a keeper?"

"I dunno, Alex. He looks like a handful to me."

"He's a good guy. He's a decent person, even if he's nuts about cars."

"What's with the scar?"

"He was arresting a drunk, Christmas before last. It was a simple pickup, just get him into lockup and dry him out, but the drunk pulled a knife and slashed him. Brian's partner started kicking the shit out of the drunk. Brian stepped in front of him and got the partner to back off."

She shook her head and sighed. "He was losing blood, he was almost unconscious, and his only thought was that his partner shouldn't beat up the man who'd knifed him."

"Yeah, Alex, he sounds like a keeper. Just keep him away from fast cars, all right?"

We took my car and drove to the spot where Robert Sankar had been found. I reviewed with Reynolds that he probably lived for a while before he died, and so he drove himself here and then died. We walked to the doorway of the office where the AA meetings were held. There was nobody in today, and the office was dark. She wrapped her hands around her face to block the sunlight and peered through the glass. The chairs and desk were still there, still in the same place. She took a step back and put her hands on her hips.

"Why did he come here?" She muttered.

"What do you mean?"

"You've just been shot. Even if you thought it wasn't serious, wouldn't you head for the hospital? Wouldn't you drive to the nearest cop shop? Or fire hall? Why come here?"

"That's the question, Alex. Why *did* he come here?"

She stood in the empty parking spot, her feet straddling the number 'seventeen' on the pavement and looked around.

"So, I've been shot. I'd be in a lot of pain, I would guess."

"Believe it." I said.

"And I took the car of the person who shot me? Or did someone else lend me the car? Gail?"

"Gail says she never met him. According to her sister, they have no idea who Sankar was."

Reynolds shrugged. "Then if we take that at face value, he took her car from her parking spot, even though she never met him. So how did he get the keys? Why did he take *that* car? Was it the car that was closest to him, or the fastest car he could find, what?"

"That doesn't make any sense, Alex. He took a car. Why not just drive himself to get help?"

"We're assuming he drove here, because he was in the driver's seat. What if he was placed there after he died?"

"OK, look, let's rewind the cassette. Victor French dies in the street after he's been stabbed. We put him in the morgue, and later he goes missing. About the same time, Robert Sankar gets shot and dies here. So far, so good?"

Reynolds nodded.

"Good. Now, are the two deaths related? They'd have to be- Sankar left French's ID in the locker at the scrapyard. Either that, or he knew who did. But either way, why was Sankar here?"

A sound behind us made us both look. The door to the Alcoholics Anonymous meeting room opened. The 'Rev', Elijah, swept dust out onto the pavement and shook his broom, then he looked up and saw us. He waved and walked our way.

"Inspector. How nice to see you again." He said.

He looked at Reynolds. "Hi. And you are?"

I waved at Reynolds. "Reverend Elijah Turner, this is Detective Constable Reynolds. She's with our investigating team." I said.

He stuck his hand out. "Hello, Detective. Pleased to meet you."

Reynolds smiled and shook his hand. "Hello. Nice to meet you, too, Reverend Turner."

"Please- just 'Rev', or Elijah." He said. "Can I help you at all?"

Reynolds waved at the empty parking spot. "Why was Robert Sankar here?"

Elijah shook his head, slowly. "He had been coming to meetings, as I told Mister McBriar, but he sort of kept to himself. He was a nice man- very warm, but he didn't say that much."

"So, he never had any altercations with any of the others in the group?"

"No, never. As I say, he was likeable, but didn't speak very much. He liked to listen."

Reynolds looked down, thinking, then smiled and looked up. "Do you remember a young woman, name of Gail, or Abigail, who might have come here?"

"Can you describe her?"

"Dark hair, very pretty, tall, thin, movie star good looks."

He smirked. "Look, I may be a man of God, but I *am* a man. I'd remember a woman like that."

"All right. So, if you do remember anything, can you call us?"

She handed him her business card. He thanked her and placed it carefully in his wallet, then he went back into the meeting room and let the door close.

"What am I missing, Alex? What am I not getting?"

"I dunno, boss. One puzzle piece out of place in the jigsaw, huh? Just one weird shape that changes it from a mess of squiggles to a picture of dogs playing cards."

"Yeah. Anyway, we're expecting a phone call. Let's meet Patrick and Brian."

We drove to the Bloor-Jane Diner and parked behind the black Porsche. Its exhaust was still clicking, making a soft crackle sound as it cooled. Reynolds walked in first, looked around for the others and realized it wasn't necessary. Walsh and Webb were sitting in the same booth we always sat in, across from each other, speaking in low tones.

Reynolds sat in the booth beside Webb and bumped her shoulder against his.

"Had some fun driving that car, did we?" She asked.

He scratched her knee playfully. "That thing is a go-kart. I just have to think about what I want to do and it…"

"So, you want one." Reynolds stated.

"Hell, yeah."

A noise from the kitchen, a door swinging open, made me look up. Walsh's girlfriend, Kelly, marched out and pulled her order pad out of her smock.

"Hi, guys. Everyone know what they want?" She asked.

We all ordered- me last. "I'll have the usual- burger, fries, coffee." I said.

She wrote this down and nodded. I looked up at her. "I hear we're losing you." I said.

She placed her hand on Walsh's head. I was surprised at the intimate gesture.

"Well, I had accepted this offer at McGill." She started. "But then I realized I'd be happier at U of T. They matched the McGill offer."

Walsh looked up. "You're staying in town." He stated.

She nodded. He smiled broadly. "You're staying. In town. Here. Toronto." He said, carefully.

She nodded again. "Yes, you're stuck with me. I'll get your food."

Walsh looked like he'd just won the grand prize. He shimmied out of the booth and walked briskly to the kitchen door. He stuck his head in, speaking softly, then a moment later came back and sat down, grinning.

"So, it's a good day, Patrick?" I asked.

"It's a great day, boss." He said.

Within a few minutes, the thrill of hearing that his girlfriend was staying in town had almost worn off, and Walsh got back to business.

He kept checking his watch, even though we were a good hour from the time for the phone call. Webb seemed calmer, cooler, but there was a nervous edge to his movements that reminded me of the first time I was in a similar situation.

We finished lunch, I paid, and the four of us got ready to leave. Walsh mentioned that if the group from Lindsay was resourceful, they might have found out the location of the phone booth, so Reynolds and I walked away first, headed away from the phone booth and went into a convenience store down the block. We browsed magazines, as the store owner watched us, suspicious. Reynolds peered out the door and turned to look at me. "Here they come." She said.

Webb and Walsh came in and looked around to see we were alone, except for the owner.

Walsh spoke first. "All right. We're supposed to go to the corner of Dupont and Osler, in thirty minutes.

I don't think they knew where the phone booth was."

"What makes you say that?" I asked.

"First question they asked was, 'how long would it take you to get to this intersection'."

"What do we do once you get there?"

Walsh pulled out an envelope from his jacket. "Got Brian's ID photos here; Let's find out as much as we can, before we pay these guys."

"What if they want to get paid today?" I asked.

Webb shook his head. "Sergeant Walsh suggested using his own cash, but I convinced him to just stall them. I don't think we should look too eager."

"Yeah, I agree, Brian. I need a map. Let's go to my car."

We huddled around the hood of my Caprice, a street map spread out between us. I circled the intersection of Dupont and Osler with a pen. "Any ideas why they want to meet there?" I asked.

Webb pointed to a symbol just west of the circled spot. "There's a railway underpass there- a pedestrian walkway. I bet they'll have us meet them in the underpass."

"Why do you think that?" I asked.

"There's nowhere there to watch them without being seen. If we were in line of sight, they'd see us. Besides that, there are escape routes in a dozen different directions from there- if they want to get away, then there are lots of roads they could take."

I rubbed my moustache. "All right. Make sure your wire is on. Alex and I will hide, and you two do your thing. Same code words as before. If you feel it's getting dicey, just leave. Got it?"

They nodded agreement. Webb took the Porsche keys out of his pocket and got in the driver's seat. We left first, and I drove along Bloor Street, east towards Dupont.

Reynolds took her revolver out of its holster and spun the cylinder. I'd never seen her actually handle her gun before. I knew this meant she was worried.

"All right, Alex, how do you want to do this?" I asked.

"No idea, boss. Got any thoughts?"

I glanced in the back seat. There was a clipboard there, from the last time I'd done something with the auto pool.

"If we're out of the car, we can pretend we're realtors; we can walk around, telling people we're checking houses for sale in the area." I said.

Reynolds looked back at the clipboard. "Got it. We'll hide in plain sight."

It took about twelve minutes to get to the intersection I'd circled on my map. I parked on Osler Street, a half block up from the intersection, and turned on the receiver for Webb's wire.

Three minutes later, Webb and Walsh arrived. Webb parked the Porsche right near the corner, looked around and saw my Caprice. He leaned forward slightly, clutching the steering wheel.

"Boss, if you see us, hit your brake light." He said.

I tapped the brake pedal. Webb came back on. "I see you. So far, so good."

He got out of the car and waited for Walsh to get out, then they both sauntered casually to the intersection.

They stood there for about two minutes. Webb turned to Walsh, and I could hear their conversation, with static, over my receiver.

"Think they'll come?" Webb asked.

"No reason to expect they won't. Just let's act casual but stay sharp."

Webb looked down Dupont Street and rubbed his nose to cover his mouth. "Cab coming. Heads up." He said.

A moment later, a yellow taxi came around the corner and stopped. A woman got out, but I couldn't recognize who she was.

She leaned in and said something to the cab driver. She handed him a few bills, said something else, and he left.

She crossed the street to join Webb and Walsh.

As she approached them, I could hear, through my receiver, the sound of clicking heels.

A woman's voice came through. "Hello, Mister Walsh. This is your friend with the problem?"

Reynolds leaned toward me. "Who's that?" She asked.

"Gillian. I recognize her voice. She runs the Starlite Motel in Lindsay."

Walsh spoke. "This is Brian. No other name needed. He'd like your help."

Gillian's voice was clear, firm. "Brian. You have what I asked for?"

As I watched him through the back window, Walsh pulled an envelope from his jacket. "Two photos. As requested."

"Fine." Gillian said, firmly.

"Where are you going, Brian?" She asked.

Webb said; "I want to go to Mobile, Alabama."

"Do you have friends there, family?"

"No, I just like the weather. Why do you ask?"

"It makes it awkward if you run into someone you know, but using a different name. We wouldn't want that kind of complication."

"No, I suppose not. Has that ever happened?"

"Once. It won't happen again, I assure you." Gillian said.

Reynolds sucked air. "That's what happened to French?" She hissed.

"Very good, Alex. I think we just got a jigsaw puzzle piece."

Webb turned around, looking up and down the street. "Look, can we get on with this? I need to be somewhere, and I don't want my wife asking more questions."

Gillian put the photos in her purse. "You have the down-payment with you?"

Webb shrugged. "No, look, a hundred and fifty thousand dollars is a lot to pull out without them noticing. Give me a day. You'll have it all when I get the passport and papers, though."

Gillian looked quickly at Walsh, then back to Webb. "I see. Very well. I'll call you the day after tomorrow at the same time. You bring the cash- small bills, nothing consecutive. I will show you the goods, and you hand me the cash. Also, bring an extra fifty thousand American."

Webb shuffled his feet. "Why is that?"

"We'll set you up with a fresh bank account in Mobile. It will have forty thousand dollars in it. It's not smart to cross the border with a bag full of cash. Also, if you have any other personal entanglements, let me know now before we go on."

"How does fifty thousand become forty?" Webb asked.

"Exchange rate, setup charges. This is a business, not a charity."

"Couldn't I just transfer it from my account in the Cayman Islands?"

She tilted her head to one side, thinking. "You could, if you had more time. I'm told you need to move quickly, though."

"Yes, before the… shortfall is detected. I need to be gone by Monday."

She nodded. "Then we have an understanding. Two days from now, I'll call your number again. We'll meet a new location and you will have full payment for me."

"The whole one-fifty, yes."

The same yellow taxi came around the corner and stopped across from Webb. Gillian glanced at it and said: "Two days. Have everything, or we walk."

She got into the taxi and it sped off past me. I jotted down the cab number, scribbling it quickly on the open map, and waited for Webb and Walsh to come over. They didn't.

Webb reached up and covered his mouth. "Hold tight, boss. We'll meet back at your place."

He and Walsh stood there for a minute, spoke about nothing in particular, then wandered back to the Porsche and drove off. I waited a good five minutes, looking in the rear-view mirror.

About the time I was getting ready to leave, a figure came out from the underpass, got into a car and drove off.

It was a rusty Chrysler. Mick's car, from the scrapyard. I couldn't be sure it was him, but it certainly looked like Mick.

I started the engine and pulled out, reaching for the microphone with one hand.

"Fifty-two zero six to dispatch." I said.

"Zero six, go." Said a man's voice.

"Zero six, I need a call placed to a cab company."

"Roger, zero six. Switch to channel one seven."

I turned the knob and switched to a different, unused channel. The man's voice came on again.

"Hey, Inspector, how can we help you?"

"Yeah, what happened to Nadine? Why did she quit?"

There was a slight pause, then, "She heard a rumor that Pascoe eats shit sandwiches. She disagreed- she said he doesn't eat bread."

I chuckled. That sounded like her. "Got it. Anyway, all my best if you hear from her. I'm looking for a trace on a cab, Yellow Taxi number three, three, eight, four, seven. It just dropped off a ride, a young woman. Where did he drop her?"

"Got it. Give me three, Inspector."

I drove back towards the diner, one ear open for the crackle of the radio.

Two minutes later, the man's voice came back. "Inspector?" He said.

"Yup. Go."

"He dropped her off at the corner of St. Clair and Weston Road. He says she paid him, then she got into a car and drove off."

"No idea what kind of car, I suppose?" I asked, hopeful.

"Yeah I asked him that. A lime green Duster. No mistake, he said, he's sure of the car."

"Man, I owe you lunch."

He laughed. "You better believe it, sir."

I pulled into my driveway just before the Porsche arrived. Reynolds was out of the car, pacing the sidewalk. We went into my house and I made coffee.

Walsh grinned, pleased with himself. "So, how'd we do, boss?"

"Really good, Patrick. How did you know you were being watched?"

He pointed at Webb. "Brian said he saw someone walk along the underpass just as we got there. I didn't think anything of it, but the same guy walked back a minute later, just before that woman showed up. Brian guessed that he was there to wave her off if he thought she was being set up. Once she left, the guy came by a third time and made sure we didn't make a phone call or anything."

"Did he look around forty, curly blondish, greying hair?" I asked.

Webb nodded.

"Yup. Mick, from the scrapyard."

We had coffee and pie, then everyone got into their cars and left. I was alone, so I decided to call Karen.

The phone rang, and a moment later I heard a click. A voice answered, but it took me a moment to recognize it.

"Hello?" It said.

"Hi, Who's this?"

"It's Ethan, dad. How are you?"

He sounded older, more mature. "Hi, son. I'm good. How are you enjoying the country?"

"Oh, wow, we're having a lot of fun. We rode horses, and we bought cheese and milk from the people in a small town, and I got to ride a tractor."

"That's good to hear. How is grandpa doing?"

"He's having fun with us, too. He took me fishing at this lake, and we caught this big fish. We ate it for dinner. It was dee-licious."

I laughed. "Great. Where's your mom?"

"She went shopping with grandpa and Charlotte. I'm here with granny Pam. We're making cookies."

I felt a twinge at him calling her 'granny'. Still, he was born years after my mother died, and Pam was the closest thing to a grandmother there for him. I accepted that.

"All right, son. Tell your mom I said hi, and that I'll call later in the week, all right?"

"Sure thing, dad. Love you. Bye."

The line went dead. I felt comforted by the call. I had raised him to be happy, competent, a good person. My father and Pam showed the children and Karen, nothing but love. We were all OK.

Chapter Twelve

At seven the next morning, I was dressed and ready for work. I did the few dishes, swilled the last ounce of my coffee, rinsed the cup, and went out to my car.

Something felt odd, out of place. It felt like someone was watching me. I looked around, but there weren't any unusual cars around and nobody was out at this time of morning. Still, the feeling was palpable.

My grandfather said that he was able to hunt well because he knew where the deer was going to be, not where it was. Good advice. I got into my car, drove off, and went three blocks. I waited for about ten minutes. Then I drove back to my house, scanning the street as I did. Again, there were no unusual cars.

I stopped a couple of houses away from mine. The same feeling that I was being watched came back, stronger than ever.

From here, I could see the front windows of the house, the living room and the hallway. I almost didn't see it, but in one corner of the living room window a shadow appeared, just for a second.

Someone walked from the dining room to the kitchen. I went quickly to the side gate, opened it silently, and moved along the side of the house.

There were no large windows along this wall, only a small frosted one for the downstairs bathroom.

I crept along to the end of the wall and peered quickly around the corner. There was nobody in the back yard, but the back door was open, the door that went up to the kitchen and down to the basement. I moved quickly to the door and stood to one side of it, listening.

There were voices, people talking. Two voices, both male. One said 'clean, nothing here.' The other responded with 'same here, let's go'.

The voices came from the front hall. I went through the door, stepped quickly up the three stairs that led to the kitchen, and poked my head around the corner. One man was facing the front door, his back to me. He was maybe four feet from me, but he hadn't noticed me yet. I pulled out my revolver and placed it against the back of his head.

"Leaving so soon?" I asked.

He turned around to look at me, making no sudden moves, moving very slowly. This man had been in a situation like this before, clearly.

"We didn't expect to see you back, Inspector." He said.

He was compact, burly, with short blond hair and cold, expressionless eyes.

"Clearly not. Why exactly are you here?" I asked.

He shuffled his feet, placing his right foot back, a sure sign that he was about to kick me. I stepped back a bit, my gun still pointed at his forehead.

"I really wouldn't try that if I were you." I said. "Get your friend over here."

The man leaned his head back. "Curtis, we've been made. Come out."

Soft footsteps from the living room got louder, then the second man came in beside this one. It was Barry Kirby's driver, the Marine. He looked embarrassed at having been caught, but not about any consequences.

I looked at the first man. "So, why are you here?"

He rubbed his nose. "Can I make a phone call?"

He stayed perfectly still until I nodded, then he picked up the extension phone in the kitchen and quickly dialed a number.

A few seconds later he said "We've been discovered."

There was a pause as he listened. "Yes, he did. No idea how."

The man put the phone on the table and backed away. "He'd like to speak with you." He said.

I picked up the receiver with my left hand. My gun was still pointed at the men.

"Hello?" I said.

Barry Kirby spoke, his voice a mixture of surprise and admiration. "Ian, how on earth did you know those men were there?"

"More to the point, why are they in my house?"

"We have to vet everyone who joins our team. That includes an assessment of their lifestyle. We needed to know that there was nothing in your life that could compromise your behaviour."

"So you were looking for what? Drugs, demonic symbols, inflatable dolls?"

He laughed. "Nothing quite so extreme. Signs of alcohol abuse, how you treat your dog, if you have a gambling habit. Things of that sort."

"And for that you had to send Laurel and Hardy into my home after I left for work?"

"Well, after all, no harm done. They'll leave now and we'll call this a successful review."

"Or I could shoot them both and say they attacked me." I countered.

He sighed, considering the statement. "But neither of them is armed."

"They will be armed when the coroner picks up the bodies." I said.

Both men looked at each other nervously. I'd hoped that the threat would hit home. Apparently, I was right.

"So, is this a regular thing, or can I expect that you won't be back?" I asked.

"No. that was it. No other intrusions, ever. You have my word." He said, emphatically.

I pointed my revolver at the ceiling. "Scram." I said.

They walked quickly out, down the steps, out the side gate, and I watched them continue down the street, in the other direction from where I'd come.

"Is anyone else in the house? This is their chance to celebrate another birthday." I said.

"No, nobody else, just those two. Have my men gone?" He asked.

"Yes."

"Now, I really have to ask you, how did you know?"

"We have a neighbor- Nosy Nellie, my wife calls her. Short of having binoculars and a deck chair, she's a people watcher. She's in her kitchen all day, watching people come and go. Most mornings, her eyes follow me as I drive to work. Today, though, she was looking in the other direction, where your guys parked. When I drove back, she was looking at my house, not me. That set me off."

"And from that you were able to figure out there was a problem?"

"Hey, from your accent and the word 'dinner' I got that you were from Missouri."

He laughed. "Ian, it's going to be wonderful having you on our side of the desk. I look forward to it. I hope you're looking forward to it too."

"Don't count your chickens just yet. You still won't tell me what's in the box?"

"As I said, I actually don't know. But I'd like to see you figure it out."

"I will let you know when I do." I said.

"And again, Ian, this is something that's required for everyone in our organization. Please don't let it colour your view of the offer."

"Sure. I'm going to kick you in the balls, but please think of me as a friend." I said.

"Point taken. As I promised, it won't happen again. Goodbye, Ian." He hung up.

I went through the house again, room by room, until I was sure there was nobody else inside, then I carefully locked all the doors and latched all the windows and drove to work.

Walsh and Webb were at their desks, tossing a tennis ball between them and talking.

"But, we have to give them a reason to trust us." Webb said.

Walsh shook his head. "They're selling a service to people who make money by being dishonest. Why would they think their clients would be any more honest with them?"

I sat backwards on a chair, facing them, the three of us forming a triangle. "So, what's the plan?" I asked.

Webb pointed at Walsh. The Sergeant…"

"Patrick, Brian. Just Patrick."

"OK. Patrick said we should just wait till they show up with the documents- fake passport, so on, then we arrest them. I say we go along with the ruse until we find out how they get people out of the country. Then we arrest them, not before. What do you think, sir?"

I rested my chin on the seatback, thinking. "Yeah, Brian, I agree with Patrick on this one."

Webb shrugged. "Why is that?"

"OK. Best- and worst-case scenarios. Best case in your plan, we get the bad guys and find out how they did it *this time*. Worst case, they take you with them and you get killed. Best case scenario for

Patrick's plan, we get the bad guys, and we ask them later how they did it. Worst case, they get away. Sounds like an easy decision to me."

Webb thought for a moment. "Well, that's why you're the boss. I see your point. I agree too."

They went off to get ready for the next day's meeting, and I flipped through telephone message slips. I tossed out the meaningless ones and answered the important ones.

I was on the phone to one of the detectives from fifty-one division, but my mind was still on the two men in my house. I didn't notice Ernest Pascoe arrive.

Ten minutes later, I was off the phone and making notes. A voice called across the room.

"Inspector? Do you have a minute?"

Pascoe was looking at me. His office door was open, and he was holding the door, ready to close it after I went in.

He stepped back as I walked past him. "Please sit down."

"Said the spider to the fly." I said.

He smiled, a plastic, 'I don't really mean it' smile. I sat down and he closed the door.

Then he sat across from me and knit his fingers in front of him on his desk.

"Well, Ian, how is it going?" He asked.

The tone, meant to be friendly, did not feel that way to me. "Fine. How is it going with you?"

He pulled a piece of paper out of his desk drawer. "I received a message from the OPP, saying that you were out in their jurisdiction. Should you have let me know what you were doing before you left town?"

I looked at the paper, reading it upside down as best I could.

"My mistake. So, who gets slapped on the wrist over that?" I asked.

"A friend of yours. Inspector Klassen. He was reprimanded for not informing his superiors about you being there. Care to comment?"

"That falls on me, not him. I asked him to keep my presence to himself. I'd be happy to call them about it, if you don't mind."

He shook his head. "No need. I told them I'd deal with it. Consider it dealt with. Good day."

I turned my head slightly. "Why the soft touch? I expected you to dump all over me about this."

He looked out the window, sighed and leaned back. "People here see me as a pencil-pusher and a cost-cutter, and nothing else. That is what I was hired to do, but I was also hired to evaluate your team, Ian.

You have a good group here. They get results, and they do it well. I'm not going to mess with that recipe."

That surprised me. "So, keep on keeping on?"

He shrugged. "You're working on two linked murders, with just four people and no extra resources. How can I complain about that?"

I grinned. "That's good to hear, Captain. I'll keep you posted."

I left his office and went back to my desk.

An hour later, I'd finished the paperwork that had piled up over the last few days. It was lunch time, and I was getting hungry. The phone rang.

"Inspector McBriar." I said, mechanically.

"Mrs. McBriar." Said the voice on the phone.

That voice brightened my day with those few words. "Hi, Karen. How are you, sweetheart?"

"Fine. Guess who I just spoke to?"

"I give up. Who?"

"Lizzie Walsh. We're flying home on Sunday, with Lizzie Walsh."

My mind jumbled the message momentarily. "Sorry? What do you mean?"

"Patrick's mother called. She's flying us home on their jet. We'll be there Sunday afternoon."

"Where? What terminal will you be at?"

"None. They fly into Toronto Island Airport. Four pm, Sunday. Can you meet us?"

"Absolutely. See you then, sweetheart."

I hung up the phone. That made me smile. Karen and the kids would be back home on Sunday.

Home. That reminded me of something else I wanted to do.

There was a parking spot out front of the big concrete and glass building on University Avenue, so I left my 'police business' sign on the dashboard and went up the steps, two at a time. The lobby was busy at this time of day; I dodged the pinball-game series of people crossing my path and went up to one of the three women sitting at a wide desk.

"Hi, Beryl. I'm just going up to see Frank Burghezian."

She looked up at me and picked up the phone. "Hello, Inspector. Shall I announce you?"

I shook my head and smiled. "No, I want to surprise him. It's for a special event."

She put the phone down. "Oh, I see. Go right up, then."

The elevator door opened on the fifteenth floor and I went down the hall, headed for Frank Burghezian's office. The tall young man I'd seen in my house, Kirby's driver, was sitting outside the door. He did a double-take when he saw me and stood up.

I pointed to him. "Sit. Stay." I said.

He sat back down. I opened the door and went in. Frank was writing something on a whiteboard, numbers and names, with different colored lines connecting them.

Kirby was across from him, making notes in a leather folio. They both looked casually up at me as I walked in, then Frank froze. Kirby just smiled.

"You were expecting me to show up?" I asked Kirby.

"It would have surprised me if you hadn't." He said.

He nodded at Frank. "He said you would show up unannounced. He knows you better than I do, I suppose. So, why are you here, Ian?"

"Detective Inspector McBriar. I'm here to find out if I should be flattered by the attention, or if I should just tell you to eat shit and die. Which is it?"

Kirby threw his head back and laughed out loud, a sincere belly laugh. He looked over at me, threw his head back again and laughed another time.

He pulled a large white handkerchief from his pocket and wiped his eyes. "Thank you for that, son. That's the funniest thing I've heard in quite some time."

"I don't get the humour in having my privacy invaded. How would you feel if I did that to you?"

He shook his head, slowly. "Well, for one, you'd have to climb a tall fence and get past a couple of formidable dogs, but I take your point. We should have warned you. If it's any consolation, our search has found you to be an excellent candidate."

"I'm honoured. Does that mean you'll pick my pocket before a promotion?"

He got serious, all at once. "Play time's over. We do serious work, important work. We don't arrest burglars and wife-beaters, and we don't put drunks in jail. Our work is of a… higher level, less direct in action, but equally important."

"Give me an example."

He thought for a moment. "The government of a country NOT friendly to us has been trying to infiltrate the R & D department of a major computer developer. No names mentioned, you understand. It's above my pay grade to even ask who they are. Still, if we can persuade the head of a certain department that a certain individual should be in a position with less authority, then we can avert the loss of some very sensitive data, with minimal involvement."

"You want me to be a spook? Is that the job?"

"Not at all. We have people who specialize in that. Men, and of course women, who can achieve the desired behaviour in a number of ways. Your role would be more in the direction of finding the vulnerability, not resolving it. In your current job, you are presented with a crime, and your job is to find the person responsible. In this job, you would find the person responsible, before they commit the crime. It's a far more satisfying conclusion. Think of it- no long court cases, no tedious paperwork, no worrying about being in danger. It's a golden opportunity, Ian."

I shrugged. "As I say, I have to think about it. Frank, see you later. Barry, good day."

The day was not as stifling hot as earlier in the week. There was a checkerboard pattern of puffy cumulus clouds in the sky, and a light breeze that made it pleasant to be outside with a jacket on. Radio chatter was light, too, as if crime and accidents had taken the day off to go for a picnic. I stopped out front of the Bloor-Jane Diner, waited in my car for a minute, and just thought.

Falmouth. Martin Van Hoeke had said that he was going fishing with his brother, in Falmouth. Why did that sound wrong? I'd think about that later. I radioed Walsh and Reynolds, told them where I was, and both agreed to meet me for lunch.

Twenty minutes later, Reynolds and Webb walked in, talking and laughing. Walsh showed up shortly after, and we ate as we discussed the case.

Webb made notes on a small flip pad. "So, boss, when do we pick these people up?" He asked.

"We'll have ghost cars and plain-clothes officers standing by, wherever they meet us." I said.

"But, what about the ones left in Lindsay? Once we pick up the person here, how do we grab them before they take off?"

"Good point, Brian. After lunch, I'll talk to the OPP, and have them stand by. As soon as we make the arrest here, we'll let them know that they should arrest Gillian and her husband at the motel, and Mick and Jeff at the scrapyard."

He shook his head. "We won't have a lot of time. If they take off, the people we arrest could claim it was all a mistake. We could end up grabbing smoke."

Walsh nodded. "Right. Boss, will the Provincials be ready to go at short notice?"

I opened my mouth to answer. Walsh glanced out the window, then his eyes opened wide. "Boss, you and Alex, get lost- now!"

I looked out the front window. Gillian, the woman from the motel, was in front of the diner, talking to someone I couldn't see.

I grabbed our plate and coffee cups. "Go. Go. Go." I said.

We raced into the kitchen and explained to a very surprised cook why we were there. Reynolds pressed herself against one side of the doorway, and I squeezed myself along the wall on the other side of the door. We could hear conversation from here, through the frosted glass doors, without being seen. The waitress, Kelly, nodded, indicating she knew what to do.

A soft bell sounded as the front door opened. Kelly put on a smile and walked through to the dining area. "Hi, table for two?" She said.

Gillian's voice was clear, unmistakeable. "No, thanks, we're with these gentlemen."

"Fine. Just let me know when you're ready to order." Kelly said.

Kelly came back into the kitchen. I whispered "What does he look like?"

She blinked slowly, took a carafe of coffee through, and I heard her speaking. "More coffee? Would you two like some as you're waiting?"

Then a man's voice, vaguely familiar, but I couldn't place it. "Nothing, thanks." He said.

Kelly came back to the kitchen. "Average. Kind of rough, country type." She said.

Then his voice again. "So, are you ready to close the deal?"

Webb spoke. "How did you know we'd be here?"

"Reverse directory for the phone booth. We have our resources, after all. Is there a problem?"

Webb laughed. "No. I've been using this booth to settles some affairs, that's all. I just need to know that it's not tapped."

Walsh spoke. "Were you followed?"

Then Gillian's voice. "Not that I know. One thirty, tomorrow. You'll be ready?"

Walsh spoke. "We'll be ready, with the full amount."

Gillian and the other man made a sound- clearly, they got up. "Good. See you then." He said.

I waited till I heard them head for the front door, and I poked my head around the edge of the frosted glass. I recognized the man with her- he was the punk I had the altercation with outside a phone booth in Lindsay. Reynolds and I stayed in the kitchen until Walsh poked his head in.

"They left. I saw them drive away." He said.

We went back into the dining area, slightly nervous, all of us looking at the door every few seconds.

Walsh nodded. "So, Gillian is definitely one of them."

"Her friend is a local yokel from Lindsay. I had a run-in with him there. I thought at the time he was just another hoser poking the new guy, but now I wonder if he was testing the water- checking to see if I was a cop or something." I said.

Webb leaned back and grinned. "Is it always this much fun in Major Crimes? I'm starting to enjoy this job more every day."

Reynolds patted his hand. "Next week, we all go to the circus. That'll be real fun too, huh?"

Webb smirked. "Sorry. It's just a whole different world from uniform."

I rubbed my eyes. "Fine. Everyone get ready- big day tomorrow. Patrick- backup ready?"

Walsh pulled out his Moleskine. "Yes. Brian will be wired. The moment he hands over the bag of cash, he'll say the code word 'Florida' and everyone will move in. At that point, Alex will radio your OPP friends. They will have cars standing by at the motel and the scrapyard."

"Bag of cash?" I asked.

Walsh nodded. "I borrowed some money from my parents. No big deal, but I'd like to get the money back, if possible."

"How much did you borrow?" I asked.

"Eighty thousand. The people we're meeting won't count it right away- I'll open the tote bag, and as soon as they take the cash and give us the forged documents, we'll arrest them."

I sighed and rubbed my eyes. "All right. You two, drive off first. Alex, you and I will stay here for a half hour and make sure we're not seen with them, in case anyone's watching."

Walsh nodded. "Got it, boss. So, as for tomorrow, what's the plan?"

"Given that they know where the telephone booth is, we can't have me standing around here with you, in case they're watching us. You two show up and talk to them. Brian, you'll wear the wire. When you find out where you're supposed to meet them, say it out loud, and I'll radio it in. Above all, everyone stay sharp, and stay safe. Got it?"

They all nodded agreement.

"Fine. Let's meet at my house for breakfast, eight o'clock."

Walsh and Webb left, strolled down the street to the Porsche, and drove away. Reynolds and I sat in the booth, watching carefully to be sure our suspects didn't come back. A half hour later, Reynolds wandered out to her car and left. I drove away shortly after and headed up to the police station.

In my phone book I had the number for Josh Klassen. I hoped he was in his office. The phone rang twice, then a familiar voice said "Inspector Klassen."

"Josh- it's Ian. I hear I caused you some grief?"

He laughed. "No. My boss said the words he was supposed to say then he bought me lunch. What's up, big guy?"

"We may have a very juicy collar for you, tomorrow. We think we've gotten to the root of the Starlite Motel ring."

There was a sound as he sat up and grabbed some papers. "Shoot."

"OK. We've told Gillian that one of our Constables here is a bad guy who's trying to disappear. She's going to meet us somewhere in Toronto, tomorrow afternoon and give us fake documents for him. When she does, we slap the cuffs on her. At that moment, we need you to arrest a couple of people at the Scugog scrap metal place, and the Starlite as well. Interested?"

"Shit, yeah. Tell me more."

I filled him in with what we knew. Finally, I mentioned that one of the men we'd seen with

Gillian was a local who had tried to pick a fight with me in Lindsay. The local cop, Zach, knew him, I said. Where could we find the local kid?

He wrote this all down. "One sec. I think Zach may be in the building." He said.

I waited for a couple of minutes, as Josh yelled to someone, then I heard footsteps coming closer. Heavy footsteps- patrol shoes, then the phone was picked up.

"Yes, Inspector?" The voice said.

"Zach? Do you remember the four guys who got into an altercation with me outside that restaurant last week?"

"Yeah, sure. They're just local goofs. I know them."

"Good. The big one, the loudmouth. Who is he?"

He sighed. "Yeah, him. That's Tyler. Tyler Westlock."

"Westlock? As in Gillian Westlock?"

"Yeah, he's a cousin- her husband's cousin."

"That makes perfect sense. Where can we find him?"

"He works at the print shop in town."

I grinned. "Can you pass me back to Inspector Klassen? I think you're going to get a very large number of guests in your jail tomorrow."

Klassen wrote down the details, and we arranged for a way to contact him after we'd arrested Gillian. We said our pleasantries and hung up.

This was going well. If we could keep it together, if the Lindsay people came through with the fake papers, we could wrap this up tomorrow.

I did some meaningless paperwork for an hour and went home. Tomorrow, Saturday, I would get these guys. Just as important, on Sunday Karen and the kids would be back home. I wanted the house to be ready for them. I'd clean up, maybe bake something special for Sunday night, or maybe take them out to one of the restaurants they liked.

I had a light dinner, turned on my jazz station, and read the paper. I wanted to be relaxed, ready for the day,

At ten o'clock, I watched some mindless news on TV then went to bed. I lay there, listening to the wind as it whistled through cracks in the window casing; it was getting stronger, it seemed. Maybe a storm was coming.

Chapter Thirteen

At seven in the morning, I made sure I had my badge, packed extra bullets and cleaned my revolver. I'd wear my holster over my t shirt, under the denim shirt that hung over my jeans. I purposely didn't comb my hair, so I could look as un-cop-like as possible. I started cooking. This, at least, made me feel more relaxed.

The windy night had brought a wave of heavy rain. It soaked the backyard flower garden, washed away the dust and grit from the road, and made the air smell fresh and clean. As soon as the sun got high the heat of the morning dried everything off, and the day started new, a clean slate, a fresh beginning.

At a minute to eight, Walsh knocked on the door. "Come!" I called.

He strolled in, sniffing the air. "Same menu as before?" He asked.

"Exactly. Any special requests, Patrick?"

"Yeah. Lots of pancakes, boss."

Two minutes later, Webb and Reynolds came in. They were relaxed, cheery, looking at each other with an unspoken intimacy.

They slid onto stools, sat beside each other, and bumped shoulders as they talked.

"Now, Brian," I started. "Any questions about this afternoon?"

"Yeah, boss. I figured I shouldn't carry my badge or gun- too much chance that we'll scare them off. And of course, we'll go to the meet in a non-cruiser."

Walsh put down his fork and patted his mouth. "I brought the Jag." He said.

"Good. I'm going to be in Karen's Parisienne. The Jag doesn't have a police radio, neither does the Parisienne. Any ideas on how we can communicate?" I asked.

Reynolds nodded. "Walkie-talkies. We could pick up some walkie-talkies at Radio Shack."

"Great idea. Alex, you'll be in your car, so you can radio in for backup, if needed."

She glanced at Webb, and her face momentarily showed worry. "Right, boss."

"Fine. If anyone has any other ideas, please speak up."

I sat opposite the other three, ate my breakfast as they were finishing coffee, and mentally went through our plans. Something stuck in the back of my head; mental chewing gum on my shoe, a piece of the puzzle that made no sense. Hard as I might, whenever I tried to concentrate on it, the thought slipped away, like one of those vivid dreams that evaporates just as you wake up.

At ten in the morning, I was outside a Radio Shack on Eglinton Avenue, waiting for it to open. The pimply-faced kid who showed me their walkie-talkies explained what they did, what the range was, and how to switch channels.

He seemed genuinely thrilled that I wanted three of the most expensive small ones he had. He cheerfully went outside to demonstrate them and walked a block away to test the sound quality. He called me from the one he was holding, and I answered that they were fine for the job.

As he bagged them and handed me my 'free battery of the month' card, he asked why I needed them. I showed him my badge and simply said 'police business'.

An hour later, I handed one of them to Walsh, and one to Reynolds. Walsh stuck his under the Jaguar's passenger seat. Reynolds radioed four cruisers she had placed nearby, and they all reported ready to respond.

I decided we should skip lunch. A well-fed person is slower to react, groggier, and I wanted us all to be as sharp as possible.

Just before one, Walsh and Webb stood by the phone booth, clutching the tote bag full of cash. I was a long block away in Karen's Pontiac

Parisienne, and Reynolds was around the corner, parked in a laneway.

My walkie-talkie crackled. "Any movement, boss?" Reynolds asked.

I clicked the 'talk' button. "No, Alex, they're still just standing by the phone booth."

Webb looked up at the phone and stepped into the booth. He picked up the receiver, spoke for a moment, then wrote something on his note pad. He rubbed his nose, a signal that meant 'stay here', and he got into the Jaguar with Walsh.

Walsh casually slid his hand down under the seat. A moment later, the walkie-talkie crackled. "We're headed for Lakeshore Boulevard and Spadina." Walsh said.

I answered right away. "Did they say where, exactly?"

"No, just that we're supposed to head south on Spadina, and park just north of Lakeshore. They said we have to be there in twenty minutes."

"Did you get that, Alex?"

The walkie-talkie crackled again. "Got it. Sending officers to the area now."

The Jaguar roared to life, hung a U-turn and drove east. I waited for five minutes, then I told Reynolds I was going after them, and I drove off.

I followed the same route that Walsh and Webb would follow; straight east on Bloor, right turn onto Spadina. They'd stop north of the Lakeshore, as directed. It was about a fifteen-minute drive, and it gave me fifteen minutes to figure out the next move.

My grandfather's hunting trips came to mind. His constant message- 'don't go where the deer is, go where it will be', came to mind. Were we doing it right? Were we going to where the bad guys were, or where they would be?

A sudden thought came to mind. Maybe we were the deer. Shit. That made sense. They would take Walsh's money and disappear, or they would give him the documents and disappear. Or they would claim we were lying.

Maybe I was being too cautious. Maybe I was wrong. I picked up the walkie-talkie. "Patrick, Alex, do you read me?"

Dead silence. I was out of range, so I continued driving. I was on Spadina now, headed south. The Jaguar was nowhere in sight. "Patrick, do you read?"

Again, no answer. I scanned the road, side-to-side, looking for Walsh's car. It was distinctive, and it would stand out from the VW's and Chryslers parked on the street. The Jag wasn't there. By now, I was south of the circle at Spadina Crescent, south of College Street, headed for Queen Street. I tried the walkie-talkie again. "Hi, Patrick? Brian? Do you read?"

Reynolds' voice came on. "I hear you, boss. Any word?"

"Nothing yet, Alex. I'll keep trying."

By the time I'd passed King Street, I could see straight down to past the railway tracks beyond Front Street. There was no Jaguar. Then, just as I was about to give up I passed a delivery van, parked on the side of the road. It had blocked my view of Walsh's jag. Walsh and Webb were both in it, waiting. I pulled into a convenient parking spot a half dozen cars up from them and sat, waiting. Reynolds' car passed me, slowly.

"Got them, boss?" She said, over the crackle of the walkie-talkie.

"Yeah, you go just around the corner and wait, Alex. Call me when you're stopped."

Her car went right at a loading ramp and disappeared. A moment later I heard her again.

"I'm parked here, boss. Let me know what to do-your call."

Her voice was calm, professional, but I could hear fear behind the calm. I pretended to read a map, opening it with an exaggerated motion in case anyone noticed me. All the time, I looked in the rear-view mirror. Walsh and Webb were in their car, waiting patiently. I picked up the walkie-talkie. "You guys OK?" I asked.

Walsh looked over at me, rubbed his nose and nodded. It was subtle, and could have just been him coughing, but I knew it wasn't.

"Any word yet?" I asked.

He scratched his head and shook it, gently.

The sliding door on the side of the delivery van opened, and someone got out. It was Gillian, from the motel. Then the big kid from the diner got out, too. He stood beside the van, and Gillian walked to the Jaguar.

She looked around, cautiously, then tapped on the side window. Walsh rolled it down and said something. She gestured to a building on the other side of the street, and Walsh nodded.

She made other motions, directions, how to go, it appeared. Walsh looked at where she was pointing and nodded again.

Gillian looked around, scurried across the street, and disappeared into the loading entrance of a building. The big kid went back into the van. Walsh leaned over as if to say something to Webb and clicked the 'talk' button on his walkie-talkie. "Too obvious to take with us. Going in, boss."

They got out of the Jag, casually pulled out the tote bag and sauntered across the street to follow Gillian in the building.

This felt very bad. I called Reynolds. "Alex, do you read me?"

She came back, a little staticky, but clear. "Yeah, boss. Any news?"

"They went into a building across the street. There's a van parked behind the Jaguar- inside is a guy that I think is the forger. At least, he's a printer for them."

She answered right away. "Cavalry's sixty seconds away. When you need them, call me."

I took my walkie-talkie and crossed the road. The building Gillian had gone into was older, a red brick warehouse with small, dirty windows on eight floors, and a ramp going down into an underground parking garage from the loading entrance. I stood at the top of the ramp and looked around the corner, peeking to see if I'd been spotted. I couldn't see anyone, but I heard Gillian's voice.

"Show me the cash." She said.

There was the sound of a zipper opening as Walsh displayed the contents of the tote bag."

"How do I know it's all there?" Gillian said.

"We can sit around and count it, if you like." Webb said. "Or are you in a hurry?"

"I'll count it later." Gillian said. "Here."

Then I heard paper rustle as Walsh opened a manila envelope.

"This is the passport? Looks pretty good." Webb said.

He snickered. "So, my new name is Robert Sankar? Why did you choose that name?"

"Because it's not in use right now." Gillian said. "Do we have a deal?"

"No. We don't. You're under arrest." Walsh said.

I clicked the mike button. "Move now. Move now. Go. Go."

Reynolds' voice came back. "Roger. Go now."

I ran down the ramp toward the voices. Gillian was looking around, stunned. She saw me heading toward her, and she turned to face Webb.

"You bastard. You BASTARD! Why would you do this? What have we done to you?"

Webb laughed. "You broke the law. Isn't that enough?"

Gillian reached into her purse and pulled out a small pistol. "No. Back off. Nobody gets arrested. I'm walking out of here right now. Nobody gets arrested. Nobody gets arrested."

She was saying it like a mantra, a chant, as though repeating it would convince us to let her walk away. She gripped the pistol tight in her hands, holding it for dear life.

Webb smiled warmly. "Look, Gillian, you don't want to point that thing at us. You'll just get into trouble. Here, put it down. Give it over."

Reynolds ran down the ramp behind me. She came up beside me, her pace slowing as she took in the situation. She stood there, mouth open, watching Gillian point the gun at Webb.

Webb glanced quickly over at Reynolds then looked back at Gillian.

He reached out his hand and smiled again. "What do you say, Gillian? Hand me that nasty gun and we'll all discuss it calmly, all right?"

Gillian looked back and forth between Webb and me, getting more and more agitated. She took a couple of steps back, inching toward a stairwell. "Leave me alone. Let me go, I said. Let me go."

Webb shook his head. "You know we can't do that, Gillian. And we've already picked up your friend in the van by now. Come on, give me the gun."

He moved toward her, within inches of her outstretched weapon. She looked ready to give up, but then she shrieked, the scream of a cornered animal, and a deafening noise echoed through the garage.

Webb winced and fell to his knees. Gillian stood there, frozen. Reynolds moved faster than I could believe, pulled out her service revolver, and pressed it against Gillian's temple.

"Drop it, bitch." Reynolds snarled.

Gillian slowly handed over her pistol. "You don't understand. I couldn't let him take me in, I just…"

Reynolds kicked the side of Gillian's leg, and Gillian buckled, falling to her knees.

Reynolds' revolver was still against Gillian's head.

"SHUT UP, BITCH." She screamed. "DO YOU WANT TO DIE HERE AND NOW?"

From the ramp, I heard familiar sounds- uniformed police shoes on concrete. Two officers came cautiously around the corner, hands on their holsters.

"Officer down, get us an ambulance now!" I called. One of them raced back up to his cruiser. The other ran over to Webb. Walsh had Webb in his arms, holding him off the ground.

Walsh spoke to him the whole time, but I hadn't noticed. "Easy, man, you're going to be all right.

Just take it easy, don't panic, breathe slowly." Walsh was saying.

The uniform bent down to look at his wound. "Looks like he's lost some blood. Here, Sergeant- I'll keep pressure on it while you hold him up."

Reynolds glanced over her shoulder. "How is he? Will he be all right?"

Webb moaned. "I've had worse. From you."

Reynolds smirked, but kept her eyes fixed on Gillian. "Stay with me, lambchop. We'll get you fixed up in no time. Right, Ian?"

"Yes, if you want to be a Sergeant, it's mandatory to get shot first."

Webb laughed, softly. "Sorry, losing it." He said. He sank back and passed out.

Reynolds' eyes filled with tears. Gillian looked up at her, then at Webb. "I'm sorry, I don't know what happened. I didn't mean it. It was an accident."

Reynolds pulled back the hammer on her revolver and glared at her. "He dies, you die. He doesn't make it, you don't live to see the jail. Get it, bitch?"

Gillian moaned and began to cry, quietly at first, then pitiful, then wailing loudly.

Reynolds backed away and pressed her foot on Gillian's hand. "You want a reason to cry? Here you go."

Gillian growled, furious that her crying didn't have any effect on Reynolds. She pulled her hand back and struggled to stand up. Reynolds kicked her in the shoulder.

"Did I SAY you could stand up, bitch? Did you hear me say you were ALLOWED to stand up?"

Gillian's expression changed. She sneered, angry, and glared at Reynolds, hatred in her eyes. Reynolds kicked Gillian's pistol away. Gillian sneered at her.

"I shot him- big deal. You think I care what happens to him? I don't. you can't put me in jail. You have no idea who I know. My friends will make sure I never see any jail time. I have friends- powerful friends. You're just a simple cop. You can't touch me."

Reynolds sighed and put away her revolver. Gillian sneered, feeling she had won. Reynolds hauled back and punched her in the jaw. Gillian spun around and landed on her side. Reynolds lifted her foot and pummeled Gillian's ribs, then she swung her foot back and kicked Gillian's spine as hard as she could. Gillian moaned in agony.

"I can't *touch* you? You still say I can't *touch* you? Huh?" She screamed.

Gillian curled up in a ball and covered her face. Reynolds huffed like a bull and stared at the woman.

I decided to calm things down. "Detective Constable Reynolds, please back up." I said.

She moved away from the woman on the ground. "Yes, Inspector." She said, softly.

I squatted down beside Gillian and she cringed, afraid of more pain. "Forgery, attempted murder, and a bunch of other charges. You're going to be someone's girlfriend for a long time, Gillian. Better learn how to make tattoos out of shoe polish."

A vehicle blocked the ramp to the garage. An ambulance, lights flashing, rolled in, and a uniform waved its driver to where Webb was lying. Two men in white jumped out and worked on him. They spoke quickly, said something which I knew to be good, then one of them went to the back of the ambulance and returned with a gurney.

He looked over at me. "We have to stop meeting like this, officer." He joked.

"Do I know you?" I said.

"Yeah. Five years ago, we pulled you out of the gutter. You'd been shot too, as I recall."

I smiled. "Four times. I never got a chance to thank you guys. Is he going to be all right?"

The man shrugged. "It looks a lot worse than it is. The bullet went right through him, and he lost a fair bit of blood, but it seems to have missed all the vitals."

The other ambulance attendant poked an intravenous line into Webb's arm and hung it from a rack over the gurney. Webb opened his eyes, just a crack.

"Does this mean I get next week off?" He joked.

"No. I expect you in the office on Monday." I deadpanned.

The two men rolled the gurney back to the ambulance; in unison they said 'one, two, three' then they lifted the gurney into the ambulance, and in thirty seconds they were gone.

It was eerily quiet in the garage. Reynolds watched it go then she pulled a pair of handcuffs from her belt and slapped them on Gillian.

"If you're smart, you'll talk. If you want to play dumb, that's fine with me." She snarled.

Reynolds turned to one of the uniforms. "Scott, can you take this piece of shit to lockup?"

He nodded and took Gillian up the ramp. Reynolds looked down, quiet. A tear rolled down her cheek and landed on the ground in front of her. She wiped her face with the back of her hand, coughed once and looked up at me.

"Are we done here, boss? I'd like to be with Brian, if you don't mind."

"Go, Alex. Give him our best." I said softly.

She ran out of the garage. Walsh took a pale silk handkerchief out of his pocket, reached down and picked up Gillian's gun.

"Boss? This is an Astra four thousand." He said.

"What caliber is it?"

Walsh popped the clip out of the gun and thumbed a bullet out. He flipped it over to read the details stamped on the base.

"It's a seven point six five millimeter, boss."

"Same as killed Robert Sankar." I said.

Walsh bent down and picked up the passport that Gillian had given to Webb. He opened the front cover and read it. "Hmph. Robert Sankar. All right, let's wrap this up and see what else we get."

I drove home and switched to my police car. On the drive to the station, the chatter was all about the OPP having picked up some suspects in Lindsay, and that they were being transported to Fifty-two division. I got on the radio as soon as there was a break in the conversations.

"Fifty-two zero six." I called. The radio went dead. Nobody spoke.

"Go, zero six." Said the man in dispatch.

"Any word on the status of the OPP transfer?"

A familiar voice came on. "Hey, Ian, you owe me dinner. I'm almost at fifty-two now."

"Roger, Josh. Meet you there in five. Zero six out." I said.

The chatter started again. I pulled up to the station, rolled into my usual parking spot, and waited. Within a few moments, a beige unmarked car rolled in and parked beside me. Josh Klassen got out, grinning from ear to ear.

He stuck his hand out and pumped mine up and down. "Ian, you are one sly fox. How did you manage to do it, huh?"

"Sorry? Do what?" I asked.

"We got the print shop that was forging the papers, the gang that was moving money and their toadies that were smuggling people out of the country, all within a week! Jesus. We've been after these guys for months, and you clean it up in a week!"

I shrugged. "I got lucky. They made some mistakes. Where are they, by the way?"

He looked down the road. A black van rolled in, drove through to the secure entrance, and disappeared around the back of the building.

I turned to look at him. "Who's in the van?"

He flipped open a notebook. "We got Jeff and Mick, two guys from Scugog Scrap Metal. We got the guy that works at Kawartha Printers. They're the ones that made the fake papers. Plus, I hear you got Gillian, and we got her husband. It's a full house."

I thought quickly. "All right. Can we put Gillian and her husband in one room, the other three in another room. I want to play them off against each other."

"Sounds good to me. Can I watch?"

"Yeah. Bring popcorn."

He looked down the road. "I hear Gillian shot one of your people. Any word on him?"

"Not yet. Alex Reynolds is there, watching him. She laid a bunch of bruises on Gillian, by the way."

He snickered and rubbed his nose. "Great. Two chicks slapping each other out and I missed it."

"Timing matters, Josh. Let's get these people talking before they have time to think."

Chapter Fourteen

We set up two interview rooms. Gillian and her husband were in one room, and I arranged for the other three men to be in the second room. I asked several uniforms to walk in and out of both rooms, dropping off stacks of folders, and instructed them to say nothing to our suspects.

I let them sweat. They were in there for almost an hour, waiting, then I got Walsh to go in and cordially ask if anyone wanted coffee or a snack or something? Everyone said no, as I thought they would. Accepting the offer would feel like cooperating in their minds. Not accepting the coffee or snacks also made them more jittery, which was my intent.

I told Walsh that I would go into each room, and after exactly seven minutes, he was to walk up to me and whisper something nonsensical into my ear.

After another ten minutes, I went into the room where Mick, Jeff, and the big kid from Lindsay, the scrappy one I'd met at the diner, were all sitting.

Without saying anything, I sat down and opened one of the thick manila folders. I made a couple of scribbled notes in the margins. I'd still said nothing to them.

The big kid spoke. "Listen, I don't know why I'm here, man, really. All I do is work at the print shop, you know? I do what they tell me, that's all."

I looked up from writing and glared at him. "Did I say you could speak? Did I ask for your opinion?" I slammed the folder closed. The kid jumped. "Sorry, man, I just…"

"Again, did I ask for your opinion?" I said, firmly.

I fiddled with my pen, leaned back and looked at a blank wall. This was where I would learn whether they were instrumental in the scheme, or just low-level employees.

"Here's the problem." I started. "We got two dead guys, and you people are our best suspects. Now, I don't care which of you goes to jail. I just want to clear my case load. How do you suggest I proceed?"

Mick looked at me with venom, his eyes incinerating me. "You feel better now, Tonto? You happy that you rounded us up for the scalping? Huh?"

"Actually, my tribe never scalped." I said. "We tied down our enemies in the blazing sun so the vultures could pick out their eyes. Far more effective, and a better use of manpower."

I looked at my watch. Six minutes. "Here's my offer. You tell me which one of you rocket scientists killed Robert Sankar and Victor French.

The winner gets a deal. If Gillian and her husband come through first, the deal is off."

They looked at each other, puzzled. "No? Fine. Have it your way."

There was a knock at the door; Walsh came in and whispered 'Brian's going to be fine.'

He turned and left. I grinned. "Well, time's up. You lose. Someone beat you to it and made a deal. See you in court, gentlemen." I picked up a manila folder and got up.

The big kid lunged forward. "Wait! Wait!" He said.

"Sorry, but a deal's a deal. They were first. We promised them a deal." I said.

"I got something for you. Something big. What's it worth?" He asked.

I sat down, slowly. "All right, impress me."

He glanced around at the other two men, wary. "I got the names. I got all the names."

I rested the manila folder in front of me. This was to indicate that I was listening to him.

"Go on."

He placed his hands on the table, parallel to each other, as though holding a box. That meant he was thinking about what to tell me.

"Ok, so, we get a picture, and they give us a name to go with it, and then we create the papers."

"Go on." I repeated.

"Anyway, I figured, you know, it takes a bunch of time to make good passports, driver's licenses, university diplomas. It takes maybe an extra two minutes, though, to make a copy of them on the Xerox machine. It didn't have to pass muster, didn't need to look good. It was just for insurance. So I copied every piece of paper we made for these guys."

"How many people are we talking about?"

"Maybe twenty? Maybe more, maybe less."

"How long have you been doing this?"

He looked up, thinking. "Maybe three years. A little less."

"Do you have the real names of these people you got out?" I asked.

"No. we never got those, just what name they were going to be."

"Who gave you those names? Was it Gillian?"

"No, man. It was Adam, her husband. He'd give us the photos and the names we were making papers for."

"Any idea where he got the names?" I asked.

"Nope."

"Well, I can tell you that part. Adam's brother, Terry, worked for the coroner. He got the names from dead guys in the morgue." I said.

I wanted them to know that I understood how their business ran. They looked at each other.

"Tell me; which of you goobers killed Victor French?" I asked.

They all shook their heads.

The big kid spoke first. "Who is that?"

"He faked his drowning on Sturgeon Lake last year. And Robert Sankar? Who shot him?"

They shook their heads again. The big kid leaned forward. "Listen, what we did wasn't quite legit, you know. We won't do it again. Honest. But we wouldn't never *kill* someone."

The other two nodded approval. I believed them. They were just opportunists, low-level crooks, not killers. Time to shake up the other room.

"I'll leave you to talk it over, then. If you can come up with any other information that will help your case, an officer will be in shortly. You can tell him."

They looked at each other, wondering how much trouble they were in. I picked up three thick manila folders and left the room.

A uniform outside the door nodded at me. "Hey." I said.

I pulled some money out of my pocket. "Listen; pick up some burgers, fries, donuts, coffee, and feed those guys in there. Tell them it's from me. I want them to feel at ease. I'm going to come back in a while, and I want to be their buddy when I do. OK? Thanks, man."

He waved at a junior officer and passed on the request. The other uniform left to buy the food.

Time to change persona: I shook myself loose, straightened the papers in the manila folders and stormed into the room where Gillian and her husband were sitting.

They were across a wide table from me, and they jumped slightly when I swung the door open.

I smacked the manila folders down hard on my side of the table, glared at Gillian's husband and smiled at her.

"How are we feeling?" I said, warmly.

"Fine, 'Mister Brewster'." She growled.

"Detective Inspector McBriar, actually."

"You lost the tattoos, I see." She sneered.

"Right. They just went away. Just like you'll both be going away."

She squirmed, wondering what I would say or do next. Good. I wanted her off balance, unsure of herself. She glanced at her husband and back at me. That told me that he was the one who made the decisions, even though he didn't speak much. He was the real boss in this family.

He glanced at her then glared at me. "Your cop, that woman, she's guilty of police brutality. I'm going to charge her for assaulting my wife. You can't do that and get away with it, you know."

I opened a manila folder, slowly took out my pen and scribbled something on the inside cover. I closed the cover and looked up at him. "Thank you for asking." I said.

"Yes, the police officer Gillian shot is in surgery, fighting for his life." I lied.

Gillian went pale. "It was an accident. The gun went off- I didn't mean…, it was an accident."

I shook my head. "I don't care. If he dies, you will be charged with murder. Even if he lives, you will go to jail for the attempted murder of a police officer."

She squirmed in her seat, rocking her butt from side to side. That was my cue to move in.

"Now, add that to the other two deaths, and you will die of old age in jail. So whatever you want to say about Detective Reynolds' actions, I don't think a judge will much care, do you?"

Her eyes widened. "What other two deaths? I don't know about any deaths. We were giving people new names, nothing more. We never hurt anyone."

"I disagree." I said.

I pointed my pen at her. "I seem to remember Mick and Jeff threatening me. That's also a Criminal Code offence, by the way. Why would you stop at murder?"

She leaned forward, ran her fingers through her hair and scrunched up her face. Clearly, she was used to being in charge, and she was way out of her depth here.

"We. Never. Killed. Anybody… Ever." She said, slowly.

"So, if the gun you shot Constable Webb with turns out to be the gun that killed Robert Sankar?"

She moaned, a desperate, sad moan. "I don't know. All I know is that Gail gave me the gun. She said I should hold onto it. That's all. I didn't even know it was loaded. Honest."

I sat back. "When did she give it to you?"

"On the day before you came to stay at the motel."

"Uh-uh. She was in Ireland then. Her sister told us so. You're sure it wasn't Abigail who gave it to you?"

"No. I've met her sister. Gail has red hair. Abby is a brunette. Obviously, it's dyed red, but they're different. It was definitely Gail."

So, I thought, did Gail even go to Ireland, or did she lie to her sister and stay in town? That would explain shooting Sankar in the Mercedes, and leaving him there, to give her an alibi. She could claim he'd taken her car when she was out of the country. It made sense.

"Does she have somewhere she stays when she's in the Lindsay area?" I asked.

"Sometimes she goes to stay with her dad at the marina."

"Is her dad Bill Fontaine?"

"Yes, that's right."

I stood up. "Fine. Tell you what; if we can prove you didn't kill anyone, I'll help you out. If Constable Webb survives, I'll reduce the charge to aggravated assault, on the condition that you drop any complaints against Constable Reynolds. If you ever do press charges, however, the deal is off. Do we have an agreement?"

She brightened up. "Yes, absolutely. Yes."

At my desk, there was a folder with details on the case. I took it to the interview rooms. The uniforms had fed the other three men; I gave them five more minutes and went in. They were chewing happily on the food, slurping drinks through a thick straw, feeling at ease, now. Good- I wanted them at ease. They would give me more information that way.

"So, how's the food?" I asked.

The big kid nodded. "It's really good. Where do you get these burgers, man?"

"Harvey's. Best in town. Now, a couple more questions and we can send you on your way."

"You mean we go home?" He asked.

"Not just yet, sunshine, but if you're truthful I guarantee you won't regret it."

The big kid squirmed, not sure if he should trust me. Jeff leaned back and folded his arms, tight. I wouldn't get anything out of him. Mick looked at me, trying to read me. I could work on him.

"Now, then. Who placed evidence in locker number seventeen at the scrapyard?"

They looked at each other. Clearly, they had no idea what I meant.

"So, that's a no. All right, have any of you seen this man?"

I pulled out the photo of Robert Sankar and slid it on the table.

"Do you recognize this man?" I asked.

Jeff leaned close and examined the picture. "Yeah. Him. I recognize him."

"When did you see him?" I asked.

"He was at the yard. He was asking about some guy, if we'd seen him around."

"What guy?"

"He showed me a picture. The guy looked sorta like him. I thought it was maybe a brother or something. Anyway, I didn't recognize him."

"Did you see the car he was driving? Was it a car you'd recognize?"

"I guess. It was an LTD or a Monarch or something. Typical salesman's car, you know?"

"Or plainclothes cop." I said.

Walsh came in and placed a hand on my shoulder. "Got a minute?" He asked.

We walked out and Walsh closed the door. He grinned.

"Thought you'd want to know- Brian's out of surgery. He could go home on Monday, the doc says. He's asking for pizza."

I patted Walsh's shoulder. "Good. Let's go see him."

I drove to the hospital. Webb was in a room by himself, with a pair of uniforms standing outside. They nodded recognition and I told them to take a break. Walsh showed up five minutes later.

Webb was propped up in bed, sleepy, an intravenous drip hovering over him. Reynolds was sitting beside him, stroking his hair. She smiled up at us, then went back to stroking his hair.

"Hey, Alex, how are you doing?" I asked.

"Shouldn't you be worried about Brian, not me?" She answered.

"He'll be fine." I said. "He's tough."

Webb snickered and opened one eye slightly. "Yeah, I'm doing great, boss." He wheezed.

"I need to borrow your girlfriend for a moment." I said.

I walked Reynolds out to the hall. She followed sheepishly.

"Listen, boss, about earlier," She started.

I held my hand up. "Not one more word. Gillian has agreed to forget what happened, in exchange for us dropping the charge of attempted murder."

She beamed. "Thanks, boss. I could hug you."

"Save it for Brian. But remember, I'm only giving you this gift once. Period."

"Never again. You have my word."

We went back in and sat with Webb; he was feeling better, he said, and he was pleased that he'd be home in two days. He still wanted pizza.

Walsh looked over his shoulder. "I thought I should spread the good cheer." He said.

Four men were going down the hall, with a half dozen boxes of pizza each, leaving boxes at nursing stations as they went.

One of the men came into our room and left two boxes by Webb's bed. Walsh pulled a wad of bills out of his pocket and thanked the man. He grinned, took the money then he waved at the other three men. They split the cash and called out more thanks as they left.

Reynolds lifted a slice of pizza from the box and held it to Webb's mouth. He took a bite and leaned back. "Oh, god, that's good." He said softly.

We watched him for a few minutes, asked questions he could answer with a nod, and made sure he was comfortable. A doctor came in wiping sauce from his mouth, and checked on Webb's blood pressure. We sat some more, until Webb was too tired to speak.

We said goodbye for the evening, walked past the two uniforms (who were also eating pizza), and left, accepting thanks from all the staff for the food.

"Way to go, Patrick. Let me chip in for that, if you don't mind."

"I sure as hell do mind, boss." He said.

"Brian is my DC, just like I was yours. Would you let someone else pay in my place?"

"Point taken. Karen and your parents will be in tomorrow afternoon. See you at the airport?"

"No, Sam will drive my folks home. I'll meet them there."

"OK. We did nice work this week. Enjoy the glory. See you Monday." I said.

The hospital was only a mile or two from Captain Van Hoeke's house. I wanted to clear up something that was still bothering me, so I parked behind his MG, strolled up the driveway and knocked on the front door

The door went dark, then opened. Rebecca Van Hoeke poked her face out.

"Ian. What a pleasure to see you again. What brings you out this way?" She smiled.

"I could say I came to see you. Or I could tell you that I'm after the truth."

She raised one eyebrow. "The truth?"

"The truth about Martin. The truth."

The smile faded somewhat. "You're a very clever young man, Ian. Come in."

She backed up and opened the door wider. I stepped in and let her close it behind me.

"I need a favour, Ian." She said, seriously.

"Name it, Becky."

"Whatever he tells you, it won't affect your job in any way. I want you to keep what he tells you to yourself."

"I'm not sure I can promise that. I'd have to tell Karen and Frank."

"That goes without saying. Just not anyone inside the force." She stated.

"Agreed."

She walked down the hall to the den, where Van Hoeke had been tying fishing lures. The door was partly open, and Van Hoeke was lying on a leather sofa, a moist towel over his face.

I sat in a swivel chair and used my feet to haul myself over beside him. "Hey, Martin, how are you?" I said.

He lifted the towel off one eye to see me, then placed the towel over his eye again.

"Figured it out, did you?" He asked.

"What's wrong, Martin? Why did you really retire?"

He placed the towel on a side table, swung his legs down and sat up. "How much do you know?"

"I figure it's not just Pascoe that made you quit. You've dealt with smarter men than him."

"What tipped you off, then?" He was smiling now.

"Fishing in Falmouth. It occurred to me later that you said you'd argued with your brother at the wedding you talked about. The only two reasons I can imagine you making peace with him is that he inherited a castle, or you're not well."

He laughed. "It's not the castle. Vey astute, Ian. I see Frank trained you well. You both came to the same conclusion."

"When was Frank here?"

"A few days ago. As they say, great minds think alike."

I smiled at the compliment. "So, what is it, and how can I help?"

"No idea, and no, you can't. The doctors aren't sure what it is. I get headaches, my hands tremble, and I have trouble standing up for long periods of time. Other days, I'm fine. All I know is that it's gotten worse lately. It was almost time for me to leave, anyway. If it does get worse, I'd rather not look pathetic in front of the men."

I had tears in my eyes. I realized that this man was almost like a father to me. He had guided me, mentored me, made me a better cop. He shook his head.

"Do you know, Ian, what I remember most at a time like this?"

"No."

"I remember when I was in the RAF, before I met Rebecca. Every day that I got into a Spitfire, every time I started the engine, I told myself that today I might die. And that it was all right.

"I was doing what I really wanted to do, and that what I was doing was the right thing to do, so whatever happened to me was the right thing to happen."

"You're at peace with whatever happens next?"

"Hell, yes. For a kid from Clapham to end up here, in this country, with this house, with this life? I'm happy."

"You know I'll pray for you, right?"

"With a yarmulke and a prayer shawl?"

"No."

Then it doesn't count." He joked.

Rebecca made coffee, and we all had more cake. Afterwards, I gave her a big hug, gave Van Hoeke one as well, and left.

Chapter Fifteen

Frank Burghezian's house was only three blocks away from mine. I parked out front and knocked on the door. The thunder of small feet got louder, then the door opened painfully slowly as a pair of three-year-old's struggled with the doorknob.

I squatted down to their eye level. They peered around the door and the girl turned back and yelled into the house.

"Mom! It's uncle Ian!"

She turned back to look at me. "Hi, uncle Ian."

"Hi, Melina. Hello, Theo. How are you guys?"

The girl spoke again. "Fine."

She ran into the living room. Other footsteps came up, heavier. The door opened wide, and Helen smiled. "Hey, Ian. You're just in time for coffee. Come in."

I followed her through the house and sat at the kitchen table. A sound from the stairs made me look; Frank came into the kitchen, a stack of papers in his hand.

"Hey, have you seen my… oh, hi, Ian. Good to see you."

"Hi, Frank. Bogged down in paperwork, are we?"

"Yeah. James Bond never had this in the movies, huh?"

Wordlessly, Helen placed a mug of coffee in front of me. She sat across from me and looked into my eyes. "You went to see Martin." She said.

"Yes." I said, simply.

"So you know."

"Yes."

"Do they know what it is yet?"

"No. How long have you known?"

"Since last week. He had us over for dinner, and I saw the signs. When did he tell you?"

"He didn't. I guessed."

Frank snickered. "OK, so I really can't let you get away that easy. What made you suspect?"

"He said he was going to visit his brother in the UK. He'd had a fight with him- the only reason he would go see him is to make peace before the end came."

Frank took a sip of coffee and stared out the window. "Well, it's always something, isn't it?"

We talked some more, reminisced about old times at the department, then I drove home, made myself something light for dinner and read the paper as I listened to the radio.

Once again, the Buffalo station was playing mellow jazz. The sun had sunk low on the horizon; light streamed in through the south windows and lit up the north wall of the living room, where the shiny wallpaper met the door frame.

I sat back, eased into my chair, and let the sounds of Grover Washington's saxophone lull me to sleep.

It was almost eleven thirty when I woke up. My mouth was dry, my shoulders ached. With some effort, I staggered upstairs, threw on my pajama pants and climbed into bed.

Tomorrow would be a good day. Tomorrow, the family would be back. Karen would be home, and Ethan, and Charlotte, and the mystery bundle in Karen's womb. Monday I'd be back at work, and hopefully figure out who had killed those two men, but tomorrow... I fell asleep.

I went to early Mass most Sundays, then I came home before everyone woke up and made pancakes. Today I went to church as usual, then I went to a diner I knew for bacon and eggs.

Around noon I found an open grocery store and picked up some staples, loaded the fridge and had lunch. By two thirty I was restless, impatient, so I parked at the ferry terminal by Toronto Island Airport and took the five-minute boat ride to the island.

The coffee shop at the airport, 'The Left Seat Diner', was open, so I bought a coffee and sat in a booth waiting.

A large form blocked the light behind me. I turned to see Sam, the driver for the Walsh family, coming toward me. He squeezed himself into my booth across from me and nodded.

"Hello, Mister Ian." He said, his voice echoing through the room.

"Hi, Sam. Waiting for the boss?"

"Yes, sir."

"Listen, can I buy you a sandwich or something?"

"You really don't have to, Mister Ian."

"No, honest, it's my pleasure. I never got a chance to thank you for the little pantomime at the motel. I appreciated you being there, Sam."

His face slowly spread into a wide smile. "Yeah, that was fun, wasn't it, Mister Ian."

"Please, just Ian."

I called over the owner of the diner and asked Sam what he wanted. Apparently, sandwiches for Sam came in threes. He ate quietly, watching the runway every few seconds to see whether the Walsh's plane had landed yet, and spoke little when I asked him questions.

Just before four I checked my watch, paid the bill and we both went outside to wait.

Right on cue, a white jet touched softly down on the runway, rolled to a stop and turned off, toward the terminal. I read the words 'Cessna Citation' on the tail, but it meant little to me.

The plane stopped by an open hangar, an opening magically appeared in the fuselage, and the opening flipped slowly down to reveal a stairway.

The first person to walk out was Kieran Walsh, Patrick's father. On this hot day, he was wearing pale cotton slacks and a light golf shirt. He turned at the base of the stairs, held out his hand and helped down his wife Lizzie.

She was in white shorts, her long tanned legs stretching down to meet the stairs, a pink sleeveless tee shirt falling over her waist. She saw me, smiled and waved.

Then Karen stepped out. Kieran was equally helpful to her. She took his hand and held her stomach with her other hand.

At the base of the steps, she leaned up to help Charlotte down. Charlotte hopped off the last step, gleefully.

Next came Ethan, gripping the cord handrail as he made his way to the ground. He seemed to have grown in the last couple of weeks. That part, I thought, was wishful thinking.

Karen looked up at the open doorway. I expected to see a flight attendant, or maybe the pilot.

My father stepped out and came gingerly down the stairs. My father came down the stairs…

I took a moment to process this. My father was in Toronto. Not in Saskatchewan.

Sam and I walked toward the clustered group.

Ethan and Charlotte saw me first, ran over and hugged me. I swept them up in my arms and kissed them both.

"Hey, guys. How are you?" I asked.

"Dad! I flew the plane! It's so cool!" Ethan gushed.

"Me too! I was the pilot. It was fun." Said Charlotte.

"You did? Both of you? Wow, that is so great." I said.

I walked toward Karen as I spoke, both children still in my arms. She held my face, pulled me close and kissed me.

"Hey, you. Missed you." She said.

"Missed you too." I said.

I looked at my father. "Dad? You're here." I said.

"Yes. Do you mind? They said they had an extra seat."

"No, I'm thrilled."

I put the children down and met the Walsh's. "Listen, both of you, I can't thank you enough. This is a terrific surprise."

Lizzie Walsh put her hand over her forehead, shielding her eyes from the sun. "Nonsense. It's nothing. How are you doing, Ian?"

"I'm well, thanks. Patrick will meet you at home later?"

She nodded.

"We had an exciting week, but he'll tell you all about it."

Sam had pulled luggage out of the plane and placed it on a trolley to wheel back to the ferry. Some of the luggage I recognized as Karen's. he rolled the trolley to the end of the tarmac and waited politely for us to come in our own time.

Kieran Walsh said something to the pilot, they shook hands and he turned back to face us.

"Good. Well, I'm exhausted. Shall we go?" He said.

We followed Sam to the ferry and sailed the narrow channel back to our cars. The children hung their faces over the side, watching the water splash under them.

Karen and Lizzie chatted, laughing occasionally as they talked. My father and I spoke about places and people we both knew.

The ferry docked, Sam rolled the trolley to the trunk of a large Mercedes and piled luggage into it. He placed Karen's bags to one side, and I put them in the trunk of her car, the car I'd brought to pick her up. It had air conditioning, after all.

The Mercedes backed silently out of the parking space and disappeared.

My father opted to ride in the back seat with the children, and Karen sat in front with me.

"It's good to be home." She said.

"It's good to have you home."

I looked in the rear-view mirror. "Hey, pops, you haven't seen our new house yet."

"No, son. I'm looking forward to it. Ethan says we have a playhouse in the back yard."

Ethan beamed. "Yeah, and we got birds and squirrels there, too. You should see it, grampa."

"I'm sure I will love it as much as you do, son." He said.

We rolled uptown in air-conditioned splendour and I parked in the driveway. Ethan opened his door and scrambled out, then turned to wait for my father to get out.

My father waited for Charlotte to climb out behind him. He lifted her gently to the ground and held both children's hands.

"Now, who's going to show me this house of yours?" He asked.

Ethan pointed to the front door and started talking non-stop.

"And we got a room just for you, and we got a piano, and I'm learning to play it. I got a train set, and uncle Frank got me a bunch of trains, and dad made a town that the train goes through."

My father nodded patiently, listening to it all. "That's great, Ethan. Tell you what, let's get unpacked and we'll talk about it after dinner, all right?"

"OK, grampa."

I lugged the bags out of the trunk and into the house. Ethan was still talking as I carried them upstairs to the bedrooms. My father's bag was an old one he'd had for as long as I could remember. We had a guest room on the main floor, with its own small bathroom, and which looked out at the back yard. I thought he might like the peace of having his own area of the house, plus he wouldn't need to go up and down the stairs.

My father followed me to the guest bedroom and sat on the edge of the bed.

"This is really comfortable, son. Please thank the Walsh's for the ride. I sure appreciate it."

"I'll pass it on, pops. Will you be comfortable here?"

He opened the drapes and looked out at the back yard. "Heavens, yes. This is lovely, son."

"Thanks. We like it."

He opened his suitcase and pulled out carefully folded shirts.

"So, how long did you want to stay with us, pops?"

"Not too long. I figure maybe a week. I need to get back, but I couldn't say no to the free flight."

"Yeah, they've been really good to us, the whole Walsh family."

He smiled softly. "That Lizzie is sure a handsome woman."

Thoughts of her shirt deflecting went through my mind. "Yeah, I hadn't really noticed." I said.

He was still looking down at his clothes. "You never could lie, could you?"

"Hey, she's got three kids that are almost my age. C'mon, dad."

He chuckled. "Really well-preserved, though, isn't she?"

"Yeah, she is at that." I conceded.

We ate early. Saskatchewan was two hours behind my time zone, and we ate at seven. My father insisted on helping with the food; he made a quick chili and baked potato dish- a big seller in his restaurant.

After dinner, the kids fell asleep in front of the TV and I carried them both up to their rooms. Karen and my father talked for a while, but he was tired too, and wished us goodnight.

Karen came over to the sofa, where I was sitting, and flopped her feet onto my lap.

"Hey, can you rub my feet?" She asked.

"Glad to, hon." I answered. "Happy to be home?"

"Uh-huh. It was a lot of fun there, though. I'm sure we'll want to do it again."

"Dad told you about wanting to retire?"

She wriggled to get comfortable. "Yeah. Some place on an island near Vancouver. Sounds almost tropical, to hear him tell it. He'll tell you more at breakfast."

"Will Pam's son run the restaurant and the hotel?"

She spoke slower this time. "Right. Take them over."

"You sound tired, Karen."

There was no answer. She lay back, her mouth slightly open, fast asleep. I carried her, like Rhett carried Scarlett in 'Gone With the Wind', upstairs to our room. She opened her eyes long enough to get into her nightshirt then slid under the sheets and fell back to sleep.

I went downstairs to lock up the house. After finding those two men in here earlier, I was taking no chances.

Something else was bothering me about the case. Those men said they hadn't killed French or Sankar, so why were the men killed? And who killed them? It made no sense. French had paid the gang to help him disappear. He had stolen a fortune and gotten away with it. He had stolen it from a bank, too, not one person.

Sankar looked a lot like French. Was it a case of mistaken identity? Was one of them the real target, and the other was in the wrong place at the wrong time?

I went upstairs, past the ticking clock in the hallway and got ready for bed.

Karen was breathing heavily; her belly now bulged even through loose clothes, as it had when she was carrying Charlotte. It must have been the same when she carried Ethan. I felt a pang of guilt that I hadn't met her at that point, that I didn't know her before she'd had him.

Then again, I'd just left the Seminary and entered the academy; I wasn't even a Constable then. My mother had died, so I left the seminary. Left the Seminary. I fell asleep.

At six in the morning, I was wide awake. I made breakfast, put coffee on, and waited for everyone else to wake up.

A half hour later, my father came into the kitchen and sniffed the air. "Fresh coffee?" He said.

"Yeah, pops. Help yourself."

He poured himself a cup and took a sip. "Mm. Everyone else still asleep?"

"I'm afraid so. We're the only early birds, dad."

He swirled the coffee in his cup, thinking. "So, what happened with you last week?"

"How do you mean?"

"Karen was worried sick; you went out of town for work, she said. She could barely sleep until you got back."

"I went undercover. It was not something I'd like to do again, frankly."

"Were you in danger at all?"

I smiled. "Not really. People thought I was an ex-con, so they gave me wide berth. You should have seen me, pops. I had these fake tattoos, and this fake ID that said I'd just gotten out of The Hill. Plus I was driving an old Valiant with Sask plates. I tell you, it was a real production."

He didn't seem amused. "So, how did it end?"

"We arrested some bad guys. There is still some cleanup, but the worst is over, we think."

He nodded, slowly. "What are you going to do now?"

"Well, I'm going to make breakfast for whoever gets up in time, then I have to go to work."

We talked for a while. He described how he and Pam had visited British Columbia, stayed with her relatives, and decided they would retire somewhere that had milder winters. It sounded very nice. I promised that wherever they ended up, we'd all visit them.

His face lit up, thinking about a third grandchild. He always hoped he'd live long enough to see them, he said, and he was delighted at how Ethan and Charlotte had turned out.

Just before eight, Karen came down the stairs, gave me a kiss and hugged my father. She insisted on a bowl of cereal and a mug of tea, and she sat with her feet on the seat of her stool as she ate.

I told her I had to go, kissed her goodbye and left. I felt bad about not saying goodbye to the kids, but I'd see them after work.

Today was a good day. It felt good, right off the bat. The sky was crystal clear, with a light breeze coming down from the north, and the faint smell of dry hay in the air. Traffic was light, and I parked in my spot just before eight thirty.

The duty sergeant told me that our suspects were in the Don Jail holding cells; I would talk to them again after the morning meeting, but I wanted them to sweat for the time being.

There were a few pink phone messages on my desk, mostly to do with the five people in custody, and a quick scan of them told me I didn't need to respond right now.

Walsh was at his desk flipping through his messages, too.

At eight thirty-five, Ernest Pascoe walked in. He plunked his briefcase on his desk and came back out.

"Ian! Good to see you. Got a minute?" He said genially.

I looked over at Walsh. He raised an eyebrow, skeptical. I followed Pascoe into his office, and he closed the door behind him.

He waved at a chair. "Please, please sit." He smiled.

"OK." I said, slowly.

I sat and said nothing. "Now, we've had our differences, I know." He started.

It sounded like what a drunk would say before he asks you for money.

"But I have to tell you, Ian, your methods…"

He wagged a finger at me, smiling. "You really get results, and without a lot of expense, too."

I had no idea what he meant. "Sorry, do you mean the arrests over the weekend?" I asked.

He nodded vigorously. "Yes. Those five- the killers, the forgers, you got them, and you solved a crime pattern that's been baffling the OPP for years. Well done, Ian, well done."

"It's not over, Captain, not yet. I don't believe they're the ones who killed French and Sankar."

He seemed to deflate slightly. "You don't? Why not?"

"Because they said so."

He laughed out loud. "For a moment there, I thought you were serious. 'Because they said so'. Good one, Ian."

I shook my head. "I don't know if you're just being expedient or what. Look, these five have admitted to forgery and fraud and to shipping the proceeds of crime across national borders. We have them on that. I don't think there was any reason for them to kill those men. It's not over."

He leaned back, tumbling a ballpoint pen back and forth in his hand. He leaned forward and pointed the pen at me.

"All right, have it your way. This morning, we'll announce that you caught these people, and you're close to wrapping up the case. How about that?"

That statement puzzled me. "Announce it to who?" I asked.

He spread his arms wide. "Why, to the media, of course. We've scheduled a press conference to tell them how we've caught these criminals."

"I'm not sure I want to tell the world that just now." I said, cautiously.

He shrugged. "No need. I'll be the one talking to the press."

"Of course. That makes perfect sense." I smiled.

Just before nine, I handed my clipboard to Walsh, and he bellowed out 'MEETING'.

The detectives in the room fell silent; Walsh read out current issues, active cases, and had teams tell him where they were in their investigations.

Then he flipped the page and glanced at me. "On a matter closer to home." He started.

"You've all heard that Brian Webb is in hospital. He's getting out later today. He will be fine, and be back to work soon. What some people will go to just to get noticed. Right, boss?"

He looked at me, and the room laughed. "Right. It's despicable." I joked.

He finished the list on the clipboard and tucked it under his arm. "Fine. Any questions?"

They all shook their heads. "We're done. Go catch bad guys." He said.

The detectives clustered into groups, organized their week and left. I was still waiting for the other disaster- the media interview. By ten in the morning, the squad room was deserted. Fifteen minutes later, a van pulled into the lot, parked in two spots, and three people got out. There was a news reporter- a woman that I recognized from TV- her cameraman and a person with a microphone on a boom.

They filed into the front area, announced themselves and were shown the squad room. Pascoe put on his jacket, straightened his tie and combed his hair back over the bald spot.

He stood upright, marched out to where the cameraman had set up, and waited for the reporter to get herself ready.

Finally, the woman turned to face the camera. She frowned, looking at the man with the microphone. He said 'three, two, one' and she smiled into the lens, as though talking to a friend.

"Virginia Maxwell, for News Nine." She said. "We're here with Captain Ernest Pascal."

"Pascoe." He corrected. "My name is Ernest Pascoe."

She scowled then looked at the camera again. "Let's start from scratch, shall we?"

She smiled again. "Virginia Maxwell, News Nine, reporting from fifty-two division of the Toronto Police Department. I'm here with Captain… Ernest Pascoe. Word has reached this reporter that Captain Pascoe's detective team has made arrests in connection with the murder of an undercover police officer, Robert Sankar."

She pivoted and poked a smaller microphone under Pascoe's chin. "Captain, what can you tell our viewers about the developments in this case?"

He looked into the camera. "We organized an operation to apprehend a number of individuals we believe were involved in a crime. My staff performed in an exemplary manner, and they have arrested the persons responsible. Once the suspects are formally charged, we will give further details. Until then we will not be divulging their identities."

He sounded very professional, very forceful. It almost sounded like he knew about the arrests ahead of time. Walsh and I sat in the back of the room, amused.

The woman swung the small microphone under her own chin. "Do you believe that this could lead to further arrests? Is there more to this story that you haven't told us?"

He looked nervous, now. She had cornered him. If he said there was nothing more, and we made more arrests, he would look inept. If he agreed that there was more to come, then she'd press him for details.

"We would be jeopardizing the development of our investigation if I comment further." He said.

"So you *do* expect more arrests?" She pressed.

He smiled. "You'll have to see later, I suppose."

This was not going the way she wanted. She looked around, and her eye caught me. She left her cameraman behind and streaked over to face me. Her cameraman struggled to catch up.

"Inspector McBriar? Hi, Virginia Maxwell, News Nine. Were you involved in these arrests?"

I nodded. "Yes, I was."

"Perhaps you can tell us- do you expect further arrests in connection with these ones?"

"Sorry, Virginia, as Captain Pascoe said, it's a developing investigation."

"When will you be able to tell the people of Toronto that they're safe again?"

"When we lock up all the bad guys."

She frowned. "You're confident that you can arrest the other people who are still out there?"

"You're putting words in my mouth. Captain Pascoe never said there *were* people out there."

"Thank you, Inspector."

She packed up her equipment, waited for her cameraman to fold up his camera, and they left, unceremoniously. Pascoe walked up beside me.

"Ian, thank you for that. Very well done, nicely handled."

"No problem. I just don't like her TV station, that's all." I said. "They run rotten cartoons."

Walsh and I went for coffee down the street. He flipped through notes in his book, trying to spot something that would help, something that made sense.

I had a thought; one I should have had before. "Patrick, did we get a ballistics test on the bullet that hit Brian?"

He flipped back a couple of pages. "Yeah. It's the same gun that shot Sankar."

"So, if Gillian had the gun that shot Robert Sankar, and let's assume she didn't shoot him, who did? And when did they give her that gun?"

That possibility hadn't occurred to him. "Ah. I just thought she shot Sankar too, but that she'd lied about it."

"Let's ask her." I said.

Chapter Sixteen

Walsh drove us to the Don Jail, weaving quickly through traffic. We showed our badges, called for Gillian, and waited as she was brought up from the women's wing.

We waited for her in the interview room, a sterile, grey concrete block wall of a room, with flat metal chairs and a slab steel table. A burly female guard brought her in, gripping Gillian's thin arm with vise-grip force, and bodily sat her down across from us. The guard faded back and leaned against the wall, her arms folded.

Walsh smiled, oozing charm. "So, Gillian, we meet again, just like at the motel." He joked.

"Except you can go outside for a smoke, and I can't." she countered.

He spread his arms out expansively. "True. Then again, I never shot a cop."

She sighed, leaned her elbows on the table and ran her fingers through her hair. "Look, I never meant to hurt anyone. Never. I was just trying to get away, that's all."

"So, you regret shooting him?"

"Yeah. Look, I know we may have done some things that were not exactly… kosher, but then again, we were only trying to get ahead, you know?"

"I notice you have yet to ask how he is- the officer you shot." Walsh said.

"Oh, yeah, right. I hope he'll be OK?"

"Like you give a shit. We have the gun that you shot him with, and it's the same one that killed an undercover cop, one Robert Sankar."

"I don't know that name." She said.

"Do you remember Victor French?"

"We got him out a year ago. How does this relate to him?"

I felt the question was genuine.

"How did you get him out of the country?" Walsh asked.

She leaned back, thinking. "He had to get out quickly. We flew him to Miami, then he went on to Nassau and opened a bank account. We took a real chance with him. Before that we put him up in a hotel and staged an 'accident'."

"The Lockview Inn on Canal Street, in Bobcaygeon." I said.

She seemed surprised. "Yes. Anyway, he rented a boat and bought a case of beer. Then he dumped the beer, swamped the boat, swam to shore. Everyone figured he got drunk and drowned. We gave him a new ID, plane ticket, and he was gone. That's the last we heard."

"The boat was from the marina that Bill Fontaine runs. So he's involved in this too?"

She shook her head. "No. As far as he knows, it was just an accident. My aunt Sandra, same thing. She's going to be livid about Mick and Jeff. She's a tough old bird, but she's one hundred percent legit, by the book."

I started putting it together in my head. "So, who gave you the gun, then? Abigail?"

"Not Abby. Her sister, Gail." She said.

"Gail is in Ireland." Walsh said.

"No. She called me from here. She said to meet her near that alcoholic place, and she gave me the gun. She said she had to disappear for a while. You already had her car, she said, and it was only a matter of time till you found her. She told me to ditch the gun, but I kept it."

"Her sister, Abby, does she know where Gail went?"

"No. Abby doesn't know anything either. Gail used Abby's modelling agency as a cover. A few times, we'd send our people to Ireland as staff, or photographers. Customs guys always ogle the girls, she said, never the guys with the girls. It was a good way to sneak them out of the country."

"Why Ireland?" I asked.

She sighed. "They speak English. They are a stepping-stone. From there, people went to Britain, or Spain, or Greece. Someone departing Ireland to retire in Greece, doesn't attract much attention. Someone landing in Portugal and retiring to Greece would raise eyebrows. Besides, Irish banks make it easy to transfer money from Caribbean countries."

Walsh sat back, dumbfounded. "Jeez, boss, I'm in the wrong business."

Gillian knitted her fingers together in front of her and stared at them. "It took a lot of work to set this up. Another couple of years, a couple dozen more people, and we could have all retired rich. In the end, think of it. Nobody was hurt, nobody was forced to do anything. They came to us voluntarily. We were just helping them walk away."

"Except that you helped a crook who stole a million dollars from a number of banks, not to mention whatever all the others have done to get their money." I said.

Walsh reached into his jacket and pulled out a thin gold cigarette case. He opened it up and reached out to Gillian. "Would you like one?" He asked.

She smiled and plucked a cigarette from the case. He reached into his jacket pocket, extracted his slim gold lighter, and in one smooth motion flicked it open and lit her cigarette.

She took a long drag of smoke, closed her eyes and smiled. "Wow, these are good." She said.

"So I've been told. Gillian, when did Gail give you the gun again?" He asked.

"About a week ago."

He sat back. "A week ago. So she was in Canada a week ago."

She nodded.

"Could she have shot Robert Sankar?"

She shook her head. "I don't know. Why would she?"

Gillian took another long puff of her cigarette. The guard stepped forward to chastise her, but Walsh shook his head slowly. The guard backed away again.

"Who took Victor French out of the morgue? Was it Terry Westlock?" Walsh asked.

She leaned back and laughed. "Well, that took you a while to figure out, huh?"

She tapped her cigarette ash onto the table in a small pile.

Walsh smiled as if sharing a private joke. "What did you do with the body?"

"We put him in with a couple of indigents that were being cremated. He's ashes now."

"Why did you take him in the first place?"

She rolled her eyes. "Think about it. We gave him a new name and made him disappear. We didn't know if he had family that could identify him, if someone would recognize him. If they did they might follow him back to us. We couldn't risk that."

"But you had nothing to do with Robert Sankar's death?" I asked.

She sighed, frustrated. "For the last time, I have no idea who that is."

Walsh slid his chair back. "Thanks, Gillian. I appreciate the help."

She stood up and leaned forward. "Hey, can I get some more of those smokes? They're good."

Walsh opened the cigarette case and scooped out a half-dozen cigarettes. "Please." He said.

We drove back to the station, neither of us talking. I had most of it figured out. Just not the most important parts. I needed to call in a favour.

I called the OPP in Lindsay and asked for Josh Klassen. He got on the line right away.

"Hey, Ian. Thanks again for the help, man. Good brownie points for both of us, huh?"

"Yo, Josh. You're welcome. I've got a question for you." I said.

"Yeah, go for it."

"So, Bill Fontaine runs the marina near you, on Sturgeon Lake. What do you know about him?"

He sighed. "Not much. I think I met him a couple of times. I can find out more if he's in the system, of course. Want me to get back to you on that?"

"Yes please, Josh. When's a good time?" I asked.

"The file on him should be pretty thin. Give me an hour."

I hung up and called Karen. She and the kids were 'terrorizing' my father, but judging from the laughter in the background, he was having as much fun as they were.

I told her I'd be home around five thirty, and did she want to eat out? She thought that would be fun. She'd decide where before I got home.

I did some meaningless paperwork, listened to Ernest Pascoe on the phone telling his superiors how the operation to arrest the forgers was 'all his idea'. It didn't matter. He didn't matter.

An hour or so later, the phone rang. "Inspector McBriar." I said.

"So, how do you cook your steaks to be that tender?" The voice on the phone said.

"Wrap them in aluminum foil, bake them in the oven at low temperature, then sear them. Who wants to know, Josh?"

"Meg said the next time I spoke to you, I had to ask."

"Give her my best. The kids too. So, any news at your end?"

I heard paper rustle. "Bill Fontaine; his wife passed away about five years ago. He got the marina from his father, and he's run it since the end of the war. They had a pair of twin daughters, Abigail and Gail. Not very original, but cute names. Both girls moved away seven or eight years ago. Beyond that, it's all foggy."

This was detailed stuff, I thought. "Was all that in your files, or what?" I asked.

"No, we asked Bobcaygeon City Hall. Bill has been a fixture there forever, so a number of the staff knew him. And before you ask, no, no criminal record, nothing out of the ordinary."

"All right, thanks, Josh. I'll keep you posted on any developments, then."

"Likewise. So, bake in foil and then sear them. Take care, Ian."

He hung up.

Walsh came up to my desk, flipping through some papers.

"Boss, I think we have a problem." He said.

"How so?"

"We pulled a bunch of prints from the gun that we took off Gillian, and from the Mercedes."

Reynolds came in and I waved her over to join us.

"Go on." I said.

Walsh placed the papers in front of me. "This set came from Gillian's gun. That set came from the Mercedes. They're identical."

"Right. Gail gave the gun to Gillian." I said.

"However." He said.

He pulled out a business card, a silver card which read 'The Gardenia Agency'. He gave it to me.

"That's the card Abigail gave to Alex." I said.

"It has the same prints as the gun." He said flatly.

I got up. "Alex, you're with me. Patrick, I'll radio if I need you."

Reynolds followed me out to my Caprice and slid into the right seat. "I don't understand, boss, what is it?"

"Abigail *is* Gail. They're one and the same person." I said.

Reynolds looked out the window, digesting this. "Holy shit. Jeez, boss."

We sped up Keele Street with the gumball on the roof, weaving through traffic.

Reynolds frowned. "But they're identical twins. Wouldn't they have the same fingerprints?"

"Nope. They are 'monozygotic twins'. And almost everything about them is the same except fingerprints. They have different prints, but the gun has the same prints as the card that Abigail gave you. Abigail *IS* Gail."

Reynolds didn't understand. "But there were two girls, twins. Why would she…"

"Remember what they do- they take the identities of dead people. Imagine if Gail died in an accident or something- why waste her identity? She can be either Abby or Gail, as she likes."

"And you got all that from just the prints?"

"Yeah, plus one thing Bill Fontaine said. He said his 'daughter' went back to the city. Not 'daughters', or 'a daughter', but 'daughter'. Singular, not plural."

We stopped at the Abigail's apartment. A black limousine pulled up behind us, and a small man in a charcoal suit got out.

Reynolds walked up to him. "Hi, can I ask you who you are here for?" She asked.

He scowled. "Why? Who are you?"

She pulled out her badge. "Once again? Who?"

He shrugged. "I'm driving Miss Fontaine to the airport."

Reynolds shook her head. "I don't think so. We're taking her in."

He looked over Reynolds' shoulder. Abigail Fontaine walked briskly out, dragging two large suitcases. She slowed down as she saw us, then smiled and came through the front doors.

She smiled. "Detective Reynolds. Hello, did you have more questions for me?"

Reynolds shook her head. "That depends. Are we talking to Abigail or Gail right now?"

Abigail shook her head. "I don't know what you mean."

"Yes, you do. We know." Reynolds said.

She tilted her head to one side, studying us. "Excuse me for a moment."

She opened her purse and handed some money to the limousine driver. "I'm sorry, it appears I won't be needing you."

He drove away. Abigail watched him leave.

"Well, at least can you be a gentleman and take a girl's bags?" She said.

Reynolds gripped Abigail's arm tight, and I loaded her cases into the trunk. We drove back to the station, Reynolds in the back seat with Abigail, neither saying anything.

At the station, Walsh cleared an interview room and sat back with Reynolds as I sat across from Abigail.

"So, do you know where you went wrong?" I asked.

She seemed mildly amused by the question. "Enlighten me."

"You said that Gail was in Ireland, but 'Gail' gave a gun to Gillian Westlock. She couldn't have been there and here at the same time. It's the same gun that killed Robert Sankar. You killed Robert Sankar. Why?"

She fumbled in her purse for a cigarette. She tapped the package, but it was empty. Walsh's hand reached around and offered her one from his gold case.

She picked out a cigarette and smiled at him. "Much appreciated. Thank you." She said.

His hand retreated and came back a moment later with a lighter. She pressed the end of the cigarette against the flame and sucked in smoke, then gave him a wink and a smile.

She exhaled, slowly, and leaned back. "I never meant to hurt Robert, but he said he was looking for Victor. I told him to back off. Victor was already dead, but he might still link him to us. I pointed my gun to scare him, and he tried to take it from me. It went off- it was an accident."

"Suppose I believe that." I said. "Why did you kill Victor?"

She shook her head. "Not me. That was not our doing. We only found out he was in Canada when he ended up in the morgue. I have no idea how he met his end."

I leaned back and rubbed my face. "What about the scrap yard? How did the scrapyard get involved in this affair?"

She laughed. "The scrapyard gave us the idea. They were crushing some old car, and Mick found a gym bag with a passport and some cash in it. I forget why, but he joked that this could be a way to leave the country. The passport photo looked sort of like him, and as a joke he took a trip into the States using that passport. We just went from there."

"You don't advertise in the newspapers though. 'Want to hide from the law? We have forgers ready to help.'"

"No. But someone heard about Mick's stunt. They wanted to get away from alimony and child support, and they paid us well. Terry at the coroner's got the names of the dead, and a contact in the print shop created papers, and the rest as they say, is history."

"You're very forthcoming. You do know what you're admitting to, right?" I said.

She shrugged. "I'll claim multiple personality disease or mental illness. A good lawyer will get me out in no time."

"Possibly, if you can prove that Robert's death was an accident."

She leaned back. "He had information about Victor. He didn't say what, but he did say, 'after all, look where your car's parked'. I had no idea what he meant. I just parked it there because I'd followed him to the meeting place for alcoholics."

"It was parked in spot number seventeen. The same number as the locker where he'd hidden documents at the scrapyard. Why did you leave his body in your car?" I said.

"After I… after he was shot, he got into my car and demanded the keys. I argued with him, for maybe twenty minutes. Then he passed out. I was going to call an ambulance, but people started showing up for those meetings, so I left him there."

"How did you get home?" I asked.

"I took a cab."

I stood up. "Fine. Sergeant Walsh will process you. Good day, Miss Fontaine."

"Aren't you going to ask me about my sister?" She asked.

I sat back down. "Go on."

"Abby was in Mexico. For real, in Mexico. She caught some tropical bug and died the next day."

"Where in Mexico?" Walsh asked.

"Cabo San Lucas."

He nodded. "Nice. We have a place there."

Abigail smiled at that.

"In any case, I brought her ashes back. She's in the vase over my fireplace. On the flight home, I thought about our side business here. Mexico can be cagey about telling foreigners that people died at a resort. I had her name and her passport now, and it was all that I needed to be either sister, one at a time."

"You're not really blind in one eye?" I asked.

"Saying that convinces people that I'm not her, and that I don't drive."

"Clever. Very clever. See you tomorrow." I said.

She looked up at me. "Ian, can I ask you something?" She said.

"Sure."

"Do you like convertibles?"

"Yes, I have a nineteen sixty-eight Fiat Spyder."

"Would you drive my Mercedes until I get out? I feel you'd take good care of it."

"No, but I'll make sure it's kept under cover."

We had a uniform transport her to the Don Jail for holding. It was the end of a long day; I felt drained, and I had almost, but not quite, wrapped everything up.

The only puzzle piece left was Victor. Who had killed French? After all, he had stolen from banks, not people. He hadn't really upset anyone.

Yes, he had. I called Reynolds to meet me where Sankar's body had been found. She arrived just as I did and parked beside me. It was three in the afternoon and the AA meeting had just broken up. Reverend Elijah was sweeping dust out onto the roadway. He stopped, leaned against his broom and waited for me to approach him.

"Hello, Elijah." I said.

"Good afternoon. I guess you're not here for a meeting?"

"No, I'm looking for one of your flock- Greta. Do you know where she works?"

He thought for a moment. "The Greta from the meetings, or Greta from the Calvary Church?"

Reynolds stepped forward. "Are we talking about the same Greta?"

"We are." He said.

"I understand. Greta from the church." I said.

He leaned his broom against the door frame and pointed down the road.

"There's a bank in the mall, across from the Zeller's store. I believe she works there."

We thanked him and drove separately to the bank. Reynolds came in with me.

Inside, the bank was all faux-modern. Plastic tables behind the tellers' wickets, glossy posters advertising savings bonds and fabric plants stuck into foam soil decorated the floor.

We walked to the side, where new accounts were opened, and waved down a middle-aged woman with glasses on a chain around her neck.

I showed her my badge. "Hi. Do you have a lady called Greta working here?" I asked.

She carefully read my ID. "She's in the sorting room. Is she in some sort of trouble?" She asked.

"Not at all." I lied. "But she may have some information about a case we're investigating."

The woman grunted, unconvinced. "Do you want to speak with her in a private consultation room? It might be less disruptive to our customers."

"That would be fine, thanks." I said.

The woman ushered us into a small room, left and returned a minute later with Greta.

I stood politely. Greta shuffled into the room, giving us the 'I'm in trouble' look.

"Hi, Greta. It's nice to see you again. This is Constable Alex Reynolds."

Reynolds stood and shook her hand.

We all sat down. "Now, Greta," I started.

"We just have some questions about your friend, Victor French. Do you have a few minutes?"

She nodded slowly.

"We arrested the person who killed an undercover police officer called Robert Sankar. Robert was looking into Victor French's affairs."

She seemed relieved at that.

"Now, the only thing left for us to do is to find out who killed Victor."

She glanced at Reynolds then back at me. "OK. How can I help you?" She asked.

"Someone stabbed him in the back, then left him on the sidewalk. I bet they thought he'd be found before he died. What do you think?"

She rocked side to side in her seat. "Yeah, maybe. I guess."

"So, the big question is, why did he come back, after he'd gotten away with all that cash?"

She looked up at me, her eyes big, anticipating. "Why?" She asked.

Reynolds looked back and forth between us, watching me work.

"I think he found religion. Or he wanted redemption, or whatever you want to call it. I think he was trying to make things right, to turn himself around." I said.

"Yeah?" Greta said, unconvinced.

"I think part of his redemption involved saying he was sorry for what he did."

She stiffened up. "Why would he do that?"

"He stole most of his money from banks. Institutions, soulless entities. But he stole from you, too. You said so- you said that he took your life savings."

"Yeah, well, I've gotten over it." She mumbled.

"But when he showed up at your apartment, what did you do?"

"It wasn't at my apartment. It was…"

"Gotcha." I said. "When you first met me, you gave me a hug. Whoever stabbed Victor stabbed him in the back, just as if you'd hugged him with a knife in your hand."

She shrank back, and her eyes filled with tears. "Do you have *any idea* how hard this year has been? The nasty comments, the looks, the jokes? Do you understand what it's like to be spat on by your coworkers, every time you walk in? That's how it's been for me. That's how my life has been for the last year."

She pulled a handkerchief out of her sleeve and dabbed her eyes.

She sniffled and glared at Reynolds. "You. I bet the guys are all over you, right? Nobody stands you up on a Saturday night, do they? You've probably got a boyfriend who just adores you."

Reynolds answered slowly. "Actually, my boyfriend is a cop, and right now he's in hospital, recovering from being shot. Don't pretend to know how great my life is- you have no idea."

Greta looked down at her shoes and shook her head again. "He was waiting for me near my apartment. He said he came back to apologize. I told him that I forgave him, and I hoped we could go back to being together, like before. I didn't care that he'd stolen from the bank, I didn't even care that he stole from me. I just wanted him back with me."

She blew her nose and tucked the handkerchief back into her sleeve. "But he said we were over, done. He said he just had to apologize, that he was asking forgiveness from everyone he'd hurt. He wanted to start a new life, even if it meant prison. When I asked about us, he admitted that it had all been a sham. He had only slept with me to get to the money. He didn't want anything more to do with me. He hugged me, and then he said 'I'm sorry, goodbye'."

She started to bawl. The woman who'd let us into the room peered in through the thin glass window to one side of the door. Greta stopped crying and the woman walked away.

"He just said goodbye." I said. "But you had a knife, and you got angry, yes?"

She shook her head. "It was a letter opener. I like to open my mail in the lobby, by the mail slot. He waited for me out on the street, and I let him into the lobby to talk. He hugged me and said goodbye. I don't remember what happened next. He staggered back. I picked him up, and I offered to drive him to the hospital. He was in pain, I could tell. We went a block or so, then he said 'get lost'. He got out of the car at a red light. I tried to call him back, but car behind me started honking. I went around the block, but when I got back to look for him he was gone."

Reynolds wrote this down, carefully entering Greta's statement, word for word. She capped her pen, looked over at me, then blinked very slowly. It was her way of saying 'yes, we've got her'.

I stood up. "Sorry, Greta. You'll have to come with us."

She shook her head. "But why? I told you the truth. I told you everything that happened. Why?"

"You stabbed a man, and he died. You killed him. That's the crux of it." I said.

She folded her arms, petulant, and shook her head. "No. I'm not going. I don't want to go."

Reynolds sighed and stood up. "Greta Moore, I am arresting you on suspicion of the murder of Victor

French. You do not have to say anything, but it may harm your defense if you do not mention, when questioned, something you later rely on in court. Anything you do say may be given in evidence. Do you understand what I have just told you?"

Greta looked at her, not comprehending. "You're arresting me?" She asked.

"We're arresting you, yes." I said.

"You mean, you're taking me to jail?"

"Yes, Greta, you get a one-way trip to the big house." Reynolds said.

We walked her out, holding her arms and sparing her the humiliation of having her co-workers see her in handcuffs. We called a cruiser to take her down to holding, then stood on the sidewalk and watched as she was driven downtown. For a brief moment, I saw her look sadly at us through the back window; I felt pity for her, but she had killed Victor French and there was no way I could forgive her for doing that.

The feeling passed. I went home.

Chapter Seventeen

I parked in the driveway and walked into the house. I expected to hear people talking, children laughing, something, but I heard nothing. That was odd.

There was a shadow- someone moving in the kitchen- and I went toward the movement. In the kitchen, my father was hunched over the stove; Karen was beside him, her hand on his shoulder, and Charlotte was sitting on the counter. All three were looking intently at something on the stove.

I wandered up to them, curious. "Hey, guys. What are you making?" I asked.

Karen turned to look at me and grinned. "Hey, hon. Your dad's making chili for dinner."

"Gosh, dad, you don't have to." I said. "I was going to cook tonight."

"Yeah, I know." He answered. "I was feeling restless. I figure I should be doing something."

Karen stroked my arm. "How is everything?" she asked.

"Good. Brian should be out of the hospital any time now. We arrested everyone, and the OPP thanked us for the help. It's a done deal."

She smiled. "That's good. By the way, what's in the cardboard box?"

She pointed up at the package Barry Kirby had left me.

"Honestly, I have no idea, hon. Frank's boss gave it to me. He said it was important, but to not look at it until I'd closed this case."

"Is the case closed?" She asked.

"Yeah, I guess. Let's eat."

We called Ethan for dinner; he thundered down and plopped himself onto his seat at the table. Charlotte was very proud of the fact that 'she made the food' and that everyone should tell her how good it was.

We cut thick slices of bread for the chili, milk for the kids in case it was too spicy. Later, Karen scooped ice cream into bowls, the adults had coffee with dessert, and soon everyone was tired and groggy.

By eight-thirty Charlotte was asleep and Ethan was playing with his trains. My father told Karen stories about me growing up. She had always suspected that I was not a perfectly behaved child, and now she had proof.

After we had caught up, laughed and reminisced, there was a long silence in the room.

My father turned to look at me. "So, what were you doing last week? Karen said you were working undercover."

I coughed. "Yes, I was 'Ian Brewster'."

He laughed. "I'd forgotten about that name. He'll tell you about it later, Karen. Go on."

"Sure." I continued. "We broke up a forgery ring. They were helping people sneak out of the country. using the names of recently dead. Very clever, very smart."

"But you figured it out. You caught them." He said.

"Yeah. Case closed. All we have to do now is wrap it up." I said.

I looked up at the box on the shelf. Part of me wanted to rip it open now. Part of me wanted to throw it away. I decided to wait till morning. I'd figure out then what to do.

"Hey, pops, do you want to come boating with us at the cottage this weekend?" I asked.

He nodded, but his eyes closed for a moment as he did. He was tired, too.

"C'mon, dad, it's been a long day for you. Bedtime."

Karen stood up and rubbed her stomach. "Yes, me too. Besides, I'm sleeping for two."

My father chuckled. "Well said, dear. Let's all get some sleep."

At five in the morning, rain poured down, one of those drenching summer thunderstorms that washes the city clean. A flash of lightning, followed a moment later by the sound of thunder, made me jump. I got up and checked on the kids. Ethan was fast asleep, oblivious to the noise. His window was only open a crack, but a trickle of water had pooled on the windowsill. I slid the window closed and checked on Charlotte. She was snoring happily. I went back to bed.

I slid quietly under the sheets, trying to not disturb Karen.

"Everyone OK?" She whispered.

"Yes. Go back to sleep."

She rolled over and threw an arm over me. "Not sleepy anymore." She said, groggily.

"No? Do you want to get up?" I asked.

There was a pause. "Yes. Up. Not, not sleepy."

She fell back to sleep.

At seven, I was already dressed. Today I would wrap up the case; today I had to tell Greta that she was going to spend years in jail, and I wanted to get as much out of Abigail/Gail as I could. There was a good chance that she wouldn't tell me much, but if I could offer her a chance to get out sooner, maybe she'd talk.

I slurped my coffee, my head tilted back, and my eyes went to the package on the shelf. It would wait. Whatever it was, it would wait. I wanted to put out one fire at a time.

My father came through shortly after that, rummaged through the cupboards and pulled out pancake fixings.

"What are you making, pops?" I asked.

"Pancakes. Karen and the kids loved 'em back home. I figure they'll enjoy them today."

He mixed the batter, let it sit for fifteen minutes to rise, then expertly poured smooth liquid onto a frypan and watched. Exactly three minutes later, he flipped the pancake with a jerk of his wrist and let the cooked side turn face up.

"Want some?" He asked.

"Never say no to pancakes." I grinned.

I pulled out cutlery and plates, set the table for five, and watched him work. For as long as I could remember, six days a week, he had worked in the diner, at the hotel, and around the house. He had mended fences, unclogged drains, replaced carpets and ordered staff, all with a calm air and a soft voice.

"Dad, I have a question." I asked.

He flipped a pancake and slid it into the oven to keep warm. "Shoot."

"How do you do it? You always seem calm; I've only seen you angry maybe two or three times. You must have had people rub you the wrong way, but it doesn't bother you. How do you do it?"

He placed an empty frypan on a cold element and turned to face me.

"Always figured this moment would come. Never quite knew when." He started.

He wiped his hands on a towel and sat down. "Do you know what I did in the war?"

"You taught unarmed combat."

"Where do you think I learned it?" He asked.

Why had that never occurred to me? Had I blocked that out of my mind?

"I don't know. Where did you learn it?"

He pointed at the front door. "Your friend Frank was a Green Beret. He went to Vietnam. I was in the Royal Canadian regiment in the big war, and we took the beach at Dieppe."

He stared at his shoes. "August nineteenth, nineteen forty-two. Never forget that day. We were supposed to make landfall in the dark of night, but the military screwed up. We got there at dawn, and the Jerries were ready for us. Some of us had trained with the Royal Marines- the British Commandos. I was one of the lucky ones- they put me through the grinder, toughened me up, made me into a weapon. I always thought that they were just being rough on us because we were Colonials, but now I realize it saved my life. Without the training, I would not have survived. Simple as that. After that I taught combat in Korea. I couldn't bring myself to kill more soldiers, but I could help other soldiers survive in war."

We were both silent. The clock in the hallway ticked loudly. "Did mom know?" I asked.

He chuckled. "She knew everything. You were too small to remember the nightmares and the cold sweats. She was strong enough for both of us. She kept us together."

"I remember when you came back from Korea. You brought us back a flag, on white silk."

He nodded. "That was a present from my CO. He thought I'd like a reminder of my time there. All I wanted to do was to get home, see you, your mother, James. Just get home."

A small sound behind me made us both look. Ethan padded into the kitchen, rubbing his eyes.

"Hi. I smell pancakes." He said groggily.

My father placed his hands on his knees and knelt to face him. "Yes. Are you hungry?"

Fifteen minutes later, Karen and Charlotte were downstairs, eating silently.

The rain had stopped; in the warm morning the street was almost dry. A little after eight I looked at my watch, said goodbye to everyone, kissed Karen and went to work.

The radio chatter was light this morning, nothing of importance to worry me. I parked in my spot at the station, walked past the duty sergeant and set case folders on my desk.

The secretary placed my usual coffee on my desk; I nodded thanks and flipped through telephone message slips.

To my surprise, the light was on in Ernest Pascoe's office. A form moved back and forth behind the frosted glass, its voice getting louder and softer with the movement as the shape moved past the open door. A minute later, the voice said 'yes, thank you, see you shortly'.

Ernest Pascoe stepped out of his office, looked around and smiled at me.

He walked up to my desk, slid a plastic chair beside me and sat.

"Good morning, Inspector." He almost sang it.

"Morning. Having a good day, are we?"

He rested his elbow on my desk and leaned forward, conspiratorially. "Guess who that was on the phone?"

"I'm guessing not your mother in law?"

He laughed out loud, a gold molar glinting in the light. "No, that was the chief. Harold Adamson himself. I've been offered a spot at the big table."

I pretended to not understand. "He's buying you lunch?"

Pascoe frowned. "He's offered me a position as Deputy Chief, based on my work here. It's a great recognition of my accomplishments, don't you think?"

I answered as diplomatically as I could. "I'm sure you deserve whatever they give you."

"Absolutely. As soon as we get a replacement here, I'm going downtown."

I had to bite my tongue to not say something too obnoxious.

"Well, I always knew that downtown is where you belong." I said.

He stood up. "Thanks, Ian. I really appreciate the sentiment."

He walked back to his office, humming to himself.

Walsh showed up shortly after that. I'd phoned everyone that I needed to call, and the other teams were working their case loads. I had very little to do this morning.

Walsh sat in the plastic chair P. "Morning, boss." He said.

"Hey, Patrick. So, where are we with the case?"

"The kid from the print shop has given us a bunch of names, photocopies of passports and documents, and in exchange we're giving him a reduced charge.

"Gillian has plead guilty to aggravated assault, forgery and fraud, and Abigail has her lawyer doing the talking."

"So she *is* Abigail, and not Gail?" I asked.

"Yep. The Mexican government came back with the information for us; Gail died of an infection, a day after being admitted to hospital in Cabo San Lucas. Abigail wasn't lying."

"Good, Patrick. Do you want to process the Lindsay gang? I'd like to check in on Brian."

"Sure. He's almost ready to go home. Alex brought him a change of clothes today. She's been in his room since last night. She could probably use a break."

"Fine. You write up the paperwork on this, Patrick. I'm going to visit Brian."

It took me about fifteen minutes to drive to the hospital. There was no rush, so it was a luxury to be able to drive sedately for a change.

The elevator door opened and a nurse at the desk recognized me. Outside Webb's room a large uniform was arguing about football with an equally large orderly. The uniform also recognized me and stepped aside.

I turned the corner into the room. Webb was sitting up, holding Reynolds' hand. They were smiling, and something he said made her laugh and cover her face with her other hand.

She put her fist up to her mouth and giggled. She did a quick double-take when she saw me, then relaxed and smiled again.

"Good morning boss. Beautiful day, isn't it?"

"Certainly is, Alex. Brian, I'm told that you're going to survive?"

He nodded. "That's the rumour, yes. I'm just waiting for the doctors to clear me so I can go home and sleep in my own bed."

The uniform in the hallway was still talking to the orderly. "I could get them to bring you something from the cafeteria, if you like?" I offered.

He shook his head. "Thanks, but Sergeant Walsh sent over stuff from one of the hotels. They brought eggs, sausages, bacon, you name it, enough to feed a battalion. I think the nursing staff will be sad to see me go."

"That sounds like Patrick, yeah. Anything you'd like me to get you before I leave?"

"How are we doing on the case? Everyone locked up?" He asked.

"Yep. Them that are talking are talking, the rest have lawyered up. Patrick's on it."

"Sorry I messed up, boss." He said, quietly.

"We all make mistakes, Brian. Ask Patrick about the time I was beaten up in my own house."

His eyes widened. "Sir?"

"A story for another day, a rainy night. Rest up. Go home. We'll talk later in the week." I said.

I drove home. There was nothing more for me to do at the station and the thought of being around

Pascoe as he cooed and preened did not appeal at all.

I parked and walked toward the front door. I expected to hear laughter, talking, something. As I got closer, even through the closed front door, I heard raised voices, yelling. I walked faster, opened the door and bellowed "Hello!"

The voices stopped. I went toward the kitchen. Karen and my father were facing each other, staring. Between them, on the kitchen table, was the package from Barry Kirby.

It had been torn open, and I could see part of the contents poking out.

I stepped between Karen and my father. "What's going on? Why the yelling?" I asked.

He poked my chest. "Is this your doing? Is this why you wanted me to come here?"

"Pops, I have no idea what you're talking about." I said.

He pushed at the package, sliding it away. "This. I can't blame Karen, but how could you, son?"

"You're not making any sense, dad."

He wagged a finger at the package. "This is why you wanted me to come to Toronto, isn't it? So you could show me this?"

"Dad, I didn't know you were coming until I saw you walk off the plane. What on earth are we talking about?"

He lunged forward and tore the wrapping off the package. Inside was a printed brochure and a textbook. I had no idea what they meant to him.

"These. Where did you get these?" He barked.

I had never seen him so irate. He was snorting with anger.

"Dad, this package was given to me, to be opened after I finished with this case. I had no idea what was in it, nor did the man who gave it to me."

He rubbed his face and took a deep breath. "Karen, hon, I owe you an apology. I should not have shown you anger. Obviously, you couldn't have known. I'm sorry."

I picked up the textbook. In block letters was the title 'Modern Typography'. It meant nothing to me.

The printed brochure was a prospectus for a company exploring in Saskatchewan. It also meant nothing to me.

"Dad, what was it that set you off?"

He shook his head. "You wouldn't know. No, of course not. You were in Toronto, in school."

"I have no idea what you're talking about, dad."

He waved at the book and brochure. "These were in your mother's bag when she died."

Chapter Eighteen

Karen sat across from my father at the kitchen table. He gripped a mug of coffee, stared at a spot on the table and spoke slowly. Most of what he said I knew, but most of it Karen didn't know.

"It was June thirtieth, nineteen sixty-eight." He started.

"Your mother, bless her heart, had gone to Yorkton. She said there was something important she wanted to check. She didn't say what. About seven that night, she called home and said she'd be a while. She needed to talk to someone in town and then she'd be home later."

"Do you know who she spoke to?" I asked.

He shook his head. "Someone on her side of the family is all I remember. She had an aunt in Yorkton, but after… your mom passed, I forgot what she was there for."

"That would be my great aunt Ruth, I guess." I said.

"I suppose so. Ruth passed a few years back. She was your grandfather's age."

He straightened up and looked at Karen. "So, Miriam, Ian's mom, gets home late, maybe ten at night. Still some light in the sky, you know, that time of year. Magpie Harris comes out of nowhere and kills her. Runs her over and keeps on going. Damn ignorant drunk."

Karen frowned. "Magpie?"

I nodded. "His name was Gavin Harris. He was an odd-job man, welder, handyman. He lived in a wreck of an old house, with fridges and bicycles and car parts all over the front yard. That's why we called him 'Magpie'."

Karen smiled slightly. "A junk man, like a scrap collector?"

"Right. Anything shiny or usable, he'd pick it out of the trash and take it home. Like a magpie."

My father shook his head. "And to think, I sold him that same truck."

"You couldn't have known, pops. Look, mom always said everything happens for a reason. If not for that, I wouldn't have met Karen. I'd be a priest in Utah or something, running a soup kitchen. Charlotte wouldn't be here. You wouldn't have married Pam. Life would be different for all of us. I'm not saying mom's death was a good thing. I'm saying that what happened, happened, and selling him that truck didn't cause him to get drunk and drive past our place."

He shrugged. "Time to move on, I suppose. Despite everything, though, you know it still hurts."

I put my hand over his. "I know, pops, it hurts me, too."

Karen looked at me. "What about Magpie? What happened to him?"

My father sat back. "He served time, then about a year after he got out he died in a house fire. They say he was smoking around a welding torch or something."

I tapped the book. "That still doesn't explain why this was left for me. What does it mean?"

He shook his head. "Not a clue, son. You're the detective."

I opened out the brochure. It stated that the 'RMR Development Company' was looking for investors. They had found kimberlite deposits, and they wanted capital to expand.

It stated owning long-term leases on its holdings in Northern Saskatchewan, and that the 'potential for return was astounding'. Their words.

This intrigued me. Beyond that, the case was now wrapped up, and I had free time. I wanted to talk to Barry Kirby.

The sun's white light scorched the concrete outside Barry Kirby's building. The glass box, two dozen stories tall, seemed to float in the air today. I resisted the urge to sprint up the steps; even that short exertion would make me sweat, and I didn't want to look eager or anxious.

I approached the wide reception desk in the lobby, the desk with three women directing visitors. Immediately, it felt cool, soothing, almost too cool, but that much I knew was only compared to outside.

The woman at the middle seat glanced up and smiled. "Inspector. Right on time." She said.

"Am I?" I asked.

She handed me a manila folder. "Yes, they're expecting you."

I pointed the folder at the bank of elevators. "Fifteenth floor?"

She nodded. "Fifteenth floor. Go on up."

I got into the elevator, waited till the door closed, then opened the manila folder.

It was a dossier on me. My name, where I lived, where I worked. It had details about my family members, my coworkers, Frank Burghezian, Walsh and Reynolds. Nothing about Webb. Apparently, it was updated some time before last week.

The elevator door opened, and I took the folder with me down the hall. Kirby's driver, the tall Marine, stepped out of nowhere and opened a door. He looked sheepish, still embarrassed at being found in my house.

"This way please, sir." He said.

I walked in and found myself in a room with Barry Kirby, Frank Burghezian, and two older men whom I'd never seen before. These were the bigwigs, I decided.

There was a chair in the middle of the floor, a low plastic chair, and the four men were seated behind a long wooden table. It reminded me of a judge's bench, or one of those scenes from the Spanish Inquisition.

Frank looked distinctly uncomfortable. He wriggled in his chair and played with a pencil as he looked at the other men.

Barry Kirby scribbled something on a steno pad, glancing up at me and the other men every so often. This was a standard action for someone who wanted to look involved without getting involved.

One of the older men smiled at me and waved at the plastic chair.

"Welcome, Ian. Please sit down." He said.

His voice was deep, fatherly, with a hint of fatigue. He waited for me to sit.

I looked around, saw a larger, more comfortable chair, and dragged it out to the floor. I sat in this one instead.

He seemed mildly irritated. "Was there something wrong with the other chair?" He asked.

"Yes. I'm not eleven years old."

Frank chuckled and rubbed his nose. Barry Kirby raised one eyebrow and wrote something down. The older man looked around, knitted his fingers together in front of him and leaned forward. "You have been offered a rather special position here, young man." He started.

"Which I have not yet decided to accept." I answered.

He leaned back, surprised. "Are you saying you don't want to work for us?"

"I'm saying I can get along just fine without this job, if it comes to that."

The other older man spoke. His voice was like a TV evangelist, smooth and warm, but with a touch of edge to it. "Would you be happy working in fifty-two division for the rest of your life?"

"I'd be happy sweeping floors, if that's what I wanted to do."

He nodded, considering the response. "Do you know why we've asked you to join our organization? Do you know how you came to our attention?"

I looked at their faces, scanning them for information, then I pointed to each man as I spoke.

"Frank put my name forward. Barry interviewed me. After that he did some deeper digging and left me a puzzle to solve. You two must know all that."

The second man nodded. "Did Frank tell you this, or Barry?"

"Neither. I got it from looking at your faces."

He smiled. "That, young man, is why we are talking to you."

There was a long, deep silence in the room. I knew they were waiting for me to say something, possibly to ask about the offer, or at least gratitude for being considered.

"So, have you been sitting here all morning, waiting for me to show up, or what?" I asked.

The two older men glanced at each other. "We can convene on very short order." One said.

"In other words, you were hoping I'd show up here today."

The other one slowly smiled, folded his arms in front of him and leaned on his elbows.

"You're a very perceptive young man, Mister McBriar."

"Again, that's why you want to hire me."

I waited for a few seconds. "So, does any of you know the importance of the package I was given a week ago?"

The second older man shook his head. "Just to be clear; we have a research team, and they assembled the contents as noted in a police report. Now, they may mean nothing, or they may mean something only to you. We have been told nothing, only that these items are a duplicate of what you might want to see."

"A duplicate, not the originals?" I asked.

"Exactly. We've given you the clay, you make the vase."

I stood up. "Will there be anything else?"

The two older men looked at each other. "Don't you have any more questions for us?" One said.

"Not right now. Good afternoon."

I turned and left. There was soft murmuring behind me, and I guessed that most people in this position didn't leave quite so quickly. I didn't care. In any case, it didn't matter. I went home.

I sat at the desk in my den, reading through the textbook page by page, trying to figure out what it meant. I looked at the cover, the names of the authors, the name of the publisher. It was printed in Chicago in nineteen sixty-seven, and from the boring content, it could only be a trade book for typesetters or something of the sort, people who produced posters and billboards.

My mother had worked in the Yorkton Public Library as a student, on summer breaks from University in Regina. That would explain why she had a library book in her purse when she… when it happened. What the book meant, however, was unclear.

I looked at the prospectus; it was simple, concise, a page dated nineteen sixty-three offering investors a chance to participate in a kimberlite mine in Saskatchewan. It said that the company had secured leases on land known to be rich in the ore, and the potential profits could be huge.

Typical hyperbole, I thought. A shadow behind me made me look around. Karen placed her hand on my shoulder. "Hey, you. You've been here for hours. Find anything?" She asked.

I shook my head. "Something's not right. I don't know why this was given to me. There has to be something here, but what?"

She read over my shoulder. "What exactly is kimberlite?"

"It's an ore that sometimes contains diamonds. There have been some diamonds found in Saskatchewan, but not in large numbers, or high quality. Certainly not worth mining for them."

"Maybe they're trying to attract investors, take the money and run?" She offered.

"You've seen this before?"

"More often than you'd think. It's a classic. We called it a 'pump and dump'. You get investors in at a fever pitch, everyone buys on emotion, then you take the cash and the venture crashes. Everyone loses, except the stock promoters."

I picked up the brochure and flipped it over. "So, why was my mother looking at this? I can't believe she'd invest in something like this."

"She wasn't a gambler, then?"

"She wouldn't throw away old light bulbs until we'd tried them in at least three lamps, just in case they worked in a different socket." I said.

Karen kissed my cheek. "My kind of woman. Come, dinner's ready."

My father had made meat loaf, and as usual had gone all the way; he had made mashed potatoes, pan gravy and a side of grilled vegetables.

Karen sat the children down at their spots, then looked at the spread of food.

"You ate like this growing up?" She muttered. "No wonder you're so tall."

Ethan ate heartily, quickly. Charlotte asked a lot of questions about the food but ended up eating everything on her plate as well.

After dinner, the kids ran to the living room to watch TV. I made coffee, and we adults sat around the kitchen table, talking.

My father sighed. "Listen, Karen, I really want to say how sorry I am for getting angry at you before. I had no right, and you didn't know, you couldn't have known…"

She patted his hand. "Don't worry. But if it makes you feel any better, if this is a boy, I'll name it after my father, not you."

He feigned indignation. "Now, just wait a minute here. You don't want me to go home with a heavy heart now, do you?"

I chuckled at the banter. "We haven't thought of names yet, dad. We're still just at the point of hoping it all goes well."

Karen smiled. "How was Ian's mom when she was expecting him? Was she nervous, or what?"

He chuckled. "She was mad for broccoli. Couldn't get enough. With James, it was tomatoes. She would pick them from the vine and eat them up, in big mouthfuls. Darnedest thing. Still, they both grew up big and healthy, so I can't complain."

"What about his grandparents? I don't think Ian has spoken much about them." Karen said.

He took a sip of coffee. "My folks were from Dundee, Scotland. They came over before the first world war, because Ian's great-uncle had a dry goods store in Brandon, Manitoba. They went further west and settled in Yorkton. I decided to stay in the area, so I bought the place in Esterhazy, where Ian was born. My folks lived in Yorkton the rest of their lives."

"They never wanted to go back to Scotland?" Karen asked.

"Never. Didn't regret moving for a moment. Loved Yorkton."

She glanced at me. "What about his mom's side of the family?"

He took another sip of coffee. "Ian's grandfather Abraham Starblanket was a full Cree, from a reservation in Northern Saskatchewan. His grandmother was Claudette Delonge, a French girl from Edmonton. They met in Prince Albert right after Abraham got back from the war, in 'nineteen. Her family was furious that she married a red man, but truth is he was the most decent, thoughtful man I've ever met."

"And then they had Miriam?" Karen prompted.

He looked down at the table. He fidgeted for a while, collecting his thoughts. "She was beautiful. Tall, lovely, smart, fierce. There wasn't a man in town thought I deserved her, nor anyone thought the less of her for being Metis. She could charm the bark off a tree, she could."

I snickered. It brought back memories to hear him say that.

"Anyway, Miriam had an older brother, Isaac. He moved to Montana, worked in construction there, then he bought the company, expanded, and built himself a real nice place in Missoula. He's a good man, too, just like Abraham."

I chuckled. "I remember going hunting with them. We got a deer once, and Uncle Isaac slings this thing over his shoulders. It must have weighed two hundred pounds, but he walked a quarter mile back to the truck with this dead thing on his shoulders, singing the whole way."

"Yep, that's Isaac, all right." My father said.

He frowned. "Can I see that paper again, son?"

"What paper?" I asked.

"The thing you got in that package. Can I see it?"

I went to my den, brought back the prospectus, and handed it to him. He read it carefully.

"This makes no sense." He said.

"What doesn't, pops?"

He pointed to a small map on the page. "Says here that they're digging for ore near Smeaton."

Karen tilted her head to look at the page. "What's so special about Smeaton?"

My father looked at the map again. "Smeaton, Saskatchewan is on the edge of Abraham's reservation. After he married Claudette, he bought some land around Smeaton. That's where you went hunting with him and Isaac."

This much was not new to me. He pointed to a spot on the map.

"This shows where they're digging for ore. Sure looks like Abraham's land."

I shook my head. "That's crazy. *'Nimosom'* would never sell that land. He left it to us."

"'Nimosom'?" Karen asked.

"Cree for 'grandfather'. Anyway, pops, he loved that land. There's no way he would sell it. He'd have said something, anyway. I never heard anything from him."

He shook his head. "No, I agree, son. Maybe it's just a bad map, that's all. Could be, that's all, just a bad map."

Something didn't add up. Why would Kirby have given me the book and prospectus? Even if he didn't know what it meant, surely the other people thought there was something I should look at.

We washed up, then my father started rubbing his eyes and said goodnight. Karen rubbed her stomach, yawned, and said she was going to bed too. I wasn't sleepy.

I sat in the den, looking at the prospectus again, then the textbook. There had to be something about them, something that tied them together, but what? I stared at the paper for hours, waiting for something to pop out at me. It was after midnight, and the words started floating off the page. Clearly, I was exhausted. Time for bed.

It is a cool autumn day. My grandfather and I have driven for five hours in my uncle's truck, up to his land near Smeaton. I am fourteen years old, and it's my first time to go hunting with them.

Last time they went up there, they came back with two deer, and we filled the freezer with venison. There were three kills, my grandfather explained, but they'd given one to a family nearby, because they needed the meat.

I woke up. They needed the meat. Of course. What was their name? I should remember. I fell back to sleep.

At seven the next morning, I was dressed and making coffee. My father got up shortly after and made himself breakfast, despite my protestations that I'd do it.

We sat at the kitchen table, talking about the old days, mostly, then I remembered my dream.

"Pops, do you remember the name of the family that lived beside Nimosom's land?"

"Sure. Giesbrecht. Oliver and Sharon Giesbrecht. We met them once."

"Right. They had a farm across from where we hunted. I couldn't remember their name." I said.

At nine thirty, I was at my desk at the police station. My mind was still on the prospectus, the textbook, what on earth they meant. Ernest Pascoe was out; he had gone downtown to accept the credit for the work my people had done. It didn't matter to me. There would always be an Ernest Pascoe somewhere, and someone would always have to deal with him.

I picked up the phone and called directory assistance for Saskatchewan. The woman on the line said that there was a phone number for O. Giesbrecht in Smeaton. She could connect me right away.

The phone rang twice, then a man's voice came on. It was older, tired sounding, but still strong.

"Hello?" He said.

"Mister Giesbrecht? I'm not sure if you remember me. I'm Ian McBriar. Abraham Starblanket's grandson."

There was a slight pause. "Yeah, sure. Ian. You were the skinny little kid that came hunting with Abe a couple of times."

"Right. That's me."

"So, what are you doing now? Are you still in Esterhazy?"

"No. I'm a police officer in Toronto. Do you mind if I ask you a couple of quick questions?"

"Please. Abe was a good man. We felt bad when he passed, but he was quite old, was he not?"

His slight German accent got thicker as he spoke. The Mennonite communities in that part of the province had deep roots, and many of the children spoke no English before they went to school.

"Yes, he was almost ninety. He had a good life, though. I wanted to ask you; do you know anything about a mining company digging near his land?"

There was a long pause. I thought we'd been disconnected. "You didn't know, then?"

"I'm sorry. Know what?"

"They came digging for something on his land, about ten year ago, I think. I asked the people who set up the equipment, and they said the old owner sold it."

"Who exactly are they?" I asked. "I don't believe he'd ever sell that land."

"I didn't think so, but they said they had a right to be there. It's a shame, because I know how much he loved the place."

I grabbed a pen. "Who are they? Do you see their company name anywhere?" I asked.

"No. they left about eight year ago. Took off in the night like gypsies. Something fishy going on, I think."

"I agree. Listen, thanks, mister Giesbrecht. I appreciate you taking the time to talk."

He sighed. "Do you remember the winter of fifty-nine?"

"No, not particularly. Why?"

"We lost most of our crop that year. Terrible rains, then locusts. Abe came out here, hunting deer on his land. He stopped by for coffee. He always liked to stop by for coffee. And he saw we were in a bad way. Anyway, he took four deer that trip, and gave us three. I swear, it hadn't been for him, we might've gone hungry. I'll never forget the generosity he showed us."

I chuckled. "Yeah, that sounds like him, all right."

"Listen, Ian, if I do hear anything, where I can get a hold of you?"

"I'm at the fifty-two division of the Toronto Police Department." I said.

I gave him my direct number. He seemed impressed by my title and repeated the number.

I sat at my desk, trying to think of what to do next. Something was definitely wrong here.

Walsh came in and sat across from me. "Problem, boss?"

"Yeah, family stuff. It looks like my grandfather sold off his hunting land. It just doesn't seem like something he'd do, though. And whoever got it was digging for kimberlite, by the looks of it. It just seems wrong, Patrick."

"You want me to do some digging for you on this, boss?" He asked.

"How?"

"I'll ask my dad's people to check on it. We should have an answer by tomorrow. Who are we looking for?"

I pulled the prospectus out of my pocket and he read it over.

"Sounds like a typical 'pump and dump' to me." He said.

"That's what Karen said, too. Why would they do this around my grandfather's land, though?"

He looked at the map. "Not much else around there, I guess. They could pretend to be doing stuff there for months without anybody coming to check on them."

"How do you mean?"

He leaned back and made a box in the air with his hands. "You want people to invest in a pie-in-the-sky scheme. You wouldn't tell them it's happening down the street- people would wander over and look for themselves. But if you tell them it's going on in Timbuktu, or Morocco…"

"Or Smeaton, Saskatchewan." I added.

"Right. Who's going to go check a project way out there?"

He wrote down the details from the prospectus and walked away. My phone rang.

"Inspector McBriar." I said.

"Hey, it's Alex." The voice said.

Reynolds sounded very cheery. "Hi, Alex, what's up?"

"Brian's home. We're just making him comfortable, then I'm going to come in and finish up the files on our Lindsay people."

"No, I've got it, Alex. You take care of Brian, I'll do the paperwork."

She sighed. "You sure, boss? I don't mind. I can do it."

"You just take care of my new detective. Make sure he doesn't make the same mistakes twice. I've got it from here. See you in the morning."

"Thanks loads, boss. See you tomorrow."

I spent the afternoon finishing up the paperwork for our case. The suspects had all agreed to plead guilty in exchange for leniency, according to the prosecutor, except for Abigail, who was going to fight us to the end. No problem; she had no chance.

There was no sign of Terry Westlock, the morgue employee who was giving out the names of dead people. I felt sure he'd turn up sooner or later. In any case, he hadn't done anything violent, so I wasn't concerned about him.

Just before five, Walsh came back to my desk. "Boss, one thing troubles me." He said.

"Yup?"

"When you opened the locker at the scrapyard, there was a passport and airline ticket for Ireland. Why? Why did Victor French have a ticket back to Ireland?"

"I wondered that myself, Patrick. Put yourself in his shoes. You've cheated a bunch of people, pissed some off, and now you want to make amends. So you walk around saying 'sorry' to the folks you've wronged."

"Yeah, I get that." He said.

"Then what? Do you get a job at the shoe store and live out your life in a basement apartment? I don't think so. I think that, if he really did want to atone for his sins, he was going to do something dramatic, completely different."

"Like what?"

"Become a monk? Join the navy? I don't know. Whatever it was, I figure he was using the last of the money to get back to Ireland and disappear for good. He had his real passport, so he wasn't trying to avoid people. He was saying 'that was me, this is me now'. I think, anyway."

Walsh shook his head. "I believe you, boss. By the way, I have an answer for you about that deal in Saskatchewan."

"Already?" I asked.

He slid a sheet of paper toward me. "RMR Development Company was set up in nineteen sixty-seven. They collected a lot of investment money, and dug for diamonds in Northern Saskatchewan for eighteen months, then they fell off the face of the earth. Disappeared."

"Sixty-seven? Sixty-seven." I said.

"Why is that significant?"

"Because they were digging on my grandfather's land. He died in sixty-six."

"Maybe he sold the land before he died?"

I shook my head. "No way. He always told us he wanted it to stay in the family. Besides, the prospectus is dated nineteen sixty-three. Why would they put out a prospectus showing his land, if they hadn't bought the land yet? It makes no sense."

"Sometimes, the prospectus comes out and doesn't tell the whole story. Maybe they were hoping he'd sell them the land?"

"I still say no, Patrick. Who the hell is RMR, anyway?"

"Ah. That took a little more digging. They are owned by Reston and Merton Rhyme, of Yorkton, Saskatchewan."

That made me sit up. "Them? Those miserable assholes are in this?" I snapped.

"Something tells me you're not feeling warm and fuzzy towards them, boss."

"Shit, no. those… those inbred little knuckle draggers were a pain for as long as I can remember. Them and their trailer-trash midget of a mother."

"Come again?" He asked.

"James had a running gag. Her name is spelled 'L-A-N-I-C-E', like 'Janice' but it's pronounced 'LanEESE'. He would always say it wrong, then she'd always correct him and call him a 'stupid Indian'. He never tired of doing it, and she never caught on."

"So, why would they have bought your grandfather's land?"

I shook my head. "He died in a nursing home in Yorkton. He'd been ill for a while, and finally age and life caught up with him. Lanice was working as a nurse's aid in the home. I wonder if she had him sign something when he wasn't coherent, or if she just forged his name. Knowing that rabble, I wouldn't put it past the miserable little dwarf."

"Even so, there's no way of proving it, boss. It's too long ago, there's no way to tell they were lying."

"Maybe, Patrick. Still, if that information was in the prospectus, what's with the textbook?"

The afternoon sun, in the southwest now, shone through the front windows and onto the floor of the detectives' room, reflecting up onto the ceiling, warming every corner of the office. I decided to call it a day and went home.

My father had made hamburgers for dinner, with home-cut fries and apple pie for dessert. The children were getting used to him being around, and Karen appreciated not having to cook.

He was happy to be around his grandchildren, and after the usual hectic days in the restaurant, this was as close to lying around doing nothing as he could do.

After we ate, the children drifted to the television, and Karen left to visit Helen Burghezian for an hour or so. I watched her car leave, the sound of the engine fading as she rolled up the hill, then we were alone. My father's body language told me he was waiting for me to speak.

He helped me wash the dishes and he sat at the kitchen table, waiting. I sat across from him.

"So, what do you want to ask me, son?" He said.

"I'm puzzled about the package that Karen opened." I started.

He put his hand up. "Not her fault, son. I saw it on the shelf. I thought it was tea or coffee. I opened it. Blame me."

"I'm not blaming anyone, pops. I was going to open it anyway, now that the case is wrapped up. I hadn't decided when, but it's a moot point. I just need to get to the bottom of this, that's all."

He sniffed, thinking back. "So, you were in Seminary School when it happened. Your mom said she'd be home late, and I thought nothing of it. 'Bout ten that night, we heard a truck race by the house. I heard her scream."

He looked at the floor. "All them years in war, all my times seeing men die, I never heard nothing sound so bad, or rip my heart out so hard, as that sound."

"I never would have thought that of Magpie, pops. He never drank much, as I remember him."

He shook his head. "Nope. I went to the inquest. He said he figures he must'a done it, but he don't remember doin' it, just remembers waking up in his truck."

I was thinking like a detective now. "Did he ever say why he got so drunk that night?"

"Yep. He said he didn't plan on it, but them Rhyme boys was buying him rounds of scotch."

That surprised me. "The Rhyme boys? Merton and Reston Rhyme?" I asked.

He looked up, puzzled. "Yeah. Why?"

"They are the ones behind the prospectus, the map with grandpa Abraham's land in it."

He sat back, digesting this. "You think they got him drunk on purpose? And then he drove home and killed your mom? Why would they do that to him?"

"That's the question. If that's what happened, then indeed why *would* he do that? But if that is the case, do you realize what this means? They certainly got him drunk on purpose."

Chapter Nineteen

I looked over the prospectus again. Every line, every word, every space between the words, every comma. I found nothing.

It was almost eleven, and everyone else was in bed. I read through the textbook again; 'Modern Typography' was hardly a page-turner.

I learned that 'Universal' was a nineteen-twenties Bauhaus design, 'Helvetica'- from the Latin name for Switzerland- was a 'neo-grotesque font' designed in nineteen fifty-seven, and that a serif was the little crossbar at the end of a letter.

Nothing there that would make for sparkling conversation at a dinner party, unfortunately.

I gave up and went to bed. In the morning, I'd look at it with fresh eyes. For now, I just needed to sleep.

I am twelve years old. My parents have taken me to Regina, where my mother went to university. She is in the front seat of our Dodge, her arm slung over the seatback as she looks at me and my brother in the back. My father drives past the library where she worked as a student. She also worked in the Yorkton library during the summer, but through the school year she worked here.

She tells us the story of someone who came in once, trying to sell a rare book. The head librarian took one look at the book and handed it back, she says.

He told the man to leave before he called the police. The man ran off.

My mother asked the librarian why he was so upset with the man, and she says he told her 'if you're trying to sell a forgery of an old book, don't print it with modern fonts.'

I sat up in bed. Karen was still asleep, so I crept out of the bedroom as quietly as I could, then I ran down the stairs, almost tripping, and into my den.

The prospectus was on top of the textbook. I flipped the pages of the book, and in fifteen seconds I found what I was looking for.

The prospectus was dated nineteen sixty-three. The font they used for the heading was a typeface called 'Impact'. Impact wasn't invented until nineteen sixty-five. The Rhymes had lied.

I looked at my watch; five thirty. It was close enough to my regular waking time that I could stay up. I crept back upstairs, turned off the alarm clock, and collected my things to take a shower.

I stood in the shower for a long while, thinking. I scrubbed my face, stuck my head under the stream, and went through the facts in my head.

What did I know? I knew that the Rhymes had fed a lot of liquor to Magpie. I knew that they had lied about the prospectus, that it was dated nineteen sixty-three, but could not have been printed before sixty-five. I knew that Magpie had gotten drunk and killed my mother. But why?

At six thirty, I was dressed, sipping coffee, stuck on the puzzle. Magpie Harris, the quiet, soft-spoken man who everyone knew, the junk dealer that had bought my father's old truck, had used it to run over my mother. He was drunk, there was no doubt about it. But why did he run her over? Was he so drunk he didn't see her? Were his lights off? Did she step out from behind her truck as she got the mail?

My mind went through the events again. Gavin Harris was in Yorkton, for some reason. He was drinking with the Rhyme's and drove home past our place. Past our place. That was it. That part made no sense.

My father came through, nodded good morning and aimed for the coffee. He poured himself a cup and put bread into the toaster, then leaned against the counter.

"Pops, does anyone know why Magpie went home by that route?" I asked.

He shook his head. "What do you mean, son?"

"From Yorkton, he would drive south on route nine, then east on twenty-two, then south again to get to his place, by the marsh. There was no reason he would detour north, three blocks out of his way, to go past our place."

My father tilted his head back. "No, you're right. Why would he come home that way?"

"Beyond that, if he was that drunk, how did he get there without driving off the road? I mean, twenty miles south of Yorkton there's that awful curve at Dubuc, where the highway zigzags. Dozens of people, sober people, in the daytime, have gone off the road there. Yet he navigated it totally drunk, and at night? That sounds unlikely."

My father smiled slightly. "You're very good at this, aren't you, son?"

"Yeah, I am. Look, I'm going to the office today; I'll be home early, but can you keep an eye on the clan here till I'm back?"

"My pleasure. You should be very proud of your family. You know that, right?"

"I am, dad. They're what keeps me going when work gets bad. And now, with number three on the way, I figure I'm triply blessed."

Karen came down the stairs, bleary-eyed, stepping carefully along the carpet. She opened her eyes just enough to recognize us and grunted in response to my 'good morning'.

"Didn't sleep well, hon?" I asked.

She shook her head. "Leg cramps. You didn't wake up though, I notice."

"Sorry. I didn't notice, no. Are you feeling any better now?"

She nodded. "Yeah. Do we have any Cheerio's?"

"Coming up."

She sat at the table, munching cereal. A little later I kissed her goodbye and drove to the station.

The overnight staff were just leaving, and some of the day crew had come in early. I poured myself a coffee and flipped through telephone message slips. By eight, the room began to fill with men and women, talking, passing papers around, making phone calls. It was a day like any other. My mind was stuck on the question I'd asked earlier. How did a man who was that drunk drive forty miles, in the dark, run over my mother, pull over and fall asleep in his truck?

And why drive past our place, instead of south towards his own house? It felt like one of those plastic puzzles Charlotte had, the kind with all the little squares in a frame, and you move them around in order to make a picture. Something was out of place. One of the plastic squares was not where it should be. Charlotte's squares- now she was learning to read, I thought.

I remembered when my mother was teaching me to read. My brother James was older, and he already had a collection of books. He read books on music and books on magic, the only subjects that interested him. He also had a magic kit that my father gave him for his eighth birthday. Inside it was a flat plastic coin holder. James would put a penny into the holder, slide the slide in, and pull the slide back out. The coin disappeared. Then he'd say a magic word, slide the slide in and out again, and the coin would reappear. He never told me how that trick worked.

Why was I thinking about that now? The two thoughts came together; the plastic puzzle and the disappearing coin.

It was like being hit by lightning. Was I right? There was one way to find out. It was nine-thirty here, seven-thirty in Esterhazy.

Ernest Pascoe came in, placed his briefcase on the chair beside my desk, and sat on the other chair opposite me. He grinned like the Cheshire cat.

"Good morning, Inspector." He chirped.

"Hi. Having a good day, are we?" I asked.

"You bet. We've gotten all sorts of good press for our work last week. It seems that a number of unsolved disappearances have been handed to other agencies- Interpol, Scotland Yard, the Mexican

Federales, the FBI. I've been contacted by law enforcement from all over the world."

That's what he craved- fame. I didn't care. "I'm happy for you, Captain. Well done." I said.

I hoped it sounded sincere. He grinned, picked up his briefcase and went to his office.

I called long distance and got them to connect me to the RCMP detachment in Esterhazy.

Three rings later, someone picked up. "Sergeant Gagnon." The voice said.

I tried to sound older, gruff. "Sergeant, this is Detective Inspector McBriar, in Toronto."

There was a pause. "Ian. How the hell are you? I missed you when you were in town."

I smiled. "Hello, David. I understand you were on course when I was back there?"

"Yeah. They want to promote me, for some reason. Go figure."

"Hey- you kept me from a life of crime. It's about time they recognized you."

He laughed. "Right. So, what can I do for you, *Inspector?*"

"We've had new leads about my mom's death. It's possible that it was not an accident."

His voice went serious. "Oh yeah? How so?"

"There are other parties that may have been involved. Do you have the incident report handy?"

"Well, we have had exactly three fatalities in the last decade- I'll find it. Can you hold?"

I heard the receiver clunk onto the table, then paper shuffling. A minute or so later, he came back on.

"You know, I always thought there was something fishy about that night, Ian."

"How so, Dave?"

"Too neat. I mean, Gavin was never any trouble. He was an odd duck, but that was all. And I never caught him drunk driving before then. It was out of left field, you know? But he confessed to doing it, and it would have been crazy to keep looking for another explanation. Besides, it would have been more painful for your family to drag it out."

"I don't blame you for that, Dave. I was only recently given this information."

"What did you get, Ian?"

"A document saying that my grandfather sold his Smeaton property to a mining company."

He snorted. "Bullshit. Abraham loved that land. He would never let anyone dig it up."

"My thoughts exactly. So, what's in the file?"

Paper rustled. "You know the details." He said, diplomatically.

"We had a statement from Merton and Reston Rhyme that at around nine fifteen that night Gavin Harris left the Yorkton bar where they had all been drinking. They later drove home, but never saw Gavin again till the trial."

"And he drove forty miles blind drunk, down route twenty-two, past the Dubuc curve, then he drove north past our place instead of south to his place, ran mom down and fell asleep." I said.

"Well, when you put it that way, I smell bullshit." He said.

I heard him switch hands, probably to pick up a pen. "What do you think happened?"

"I think the Rhymes got Magpie drunk, then one of them drove his truck, ran down mom and left him to take the fall."

"Well, that certainly makes more sense. Why would they do that, though?"

"Best guess? Mom was in Yorkton picking up something she had on her when she died. It proved that the Rhymes had lied about their activities. I bet she told them she had proof they were breaking the law. They panicked and ran her down, leaving Magpie to take the blame."

"That makes more sense than anything else I've heard. It also explains Gavin's death." He said.

"How so?"

"He died in a fire. The verdict was that his torch set off an explosion and he was knocked out. The coroner said it could have been that he was unconscious, and someone started the fire after. Trouble is, there was no way to prove that theory."

"Who found him?" I asked.

"Lanice Rhyme. She was driving by when she saw the smoke and called the fire department."

"Again with the Rhyme's. This is starting to smell really bad, Dave." I said.

"I agree. You got something I can sink my teeth into?"

"Not yet. What about the boys? Can you question them?" I asked.

"The boys? They moved away. They're in your neck of the woods now." He said.

That made me sit up. "What do you mean, my neck of the woods? Where, exactly?"

"I heard they're in Ajax, Ontario. Word is they have a trucking company or something- moved there about four, five years ago."

"Right after Magpie died?" I said.

"Right after Gavin died, yes."

"Sergeant Gagnon, I will keep you apprised of any developments."

"Godspeed, Inspector." He said.

The yellow pages for Greater Toronto listed several companies in Ajax. Right near the end of the 'R' was a listing for Rhyme Brothers Trucking. It gave an address on Station Street and on the map it was a short dead-end street across from the railroad tracks. I would go there myself, but I needed someone to go with me.

I dialed a number, and a familiar voice answered. "Inspector Klassen." It said.

"Josh- it's Ian." I said.

"Hey. Got any more arrests for me to make?" He joked.

"Actually, maybe." I answered.

There was a pause at his end. "Go on."

"This might be one you hand off to the Mounties, but you have jurisdiction there and I don't, so I'd like you with me."

He sighed. "All right. You buy lunch."

We decided to meet on Harwood Street, a main road in Ajax. Josh Klassen described the spot- it had a gas station on one corner and a coffee shop on the other. He would be at the coffee shop. Since this was outside my beat, I thought it best if I left my gun at home.

It took me half an hour to get to the coffee shop. Josh's brown Coronet was already there, flanked by a pair of black and white OPP cars. I walked in, looked around and saw three men in a wide booth- Klassen and two uniforms. I slid in beside Klassen.

"Inspector Ian McBriar, Constables Mark Schneider and Vern Hamilton." He said.

I nodded. "Thanks for coming, guys. Anyone hungry?"

One of the uniforms waved at the kitchen. "We ordered already, Inspector."

I picked up a thick, laminated menu. "Great. What's good here?" I asked.

Klassen waved at the counter. "Club sandwich is good. They make their own fries, too."

I put the menu down. "Perfect. Where's a waitress?"

A woman appeared beside me. She was middle-aged, with a cheery smile and a kind face. She nodded at the other men. "Lunch will be right up, boys. What would you like, hon?"

"Hi. Just a club sandwich with fries, please, and a coffee."

She scribbled something on a pad. "Coming right up."

I waited till she had gone then leaned forward. "I don't know what the Inspector here has told you." I said.

The one who'd spoken shrugged. "Pick up some perps, I heard. You got some people you can't touch, Inspector?"

"Yeah. Now, this may be a wild goose chase; my mother was killed a decade ago, and I think that these guys did it. Beyond that, it's guesswork on my part, so I appreciate you being here."

The other one shrugged. "That's what we do for a living. Glad to help."

We ate, talked small talk, shop talk, cop talk. Josh Klassen set up the scenario; the two uniforms would wait down the street, hidden from sight.

Josh and I would drive to the Rhyme's office, then call for backup. I paid for lunch, and we left.

Rhyme Brothers Trucking was near the end of Station Street, past where the asphalt ended, past the gravel street beyond that, on a bumpy stretch of compacted dirt road.

The company name was written on a tin sign, hung on a long chain link fence that surrounded a rusty metal building. Beside the building sat five or six truck cabs, lined up inside the fence.

On the other side of the property was a Quonset hut, a corrugated half-pipe of a building with a plywood end wall and a metal door that had the word 'office' stenciled on it.

Klassen parked his Coronet outside the fence and we gingerly stepped over the shallow puddles in the yard as we walked to the office. I told myself to be calm, stay collected.

He opened the office door, went in and I followed. Inside, the furniture looked like either Salvation Army castoffs or very old hand-me-downs. There was a bullnose metal desk with chipped beige paint decorated in coffee rings, covered by a stack of bills of lading and gas slips. On the other side of the room, a wooden swivel chair- a nineteen forties throwback- pressed against a tall metal filing cabinet.

At the far end of the office, which I noted was only half the Quonset hut, was another plywood end wall with a newer, cleaner door in it.

The door opened and I stiffened up. A young woman came out, rummaging through a purse. She glanced up at us, indifferently, and went back to looking through her purse.

"You the guys from diesel sales?" She asked.

"Not exactly. We're here to see Merton Rhyme."

She shook her head. "He's in North Bay till later this afternoon."

"How about his brother, Reston?" I asked.

"He went to lunch. He should be back in about twenty minutes. Are you friends of his?"

"Not really. I knew him back in Esterhazy." I said.

I looked around. "How is he to work for? A pretty good boss?"

She closed her purse and looked me over, reading me. "You knew him back when?"

"Yes, I did."

She snorted. "I can't believe he's changed much."

I smiled understanding. "Probably not. How long have you worked here?"

"Six months. I figure that's about the lifespan for a woman in this place."

"So you're not happy here?" I asked.

She grinned. "I found a better job. I start tomorrow."

"I guess there's no love lost between you two, then?"

"He's a slimy weasel with sticky hands and big eyes. Does that tell you how I feel?"

She pulled open some of the desk drawers, took out various papers, put them into her purse and snapped it shut again.

"Mind if we look around as we wait here for him?" I asked.

"Be my guest. I'm leaving anyway." She said.

She walked out; I heard a car start up, then gravel being sprayed against the door as she left.

Klassen went into the back office. It had several low filing cabinets, and a large, nicer metal desk with a leatherette swivel chair. He pulled out drawers in the cabinets. Most were empty, but one had a series of maps and documents in it.

We flipped through the documents; I stopped when I recognized a name on a paper.

"Jackpot." I said.

The paper said that my grandfather had leased his land to the RMR Development Company for twenty years, in exchange for a percentage of diamonds found on the property.

The document was dated nineteen sixty-seven. I showed it to Klassen.

"What about it?" He asked.

"It says my grandfather signed this over to them in sixty-seven. He died in sixty-six."

He chuckled. "We now have a crime. We also have a motive. Jeez, Ian, I really want you on our team. Do you want to leave the city and go provincial?"

"That's a discussion for another time, Josh. Let's just take these bastards in, all right?"

Ten minutes later, the sound of a truck engine got closer then went quiet. Reston Rhyme was back from lunch. The outer door opened, and I heard a voice say 'hello?'.

I knew that voice from when we were children together. He was the meeker brother, the follower, but always ready to blow up a frog with a firecracker or shoot a dog with a BB gun.

Footsteps came toward our inner door. A moment later, Reston Rhyme walked in.

He was taller than I remembered, almost six feet, skinny, with stooped shoulders and an expression like he didn't get the joke. He looked at Klassen, then he recognized me and turned to walk away. He got almost to the front door before I could grab his arm and pull him back.

Klassen swung out the swivel chair. I glared at Rhyme. "You. Sit." I said.

I pushed Rhyme down into the chair. He looked up at us, terrified.

"We got you, Reston." I said.

I bared my teeth. "We got you for murder. We have proof."

He sat up straight, suddenly belligerent. "Why are you here? This is private property. You got no right to be here. Get out!" He shrieked.

Klassen held up the document we'd found. "This proves fraud and malicious intent. It gives us grounds to arrest you and to search for other evidence. You want to tell us what happened?"

Rhyme glanced at the document and shook his head. "I don't know what that is. I've never seen it before. You're making this up."

Klassen looked at the paper. "It has your name and your signature on it. Want to try that again?"

Rhyme shook his head, firmly. "I don't believe it. You're lying."

Klassen sighed and looked at me. "Was he always like this?"

I nodded. "Yeah. It was never him, he never did anything wrong, nothing was ever his fault."

Klassen snorted. "Typical. So, *RES*-ton, we arrested your brother earlier in North Bay, and he says you drove the truck that killed Ian's mother. We have you both for murder."

Rhyme got nervous. He looked around, trying to find a way to escape.

"It wasn't us. It was our mom. She drove the truck. It was all her idea."

"Your mom, your mom who died three years ago?" I asked.

"Yeah. She done it. It wasn't us. It was all her idea."

Klassen looked at me, checking my reaction.

"You do remember that my father sold that truck to Gavin Harris, right?" I said.

I leaned down. "Do you know why? Because the seat was broken. The seat kept moving back and forth, and it was hard for my mom to drive it. Gavin welded it in place. He was your height. Your mom was under five feet- there's no way she'd reach the pedals. It was you two cretins."

Klassen pulled out his handcuffs. "Reston Rhyme, I am arresting you on suspicion of fraud, uttering, forgery, and homicide."

Rhyme pushed against the desk and his chair rolled back four feet. "No! You can't! it's been more than seven years- the statute of limitations- you can't touch me." He cried.

Klassen shook his head. "God, I hate American TV. There is no statute of limitations on serious crimes in Canada. We've got you, sunshine."

Rhyme held his hands up in front of him, desperate. "Wait, wait. Wait, just wait a sec. Wait. It wasn't me, it was Merton that drove the truck. It wasn't me."

Klassen nodded. "Right. You say it was him. He says it was you. You both walk. No deal."

Rhyme shook his head. "I can prove it was him. I can prove it."

I sat on the edge of the desk. "How?"

He looked up at me with a desperate expression. "Listen. Your mother went to our office in Yorkton. She said that we had lied about buying Abraham's land, that we didn't have any right to dig there. Merton tried to reason with her. He offered her a share of the profit.

"She said no, that it was 'sacred land' or some such shit, and it should stay that way. She said she was going to the police in the morning. That's when we saw that Magpie in the bar. He only had enough money for one beer and that's when Merton had the idea. He bought Magpie a bunch of drinks, got him totally pissed, and he drove the truck with Magpie asleep in the right seat."

He pulled out a handkerchief, mopped his face and continued.

"So, he just wanted to scare her, you know? But he hit her. It was an accident, so he figured that the loser was already drunk- let him take the blame. That's what happened, honest."

Klassen looked at me, waiting for my reaction.

"Pure bullshit." I said.

"If you did only want to scare her, you'd have done it in your own truck, not Gavin's. And I still don't believe that Merton was driving it, not you."

He pointed at me, triumphant. "I can prove it. Like I said, he drove Magpie's truck. I followed Merton in our truck. Magpie's truck had a burned-out taillight. Every time Merton hit the brakes, only one light came on. There's your proof."

"And Magpie? Why did you kill him?"

Rhyme shook his head quickly, trying to brush off the question.

"He got suspicious. He asked us why we got him drunk. After he got out, he stopped drinking, and he started asking a bunch of questions. We just wanted to shut him up."

"By killing him?" I asked.

"You don't get it. We told him it would be bad for him, that he'd be arrested, that he'd go back to jail, but he wanted to tell the cops what happened. It would have ruined everything."

"So you knocked him out and burned him to death?"

"It was Merton's idea. He said we should scare him. It just got out of hand, that's all."

It was getting hard to keep my anger in check, but I wanted to hear the whole story.

"You were with him- you helped him. You helped Merton kill an innocent man." I said.

Rhyme's face turned red. "You don't get it, do you? You don't get what we were trying to do. We were trying to build a mining business. We were trying to make something important, something big."

I spoke in a measured voice. "By stealing my grandfather's land and killing Magpie." I said.

He exploded with anger. "The old man was dying! What good was the land if it just sat there! What harm was there in what we did?"

"And killing my mother?"

"We killed one stupid squaw! Big deal!"

He never saw it coming. My fist hit the side of his head, spinning him around in the chair. He fell onto the floor and I sailed over the desk, landing on him. He squealed like a dying pig, curled up into a ball and tried to protect himself.

I grabbed his arm, pulled it back like a pitcher preparing to throw a ball, and got my elbow around his neck. I could snap his spine. In a moment I could kill him. I'd finally get revenge.

Klassen roared like a drill sergeant.
"INSPECTOR!"

He was looking at me, I realized, with pity. I let Rhyme go.

"Inspector Klassen, would you please arrest this man?" I said, calmly.

I dragged Rhyme onto the desk. Klassen cuffed him and went out to his car. I just stared at Rhyme and said nothing.

Five minutes later, one of the uniforms from the coffee shop bundled Reston Rhyme into his cruiser and drove him to the holding cells in Peterborough.

We sat in Rhyme's office, went through more documents and found a few other papers that would assure a conviction. There was a letter sent to a farmer near my grandfather's land, warning him not to complain about the mining activity.

There were invoices, bills, statements that described the operation- notes for workers and equipment sent to our land, things of the sort. It was damning, and it was irrefutable.

Around three in the afternoon, another sound came through the door, a lower, gruffer sound, a big truck motor. It rumbled for a long time then went quiet. A minute after that, the outside door opened again.

Merton Rhyme walked in, reading something on a slip of paper. He didn't even look up.

"Res, you got to find us some cheaper diesel, man." He said.

He looked up. His eyes went back and forth between Klassen and me.

For a brief millisecond, a fraction of a moment, he froze. Then he threw the piece of paper in the air, spun around and raced out of the Quonset hut. I heard him go 'oof' then the sound of a pair of hard shoes, cop shoes, came toward us.

The larger uniform from the coffee shop had Merton in an arm lock, pinning his head down.

"This one of the guys you were after?" He asked.

Klassen held Merton while the uniform cuffed him. "Thanks, Vern. We'll be right out." He said.

The uniform smiled. "Say the word." He said.

He walked out to his cruiser. Klassen sat Merton on the edge of the desk and sat next to him.

"Now, Reston has been very cooperative. He has already signed a confession which implicates both of you in the death of Miriam McBriar. You don't have to say anything, of course, until you speak to a lawyer, but if you do wish to make a statement, it could help your case."

Merton glared at me. "I got shit to say to you. You can't prove nothing."

I shrugged. "Actually, your brother was very forthcoming. He showed us the documents relating to my grandfather's land, the forged signature on the lease, everything. We have you dead to rights, you stupid little dipshit."

Merton leaned back and groaned. "That moron. He never could keep his mouth shut."

He shook his head, clearing his mind. "No matter. We won't even get to court, and if we do, we won't do much time. I got friends that will sit on the jury. We'll be back here in a few months. Then you just watch out, Tonto."

Klassen watched my reaction. I didn't show anger, or rage, or pain.

I looked at Klassen. "Give us a minute, Josh."

He looked back and forth between Merton and me. "Fine. I'll be right outside." He left.

Merton sneered. "So, what now? You gonna rough me up? Slap me out? Will that make you feel like a big shot? You think that'll bring her back?"

I sat in the chair with my hands on my knees, looked up at him and smiled.

"You know, before my mom died, I was in a seminary, studying to become a priest. Because of your actions, though, I became a police officer."

He rolled his eyes. "Whoop-de-do."

I continued. "In the years I've been a cop, I've put a lot of violent criminals away. I kept track of them. Twenty-six. Fourteen of them are in Prince Albert, and twelve are in Kingston. Whichever place they send you, you'll run into some very brutal men I've put away."

He laughed. "Great. We can form a 'screw you, Ian' club."

"Yeah. You be sure to tell them who you are. Even the most stupid ones will put two and two together, Merton."

His expression changed. "What do you mean?"

"Twenty-six men, twenty-six violent criminals, that I put away. And the only reason they're in jail is because I'm a cop, and the only reason I'm a cop, is because of you. I wish you well, Merton. Good luck on the inside."

I stood up. "Josh, can you come in here, please?"

He came back into the room and looked at Merton's face. "What did you say to him?" He asked.

"I told him that he'll be in jail with men I put there. Because I became a cop. Because of him."

He took Merton's arm and led him out of the Quonset hut. "Come, let's go." Klassen said.

Merton dug his heels in, trying to slow Klassen down. "Wait! We can't go! My life's in danger! You can't put me in jail! They'll kill me!"

The uniform came out to meet us, and together the two men forced a squirming Merton into the back seat of the cruiser. Klassen closed the door, the cruiser left, and he turned to face me.

"OK, so, what now, Ian?" He asked.

"I'll call the Saskatchewan RCMP. They'll want these two transported, and they'll handle it from there. Open and shut case."

"Open and shut case." He agreed.

He held out his hand. "You realize this is more brownie points for both of us, right?"

I shook his hand. "You deserve it, Josh. Keep in touch."

He walked towards his car then turned back. "The steaks turned out great, by the way."

Chapter Twenty

I got back to the station house around three. Ernest Pascoe was in his office, talking animatedly on the phone. He bounced up and down on the balls of his feet, barely able to contain his excitement, but he spoke softly, calmly. Finally, he said 'thanks, I will' and hung up.

He saw me come in, did a quick double-take and strutted over. I sat at my desk and he slid a plastic chair around, sat and leaned toward me.

"Ian! Good work, Inspector, well done. Well done." He gushed.

"Excuse me?"

"You just cracked a decade-old cold case. And you did it with the thanks and cooperation of the OPP and the RCMP, too. I mean, how much better can it get?"

"It would have been better if they hadn't killed my mother." I said.

He pasted on a sympathetic frown. "True, true. But still, your work has been sterling. Having you on my team helped solidify my right to that job. You know what that means, don't you?"

"More money for you?"

"Beyond that. You can write your own ticket in this department, son. You can have my desk, if you want it."

I shook my head. "That's just it, Captain. I'm not sure if I want that. Maybe I'm happy doing what I'm doing. Maybe that's where I'm meant to be."

He leaned back, puzzled. "I don't understand. Are you saying that because you don't like me?"

"Why on earth would you have anything to do with my decision?" I asked.

"Then, why not just take the job? It's by far the best offer you could hope for, considering."

"Considering?"

"Listen, you're seen as an outsider in certain circles. But even so, you have been mentioned downtown- they're taking notice of you. Take the position. You deserve it."

"I was under the impression that we didn't get along, Captain. Why the sudden change of tune?"

"In my new role, I'll liaise with a number of captains, so I'd prefer our relationship to be cordial. What do you say- how about we bury the hatchet, smoke the peace pipe?"

"Should I build a teepee and skin a buffalo while I'm at it?" I sneered.

"No, no, look, that's not how I meant it. It was just an expression. You know what I mean."

"You mean that as a Metis, this is the best position I could expect? Or does promoting me fill a minorities quota for your portfolio?"

He spoke slowly. "I'd view it with the perspective that your work is being rewarded, that's all."

"Yeah, fine. I still haven't decided. However, I do have a bunch of vacation time available. I'd like to take a week off and think it over."

He stood up and patted the desk. "Fine. Sure. Good idea. Take a break, clear your head. We'll talk more when you get back."

I stood up. "I'll let my team know I'm taking the time off. See you in a week."

I got home around four. There was an unfamiliar sedan in my driveway, parked behind Karen's Parisienne. I stopped on the street and walked down the path to the front door.

As I opened the door, I heard men talking, then laughter, then more talking, so I followed the sound to the living room. My father was sitting in one easy chair, laughing and wiping tears from his eyes. Barry Kirby sat opposite him, also laughing, wiping his eyes with a handkerchief.

"Hey everyone." I said.

Kirby stood up and stretched out a hand. "Ian. It's nice to see you again." He said.

I shook his hand. "Hello, Barry. I see you've met my dad."

My father nodded. "We were just swapping stories. Barry and me got a lot in common."

"I see." I said.

I pulled out a chair and sat beside my father. "It's all over, pops. We got them." I said softly.

His smile faded. "Who did you get?"

Kirby watched us speak but said nothing.

"Merton and Reston Rhyme- they're the ones that ran mom down. They pinned it on Gavin Harris- they got him drunk and left him passed out in his truck to take the blame."

My father stared at me. "Gavin didn't do it? You're sure about that?"

He shook his head. "I blamed myself so many times for selling him that truck. I saw it as somehow my doing that she was taken away too soon."

"He was just a poor, sad man that the Rhymes duped, and they killed him when he started asking questions. The irony is, that truck had a loose seat track and a burnt-out taillight.

Those two silly things helped us catch them. Funny how that works out, huh?" I said.

My father was still staring at me. "What will happen to them? Will they go to jail?"

"They are going to jail, dad. They will be in prison with the men that I put there. The brothers will never feel safe, no matter how much time they serve. Still, it doesn't make up for losing mom."

He looked down sadly. "Ain't a day goes by that I don't miss her. I love Pam to the bottom of my toes, you understand, but your mom was the one what made you and James into the men you are. I'm just glad she'll have peace now that you found out who really done it."

Kirby leaned forward. "What are *you* going to do now, son?"

"I'm taking a week off. I need to decide where I'll go next."

"What about the two men you arrested? How are they?" Kirby asked.

"You mean, did I beat them up or anything? As I told dad, they'll be in jail with criminals I put there, thanks to their actions. That will give them something far worse to worry about."

Kirby chuckled. "Serves them right."

Something suddenly made sense. "You said there were three parts to the test. The first part was in your office, when I figured out who you were. Part two was figuring out what the book and the prospectus in the package meant. Am I right?"

"As I say, I had no idea why they were in the package, and the people who put it together didn't know either. It just seemed odd that she should have those things. We left the rest up to you."

"But you said that there was a third part to the test. You also said that if I passed, I'd realize it, and if I failed, it would be irrelevant."

"Correct." He said.

"I didn't take my revenge, even though I had the chance. That was the final test."

"You never cease to amaze me, Ian. As I say, we have a place for you in our organization."

"I've been offered the Captain's desk, as well. I can choose whichever job I want." I said.

My father looked over at me. "Well, Ian? Have you decided what you're going to do?"

"Not yet."

I could hear Karen and the kids in the back yard, laughing, playing. The big clock in the hall was equally loud, though, and its tic-tic-tock sound seemed to demand attention.

Barry Kirby handed my father his business card and promised to stay in touch. He drove off, then the house was strangely quiet.

My father read Kirby's business card carefully. It was a plain white rectangle, with 'B. Kirby' in block letters and a phone number below it, nothing else.

He opened out his worn leather wallet and placed the card behind his driver's license.

"Son, I'm going back home day after tomorrow, you know that, right?"

"Yeah, dad. I'm so glad you came. It means a lot to us that you were able to visit."

"Next time, I'd like to come back with Pam. What do you think?"

I understood immediately what he was asking. "I'd love for her to visit, too. The kids are already calling her 'grandma Pam'."

He smiled broadly. "Yeah, she said that made her feel like a real part of the family. Listen, we got time before supper. What say we make a meal to remember?"

"Good idea. What do you have in mind?"

We went through the refrigerator and pulled out foods, stacking them on the counter as though planning an expedition. My father casually mentioned that there was enough there to feed an army, so I suggested we make it a party- a spur-of-the-moment party.

I picked up the phone and dialed a number. Frank answered in two rings.

"Yello." He said.

"Hey, it's Ian. How would you guys like to come over for dinner tonight, around seven?"

"Who's cooking?" He asked.

"My dad and me."

"We'll be there early."

"See you then, Frank."

I made another call. Rebecca Van Hoeke answered.

"Hey, Becky, it's Ian."

She sounded puzzled. "Hi. How are you?" She asked.

"Great. We're having a 'bon voyage' dinner with my dad and Frank's family. Would you two like to join us?"

"Who's cooking?" She asked.

"Have you been talking to Frank? Me and my father."

"What time?"

"Seven-ish?"

"We'll see you at six forty-five." She said.

By six-thirty, everything was ready. The big dining table normally sat eight, but we had an extension leaf in the basement that added four more places.

I pulled three kitchen chairs into the dining room, and my father set eleven places. A few minutes later, Frank Burghezian knocked on my front door. He waited about two seconds then opened the door and called 'hello?'

"Come!" I yelled.

Frank shooed Helen and his kids into the front hall in front of him. He was about to close the door, when he did a double-take as Martin and Rebecca Van Hoeke walked up the path. He waited for them to catch up, then he put an arm over Martin's shoulder.

"Hey, boss. Good to see you." He said.

Van Hoeke nodded. "Good to see you too, Frank. You going to leave us any food?"

"Not if I can help it."

Karen and Helen settled the children into their seats, then the adults sat. My father and I made sure everyone was comfortable, then we went into the kitchen and brought out food.

Frank craned his neck, looking around Rebecca Van Hoeke to see into the kitchen. My father came out first, carrying a large plate of grilled vegetables. I followed, balancing a platter in one hand and a large bowl in the other.

My father rested the vegetables in the middle of the table, then clasped his hands together and addressed everyone.

"Now, then. We have carrots, zucchini, and eggplant in olive oil. After that, we have meat loaf and mashed potatoes. Dessert will be later. Everyone, please dig in."

There was a subdued rumble of voices, requests and responses as plates floated back and forth over the table. The children grudgingly accepted the vegetables, but only after being told that they'd get meat loaf and potatoes after they finished the veggies.

Frank piled some of everything on his plate. He ate quietly, his head down, and only looked up occasionally to see how his family was doing.

A half hour later, I cleared the empty plates away and took the dirty dishes into the kitchen.

With almost ballet-like choreography, I placed a stack of dessert plates on the table as my father brought through two steaming apple pies and a bowl of ice cream.

We sliced wedges of pie onto the plates, spooned ice cream beside them and served dessert.

I brewed a very large pot of coffee, poured milk for the children, and again there was a muted rumble and clattering of plates as everyone ate.

By eight-thirty, the food was gone, the dishes cleaned, and the children were all in the basement watching TV or asleep on the floor.

We adults were in the living room with our coffee, all talking.

Van Hoeke and my father talked about their youth; Van Hoeke had grown up in a tough part of London; the war and the RAF had turned him around.

My father told stories I had never heard; about growing up hungry and poor during the depression, having to work on the farm as a child to help the family survive, watching his father reluctantly put down their pet dog because they couldn't feed it.

It made me realize where he came from, why he had always worked so hard, why he always made sure we had food in the house.

I saw him in a different light now. He was a hungry little boy, scrapping with other hungry little boys, trying to survive.

We talked late into the evening. After eleven, everyone said goodnight, wished my father a safe trip and left.

Karen and the kids were in bed and I was in the kitchen, eating a small bowl of ice cream. My father leaned against the sink and sipped a glass of water, looking out at the back yard. The scattered clouds lit up like neon as they drifted in front of the full moon, little puffballs of light which disappeared after they passed by it.

I pointed my spoon at the window. "Pretty view, isn't it?" I said.

He nodded. "Yep. It's been quite a trip, hasn't it, son."

"Sure has. Did you enjoy it, dad?"

"Not what I meant. I was talking about what happened with your mom."

I put down my ice cream. "It healed a wound that's been open for a decade, dad."

He turned to face me. "You know, sometimes things like that drive you forward. Other times, they burn you up."

"Which one was it for you, dad?"

He shrugged. "Ten years ago, five years ago, maybe, if I knew what you know, I mighta killed them boys. Now, I'll just let God punish 'em. Life did what it had to do. That's all we can say."

I put my hand on his shoulder. "I miss you, dad."

"Miss you too, son. Let's not have so much time pass till we meet again."

He rubbed his eyes, said goodnight and went to bed.

I went upstairs, sat on the edge of the bed, undressed and listened to Karen, her breath making a soft 'whssh' sound as she exhaled.

Despite the day, or perhaps because of it, I was restless.

I got dressed again. Karen sat up and looked at me.

"What's wrong?" She asked.

"Something I want to do, hon. Don't worry, I'll be back in a little while."

At the bottom of the stairs, I turned and went into my office. I picked up the phone and dialed a familiar number, barely looking at the dial pad.

After three rings, a sleepy voice answered. "Hello?"

"Frank, can I buy you a coffee?" I asked.

There was a brief silence. "Sure, kid. Ten minutes?"

"Yeah, see you out front, Frank."

I was at his house in seven minutes. A minute later, he stepped out, pulling a sweater over a tee shirt.

He ran his fingers through his short hair and shook himself awake, then he hopped down the steps to the sidewalk and jumped into my car.

"Hey. What's up, kid?" He asked.

"You haven't called me 'kid' in years." I said.

We drove to an all-night diner we knew and I parked. Frank got out and waited on the sidewalk for me, then I joined him and we went in together.

The inside of the diner looked like a modified streetcar, with booths down one side, a long counter with swiveling stools on the other. There was a tired man in white behind the counter, and the only other patrons were three uniformed cops sitting at a far booth, eating burgers.

Two of the cops recognized me and waved. I nodded back. One of them explained to the third cop who I was.

Frank shimmied into a booth and I slid in opposite him.

"So, what's on your mind?" He asked.

"Do you remember the last time we did this, Frank?"

"Sure. You had just rescued Patrick Walsh."

"I'd killed one of his kidnappers." I corrected.

"Matter of perspective, Ian. Which was a better solution?"

"No, I've made peace with what I did, Frank. I don't feel any guilt about that anymore."

"So why are we here?"

The man in white came out from behind the counter and handed us a pair of laminated menus.

"What can I get you?" He asked.

"Just coffee." I said.

"Same." Frank answered.

He looked at us and snorted.

Frank glowered at him. I waved the man back.

"Actually, I'd also like to pay the tab for those officers." I said.

He looked at them and back at me. "Yeah?" He asked.

"Yeah." I answered.

He shrugged. "OK."

The three uniforms were sliding out of their booth, and the man in white spoke to them, pointing at me. One of them grinned and waved at me.

"I got yours next time, Inspector." He called.

The man in white brought us two mugs of coffee. "Here you go, sir." He said softly.

He went back into the kitchen behind the counter.

Frank poured sugar into his mug and stirred it. "So, why the invite?" He prodded.

"Where do I go, Frank? What should I do?"

"You're asking me for career advice, are you?"

"I guess I am, yes."

He took a sip of coffee and poured some sugar into the cup. "Of course, I'd like you to join our merry band of men. You know that."

"However." I said.

"However. You got to make your own choices, man. You got to do it because it's right for you. If you're working with me cause you figure you owe me something, forget it. I don't want to work with you that way."

"Pascoe told me I should take the promotion in the department because it was the 'best I could expect, considering'." I said.

"That bluntly?"

"He suggested we bury the hatchet and smoke the peace pipe, in his words."

"Asshole. He can sure open his mouth and change feet, huh?"

"Frank, part of the reason I became a cop was because of my mother's death. Now that I know what really happened, it feels like I don't need to be a cop anymore. Does that make sense?"

"Yes, it does. So, what *do* you want to do when you grow up?"

Outside, a street sweeper rolled past, swishing the gutters clean and spraying them with soapy water. We watched it disappear into the distance.

"I'm good at being a cop, Frank. I'm good at being a dad, and I know I'd be good doing what you do. The question is, though, what *should* I be doing?"

He shook his head. "That's up to you, kid. Whatever you decide, remember that I will still be your friend, no matter what. Does that help?"

I looked down at my coffee. "Thanks, Frank. Yes, that helps a lot."

"Have you decided what you want to do, then?"

The man in white came out from the back room. I waved at him and made a motion like signing a check, and he nodded understanding.

"Yeah, Frank. I know exactly what I'm going to do." I said.

THE END.

CPSIA information can be obtained
at www.ICGtesting.com
Printed in the USA
LVHW060557050623
748254LV00005B/8

9 781778 010941